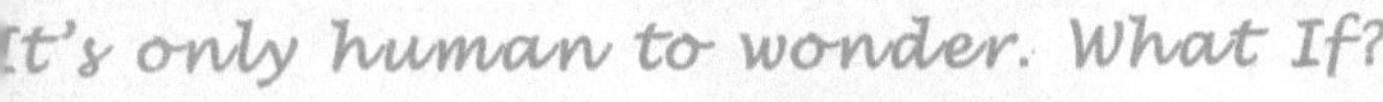

'The One'

A Deedra Lee Saga

It's only human to wonder. What If?

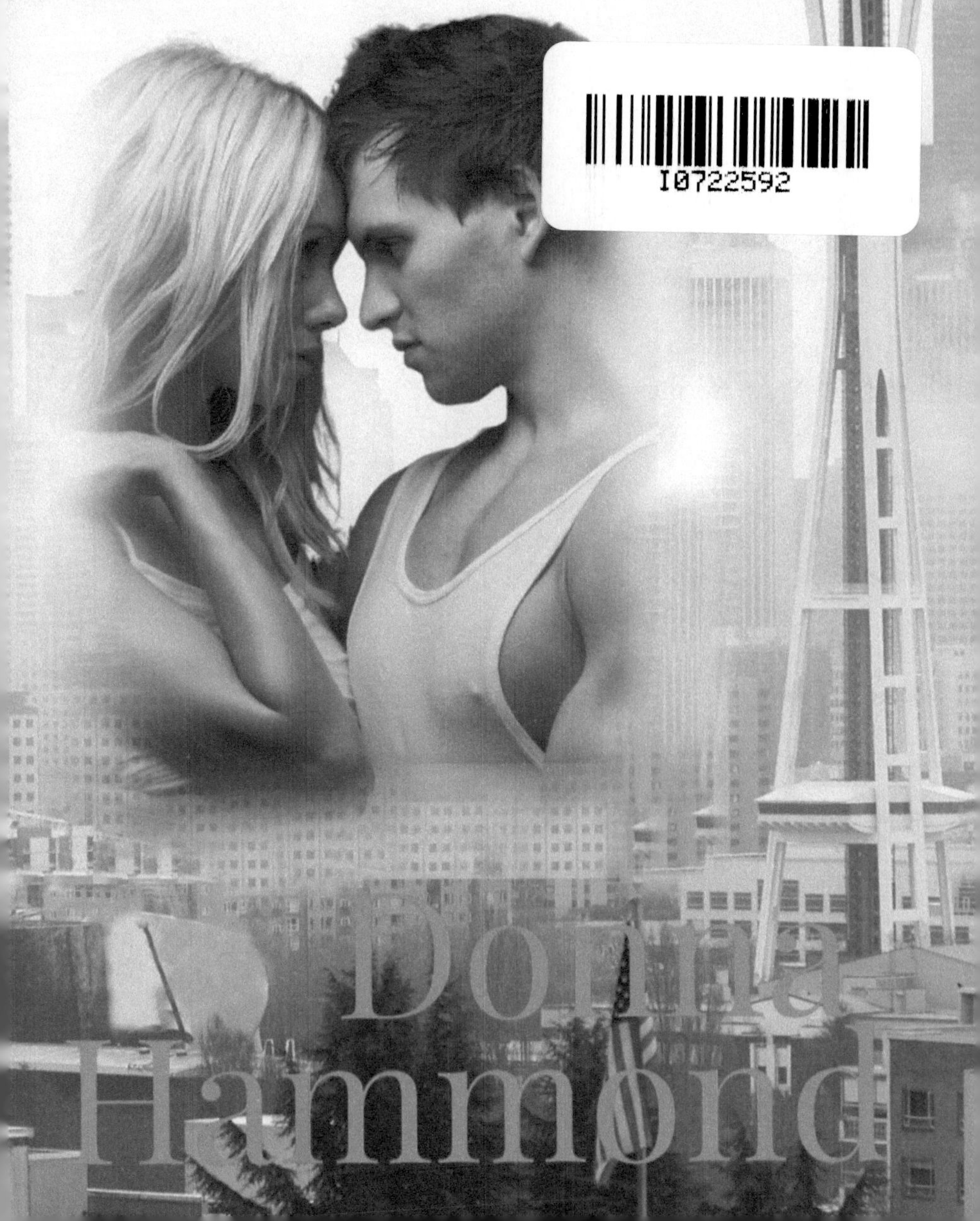

Dona Hammond

WORKBOOK PRESS LLC
187 E Warm Springs Rd,
Suite B285, Las Vegas, NV 89119, USA

Website: https://workbookpress.com/
Hotline: 1-888-818-4856
Email: admin@workbookpress.com

Ordering Information:
Quantity sales. Special discounts are available on quantity purchases by corporations, associations, and others. For details, contact the publisher at the address above.

Library of Congress Control Number: 2016919643
ISBN-13:   000-0-00000-000-0 (Paperback Version)
                     000-0-00000-000-0 (Digital Version)

REV. DATE: 03/10/2022

'The One'

A Deedra Lee Saga

Its only human to wonder what if?

By

Donna Hammond

Prologue

In 9,000 BC, Immortals arrived from the capital of Atlantis. This group of Atlantean went on a mission to conduct exploration of the present populace of mortals. By the time the party regrouped and headed back home, Atlantis had disappeared permanently. The six warriors divided up and assimilated into the modern civilization. When the society grew, they considered some to be gods. They worshipped others from afar. The Atlantean, now, were the immortal populations. Where the corrupted rose to the surface, they ran in secret societies such as the Knights Templar, Skull & Bones, Illuminati, Freemasons. The ancients carry a story from their old beliefs; 'The One' would come to set the immortal world straight. In the 1800s, they incorporated into the wealthiest of circles: Forbes, Carnegie, and Rockefeller. The corruption ran deep taken over in the economic wealth of the United States. Remarkably, the besmirched leaders of the immortals remained in their antiquated practices. New highbred immortals called themselves Renegades, they worked for the cartel. They successfully pushed out the original six by putting them to death. Yet, one hid making society's life altering choices from the security of the burnt-out abandoned city below Seattle, Washington. Effectively, he had manipulated.

Immortal and mortal lives for centuries.

Until now!

Chapter 1

Life's Little Moments

Have you ever had a déjàvoo moment? Has someone called you when you are thinking of him or her? Have you ever had a dream about someone from your past and didn't know why, after many years, he or she is in your dreams? Magic is a part of all of us. Sometimes the universe just chooses us when we least expect it.

My name is Deedra Lee. I believe that magic lives in all of us. I also think fate has given me a little more chutzpa. My intuition is as good as it gets. I can sum you up in the first sentence out of your mouth. When I try to second-guess myself because I am looking for the good in all people, I always regret it. My dreams are so real it is like going to a 3-D movie theater with all the color and sounds of a live-action thriller. I have had trouble awaking from some of my dreams. When I do, I experience confusion; I am disoriented, like when you wake up in a new place, and you take a minute to remember where you are. Swinging my fist into the air is my first response. Fight or flight is an instinct in most humans, safety first, then trying to figure out where you have landed.

Sometimes a dream leaves me uneasy long after I am awake. Some are violent and profoundly disturbing; they are still with me the longest. I repeatedly dream about a group of six, oddly; they come to me dressed in scarlet robes; I feel a profound sense of authority; the six of them are godlike, but their faces stay blurred, hidden behind hoods that cover most of their features. Sometimes they are in the distance; I can feel them watching me. I know what they are thinking even if I can only see some small pieces of red cloth in my dreams. However, the feelings of death, fear, and loneliness are none the less real. Making my days long, because of sleep deprivation. Some of my dreams are sexual; a hallow pain that leaves me with an empty yearning. An aching for something or someone I have lost. I can emotionally feel it in my soul. Moody doesn't even describe what happens in those dark days that follow. Growing up in Cherokee, North Carolina, time runs a little different here. I was still living at home with my parents. I had turned twenty-nine and needed to be on my own. They didn't mind, but I had been feeling it might be time to spread my wings and fly the coop. Deciding, with all the weirdness that is my life; I had to go looking for answers. Truth be known. My family thought evil spirits possessed me. Friends thought I was maybe a bit off. Always looking for answers to my weird life. I saw an ad in the Cherokee One Feather local newspaper that read Asheville's oldest authority on supernatural reading for free. Donations accepted. Then it gave a vague address outside the city limits on a rural road. I would never recommend someone doing this. Yet, I am on my way to visit a gypsy's camp. Is it safe? I don't know, but my intuition took over, and I went into the unknown. It was fifty-two miles from Cherokee to Asheville and then another ten miles on the other side of the city. Her name was Syeira, or so said the tent that I was standing in front of. Suddenly, a woman appeared in front of me. Her long red hair was wrapped in a traditional coined dickhlo with flowers on the side of the scarf. Her long, pink, full skirt was covered in red roses at various stages of blooming. Over her shoulders was a pink and red lace shawl over her fitted shirt. Holding out her hand, pulling the tent back to invite me to enter; she bowed her head…"

"Funny, her ad claimed she was born with the bloodline of an original witch of Salem in 1692; Did they all have a way of dressing? Witches and gypsies are different, aren't they?"

"Please come in. Deedra Lee, I have been waiting for you

to show up."

"Interesting... how did she know my name?"

She didn't look any older than me, in her late thirties. She also wore markings that scrolled in an extraordinary design around her hairline. The markings were like looking through a stained-glass window as the scrolling illuminated her face. The colors are more vivid than any tattoo I've ever seen. I held my breath for a moment, transfixed on who she was and how elegantly she moved. She truly was mesmerizing. Her aura was so powerful I could see it shimmering like the aurora borealis in many colors waving all around her as I stepped into the tent and commented.

"Your markings are so radiant I can feel the power you hold."

She looked deep into my eyes and smiled. I didn't even hear her move. The next thing I knew, she was standing in front of me, studying me, reaching inward, and trying to read me. I could feel her pull on my senses. Then she spoke again with a heavy accent. Her voice was low and sensual. Or maybe it is the accent that made it so sexy.

"Tu... ... prietenul meu, deține un spirit foarte vechi."

"Sorry I don't understand. I only speak English and a little Cherokee."

"You.... My friend, you hold an incredibly old spirit. Your gifts of magic have immeasurable potential when you learn to control them. You have yet to discover who and where you belong. Please sit, what can I do for you?" Taking a deep breath and wondering what in the hell was she talking about holding an old spirit; I was barely twenty-nine. I cleared my throat to speak.

"Are you able to explain the voice in my head?" her eyes narrowed and the crease between her eyes pinched together as she scowled.

She paused for a timeless moment, just watching as her surrounding aura got brighter. The scrolling in her hairline looked like it was moving. Her pattern swirled as it went to the same colors as her aura. I stepped back. Then she asked.

"You can see my markings, can't you?"

I nodded as if I had lost the ability to speak. I released a breath I didn't know I was holding.

She smiled. "They are ancient; they represent my heritage

and carry some of my magic. Most mortals cannot see them; only someone with an extraordinary gift can see them. Who are you?"

I could feel the warmth coming from her. I stepped back further as I stuttered out the words.

"That's… aaah. ah, what I am here to ask you. I am not magical that I know of."

Then she whispered.

"Come in and sit, do not fear me? I will try to read you. However, for someone with dormant magic, it will not be easy. I may only confuse you further, for the reading may come in a puzzle more than an answer to your many questions."

We stepped further into her tent, where Syeira had a sitting area with a small table.

"I all most expected to see a crystal ball sitting there, but no such luck."

Quietness fell in the tent for an exceptionally long time. I could smell sweet vanilla, lavender, rosemary with something more exotic, perhaps verbena. I could feel the warm, fragrant air as it swirled around my senses. Then she spoke.

"Evergreens, saltwater, violence, blood queen, lover, friends, enemies, death." Then her eyes rolled back into her head. I could see the whites. Was she in trouble having a seizure or something else? I stood up and went to get help and then she let out a blood-curdling scream of pain, then she fainted. I grabbed for her, catching her just before she hit the floor. When she woke up, she seemed frightened, trembling, and pale, with beads of moisture forming on her brow. Her whole body stiffened as I helped her stand. We looked into each other's eyes, and I saw the fear and horror. Syeira pointed towards the front of the tent where I had originally come in.

She grabbed my forearm, my skin burned. "I leave you with a gift of protection. The markings you will now carry have powerful magic and when the time is right, you will know how to tap into this magical energy. Now you must go. I have nothing further to reveal to you, only that your life is going to take a violent turn. Remember what I have told you of the magic you hold. It is not your only power. Deedra, you are going to change the existence of your people."

A man appeared from nowhere, holding the folds of the tent open for me to leave.

"You have to go; Madame Syeira has nothing more to show you." Trembling and shaking her head as she was pushing me out of the tent. I stumble to gain my footing.

I yelled back to her, looking over my shoulder. "What happened? Who are my people? What am I? Am I not human?"

Madame just disappeared back into the tent. Then another man came out and pointed to my car. I got the message that they wanted me to leave.

Again, I got nowhere fast and still had no answers for my ever-changing abilities, and she could not explain the voice I heard in my head. My arms still burning, I pulled up my sleeve. There on both of my forearms were some of the same tats that were on her face. The green Ivy shaped like hearts, with small soft pink and periwinkle blue flowers that wrapped my forearms from wrist to elbow. They were beautiful, but how did they work? I guess I will find out.

A few months later, in Montréal, Canada, I met another gypsy. She said her ancestors were direct descendants of the gypsy movement from Austria-Hungary in the 1880s.

She told me my future would be violent and that they had chosen me to lead. Lead… what or whom? She was unambiguous about that part of the vision… This time I left with a blessing of safe passage, and she placed an amulet around my neck to protect me. She told me to never take it off, for its magic would someday save my life. The silver teardrop-shaped necklace was the size of a small egg. Hand carved vines and small flowers wrapped the amethyst. I left another tent with at least a blessing and a necklace from complete strangers. Yet still not an answer that I understood. Thinking to myself, the two supernatural experts, one a gypsy and the other a witch. They seemed similar in their messages. Yet different in their approach in telling me I was S.O.L. That my future was rocky.

For many years, I have searched for anyone in the mystical world to give me insight into the mysterious occurrences that keep showing up in my life. I think I might just be imagining all of this, although I may need to change my diet and watch what I eat before I go to bed. I could be just delusional and need to be locked in an institution.

I am bewildered and vexed by all the strange feelings that I am having and the voice in my head that talks to me as though I am a dim-witted child. Oh, and then there are the queen-like words that my voice in my head uses to make unnecessary rude remarks about the surrounding people. I have decided the voice is not my sub-conscious mind that is speaking to me; it is another entity all together. Perhaps I have a split personality and should turn myself in at the next psychiatric ward or better yet, should I find a Catholic Priest and have them perform an exorcism. None of those thoughts made me feel better about the voice in my head that was sometimes annoying and not very helpful in my quest to figure out what was happening to me. She never responds to my questions; just makes condescending remarks, and now she is silent. I haven't heard a peep for days. In the past few months, I have been having vivid dreams of a place with evergreens and rhododendrons, an immense white house with a wraparound porch, a room with a painting of me, but me in a different time and place.

My life had been full of adventure because of the weirdness I call my life. Never having a dull moment, not for as long as I can remember. A packet arrived in the mail with my name on it. Inside was a scholarship form for out-of-state student for scholastic achievement to apply for a full ride to the University of Washington. Coincidence? I don't believe in them…. Fate somehow figures a way to give you choices. There was a brochure showing pictures of the campus. One picture showed the doors on the Suzzallo Library. The same hand carved doors, with a language that seemed familiar. The doors I have been showing up in my dreams. I never thought to further my education. Is fate directing my next move to find out what purpose to this peculiar life? My dreams have led me here and getting an education seemed the right path if I was reading my dreams correctly and if I wasn't, maybe I would find someone there who could help me. I filled out the paperwork that would allow me to enroll at the University of Washington in the land of evergreens and rhododendrons. We waited for about six weeks before I got the response I had been accepted into the program. I came from a small town in the hills of North Carolina where my graduating class was seventy-six, and the town had a population of 29,850. I was an honor student. Had received several awards for academic achievement. You must understand I have done some traveling, but nothing like going back to school at twenty-nine seemed like I might be too old to fit in. Seattle was an immense city showing up there was the scariest thing that I had ever done, even scarier than going into a gypsies' camp. I have always had a great imagination. I know I inherited that from my dad. Don't remember the first time I dreamed in three-dimensional color images. Knowing I have always dreamed beyond the normal person. When someone is describing their thoughts to me, I can visualize it at once in my mind. I never thought about it being a gift. However, I understand not very many people can see in their minds this way. I believed in the possibility that magic stays in this world. It can't all be explained away by science. Otherwise, I am looking to be locked up... I also hear a voice in my head that sometimes she tells me what to do and where to go and sometimes she tells me random knowledge of my family that no one else knows.

I hear nothing from her for months on end. Then **voilà**, she is speaking to me again. I know it's crazy, right... I sometimes think so too.

Regrettably, to share my secrets with my family and all their superstitions, they would have me locked up for sure.

In December, I was stuck at home in a snowstorm. Severe weather is common in our state. I live with my parents in the mountains of Cherokee, North Carolina.

I booked my flight to Washington through Portland, Oregon. Taking a road trip through Washington State on my way to Seattle. I had received a full-ride scholarship to attend the University of Washington.

The snow let up, and I could get a ride to the airport with my cousin. I boarded the plane on time and was to arrive in Portland around lunchtime. Looking at my phone, we were going to depart on time. We had been in the air for some time. I must have fallen asleep when the pilot came on the speaker.

"We are currently making our descent to PDX. Please pay attention to the seat belt signs and return to your seats. The weather is cool and rainy. It is approximately 12:00 pm and the week's weather looks like typical Northwest rain, I am afraid. Welcome to the Pacific Northwest." Then the flight attendant came around, reminding everyone to return to their seats and put their seats and tray tables in the upright position. Also asking for any trash left in your area. Disembarking the plane, went over to the rental counter. I had reserved an SUV. When checking in, they gave me a choice of a Tucson or Blazer, knowing both vehicles I chose the Hyundai Tucson. Walked out to the elevator. The doors opened as soon as I approached. Waited for the other passengers to vacate, then stepped on. The elevator took me to the fifth level. I walked across the sky bridge to the rental part of the garage. Stopping at a kiosk, picking up my keys and having them direct me to the rig. Key ring said Sedona Sunset Tucson 2016. How could I miss that? And sure enough, the only burnt orange SUV left in the lot was mine. I walked around her, checked for dents, dings, and scratches. Then checked the interior. I filled out my sheet and stuffed it in my visor along with the rental agreement. Got in, adjusted my seat. Set a radio station, checked my mirrors and off I went. Following the signs leading out of the airport and on my way north on I-5. While I drove up I-5 for about a half-hour, my stomach rumbled. There was a Polynesian-looking building that I could see from the freeway. The sign read Kalama Harbor Lodge-McMenamins. I pulled off at the next exit. I was tired with the time change and hungry. Thinking to myself, lunch sounded good walking through the front doors of the lodge. You couldn't help noticing rough-hewed planks of cedar lined the walls, from floor to the ceiling. The gnarly wood sculptures were beautiful. Then I looked through the lodge to the all-glass windows that showed the mighty Columbia River. I had to check it out. I stopped at the desk and asked if they had rooms available. While I was checking in, the smell of food from the restaurant made my stomach growl loudly. The staff gave me a key and directed me to the elevators.

They gave me a room on the 4th floor overlooking the Columbia River. I unpacked a few items and hung them up in the bathroom, so when I took my shower. It would help the clothes unwrinkled before I had to wear them tomorrow. When done, I stepped out into the hall to take the elevator down to the restaurant. I asked to be seated by the window. The server placed me on the end with a view of the Columbia River and the Totem poles. The brochure on the table I picked up and read;

"The totem poles featuring mythical forms, symbols, and creatures of the Pacific Northwest Native American culture are in Marine Park. Marine Park borders the Columbia River just west of Interstate 5 and downtown Kalama. The tallest pole is carved from a 700-year-old Western Red Cedar, and, according to the Cowlitz County Department of Tourism website (2008), at 140-feet, this totem is the largest one-piece totem in the world. 140 feet high. Local Native American artisan Don Lelooska began work on them for the display at the Seattle World Fair in 1962 but did not finish in time. Refinished and rehabilitated twice, they stand as a proud landmark of community involvement and pride."

Having the blood of Cherokee running through me, I sat there staring at the totem poles, letting my memories take me back to the time as a little girl listening to my grandfather's stories in his native tongue. His stories told of a race of spirit people. They were invisible unless they wanted to be seen, at which times they appeared physically to resemble the Cherokee. Or the spirit people would come as your spirit animal. A few people still believe an invisible supernatural being exists. Didanawisgi is the Cherokee word for traditional healer. The traditional healer was the historian or the keeper of myths, legends, traditions, and tribal wisdom that they learned from the supernatural. The shaman used magic along with special plant and herbal recipes to help the sick. I believe in magic and wish for it to always be a part of my life. Maybe the animals on these totem poles were the spirit animals of the indigenous people of the area.

"Excuse me, ma'am, can I get something started from the bar?" Taking a deep breath, I turned my head to face the server and sighed as I came back from my daydream.

"I was just marveling over your totem poles."

"Yes, they are magnificent. Did you know that one common misconception about tribal artwork in Washington State is that totem poles are traditional art forms from the

Coast Salish people. Totem poles are actually crests that represent clans from the indigenous people of Coastal Alaska and Canada. The reason totem poles are associated with Seattle and most of Washington state is because on October 18, 1899, a 60-foot totem pole from Fort Tongass, Alaska, was unveiled in Seattle's Pioneer Square and greeted by cheers of a multitude of people. The totem had been stolen from a Tlingit village several weeks before and was presented to the City of Seattle by the Chamber of Commerce "Committee of Fifteen" - the group of Seattle vandals (who were prominent citizens) that had taken the totem. It was not their place to have taken the totem. The Tlingit Nation later sued for the unlawful removal of the totem and the courts ruled in favor of the Tlingit people."

"Wow, that is an interesting history. The brochure says a local craftworker carved the totems here. "

"You are correct. Local Native American Craftsman Chief Don Lelooska carved our totem poles. He began work on the totems for display at the 1962 Seattle World's Fair, but he did not finish in time.

Did you need anything from the bar before I place your order."

"Yes, I would like to try a glass of the Cuvee De Labri. I also would like the steak bites rare with a house salad with blue cheese dressing. "

"I will get this order in right away. Would you prefer the wine with dinner or while you wait?"

"Yes, I will have a glass of wine while I wait."

The server left, and a short time later, the host came with my glass of wine. Sipping my wine and looking out the window. I heard the buzzing that lets me know just before she enters my mind. *"What could she possibly have to say to me, at this time?"* I stilled my mind to receive the intrusion. When I paused, my mind didn't cause the headaches that usually follow her abruptly popping into my thoughts.

"Take a trip up to Chief Lelooska lodge."

"What the hell? Now you decide to tell me where I should go."

Then silence, as always. The buzzing stopped, and I was alone in my head.

I am about ready for a straitjacket listening to this random voice I hear in my head from time to time. It is not my voice. It is a woman I feel I know, but how?"

After dinner, I returned to my room, needing more sleep for the drive up the highway to Seattle tomorrow.

The next morning, I got on the freeway and decided I was going the wrong way when I saw the Starbucks at the Woodland cut off. So, I took the turnoff and stopped for coffee and scones to wake up so I could get on the freeway going the right way up north to Seattle. As I am paying, I asked the clerk. "How far is Chief Lelooska?"

"Not far, maybe twenty minutes. Do you have GPS in your rig? Just enter Chief Lelooska interpretive center. You'll have to go south on this access road to the freeway intersection. Turn left up the Lewis River Highway about fifteen miles." The buzzing started again. Bracing myself, she slammed into my thoughts.

"Better hurry or you will be late."

"Be late for what?"

Then the silence that lets me know I am alone with my

thoughts again. I am in my rig in the drive through line. The second window was coming up. I headed out of the drive and back up the Lewis River hwy. Just like the Clerk said, a sign and arrow. Merwin Dam state park and Lelooska Interpretive center. My mother says that Eagles are a sign of luck. That you will have a blessed day if you find you are on the path of an eagle. Driving further up the road, I see the lodge and pull into an empty parking lot. I get out and walk up to the lodge. The door swings open, and a woman dressed in what looks like she is in a white ceremonial gown with beading of many colors. Her head band is adorned with three feathers and her long white hair was braided and hanging over her shoulder. She doesn't appear to be in her 30s, but in her dark eyes, you can see the wisdom of many years. She is beautiful, with a white aura that is warm and inviting.

Welcome, Deedra Lee. I have been waiting for you. My name is Loleatta. She stepped aside and ushered me to enter. It took a minute for my eyes to adjust. There in the middle of the room was a huge fire pit with a large fire blazing away. I could smell herbs in the smoke that floated across my senses. She walked over to the bench that was at the fire's edge and sat down. She patted the bench, encouraging me to sit with her. The heat from the fire was a pleasant change from the sodden day outside. I could hear the slight beat of a drum along with some chanting.

"Please join me, won't you?" Loleatta said as she patted the bench again.

I sat next to her on the bench. The amulet on my neck warmed slightly.

"How do you know my name?"

"I know many things about you child and your world. You will also understand more when you listen to your spirit guide. You have a lot of training to complete with your team."

"You will cleanse the evil from the land. Make the people abide by the rules their ancients have set forth for living in this world."

"You're talking about the woman's voice in my thoughts, aren't you?"

"Hello ma'am, we are closed. You can come back at 7:00pm when we open. I am going to have to ask you to leave." I stood up and turned to talk to the man in the back.

"Loleatta invited me in."

"That is not possible. She was my great grandmother, and she has been dead for many years. Who are you?"

I looked around. The drums and chanting had stopped. I turned slowly and there wasn't a blazing fire and no Loleatta. The amulet was cold. I shook my head in disbelief.

How could this be happening? I was just talking to her and the fire. I stopped my thoughts, took a deep breath. "Funny farm here I come."

I cleared my throat and turned back to the man in the back of the room.

"Sorry to have bothered you. I will be on my way now."

"Wait, who are you? How do you know my grandmother?"

I took a couple of steps to the door, out I flew, almost running to get into my rig. "What the hell was that? Was I talking to a ghost?" Pushing the start button and throwing the car into reverse, I backed out of the parking spot. Hitting the drive, I gave the car some gas and headed out of the center's parking lot. My hands hadn't stopped shaking and my heart was beating out of my chest.

As I was trying to take deep breaths and calm down inside, I was screaming in my thoughts, trying to make sense of what had just happened.

"What in the H E double L is going on, oh spirit guide?"

"Keep heading north, they know you have arrived… Hurry, time is short. Find the others. They will keep you safe."

"Who knows? I have arrived and who cares? Who or what are the others?" I was by now screaming out into the nothingness of the rig. I knew I was alone with my thoughts again. No humming in the back of my head when I hear her voice.

I drove up I-5; I was about an hour north, and my brain finally started functioning again after my supernatural experience. My hands had stopped shaking and the death grip on the steering wheel had let up. My back was tight, my hands hurt from gripping the steering wheel so tight, my neck was stiff, and the rain turned to drizzle along with an eerie fog that floated around, making it hard to see. I pulled into the rest area at Maytown for a cup of coffee. Pulling up, the fog seemed to engulf everything. I couldn't even see the trees in the rest area or the building to get my coffee and go to the bathroom. As I pulled up, finally connected with the curb to let me know I had pulled completely in the parking spot. A tall, thin man appeared out of the fog and was headed towards my rig. I reached down and locked all the doors with a click. My amulet lying on my chest warmed up again. Was it a warning of danger? Sitting in the fog, my imagination was running wild with the warning from my spirit guide before I turned off at the rest area.

"Now I am headed to crazy town calling her a spirit guide."

I watched as he walked between the cars without paying me any attention. Then he disappeared into the fog as fast as he appeared. Opening my door, I stepped out into the fog, I headed towards what I hoped were the restrooms and the coffee station. Hearing the laughter of people, I figured I was going in the right direction. Fifteen feet in front of me, I could finally see the building and smell the coffee. Went in the restroom, did my business, and washed my hands. The dryer echoed loudly off the metal and concrete walls. I stepped out and went to get the coffee that smelled so good. I waited along with the other travelers that had pulled off talking about the weather and getting their coffee. The Rotarians that staffed the rest areas had cookies and bagels with cream cheese. Yummy, I bought a raisin cinnamon bagel. I picked up two cream cheeses. They were small and I like cream cheese. They had a microwave set up to warm the bagels. I had the guy behind the table cut my bagel in half and warm it in the microwave. Warmed, he placed it in a sack.

I walked carefully back to my rig, so I didn't trip on anything. The fog was so dense you couldn't see 3 feet in front of you. The drizzle penetrated my coat, making me shiver. I was getting cold and wet quickly. I opened my door, took off my coat, threw it over the passenger seat to dry and then got in the rig and turned up the heat. Taking a sip of my excellent coffee and biting into the bagel. My mood was improving even if the weather kept on. I sat there waiting for the weather to lift. I tried to figure out what was happening to me. The voice in my head, or now we are calling her a spirit guide. Then what was with the Native American princess? Was she a ghost? Was I taking advice from a ghost? Or was heading for a straitjacket and the nearest lock up for the mentally insane... I had taken the last bite of my bagel and a finishing my cup of coffee. The fog was thinning; the sun was trying to come out, what weird weather. Even the drizzle had stopped. I stepped out of the rig to give a good stretch and throw away my cup and napkin. Back in the car, reaching to put on my seat belt, started the rig, backed out and headed to my next destination, the Silver Cloud Hotel University district.

I had booked a room for a couple of days until I could find an apartment close to campus. The rig I was driving had to be returned in a week. I passed the Sea-Tac airport sign as I traveled further up I-5. Looking west, I could see downtown Seattle, then I heard the GPS. "Take exit 70, NE 65th South Ravenna Boulevard. Turn right 25th, in ½ mile, the hotel is on your left. I pulled into the hotel. I drove under the brick arches and stopped, got out of my rig, and walked into the lobby. The lobby was busy with people checking in. I got in line for a brief wait to check in. I was given a double queen on the 3rd floor, room 314, going back outside to get into my rig. Was told to park in the lot out back and my key card would let me in any door. Finding the lot full, my parking spot was in the last row. The amulet warmed again. I looked around the lot, seeing nothing. Maybe it wasn't a warning, maybe it was on the fritz, it didn't come with any instructions and the gypsy wasn't helpful. The lot had tons of lights with a six-foot fence around the parking lot. It seemed fairly safe. I grabbed my overnight bag and locked the door. As the clerk told me my key card let me in on the ground floor. I followed the signs to the elevator just past the noise of the indoor pool and the smell of chlorine. Pushing the arrow for up. I waited, listening to the families having fun in the pool. The ding at the elevator alerting me the door was about to open. The elevator was empty. I stepped in the elevator, hit button number three, for the third floor. I wasn't sure I was on the right floor. The numbers seemed backward to me. My room was at the end of the hall. I opened the door to a large room with two queen-size beds, a desk, chair, and TV. Bathroom was very nice with a granite counter and two sinks, tile shower and flooring.

I was getting hungry. I pulled the book that has all the info of the local area out. I didn't feel like going to the restaurant to eat. I just want to stay in my room and have something comforting and delivered. Found Delfino's Chicago deep-dish pizza. That should work. All that delicious bread ought to put me in a coma. I called in the order and gave the address of the hotel. They said they would leave the pizza at the lobby front desk.

Then I opened my bag to pull out the clothes I intended to wear tomorrow for registration.

An hour later, the phone rang to let me know I could come and pick up my pizza at the lobby desk. Dressed in yoga pants and a sweatshirt, I walked down to the lobby to get my pizza. The smell was wonderful as it filled the elevator. Arms full of a pizza, a liter of diet Pepsi and some cinnamon dough for ordering the special. They covered the pizza with Canadian bacon, pepperoni, and pineapple. The smells of the pizza and the cinnamon dough were making me salivate. I stepped out of the elevator onto my floor. Getting the key out without dropping the pizza was harder than it should have been. In the end, I sat down the soda and the cinnamon dough on the floor to pull the key free from my sweat-shirt pocket. The door opened with a beep and green color for go. I pushed the door open with my shoulder. Bent over and picked the cinnamon dough and the cola off the floor. I set the pizza along with the dough and Pepsi on the desk. I went back out to the ice machine around the hall by the elevator. To fill the bucket with ice to cool off the soda. I headed back to my room. After finishing a couple of slices, my tummy was full, and I drifted off. An arm pulled me close to a hard body. The smell of spices and earth invaded my senses. His warm breath caressed my neck as he whispered, "I have been looking for you all of my life." I rolled over to look into the most beautiful blue-green eyes; they were pools of lake water that took my breath away. He had chiseled features and hard smooth abs, broad shoulders that met his narrow waist.

I knew I was dreaming, but it felt so real. His essence was so intense; with his earthy smell and the hint of spices that was all man. His arms snug around my body as his warm breath spread across my lips. Then, with a slow desperation, he devoured my mouth, his warm lips pressed to mine and then sliding his tongue gently into my mouth. A moan escaped. I was melting into the stranger; my breathing had become faster; my heart beat out of my chest. Warmth pooled lower in my belly and a small throbbing was causing me to peek towards a climax. Reaching up to grab his dark hair and pull him closer. I knew somewhere in my brain this was a marvelous fantasy. That's what I get for holding out and being picky about my partners. It had been a year without even a kiss. I was going to let this dream play out. Pulling him closer, I could feel his hardness press against my belly. He whispered, "I have to be inside of you."   I couldn't wait. He reached down, putting one finger at a time into my wet folds, stretching me, making room for his massive shaft. Curling his fingers back, hitting the G-spot every time. He was sending shivers up my spine as he brought me to the precipitous of a climax. He placed his mouth on my erect nipple and began tugging with his teeth, sucking, and pulling, then pushing in one finger, then another, in and out repeatedly as his thumb still rubbed on the button at my core.

He whispered in my ear, "Just let it happen, love." as I hit the edge and fell off floating on the waves of pleasure that have never happened for me with any of my partners, euphoria like nothing I have ever experienced. I did not want to stop. Not able to catch my breath somewhere in the distance, I hear a phone ring over and over, never stopping. I was trying to pull myself out of the haze of my erogenous dream. I reached over my head, fumbling to find out what was making all the noise, and then lifting the phone receiver up to my ear. I heard a woman's voice.

"It is 7:00am; this is your wake-up call."

I opened my eyes to find I was alone and fully clothed as

I was last night when I must have crashed after the carb overload of pizza. I got up and took off last night's clothes to get into the shower. The hot water ran over my body when it hit my nipples. I pulled back… they were tender. I looked down and my nipples were red and chaffed, as if they had been worked over. But that was not possible. It was just a dream. Washing my hair, I thought of the luscious man that I fantasized right into my bed.

"Ouch!" I was trying to be careful not to let the shower run on my nipples full on. Reaching to shut off the shower, I thought how nice it would have been to actually have the man of my dreams in the shower with me.

"Stop thinking like that, get your thoughts together, registration is today; you don't have time for daydreaming about Mr. Hotness, like a 16-year-old pubescent teen."

After I chastised myself, I pulled the shower door back and reached for the plush white towel that hung on the bar outside. Drying off, I looked at my reflection in the mirror. I had bags under my eyes and dark circles from my sleepless night.

"No more pizza before bed."

I hung the house keeping sign on the doorknob and left. Walking to the parking lot, the hairs on the back of my neck rose. I stopped and looked around, taking in my surroundings. My amulet heated again. I wish I knew if it was a warning or something different. I didn't see anyone but picked up my steps getting to my car. Got in and locked the door.

"This is ridiculous. I am dreaming sensual dreams and imagining I am being watched." Turning on the rig, a guy stepped out of the shadows in the back of the parking lot. He was tall and slim, like the guy in the rest area. I got that weird feeling again. My amulet heated on my skin. I watched him just like the guy who disappeared into the fog in the rest area. This guy disappeared into the shadows of the hotel. I put the rig in drive and took off. I went out of the parking lot onto 25th heading South, then left on 44th, then pulled a U-turn on NE 45th to pass Riley's auto parks, then University. Just as the Clerk said as I picked up my pizza from the lobby last night when I asked for directions to the university. I pulled onto University Way NE "The Ave." Head to the Central Plaza Underground parking. I parked and got my campus map out.

Chapter 2

University Campus

It was a sodden, frosty January morning in Seattle, Washington... The snowstorm had been on the ground for many days when it drizzled. The silvery clouds swirled around with the swell of dancers in the sky. The rain fell sideways with a bite that seeped into the bones. I was beginning with my first quarter at the University of Washington in Seattle. "Go Huskies."

When I had dressed this morning at the lodge, I plucked out my comfortable jeans with a blue ribbed sweater.

The amulet the gypsy gave me still hung around my neck for protection, just in case. As I headed out, I didn't have an inkling which way was registration. The college grounds were huge and gothic; it had to have gone on for miles. I thought as I wondered along the pathways of this traditional school. If these walls could tell me what they have seen.

"What secrets could they tell?" Thinking about campus loss, and I was too proud to seek help. I sat down on a stone bench at the edge of the brick paved circle. The seat was numbing. I shuddered as I got out my campus map, looking at it lost. When a lovely red curly-haired young woman stood in front of me, she smiled as though she knew I was lost. "Hey there, you seem lost. Can I help you?" I puffed out a gust of vapor from the warmth of my breath. The air was very crisp.

She was about 5 ft tall, maybe 90 lbs., and her hair was pulled back in a ponytail. Her bright blue-green eyes were gentle and peaceful. She couldn't have been over 20 years old. As I watched her, she was grinning as if she knew something I didn't know, but perhaps I should. Thinking to myself.

"She looks normal enough!"

"Ahem, looking for the registration building. I have figured out it was called Kane Hall." Was looking up and staring at the gargoyles instead of my map as I walked around. Small confession to make. I am lost." Smiling, hoping she wouldn't think I was a dimwit.

"They are distracting and beautiful, aren't they? Did you know most gargoyles are mounted on structures to used to divert water off the roofs, like our modern-day gutters? The water flows through their mouths or beaks. Unfortunately, with a few exceptions, most of the grotesque figures on the University campus are not true gargoyles. I apologize I can't stop myself when it comes to the Gothic Architecture of this campus. Finding it fascinating. I tend to over explain I have been told. She laughed.

"Well, maybe not so normal, but who am I to judge?" I chuckled under my breath. She motion with her hands to follow her. *"Ok, sort of normal. At least she is helpful."* I grinned to myself. She studied me, scrunched up her nose, and laughed as though she heard what I felt about her.

"I am headed that way. I'm Amanda. What is your name?"

I stared at her, not answering for a minute like a loon, gawking at her for a few seconds longer, like her question didn't register. It wasn't that I didn't hear her question; it was the static she was putting off; I heard in my mind; it was coming from her. Like a shield on an old Syfy movie all wavy and staticky. The noise of an old 1960's tube radio, as you tuned into a new channel. I shook my head to clear the interference. "Oh, umm… sorry, my name is Deedra…. But just call me Dee." *"Hmmm, is the static her blocking her mind from me? Or I am causing it? Maybe she is trying to enter my mind."*

We arrived at the registration building, where she turned and smiled.

"Here you go, Kane Hall. You should check in over there. I'll see you around campus." she had pointed to the long line that was full of students.

She turned and headed off across the square.

"Thanks Amanda, see you around campus."

A guy on a megaphone caught my attention.

"Freshman Orientation and class assignment are going on in Kane Hall. Inside to the right are tables set up alphabetically by last name, pick up your packet and then meet with guidance counselors to make sure of your classes and their helpers will inform you where to go. The orientation in the main hall begins in two hours."

I was taking three classes, trying to ease my way back into the learning process. My first class was at 10:00 am Monday, Wednesday, and Friday. Taking mythology in the gargoyle building. I really was not sure what to expect, but it covered the English credit and it looked interesting. Really needed to finish my associate's degree. My second class was a math credit in the Gowen building; my third class was creative writing in the Parrington. So, all my classes took place one right after the other. That way, I could find some source of employment at one of the local restaurants. It took most of the afternoon to be done with the registration… The aide told us there was going to be a tour of campus to help prevent you from getting disoriented and to help you arrive at class on time.

"Like that was going to save me, with my non-logical capacity for direction."

We all clamber aboard the campus bus that headed south.

We passed by the Suzzallo Library. The bus halted and let us out at George Washington bust, where we cruised through Red Square. We left the Gargoyle building. Then we wandered down to the Drumheller Fountain, and then another bus took us up and got us back to Kane Hall, where we came out for our one-hour orientation. They brought in two speakers to inspire us. The tour of campus thoroughly put me off balance and drove my sense of direction further off. I could never negotiate the first day I was leaving two hours early, so I wouldn't become lost. Stressing over the day, I heard a growl then a rumbled. It was my stomach letting me know how starving I was. I wasn't sure I could sit for an hour. I wondered if they would notice I wasn't there? Looking across the square, there was Mary Gate Espresso. I inhaled the smell of coffee as I strolled across the plaza.

Walking towards the coffee shop's doors, one opened, and I gasped. There he stood, holding the door for me. The guy from my dreams. The same sculptured body. His face was chiseled to perfection. Same broad shoulders with narrow waist. His t-shirt showed off the definition of muscles as it strained to keep them in. His hair was chocolate brown, wavy. It was a little messy around his flawless face. His full lips look ready to kiss. My mouth went dry, and then I looked up into the pools of blue-green of his eyes. A flush ran up my neck and across my face, a blush like a schoolchild, which I was not. My body became warm and tingly all over. My heartbeat so hard it felt lodged in my throat.

As I drew closer to him, my heart skipped a beat or three. Chills intensified going down my spine, and when he smiled, his eyes sparkled in the light. I could barely breathe, let alone look away. The electricity in the doorway could have blown the circuits in most of Seattle if turned loose.

No one has ever spiked my awareness of a single individual, as he did at this moment. When I met his eyes, I was in stasis. I couldn't for the life of me stop ogling. Then, in the next second, he looked up long enough for me to shake my head and clear my thoughts.

Then I heard him whisper into my ear or my mind. I wasn't sure which or if I really heard him or not.

"It's you!"

I continued to pass him and into Mary's. I was so bewildered I could not even think about why I was even there. After a few seconds passed, I had time to regain my composure and was not hungry anymore. Well, not the kind that nourishes my body. Turning back to look for him, he had disappeared into the students on campus. I headed back out the door of Mary's, seeing if I could find him. He had vanished.

"I swear, I heard him whisper. *It's you! But that is ridiculous. Isn't it?"*

 Standing there in disbelief, who would believe me? That the man of my dreams exists? *"Another coincidence? Fate was messing with me. Life happens for a reason."*

Stepping back into Mary's gates espresso, I was trembling. I stepped up to the counter to order a coffee. "Ma'am can I get you something started?" It took me a minute before I could speak. "Yes, I have a large vanilla soy latte, thank you."

While waiting for my coffee to be prepared. I looked at the wall with jobs and apartments posted. I pulled off numbers and took several flyers. After picking up my coffee, I sat at a table with my thoughts; I remembered why I had come to Mary's. I made few phone calls about places to rent. All I got was, "Sorry we have rented that apartment." I felt pretty bummed when I heard the bell at the top of the door coming into Mary's open and looked up. It was Amanda. She saw me and smiled and came walking over.

 "Do you mind if I sit?"

"No, of course not." I smiled up at her.

"How is it going on your first day on campus?"

"Pretty decent, had the classes taken care of, and now I need a place to live."

"Actually, I have an acquaintance that just moved out. How about I give the proprietor a call for you?"

"Wow Amanda, that would be great. You must be my guardian angel. You have been so helpful to me on my first day here." Then I thought I heard her say.

"Those were my orders, to keep an eye on you." I looked at Amanda to see if I could read her.

"Did you say something?"

"Um, no, what do you think I said?"

"Oh, nothing, never mind."

"I am just going bat shit crazy thinking I can hear people's thoughts."

I was excited she knew someone. Maybe this was it and I could start looking for a job.

"Amanda, thank you, but I must confession. I have some parameters.

Number one in importance needs to be close to campus. Number two walking distance from school, job, and food. I only have the rental in a few days. Oh, and rent needs to be very inexpensive. I'm running out of savings and need to find a job. I'm not asking for much." Laughing, I bated my eyelashes and gave my most endearing smile.

"It is just on the other side of campus up towards Ravenna Blvd. I'm sure the maintenance guy is there. Let me check. He would have the keys to show you around the apartment building."

"Are you sure I don't want to be in any trouble?"

"It's no trouble at all. Just let me text my friend."

A few minutes later, she stared up at me. You can see it today before 5:00 pm and have the keys and sign the lease if you like it tomorrow. She wrote the address on my coaster.

"I have to be going; do you think you can find the address?"

"Sure, my rig has GPS. I'll just plug it in. Thank you, I owe you big time. Anything I can do for you, just ask." Amanda waved it off. "What are friends for? I will see you later around campus."

Then she went just as fast as she showed up. Oddly, she didn't buy coffee. *It seemed odd that Amanda seemed to pop up when I needed help. Was she following me around? That's ridiculous.*

Chapter 3

New Life Begins

*W*alking back to my rig, I was recounting my run-in with Mr. Hotness, then running into Amanda twice in one day and to get her help. I should buy a lottery ticket with this much good luck.

She is a lifesaver. I was getting a ton of *"Already rented."* from my phone calls.

I sipped my coffee and looked back at the ad wall. A flyer appeared that wasn't there before when I walked in. The flyer read host wanted in a small establishment called BJ's. The address looked familiar, so I pulled the fly and shoved it into my pocket as I left Mary's.

I was just alone with my thoughts the rest of the day, not a sound from my spirit guide all day. Getting back to my rig, I put the address in my GPS that Amanda had written on the coaster and drove off to meet the maintenance guy to see the apartment. I pulled up to the curb and shut off my mortar. There was a guy who was waiting in front of the apartment complex, dressed in overalls. I was hoping he was the Maintenance guy, not some weirdo standing around an apartment building. I got out of the rig and looked around and felt nothing weird. My amulet didn't warm up. I stepped up and asked,

"Are you Amanda's friend? She didn't tell me your name."

He reached out his hand.

"Yes, I am Amanda's friend. You can call me Mannie. Amanda said you would be by." "Hi, I'm Dee."

"You're here to see the apartment?"

"Yes." We headed down the sidewalk, he was explaining.

"This is the smallest place we have. The rent is 700.00 a month. First and last month's deposit waived for any friend of Amanda's."

It shocked me. I just stood there with my mouth open.

He opened the main door and ushered me into an alcove with mailboxes that lined one wall. Further to the left of the mailboxes was a staircase and around the corner was a wrought iron wire- like bird cage elevator. It was larger inside than it looked. Mannie raised the overhead safety gate then opened the door. I stepped in and stepped to the back. Mannie shut the door; the elevator groaned as it ascended to the 4th floor. Mannie manhandled the door, then the safety gate, and walked out and I followed him out of the elevator in a hurry, not sure how safe the elevator was. I was walking down the hallway with hardwood floors and carpet runners up the middle of the hall, like in an old hotel.

"Hey Mannie, is this an old hotel?" He smiled up.

"Yes, it was back in the 1800s. Then, in the 1950s, the owners converted into apartments. The new owners wanted to make low-income rentals for college students." Mannie stopped in front of the door marked with number 403, took the key ring out of his pocket, and turned the keys around until he found the correct one. Placing the key into the lock, he turned, and the door fell open. The room had two double-hung small windows. Outside those windows was an old metal fire escape. There was a Murphy bed behind the mahogany cabinet that sat against the wall just before the bathroom. I was fortunate again; I had a bathroom. Some apartments had to use a communal bathroom on the second floor. The room was small, but the 10-foot ceilings and the crown molding made the room feel much bigger than it was.

"I will take it. When can I pick up the keys?" Mannie handed me the keys and said he would meet me tomorrow to sign the lease. With keys in hand, I went back to the small storage I had rented to get my belongings

I had a small stereo speaker for my phone; I bought a small old green couch that I picked up at a garage sale and a small table with two chairs to eat at and do my homework. My dad had bought me a laptop for Christmas. I had the basics. I opened the garage door to my things. Lucky for me, the maintenance guy walks by asked me If I need a hand. I smiled. "That would be great if you could spare a minute or twenty to help me."

"Sure, let's take the legs off this table first." We finished loading my rig when out of nowhere an oversized tabby walked over to me and said hello; I wondered where he came from. We were in an industrial area, not residential. He talked too much, rubbing my legs, going around in circles. I reach down and picked him up. His purr got louder, and he nuzzled my face. The maintenance guy piped up. "That damn cat has been around here for weeks. I'm pretty sure someone just left him. It's a shame when people store their stuff and pay dearly for it and just drop off their animal when they want to move on. We get a lot of that; I usually have to call the humane society to come get the poor things." Falling in love with him. I no longer wondered where he belonged. I would guess he was around eight months old. We just hit it off. He was hungry, and I was lonely. I now had everything a girl could want but a job. I put the cat in the passenger side, and I got in and headed to the apartment. Driving over to the apartment, I asked him if I could call him DC instead of dam cat. He looked at me and meow. I took that as a yes. Getting closer, I sure hoped Mannie was still hanging around to help me unload all my earthly belongings. I was surprised I didn't get a ticket. The couch the size of a love seat hung out of the back of my rig. I wasn't sure how I was going to get it to my apartment. I couldn't have loaded it myself. Good thing the maintenance guy was at storage place. Helped me load it into my rig. My day was going so well, I just hoped someone would help me take it up to my apartment. Pulling up, Mannie was still working in the landscape. I rolled down my window and asked him if he would help me. He smiled pointed to the unloading zone in front of the apartment. Mannie met me with a cart. We unloaded the couch and left it on the grass. We filled the cart with the table, one chair, and all my clothes. He helped me unload all my belongings and get them in to my studio apartment. Then we came back down to get the couch. You could tell Mannie had done this before. DC just followed me around, riding in the elevator like he owned the place. I was surprised I didn't have to pay a pet deposit. My day was full of surprises. After I got the furniture placed, I was hungry and remembered I still needing to look for a job to help with the rent. I thought I would just be a server. It was hard work, but the tips made up for the crappie pay. Remembering, I shoved a flyer in my jacket the day after Mary's. I began looking for my coat, which was on the floor by the bed. I hadn't put all my clothes away in the oversized closet with a built-in dresser. Pulling out the flyer, it read BJ's. I noticed while picking up a few dishes the other day there was a charming bar around the corner from my apartment called BJ's nightspot. Could this be the same place?

Grabbing my coat off the hook headed out. Yelled at DC, "Be good," on my way out the door; I went. Walking down the block and came around the corner. Half the way down the block on the left was the nightclub.

Suddenly, the hairs on the back of my neck stood up. The buzzing like the fluorescent lights when you turn them on started in the head. I braced for her intrusion.

"You must hurry inside. You are being followed, and they know you're here."

"Who is following me? Who knows, I am here?" Then nothing, of course, just silent's of my mind.

 I looked around. I didn't see anyone, but I could, since someone was watching me. My amulet was hot, almost burning my skin.

The nightclub was 10 feet away, so I hurried to the door. I stopped, taking another look around. A tall, slim man stepped out of the shadows.

Was that the third time I noticed the same man, first in the rest area and then in the hotel parking lot? As I passed the window in front, the signed read HELP WANTED. I hurried in. The aroma of cigarettes, cigars, and wine wafted out the door as I opened it hit me. Sure, the law was no smoking, but I could still smell the residue left from the years that many people had smoked in here.

The door swung shut behind me and I waited for my eyes to adjust to my surroundings before stepping further in. My hands were shaking again. I felt so vulnerable; I had never taken self-defense classes. Maybe I should enroll in one. It was a bigger city than I had ever lived in. Was I being followed? If so, who was following me? Looking around the room, I could see the room that had several tables set for dinner.

The energy said welcome, knowing I would be safe here. Don't know why I just could feel it and the voice in my head gave no more warnings. I rub my hands up and down my arms and try to get them to stop trembling. Shaking a shiver away, I walked further into the nightclub.

 The room was small but had that old-world charm. The bar spanned the full length of the wall. They cut the ceiling slat mahogany that made diamond shape patterns all the way across the ceiling. Behind the bar that spans at least 30ft with ornate arches over each mirror with gold ornate inlays, it looks like it could possibly be Irish around the turn of the century. A teardrop chandelier hung over the white marble. The marble also ran around the back of the bar, where they stacked the bottles of liquor just waiting to be made into a special drink. The hardwood floors had the character of an old establishment. At one end of the bar was a black Steinway grand piano. I walked over and ran my hand across its sleek service. Off-white chipped ivory keys showed their age. It had a date of 1912. The music of the keys was melodious to my ear as I pushed the keys one after the other, dragging my fingers over them. The piano seemed to talk to me as I ran a single digit along the keys. A tingling sensation came from the piano. It pulled Mr. Hotness to mind.

"Wow, I have to let that go."

It was almost spooky. I could almost smell the earthy spiciness of the man.

"I must be losing it!!!!"

This place felt familiar. Peacefulness came over me, the warning disappeared, and I felt safe. Yet, I could just be losing my mind to onset of senility.

Standing in front of the piano, looking at its beautiful curves, I heard a woman's voice.

"Do you play?"

The pleasant voice floated out from behind the bar.

"I wish…. I love piano music, but never had the talent to put my fingers to the keys and make them sound the way they should. No, I'm looking for a job?"

Pulling a flyer from Mary Gates Espresso out and showed it to her.

"Also, I saw the help wanted in the window. I just rented an apartment around the corner. Oh, *my god I am rambling. I do that when I get nervous. I should just let you talk.*"

I looked towards the bar. She was standing behind it with a towel in hand, and she was pulling out and wiping glasses from the dishwasher, drying and rubbing off the water spots.

"So, what do you go by?"

"Deedra, but my friends call me just Dee."

"Ok, just Dee, it is." We laughed.

"My name is Mica."

She was in her mid-thirties, about five-seven, with long brown hair with red highlights and her eyes were aquamarine blue like none I have ever seen. Her figure was lean, yet muscular, with long legs. Built like a yoga instructor. She seemed like she would be great to work with.

Holding herself with the energy of a strong an independent woman; take no prisoners. She was dressed in jeans, boots, t-shirt, with a black apron over the top that had the BJ's logo on the front. Putting the towel down, she stepped forward with a bottle of wine and corkscrew in one hand.

She held out her other hand.

 "I am the manager, so you are talking to the right person to ask for a job." Curiously, I asked.

"Who owns the club?"

"A long-time ago a group of friends and I, bought the club. We all work here at various jobs. We employ about seven students and have other staff to cover in the owner's absence." She gave no names, just short and to the point. Then she elaborates as if she could feel her answer disappointed me.

 "Our primary investor comes in once a week to check on the bar. He checks out the books, places orders for supply and keeps the liquor inventory. He sometimes listens to music and has dinner. There are times, if it is late at night, after closing, he will play the piano. He has a room above the bar that he stays in." She changed the subject back to me.

"Have you waited tables before?"

"Years ago, but I am a hard worker. In high school, I worked at a drive-in burger bar A & W. As a carhop, we were on roller skates. Cars pulled up to place their order, by looking a huge Plexiglas menu, then speaking into a little box. The person on the other end took your order. Balance was the trick to delivering root beer in glass mugs with little blue animals hanging off the edge of the mugs.

The key to being a great server was making it to the car without spilling the soda. That counts, doesn't it? I can really use the job."

Mica smiled.

"If you cannot keep up, you will only last one day."

 I nodded in agreement and smiled. "Um, what smells so good? "

"Hungry? Jerry is preparing a Prime rib for the special tonight. Would you like to try some?"

"If it's not too much trouble, I just moved in around the corner and didn't have breakfast or lunch."

"It's no problem. I will be right back." She was so nice. Mica returned with a prime rib sandwich on sourdough and a Pepsi. While I ate, she told me about Jake and Jerry that also collaborated with her. Jake would be training me tomorrow.

"Mica the sandwich was fantastic. What do I owe you?"

"I will take it off your first check."

"Really? Are you sure?"

"Yes, then you will start tomorrow evening at 5:00 pm sharp." I got down from the bar stool to leave.

 "See you then." I smiled and hurried towards the door. I

turned back to her.

 "Thank you again for giving me a chance. I will see you tomorrow."

I stepped back out the club's front door. I stopped, took a deep breath, looked around to see if I saw anyone in the shadows. My amulet warmed a little, just enough warning. I stepped onto the sidewalk at a good pace, heading around the corner back to my apartment. Just as I reached the door, that eerie feeling that I was being watched came over me and I stepped inside. I turned and looked out the window of the apartment door. I couldn't see anything in the shadows.

When I opened the elevator door and stepped in, it reminded me of how grateful I was, with a full belly, and that Mica would take a chance on me to be a host for the nightclub. I had forgotten all about the warning from my spirit guide or whatever the hell the voice in my head was.

To keyed up, I couldn't sleep. Tried to focus, asking each part of my body to relax first my shoulders, arms, down my body to my feet soon I drifted off. I was somewhere between sleeping and awake. I saw the exquisite man that had held the door for me at the cafe. This time, I was frightened. I could hear all his thoughts and he was so drawn to me he wanted me; he felt an uncontrollable urge to grab and take me.

I wanted to run but I could not… Frozen in place, I could hear someone calling to me. Not the voice in my head. This voice was like melted dark chocolate, velvety, hypnotic. It overwhelmed me with the smell of earth and spices. It was intoxicating, all-male and the voice that kept calling my name. I wanted to scream, and nothing would come out. Finally… squeaked out a mousy scream, and I set up in bed; the alarm was going off.

I could not shake off the feeling that the dream had left with me. I continued to be in a state of utter frustration, like having sex and never having an orgasm. First the erotic dream at the hotel, then I run into him at the coffee shop and now a scary dream.

"Hello, spirit guides any thoughts why I am dreaming about Mr. Hotness?"

As usual, silence, nothing going on in my head but my own confused thoughts.

I had to stop with the Mr. Hottie and get my head on straight and stop fantasizing about a man I don't even know.

My first class was mythology. I walked in and saw Amanda. I went over and walked up to the level she was on and sat down next to her.

"Hey, Amanda."

"Hi Dee, how is your apartment?"

"It is perfect. Didn't know I would have you in any of my classes. I am glad to see a friendly face. Also, glad you have friends. Mannie waved me first and last month's deposit because of you and no pet deposit. A cat adopted me. I couldn't turn him away."

She looked at me and smiled. "Yeah, he is great that way; he likes to give the students a break."

"Do you know what this class is all about?"

"It's about the local Indian legends. We are close enough to the reservation that knowing about their beliefs was an important history to the local area. It is also a required credit for any degree."

The professor stepped up to the front of the class.

Hello Class, my name is Professor Jacquelyn Bluestar. You may call me Professor J. Before I give out my assignment for the quarter, look to your left. Starting with the outside row looking left, that will be your study partner for the duration of my class. Those of you who don't have anyone to your left meet me after class and we will pair you up. I was on the end of the row and Amanda was on my left. They assigned us to gather information about the many tribes. Snohomish, Snoqualmie, Puyallup, Skagit Quintal, Quileute, Oh, Makah. We are supposed to discover something unique about the tribe. What they had in common. Our first semester paper had to do with folklore and legends; it had to be a 1500-word report. This was going to be our semester grade. The paper was due on the last day of the semester.

"Amanda, you're from around here. Where do we start?" She suggested the library. I had not been there yet. After class, we went over there. I only had an hour and then I had to leave for work.

It was the most beautiful building on campus, the oversized doors with the etching on them. As I pushed on the heavy wooden door, my hands tingled a familiar feeling going through my mind as I pushed past, letting go of the door. The tingling stopped. Could these be the doors in my dreams? They etched the door with strange writing and some interesting carved pictures. Again, I had a strange feeling when touching the doors. It somehow had something to do with the land and its people. I could read parts of the words that looked like a Cherokee dialect my grandfather taught me when I was seven. So many curious things have been happening since I started my trip to Seattle. Weird energy I picked up left me with a bizarre feeling I am being followed and or watched. The amulet warms up against my chest like a warning system to be careful. The voice in my mind, the energy the night club gives off. Still, the possibility I am headed for the nearest institution hasn't been ruled out yet.

Suzzallo is the name of the library. I wondered if the name of the library and the doors had some significance. It was a story of the one who would save them.

"Whatever the one is… and who would save was about. I would have to study the doors later."

I apologized to Amanda because I had to leave almost as soon as we got there. I did not want to be late for work.

"I am so sorry, but it is the first night at my new job. I want to be on time. I have to go."

"I think I'll stay awhile and do some more research." Anyhow, that's what I told her as she left to go to be with the guys at the club for safe keeping.

"Now that I have you squared away at the club and in the apartment, I think I will take the night off." Dee turned around and gave me a funny look. "Did you say something?"

No, why? What do you think you heard?"

"Oh Nothing, do you know anyone that might tell us about the carvings on the doors of the library?"

"Why?" she asked

"It looks familiar somehow to me. I can sort of read the writing and symbols on them. Weird huh?"

My Grandfather taught me this dialect when I was seven

years old.

"Sure, I will check around and see if anyone knows anything about the doors."

"Thanks, I'll see you tomorrow."

That was weird. The same static wavey sound came at me with a few words. *(Have you squared away, keep her safe.)* Just shaking my head to clear my mind. Could that static noise be coming for Amanda? With my thoughts taking a turn down batshit crazy avenue. I hurried off to work and arrived ten minutes early. When I got to the club, I hung up my coat on the rack by the kitchen and then got an apron on and reported to Mica. She told me to work with Jake.

"Jake, this is Deedra, and I want you to see how she will fit with our little group keeping the club running smoothly."

"Hi", I smiled.

"Hey." Jake was tall, about 32 years old, with strawberry blonde dreadlocks that went down to his waist. He had it pulled into a ponytail at the back of his head. When he smiled, his dimples made his face light up. He has that surfer guy vibe, with an underlying strength. I knew instantly we would hit it off. I asked where he wanted me to start. He just pointed to the area in the club's front.

"You can start in the dining room. Do you think you can

oversee the dinner crowd?"

"I will give it my best shot…. "

As I grabbed a couple of menus, I looked it over. They only had a few items on the menu, and the bar could manage the rest. There were two couples sitting at a table and they appeared as though they had stopped in after a bad day at work.

I went over to ask them if they wanted anything to drink, just my luck. They ordered four unique drinks. I took my order to the bar.

"Hey kid! You must be the new gal?" I was sure I was older than he was, but I had to remember I only looked 18.

"I'm Jerry." He put out his hand, and I shook it. I let go faster than I should because I could hear him say. *"Boy, is she young and uncontrolled, wide-open thoughts."* I just stood there, staring.

"I'm Deedra, but you can call me Dee."

 "Is everything alright Dee?"

"Oh yeah, a sorry… I thought you looked familiar."

"I couldn't say. Did you just think? "Boy, she is young and uncontrolled, has wide open thoughts."

Jerry was tall & dark with blue eyes so dark they looked

black until the light hit them just right. They were midnight blue and a sweetness that just made me melt in his presence. I was not the only one who had noticed I had a feeling he had groupies that came in just to flirt with him at the bar. He looked to be in his mid-30s.

The night got busy for a while, and then it slacked off around 10:00pm. I was cleaning up and refilling the salt and pepper shakers. I also was checking to make sure all the ketchup was full. Jake came over.

 "Dee, you did an excellent job. Have you waited tables before?"

   "Thanks, not really. I just needed the job." As I looked down, I couldn't take compliments well. They always made me feel uncomfortable.

I heard him yell in back to Mica.

"She is the best you have hired so far."

"Good, then I can take the sign down."

"Deedra, you have the job." I smiled.

Mica called out from back in the kitchen area.

"Jake and Jerry, you guys need to get busy so we can get the hell out of here."

"You don't know how good it feels to have a job. Can I help

you close up the club for the night?"

"Sure, that would be great." We finished cleaning and set the chairs on top of the tables so the cleaning people could sweep up after hours. As we walked out the front doors, Jake locked it behind us.

 Jake smiled. "See you tomorrow. Do you need me to walk you home?"

"No, it's not far. I'm fine good night" I smiled, thinking I was a big girl, and I didn't need him to walk me a couple of blocks. He smiled back at me. "You need to be careful in this neighborhood. I'll walk with you. Mica will kick my ass if I lose her extra help." We walked around the corner to my apartment, about two blocks from the club. When we arrived, I smiled and winked at him. "We wouldn't want you to lose your ass to a woman now, would we?" Jake made sure I made it home and even walked me up the fourth floor right to my door. It was so sweet that he was so concerned about my safety when I had only just met him. "Thanks Jake, I will see you tomorrow" he smiled and winked, "See you then. Good night, Dee." I was kind of thankful for Jake after the voice gave me the warning and the guy, I have seen in the shadows several times.

Wow, I was beat. DC was waiting for me, meowing the minute I walked in the door looking for his dish of milk. I opened the refrigerator and poured him some canned milk. Then I went straight to bed.

The night was moonless. The darkness engulfed me as I lay with DC on my bed. I drifted off and was dreaming of the club. It was dark when I arrived. I could hear Jake talking but could not see him. I listened for a minute or two and then called out again, Jake, are you there? There was no answer. Then I heard my name. "Deedra." It was the same velvety voice that had enticed me in my other dreams. Just like before, I knew I was in a dream. I was trying to see what would happen if I moved forward, then a scream. A man stepped in front of me out of the shadows.

Waking up with a scream looked around, still in bed. It was my apartment. I was going to have to pay attention to what I was eating late at night.

Needing to pull it together and get to school. I got up and took my shower, was blowing dry my hair when I felt a breeze brush my naked skin. It was strange; it made me stop what I was doing.

I felt weird and tingly all over, as though I was being watched. I grabbed my robe off the back of the door and looked around my apartment. Being so small, I could scan the room from the bathroom door so there was nothing there... Then DC hissed it was still dark out at 6:30am in the morning. He growled. I walked over to the window where he was by the fire escape. Reached up to check the lock at the top of the window, looked around and saw nothing. It was probably another cat. I was running late and had to finish getting ready. It was rainy and gloomy outside on my walk to school. It poured. My umbrella helped keep me dry as I drudge on. I did not want to be late for class.

Amanda was waiting to tell me she had found some information about the legends of the local area. There was one she liked about the supernatural creature that moved like a ghost and had powers. The ancestors called them the quiet ones. She said her dad used to tell stories about the Indian legend because we lived so close to the reservation.

 "I never paid them too much attention. They were just scary stories. I think my parents thought if they told us stories of the quiet ones visiting terrible children, we wouldn't behave. "

"Did you?" I laughed at her. She shook her head.

"No, we still misbehaved."

Amanda told the story as we walked. She talked about her father's stories. We know James Island as a source of spirit power for the Quileute people. The quiet ones came from the gods. They are here to protect us from the evil immortals.

"So, are there good immortals? What evil immortals did they believe were here?

Immortals, huh, really!"

"Do you believe in the immortals?"

"Oh Dee, those are just stories passed down from my grandfather."

"Funny thing is Amanda, my grandfather, used to tell me about the immortals, too. Don't you find it interesting that I grew up in North Dakota and you grew up here in Seattle and yet our ancestors spoke of the same beings? You know all wonderful stories begin with some form of the truth."

"I am not sure my grandfather even knew what he was talking about. Who knows? You know how stories get embellished after they have been told so many times."

"That is all I can remember."

Well, what do you know about the carvings on the doors of the library and what is the story about them?

"Maybe we could talk to Professor Jacquelyn."

"She is still part of the tribal councils."

"Maybe she can help us with the stories or tell us where to get more information."

We walked through the doors to the great Hall. Everyone was getting ready for our class. Amanda and I were still talking.

"I did some research after work last night. I looked up this class last night on the internet. Did you know this is the only class in the country? According to my research, sometime late in the 60s, the Indian nation donated the hand carved doors to the library as a token of appreciation for keeping their legends alive by the Mythological class. They placed the doors on the library to protect the mortals and all who walked through them." Amanda had this funny look on her face…. The professor walked by Amanda and me in the hallway to her class. "Professor, I called out as she passed. I have been looking into the information of the doors on the library." She stopped and turned to look at me.

"Deedra isn't it?"

"Yes, but I go… by Dee."

"There have been many stories that have been passed around the college for many years about those doors. They are their own urban legend. They have changed the stories many times, so who knows the truth? No one has translated the dialect of the writings and the picture could mean anything to anyone in their own interpretation." The professor kept walking to class. I hurried to catch her as she opened the door to the class. She turned, looking over her shoulder.

"Good luck with your paper, ladies."

I could read some of the etching and they spoke of someone's arrival to save the mortals... but that is impossible because it was the teaching of my grandfather's ancient language. We are in Quileute territory, not Cherokee. I must be wrong.

Amanda and I walked into the class. It was filling up. Professor J passed us and just kept her steady pass to the front of the class, getting her papers ready for her lecture. I watched her closely, wondering what she really knew about the doors.

Amanda poked my side. "Dee, are you still with us?"

"Oh, yeah."

I turned my head and looked her way.

"Sorry, just over thinking."

Our professor was a tall, thin woman with the blackest hair. It was almost midnight blue. She wore her hair in a braid down her back. She has high cheekbones, beautiful skin and her eyes somehow seem familiar, piercing blue pools of water. Her skin looked sun kissed. She is part of the Puyallup tribal nation. She has a quintessence about her that is hard to explain. I could feel her energy when she was too close. Her essence almost pulsed about her. After, the professor's lecture on the tribal nation finished. I walked down to the base of the hall. Amanda followed me. I was all ready to tell the professor I could read parts of the dialect on the doors to the library. Then the buzzing began with a low hmm, then the voice inside my head.

"Patient not yet, we will reveal all in good time."

I had to stop walking as she pulled out of my thoughts, leaving me a little light-headed. Then looking up saw the Professor was staring right at me from her podium. She stared with those blue eyes, looking right through me. It was unnerving.

"Where had I seen eyes that blue before?" Then it hit me that Mr. Yummy has the same eyes. Hmm… Related…? Then again, out of nowhere, I heard someone say.

"That girl is going to be hands full. She is too young to have the gifts of our ancient ancestors. "

Not the hum of the inner voice. These thoughts seemed to come from someone in the room. I looked around to see if anyone was deep in thought and no one stood out and accepted the professor up front. She was still staring at me.

I stopped ahead of Amanda.

"What is it, Dee?" She scrutinized me.

"You look so serious."

"Oh, it's nothing. Just over thinking again." as I laughed and shook my head, I started walking towards the door.

"Did I just hear the professor rumbling about how I was too young and something about the powers of the ancients surely can't be referring to me?"

Amanda and I walked to our next class.

"Hey, I think I can translate the doors into the library."

"What?" Amanda just stared at me in disbelief.

"Well, not all of it, but I think it is an old Cherokee dialect that my grandfather taught me. I need to take a rub of each door so I can study them. Then I can do some research on the rubbings. Aqaba is a brand of rubbing paper that works best. Do you know of a store that might carry a brand? I would like to do it tonight late, so no one knows I took the rubbings. Can you help me?"

"Sure Dee, I would love to be arrested on Tuesday night by the college security. The University bookstore has rubbing paper."

"We won't get caught; you'll be the lookout."

"Oh, what the hell, sure, what time do you want to meet me back here for our B & E?" she giggled.

"Technically, we are not doing a B & E, just an etching of the doors."

"How about 12:00 pm? I get off work then."

Standing with her hand on her hip, she chastised me.

"Alright, but I better not have to bail us out of jail."

Our math class was just a computer lab. The teacher was ill, so instead of a substitute, we just did labs for an hour. I was still thinking about the thoughts I heard from the professor.

"Ok, so let's be rational. I cannot hear others' thoughts. But if I can, I had better figure it out by putting it on the test; Picking someone out of the crowd and see if you can hear them. I focused…. A couple of minutes passed…. nothing.

"I need to be put away. Perhaps my family is right. I am going totally mad…."

Amanda was giving me one of those looks I was so familiar with, like, who is this crazy person?

Then Amanda stopped. She turned and looked at me seriously.

"Deedra, I got the feeling the professor wanted us to change our report?"

"Yep, so did I. That is why we will not change our report. We need to find out what the professor is hiding."

"What do you think you'll find?"

"Maybe there is a secret that is being hidden. I think maybe immortals might just be here in Seattle living among us right now."

"You think you will find the secret about immortals?" She just stared at me with the pained look on her face.

"You understand how crazy that sounds, right?" I smiled at her.

"But what if they exist? What if I right?"

Shrugging my shoulders, I turned to look at her as she walked away.

"I will see you later. I have to go to work in an hour."

 I hurried down the stairs and across the plaza. I yelled back at her.

"I will see you tonight at the library at 12:00pm sharp. That is when the guards change shifts." Amanda put her hands to her mouth like a megaphone and yelled at me.

"Being arrested should be on time. I will be there."

"Oh, hilarious Amanda, don't say things like that. The universe will hear you and give you what you want, and we will get busted. Are you going to be there?" With much attitude, she yelled.

"Yeah, I'll be there."

I arrive at work just in time, still thinking about the bizarre conversation in my head.

What is the professor hiding? Who did the carvings on doors in the library? Why did they make my hand tingle? Why am I having so many strange experiences here in Seattle? Then my mind took it a step further. What if the immortals existed among us? What does the professor know? Why do I feel so many emotions in this place? As if I can hear people's thoughts. My head feels like it will explode.

Jake startled my thoughts when he came through the door behind me.

" Hey Dee," I jumped out of my skin with a squeal. I turned and looked up at him.

"Oh, hi you startled me."

"I'm sorry." As he scooted by me with an enormous smile on his face.

"You think that was funny, don't you?"

"Well, yeah, kind of. You squeak like a mouse."

"I do not sound like a mouse."

"What are you so serious about?"

I walked over and hung my coat on the wall and grabbed an apron.

"Nothing much. I just had a weird day, and I was just re-thinking it."

"So how weird of a day can freshmen have?"

"You wouldn't believe me if I told you anyway and you might even be sorry you hired the crazy girl."

Jake was looking at me with that twinkle in his eye. I just smiled back. If only he knew how crazy my day was.

"Ok, so do you think you can pull yourself back to reality and make the coffee while I made sure all the table settings were complete? It is Friday night, and we will start getting busy around 4:00pm. Then happy hour from 6 to 7 and then at 9:00PM we have a jazz band coming in to play."

"Let's get to work."

As he smiled, he nudged me with his elbow, and then pulled me in for a side hug as he walked me further into the club.

"Come on, let's get started."

I laugh, thinking I am being ridiculous, and I need to keep my imagination in check when I am at work. But the teasing and the hug were nice. I needed it.

I pulled away from Jake's hold and said,

"I get it; we are going to get busy."

I stepped over to the counter and started making coffee.

I couldn't stop thinking about how weird the professor was acting. I couldn't wait until tonight when I could get the etching of the doors so I could study them.

The night got very busy; it helped keep my mind from wandering. We ran late; It was jazz night. The band played late into the night. The music helped keep me relaxed. A table of young women came in and they talked about an array of normal topics that most women talk about hair, makeup, aging excreta. I enjoyed listing to the normalcy because my life was steering towards weird and unusual.

Finally, the night was over, and the clubs were shutting down.

Jake, Jerry, and Mica were having a glass of wine behind the bar, and they asked if I wanted a glass to celebrate, having a good night and making a record receipt for the month. I sat down on the other side of the bar, and they poured me a glass. They had opened a Shiraz from Australia. It was wonderful, full-bodied and with a hint of fruit and a wonderful pepper finish. Jake was talking about the women who talked all night about all the normal girl's stuff and how much they spent on their clothes, shoes, and makeup. Jake made some comments on their style. I found it interesting that he would notice what style that the women were wearing. He seemed too approved of the way they all dressed. The women appeared as if they were on the front of Harper's Bazaar. They like Jake and tipped him… really well.

We finished the bottle of wine when Jake made a toast.

 "To keeping the team together, to having bigger nights in the club." Then we raised our glasses and clinked them together to make our toast.

When we finished, we all walked to the door. Jake asked if I needed him to walk me home. He was so thoughtful after my weird day I welcomed the company. Once again, he walked me up to the fourth floor and waited until I was in the door. Said good night, then he was off. I waited until I heard the elevator doors clang shut. Giving him a few minutes to make sure he had left. I headed out the door to meet Amanda to get the rubbings on the library door. When I got there, Amanda was waiting in the dark just before the library. She stepped out and scared me. She thought that was funny.

Amanda stayed there, and I took the paper and went to get the rubbing. When I had done the rubbing on the large paper, I walked back to Amanda and the security guard walked past me. I caught up with her and we walked off campus.

"Thanks Amanda, I'll see you tomorrow."

"No problem, Dee, see you later."

I turned and walked back to my apartment. Back home, I was hoping to get some sleep. I was pretty keyed up from our adventure in getting the rubbings off the doors. I needed a good night's sleep. DC met me at the door, meowed, and wanted his milk. Shuffling to the refrigerator to get his milk. I went to the bathroom, washed my face, brushed my teeth, and then pulled the bed out of the wall. I hit my pillow and did not move until the alarm went off.

It was Saturday. I called Amanda to ask her if she thought James Island might have something to do with the doors.

 "I don't know." Sensing my friend hiding something from me or was just getting paranoid. I had to get a grip on my imagination.

"This morning while I was drinking my coffee, I looked up some Indian legends of Washington State on the internet. The article talked about James Island, and I thought we could drive out there. Maybe it has something to do with the carvings on the door. I noticed an island on the doors. It also looked like a cloud, but I was sticking with an island. I think there was fish jumping, but again, they could be birds flying."

"Dee, Hello Island means we need a boat. She was laughing at me. I don't own a boat or know anyone that does. Do you?"

"Hum… I will call Jake."

"Who is Jake?"

"Oh, the guy I work with."

"Ok, call me back if you get us a ride."

"Ok, talk to you soon. "

 Shit, what is Jake's phone number? Dammit, I don't even know his last name. I will just run down the club, and somebody must be there.

I got dressed and went down to the club; it was early. Mica had given a key to me, so I let myself-in. Opening the door, the smells of the bar swirled around my head; I could hear someone in the back.

"Hello," I yelled into the club.

"Is anybody there?" From the back came a dark figure. He stopped just inside the shadow so I couldn't see his face.

 "Hello." Came from the voice in the shadows of the doorway.

 "Jake, is that you?"

"No, he isn't here" the man was still standing in the shadows.

"Maybe I can help you."

"Um, I need Jake's help today, and I don't have his phone

numbered. Do you know his number?"

He was still standing in the shadows. Why was he standing there where I could not see his face?

"Yes, we must have it around here somewhere. Who are you again?"

"Oh, sorry, my name is Deedra. I am the new hire. I just started last week. I was hoping Jake knew someone with a boat or access to a boat."

Then the stranger stepped out into the light.

"Oh My God! Gasped… It was him from the Mary coffee café, from my dreams."

Our eyes locked. I froze, and then every nerve ending in my body was tingling. He was so intoxicating. The smell of earth, spice and all men filled my senses. He smiled at me, and I couldn't move. All I could do was stare up at him. I hoped my mouth wasn't open and if it was; the drool remained in my mouth. I could feel the flush of my face and the heat pooling in all the wrong places.

He looked away just long enough to let me take the breath I evidently was holding. I stepped back in my big girl voice, reminding me of my mother. "Who are you?" His smile got bigger, whispering.

"I am the owner of this place." His voice was familiar. He took a step back, almost into the shadows again.

My head continued to spin out of control. I leaned against the door, gripping the handle.

 I shouted in my head *"Get a grip girl!"* once again talking to myself like a loon.

 I wanted him; the urge scared me. I just wanted to rip off his clothes and go to the floor and have my way with him. I was even ogling him. I do not ogle. But there I was, looking at him from the top of his chest to the way his jeans hung at his narrow hips down his zipper where a nice bulge was building. When I looked back at him was smiling at me. I swallowed and cleared my throat and tried to talk, but nothing would come out. The humming and then buzzing I prepared for her.

"Oh, sweetie, he is very handsome. I see he is taken by you as well. Don't just stand there…. talk to him."

"Now you have something to say."

 looking down, blushing; I was sure I was red and blotchy from running down my neck from my cheeks. I have never in my life wanted to run over to this stranger and jump into his arms.

Then the door opened behind knocking me forward. It was Jake came through the door. Thank God, before I made a total fool of myself.

 "Hey Dee, I didn't hurt you, did I? Why are you so close

to the door? You're going to have to move further into the club when you get here. I seem to always have to knock you out of the way to get in."

Jake looked further into the club and saw the problem.

"Oh, I see. Hey…Blaine." Jake turned back to me with a twinkle in his eye, smiling and showing off his dimples.

"Dee, what are you doing here? Isn't your day off?"

Jerry bopped in behind him.

"Hello Dee, isn't it your day off?" Both of them had those little boy smirks as though they had been interrupting something.

"Yes, it is my day off. I was looking for you because I didn't have your number or your last name. I wonder if you would give me a ride somewhere today and if you knew someone with a boat?"

"I have to open today, but this afternoon I'm free. Where did you need to go?

"I'm doing some research for a paper with Amanda, a friend from school. I have to turn in the report at the end of the semester for my grad in mythology.

"We need a ride out to James Island to see if we can find any proof of our theory about the immortals that lived there. Or proof the legends are not true. I think the doors on the library tell the story of the island, but I need to study them more to understand the dialect that is written and what the pictures mean."

"Dee, what do you expect to find out there on a deserted island? I have only heard of the old chiefs telling stories of the immortals. I have lived here for a long time, and I have seen no actual proof of a race of being living on a deserted island in the sound. The Island is for camping only and no vehicles allowed only hiking and you have to pack in all your gear, really a remote destination."

Jake laughed at my suggestion of finding any evidence on immortals.

"Hey Blaine," Jerry walked back behind the bar.

"What are you doing today?"

"I'm doing inventory on the liquor for the quarterly inventory taxes."

"What do you think about immortals living on James Island?"

Blaine stepped forward close enough that the smell of him swirled around my senses.

"Just his smell had me think of naughty thoughts. Taking him on the bar, the floor, or the kitchen counter? Need to be closer. I have never had such an uncontrollable urge to rip off a perfect stranger's clothes. What is with me
78

smelling of him and why do I feel out of control around him? What the hell, I am smelling him now, are my senses improving? He isn't really even that close. God, I am as mad as a hatter."

"Are you talking about Professor Jacquelyn Bluestar class at the college? Yes, I am taking the Native American in local mythology class. Why do you know the professor? "

Blaine got the same pained look on his face as my professor did.

"Hmm,   what   does   he   know?   "
"So, you know about the legends?"

"I have heard some stories." Jake cleared his throat.

"Dee, Blaine is Jacquelyn's brother."

"Oh, hell, that explains her familiar eyes. He has her blue eyes. "

"Blaine, this is your new server, and her name is Deedra."

"We were just getting acquainted before you guys came through the door."

"I'm done for now with the inventory. I have my car outside, but it only holds two people."

"Did he just ask if he could take me out to James Island?"

"Would you like to ride out there with me? I have a couple

of stops to make. I need to check out a couple of wineries tasting rooms."

Before, I could think about it or say anything.

Jake jumped in.

"Thanks Blaine that would be great, if you could help me out like that."

"You need to know the only way out to the island is by boat. No Vehicles allowed. You will have to walk the island to see it. We might not get very much time out there. We will probably only be an hour before dark and then we have to cross back to the dock to get the car. Looking up to look into those gorgeous eyes, the warmth was spreading in my lower region again.

"You seem to know an awful lot about the island."

"As a kid I would spend my weekends camping there with my father."

I gave Jake a dirty look.

"What????..." He mouthed, shrugged his shoulders and held his hands up in an innocent gesture. Looking back to Blaine, I smiled.

"Sure, your expertise on the island will be helpful. I will text my friend and let her know about the change in plans."

I pulled my phone out of my pocket and texted Amanda.

"Getting a ride with Blaine, the owner of the nightclub I work at. His car is two seated. There isn't any room for you. Wish me luck."

"Good Luck. Call me when you get back."

"All right, I will get my coat from the back, and we can be off." Blaine headed to the back of the club.

"Jake! What the hell was that all about?"

"Well… I could see you think he is hot. I just thought I would help you out. Isn't that what friends do for each other?"

With that twinkle in his eyes and those dimples, I couldn't be mad at him.

"Have fun." He and Jerry went to work.

Blaine returned from the back room with his coat. He was standing at the door waiting for me; he opened the door.

"After you." My car is just out front. There were three different cars sitting in front of the club. Hmm, so which one does he drive: the Hummer, Land Rover, and a Tesla Roadster?

He was standing in front of a Red Tesla. He came around and opened my door. The smell alone was expensive. Walking towards him, his hand extended out for me to support myself as he lowered me into the leather seat of the car. I was spinning again just by his touch. I was glad for the help.

"Oh, my, a gentleman, very few of those kind of men around these days."

He shut my door, came around, and got in to put on his seat belt.

"Your seat belt?" As I sat there just staring at him like an idiot.

"Oh, yeah, seat belt." Putting it on, I was mumbling to myself.

I really need to pull it together. It's not like I have never been alone with a man. I had many relationships over the years. None of them lasted very long; most of them bored me after a while. What is it about this man?

All I could do was stare at him. He is perfect in the way he moves like a cat. Sleek like his body. The teal blue sweater he had on showed his broad chest and his narrow waist. His well-worn jeans fit him like a glove. The blue in the sweater set off his eyes when he looked at me. I got lost in them. What was he doing to me? I was myself, but not myself... almost as though I was out of my skin and watching from the outside. I needed to focus. This was just a little chemical crush, was all? Then the buzzing started as she invaded my thoughts.

"Pull it together dear, you're not a prepubescent teenager with no control over your emotions. This behavior is beneath you." No buzzing, no light-headedness, just in and out of my thoughts with her barbs.

He pulled away from the curb and we were off. He was driving through the area at speeds that made most of the trees a burr.

I cleared my throat.

"You seem to be in a hurry."

"I have an appointment to check on the last case of a very special wine I want. I forgot until after I told you I would help. It's on the way and it won't take long. You don't mind, do you?"

He looked at me with those blue eyes that looked into my soul. I glanced away, facing the window, watching the landscape pass by. I turned back to his stare at his beautiful face.

"No, I guess not." Thinking how I couldn't say no to anything, he asked.

"Can I ask you a question?"

"Sure."

"Do you think immortals exist?"

" You mean, do they live on the island?"

"Why is everyone so afraid to talk about the myth? Or the stories that have to do with the myth. All stories have to come from some form of the truth. I am just looking to do a paper on the myth but with everyone I talk to acting so weird, I think they exist and all of you know it and are hiding something."

Calmly, he looked at me.

"That's over one question and quit the statement."

Then he asked, "Can you read the doors?"

"You're the second person who has asked me if I could read the dialect like I am crazy. It looks like the language my grandfather taught me of an ancient Cherokee dialect."

The car got silent, so I just stared out the window. It was a beautiful day in Seattle and the sun was out, but it was only 42 degrees. Still cold, it was good to see the sun. Then I thought I heard him say,

"It's time. I should just tell her the truth."

I turned to look at him. "Did you say something?"

"No, but I was wondering if you want to stop for lunch, my treat?"

The appointment I have is with a wine tasting room inside

the restaurant and I wanted to pick up the case for my personal use and then try some of the wine for the club.

I spaced off and thought about hearing his voice inside my head. I could swear I heard him hmm… was I hearing his thoughts? Telling me the truth, the truth about what?

Then I heard Blaine say.

"Earth to Dee?" I turned to look at him.

"I'm sorry. What were you asking me?"

"Lunch? Are you hungry?"

"Sure, sounds good."

We pulled into The Secret Cove restaurant. Exterior was nice. Sitting on the bay gave an angler's charm to the old house turned restaurant. We arrived at Anacortes around 1:00pm. It was a four-hour drive from the club. Getting out of the car, I had to stretch. After getting all the kinks out, I followed Blaine to the front door of the restaurant. Blaine opened and held the door for me then placed his hand on my lower back as he guided me past the check in sign that read: Allow the server to seat you please. We walked in through the restaurant to the back corner, through another door to the wine room. A beautiful woman stood behind the bar. She knew him. I will bet he really gets around.

"Hello Sarah, did the shipment of wine I ordered to sample come in?"

"Yes Blaine, they came in just before you got here. I was worried you might come earlier in the day and be disappointed, but they are all here." Then Blaine turned to me

"Do you want to help me choose a superb wine for the club?"

"Sure, what are you looking for?"

"I need a medium price wonderful wine to serve."

Sarah started pouring samples in the glasses she set in front of Blaine and me. She opened a Hard Row to Hoe. Good in bed 2016 Sparkling wine. Um, yummy. Then Shameless Hussy 2017 Chardonnay,

The Chardonnay was really delightful.

Next, she opened a Benson Vineyards 2018 Viognier, and then switched to the Reds Benson 2018 Syrah, Back to Hard Row to Hoe Tempranillo, and then she pulled from a case on the floor Ryan Patrick 2015 Malbec, 2017 Red Island Red Cabernet Sauvignon. Finally, she pulled out a bottle of a Hard Row to Hoe, 2016 Burning Desire Estates Cabernet Franc Reserve. As she poured the final tasting, Sarah pointed out.

"They only have a few cases of this one left if it isn't sold out already. "

I took a sip. This was one of the best, smooth, full body, finish was dry but still with the hint of fruit. I look at Blaine.

"Burning Desire. I love it. What do you think? "

"If this is what you recommend, I am all in." The twinkle in his eye said he was talking about more than the wine. My mouth went dry, my face felt as though it was burning off. The heat pooled in all the wrong places, or maybe the right places. Then the thought of having my way with this gorgeous man. I was doing so well until the wine began kicking in and felt a little buzzed. Tried to take my mind off Blaine or what I wanted to do to him.

"Think about the wine again. Stay focused."

"I like this Cab/Franc for meals that will hold up well with food. Actually, all of them were outstanding and a great selection of wine."

"Sarah, how much is the reserve?"

She dug around in the drawer, finding her price sheet. The Reserve if I can get it is 55.00 a bottle, case is 60.00 a case. They discount the case.

You like expensive wines, don't you?"

"Price too much for you?"

"No, I will take two cases. I would like a case of all the ones we tried. You have the address to ship to and my card number. I will take two cases with me now and you can ship the rest. Thank you for the wonderful selection of wine. Then he turned back to me and smiled

" Are you hungry?" I bobbled forward. He put out his hand on my arms to hold me steady. Then he wrapped one arm around my waist and walked me back into the restaurant, over to a booth by the window. He sat me down and pushed the glass of water in front of me.

"You need to drink about three glasses of water and get some food in you. Would you like some coffee also?"

"Nope, then you will have a wide-awake drunk on your hands. Then I look at him and giggle. I grabbed the water and watched him over the top of my glass.

 The server showed up with menus and asked,

"Can I get you something to drink?"

 "Oh no, I have had enough for now, just some water, please".

"Do you need a moment before you order?"

Blaine smiled with that voice that got him on his way. "Yes, thank you. We haven't decided just yet."

She turned and left.

"So, Blaine, do you know how you affect women?" *Oh boy,*

was I tipsy and bold? Evidently, I was going to regret this tomorrow.

"Oh, how is that?"

"You have to be kidding me…. they melt around you."

He blushed and smiled at me. "What about you? Are you also melting?" he laughed.

"I really don't know what you are talking about. The ladies here know me. I come up to sample wine and have lunch about twice a month. "

"Jealous much?"

"Did you say something?"

"No, why? What do you think you heard?"

"Never mind. You must leave a good impression on them."

"I didn't just hear him accuse me of being jealous of him. I barely know him."

 Feeling bemused. I looked down at the table, trying to clear the interference of too many voices in my head. I changed the subject

"What's good to eat here?"

He was still smiling at me. He looked at me inquisitively.

 "The fish is always good." He was gazing across the table

at me again, making me feel all kinds of knotty thoughts.

"Stop it Focus."

"That sounds good. I will have the fish and chips."

"Good, I think I will too."

He was still watching me with those beautiful eyes and the perfect smile.

 "Ok then, it's settled." saying nothing to the server, she just showed up.

 "We'll have the fish and chips."

"Excellent. Would you like the Bensen Pinot Gris to have with your meal?"

"No, you can bring the bottle and leave it before the meal."

The server left and went to turn in the order. She was back with a cooling buck with the bottle uncorked and sitting inside. Reaching for the bottle to pour and Blaine stopped her.

 "I have got it, thank you. Linda."

But before she left, she bent slightly so she could show him all of what she had bulging out the front of her White blouse. Blaine seemed to ignore her and just pulled the bottle out, lifted the cork, put it to his nose and inhaled the fumes. Satisfied, he set the cork on the plate under the bucket. He reached over and filled my glass and then poured some in his glass, setting the bottle back into the bucket. He tasted the wine. I was still drinking my water. I let my wine sit.

"So, Dee, what are you majoring in?"

"I'm not sure. I'm just getting started."

"You don't know what you want to be when you grow up?"

"No, not really." I straighten my shoulders and asked Blaine,

 "What do you do for a living?"

"I'm a business owner. With a master's in global economics. I like music, fine wine and beautiful women."

"What does a girl say to all that? Shit, he is smart and gorgeous, way out of my league."

Then the buzzing hit me. I braced for her intrusion into my thoughts. *"That unadorned man doesn't even know who you are, and he isn't way out of your league, my dear. He is not even good enough to be in your presence. You're from a royal bloodline."*

"What are you going on about? I am only a girl from a small town. Not even sure how I got here." Then nothing, just silence of my mind again.

I gritted my teeth at her announce and tried to pull off a smile. The food came arrived just in time. The fish was mouth-watering. I took a drink of water to wash down all the yumminess down. As I wiped my mouth.

"How much further is it to the island?"

"Only an hour from here. What do you expect to find?"

"I'm not sure, perhaps a clue. All stories begin somewhere, don't they?"

"You realize your story is over 500 years old. What clues do you think are left after all that time?"

"I am not sure."

"He made some since. What did I think I was going to find?"

I just finished my lunch, letting my wine sit until I drank my glass of water. Still trying to sober up, he asked for the check. The server was all over him; she slipped him her phone number. "Unbelievable," Shaking my head, I muttered under my breath.

He looked up as he was getting his wallet out and asked,

"Did you say something? "

"Nope, nothing." He was making me uneasy, and in the next breath, I wanted him to get closer. He loaded the two cases of wine in the car. "I need to go talk to the boat captain."

"Hey look, here is a brochure on the island, maybe it has a clue." smiling at me the way you patronized a spoiled child. Was I looking for something that really did not exist?

I look at the brochure. Blaine went to talk to the owner of a boat that would take us over to the island. The boat owner's name was Noah. He also had the same blue eyes with dark hair with darker skin. As I looked over the brochure, it read.

James Island State Park is 1/2 mile east of Decatur Island on Rosario Strait, San Juan County. Township 35N, Range 1W, in parts of Section 14 and 23. Has 113.65 acres with 12,335 feet of saltwater shoreline on Rosario Strait. James Island State Park was acquired from the Federal Government in 1964 at no cost. The island was named by the Wilkes Expedition in 1841, possibly to honor the earlier heroism of an American sailor, Reuben James. There is 1 water trail site, 13 primitive campsites, picnic shelter, 1.5-mile hiking trails, 121-foot pier, 4 mooring buoys, 12 x 45 ft moorage float, 2 vault toilets, 3 pit toilets, 1 bulletin board, and a pay station. No drinking water. Garbage: pack-it-out Primitive camping, picnicking, hiking, saltwater fishing, and scuba diving.

Hmm, so primitive. How was I going to find any immortal clues? Blaine walked back over to the car and asked if I was ready.

We needed to head out by the time we arrived; it was already getting dark. In the fall, it was dark by 4:30. I hated this time of year. There was never enough time to do anything in the daylight. We walked down to the dock and climbed aboard a 62 ft a small ferry with room for six cars and a couple of motorcycles. The passenger cabin was beautiful with teak trim, wooden floors that gleamed with wax. There were benches to set on with tables that were secured to the deck to prevent them from sliding if we hit rough water. By the time we got across to the island, it had rained and got dark. The water churned, tossing the ferry left and right. There would be nothing to see, anyway.

"You knew I wouldn't be able to see anything out here, so why did you volunteer to take me out here?"

"Your story amused me, and I wanted to see what you thought you might find."

"I just felt truly ridiculous. He must think I have lost my mind. I do…."

"You must think I'm a bit off?"

"No, not at all. I find you irresistible charming."

"Charming huh? Who was under a spell?"

"I must be under your spell. I think you're the most interesting woman I have ever met."

"Interesting huh, is that his way of paying me a compliment?"
94

"I also think you're the most beautiful woman I have ever enjoyed the pleasure of spending my day with." He reached up and ran his finger down my cheek and across my lips.

"Ugh, are you looking at me?" I step back from him not because I didn't want him to touch me but afraid, I would jump him here on the ferry ride back.

"Does he need glasses? I am five foot, three inches, with weird lavender blue eyes, long curly blond hair with a medium build, short legs, long torso and a peasant butt. Nothing a beautiful woman has."

"Yes, I am looking at you. I have been looking at you all day and I think you're amazing. Deedra, I think you are as desirable as anyone I have ever come across." He leaned in closer. I could feel his breath on my lips. My heart was pounding out of my chest. Then he pulled back. Hearing the captain, Noah asked if we should head back with the storm coming on shore. Blaine turned towards the captain. "That is probably a good idea." he moved away long enough to regain my composure. I thought I was going to pass out.

"Was he going to kiss me? Did I want him to? Oh, hell yes!"

I had to grab the rail on the boat and sat in the seat as the ferry rocked side to side as the ferry turned around to head back to the dock. I was still tingling from his breath, so close to my lips. All I could think of is how much I wanted him…. Then the humming sound in my head began as I prepared for her invasion of my thoughts.

"My dear, you don't even know him. We have better manners than to be giving ourselves to every stranger that piques our interest, but you're right, he is a very gorgeous man."

I laughed and shook my head. She just has the opinion when it isn't needed and does not help when I could use it. I could tell she pulled away just in the silence again, knowing I was alone with my thoughts.

When we got back to the dock, we walked silently to the car. He arrived there first, holding the door for me. It had started to drizzly, and I was getting wet. I looked up. "Thank you." Again, he made my head spin as he held out his hand and helped me slide into the car seat. This time I put on my seat belt and stared out the window. Blaine got in and started the car. I looked his way, and he was gazing at me.

I tried to hold eye contact, but the naughty thought sprang up and I had to turn away and just kept looking out the window. I heard the tires crunch as they ran over the gravel parking lot. We drove for hours in silence.

Next thing I knew, we were back at the club. I must have fallen asleep. He drove right by, and he pulled in front of my apartment and turned off the car. He came around and opened my door. I looked at him and he smiled.

"Thank you for taking me out to the island, even though the weather turned bad. It was a lovely day."

"You are welcome. We should do it again soon."

"When do you work again next?"

"Tomorrow after my last class."

"I will be in town for the next couple of months, so I will see you then." He reached up and tucked my hair behind my ear, then stepped back, turned and got into the car. I was standing on the sidewalk as he pulled off.

Riding the elevator up to my apartment, my thoughts consumed me.

"How did he know where I lived?"

I was exhausted from trying to fight off the urges to rip off his clothes from his gorgeous body. Too tired to analyze the day, all I wanted to do was shower and go to bed.

I was still feeling a little light-headed from being so close to him. I let myself in and DC was in the same meowing routine. He wanted his milk. *What just happened? Why was I so confused? What power did he have over me? I was so exhausted trying to fight keeping some normalcy to my thoughts as I tried to continue a normal conversation with him.*

After taking care of DC, I showered and went to bed. I dreamed all night about nothing that made any sense. The next morning, I was still tired, but had to get to school. I had trouble all morning. I could not get my thoughts together, and it was as if someone was in my head stirring my thoughts.

 "Who was Blaine Bluestar?" I was so tired and confused. I just wanted to take a nap and I just got up. "Oh, crap Amanda."

I called the phone rang for a long time, then finally she answered

"Hello."

"Hey, I am so very sorry I didn't call you back. You will not believe what happened to me. "

"So, spill… it was a guy, wasn't it?"

"Not just any guy, but the Professor's brother."

"Whose brother?"

"The club I work at is owned by the Professor's Brother."

"She has a brother?"

"Oh my god yes, but he is different, not anything like her and has a way about him a sort of persuasion. The only thing they have alike is their blue-green eyes. You'll see meet me at the club tonight.”

“What do you mean, he is different?”

“He has some kind of power over me.”

“Oh, Dee, are you in Looovvvve?”

“No, it’s weird you’ll see. Come over after school today and meet me at the club. Promise you will come to the club and check it out for yourself.”

“I have to go, or I will be late for school. Remember, I have a surprise quiz in math today…I will see you in mythology.”

“Find any clues about immortals. I Found nothing on the island?”

“I will see you after my math class. We can talk then.” I hung up the phone and threw it in my backpack. Turned off the lights and locked my door.

The math exam went well. I think I got them all right. I was on my way to mythology when I thought I heard Amanda.

“Where is she?” As I came around the corner, she smiled, somehow relieved to see me.

“I thought you got lost again.”

“Oh, you’re hilarious.” I looked at Amanda. “About our report…I think we can just use the legend about the little people and compare them to the Irish legends that will make Professor J happy and get her off our backs. Besides, what made me think about a legend over 500 years old? That I would find some proof of life on a deserted Island. Are you sure you do not want another mythology partner?"

 "So, what has changed?"

"Nothing, except what our paper is about. I still need to know about the Island and the doors." Amanda and I walked into mythology class and sat in the second row.

"Good morning, ladies," As the professor passed us on her way to the front of the lecture hall.

"How are you today?"

"Good."

 "Do you have your report almost ready? It has to be in on Thursday."

"Wow, the end of the quarter was already here?"

"We will. It is still a work in progress."

Amanda was coming in around the club at seven. I arrived about 15 minutes earlier. Jerry was setting up the bar.

"Hey, Dee."

"Hey, Jerry. I have a friend coming to visit with me during my break. Can you keep her company for a while? You'll like her. She is a spitfire." I went to the back and grabbed
100

my apron off the rack and hung up my coat and backpack. Jake was in the kitchen getting a bite to eat.

"Dee, did you have a good time yesterday with Blaine? Tell me everything."

"Well, it was interesting." I smiled.

"So that's it."

"Not even a crumb."

"Yep! That's it."

"Did I just hear him say? Not even a crumb?" His lips didn't move.

"What did you say?"

"I didn't say anything. What do you think you heard?" he smiled mischievously.

"Oh, nothing. I must be hearing things."

I put on my apron and headed out to the dining area. I swear I can hear everyone's thoughts. When I am close to the professor Jacqueline, Mica, Amanda, Jake, Jerry, and Blaine but not anyone else. I have tried to listen to strangers and nothing. It's so weird.

Jake was too interested, and I was not sure yesterday even happened. I wondered if Blaine had said anything.

As I grabbed my pad, I already had some customers in my area and the night began.

I could see someone in the corner booth, so I went around the corner to see if I could help. There he was.

I cleared my throat. My heart was pounding out of my chest; I really needed to know why Blaine affects me in such a way that I cannot function.

"Can I get you anything?"

"Hi Dee, how are you today? Can I call you Dee? Mica said that is what your friends call you.

"So now he thinks he is my friend. You know they have medication for people that cannot make up their minds. No kiss… just drove off."

"Oh, um I'm great. Can I get you anything?" He smiled up at me with a twinkle in his eye. "No thanks, I already have a bottle of the wine you picked out yesterday, and it is very nice."

"Oh, yeah… I guess you do, so you like it?"

"Yes, I will have to take you to pick all of our wine."

"Well, I have to get back to work before the boss fires me. Enjoy your wine. Let me know if I can get you anything else."

"I'm sure your boss would forgive you for a minute to give a customer a smile." Then he winked at me." Looking into his smoldering blue pools, I turned five shades of red. I was so fluster, how naïve he must think I am. Truth be told, far from it. I laughed to myself.

"All I could think of was how I just wanted to press my lips against his lips. I wanted to just run my hands down through his hair and down his chest. STOP IT!!! I am NOT going to lose control."

As I backed away from him. I heard him ask.

"Would you join me when you get off? We can share a glass of the wine that you picked out?"

"Sure, why not? I'll see you later than…" I smiled and kept backing up. I turned and hurried back to the bar.

"What was I doing? Why couldn't I say no? Where was Amanda?"

Other customers had come in, they kept me busy. I could see Amanda had arrived and was at the bar. Walking over, she was talking to Jerry. Hey Amanda, I see you have met Jerry. She smiled. "When is your break so we can talk?"

"Silly girl, I have been with Jerry for many years."

"What did you say?"

"When do you get a break? No, not that, the other thing?"

"What are you talking about?"

"Oh, nothing. In a half hour."

"Ok, I'll just wait here at the bar for you then."

The night slowed down just before my break, and suddenly music filled the air. I could hear someone playing the piano. It was Tuesday night, and we rarely had any music. It was classical, so soft and passionate. I stepped around the corner from the front of the club and there he was, playing. I could not stop watching him. He was so perfect.

 "Is there anything he can't do?"

Amanda had just spotted him for the first time. I could tell he affected her the same way he affected everyone. What was it beside the obvious that made women drawn to him?

The music rang through the air. I was so taken I had to lean against the bar.

"Dee, are you alright?" Jerry reached across the bar and touched my arm.

"Oh umm, I'm good." as I straightened up and backed up into the front area, the music kept playing. Tears ran down my cheek.

"What was happening to me? Why, did everything that

Blaine do have such an effect on me."

Amanda looked up at me.

"Dee, what's wrong? Are you OK?"

"I don't know."

I ran off to the bathroom. Then the buzzing sound in my head. I braced myself for her intrusions.

"Oh Dee, I am so sorry I haven't heard that song in many centuries. It still stirs all kinds of emotion in me. I couldn't hold it back from spilling into your emotions"

" Who wrote the song? Why do you know a song written centuries ago? Who are you?"

Then there was nothing. I knew I was alone. Looking in the mirror, my face was blotchy, and my eyes were red. I looked like I had been crying. I splashed some cold water on my face as Amanda opened the door and came in stood beside me. She put her arm around me. I leaned into her hug.

"What happened?"

"Not sure. The music just moved me to tears."

"I couldn't tell her my spirit guide knew the song from centuries ago and they were her tears."

"Are you ok now?" I took a deep breath and sighed. Then turned and held the door, ushering her out into the club and back to the bar. Sitting down with Jerry and Amanda, I took my twenty-minute break at the bar. Let her know I was having a drink with Blaine after work.

"I will get my notes on the paper to you at lunch tomorrow and we could stay later at the library and finish our assignment if we have to."

She smiled. "That works for me."

The night drug on and on, customers kept coming in for a drink. I thought it would never end. Finally, Jake put the closed sign in the window and locked the front door. I turned when I heard my name from the corner booth.

"Are you ready to join me for a glass of wine?"

I really needed to find out about the song; just one drink might help me keep it together.

"Sure, be right there." taking off my apron and hanging it up, I grabbed my coat, backpack and headed to the table where Blaine awaited me.

"So, what was that last song you played?"

"Why did you like it?"

"Well, let's just say it moved me".

"A teacher of mine wrote it many years ago for the woman he loved."

"Really, the song was moving. I could feel the love and loss in the melody."

"Could my inner voice be that woman? That might explain my intense feelings about the song. But damn, he plays the piano, he has a business degree, owns a nightclub, he's magnificent to look at. What in the hell does he see in me?

Many years ago, my professor of music wrote the song because he had found his soul mate. Then he lost her in a tragedy."

"That's terrible."

"Is the wine as good as it was yesterday?"

"Hmm, he changed the subject. "The wine is decent."

"Are you hungry?"

"I could eat, but there isn't anyone in the kitchen."

"It's Ok, just follow me" as he took off through the kitchen doors, I trailed behind him.

"Oh, don't tell me he also cooks. If he does windows, I am going to ask him to marry me …. He is way too perfect to let go."

He turned on the lights and pulled food out of the refrigerator.

"Do you like pasta?"

"Sure."

Grabbing a large crab, goat cheese and spinach ravioli out. He pulled down a frying pan, added oil to the skillet, and while the oil heated. He made a pesto mayo dipping sauce. Oil was bubbling, showing it was hot. Placing the ravioli in the hot oil fried the ravioli it until crisp. Took it out and set it on a paper towel to wick away the oil and cool off the ravioli. He picked it up, still warm and dipping the ravioli in the sauce. He fed it to me. "Here, try this."

Eating out of his hand, I wanted to lick and suck on his fingers. Oh, man, so sensual. I needed to focus. *I think I let a moan escape my lips.*

 "Wow, this is fabulous. It should be on the menu. You know, you make it hard to be around someone who does everything so well."

"I have had a lot of time to practice."

"What are you, all of thirty-five? How much living could you have done?"

 "Maybe he is older than thirty-five? He seems to have an old soul."

"Dee, tell me how your paper is going?"

We have written about the little people's legend."

"Really? What changed your mind?" A huge smile came to

his face.

"I need good grades and the professor she didn't really like my idea about the immortals of James Island. How the doors are part of the legend of the immortals? That does not mean I have given up looking into the stories. Did she tell you about me?"

He got quiet, and he had that constipated look on his face again.

"What was with the story that made him so uncomfortable? What are his sister and him hiding?"

"Blaine."

"Deedra."

"Why do the stories of the immortals bother you and your sister so much?"

"It doesn't bother me."

"Really? Then why do the two of you always have that pained look on your faces when I bring it up?"

"You picked up on that from both of us."

"Both of your aura's change, and I am picking up a fear vibe from both of you. It happens every time I bring it up with the two of you. What are you hiding, and would you like to explain?"

"You would not believe me even if I told you."

"Try me."

He turned and walked into the club and sat down at the piano and played.

I followed him into the club. We were the only ones there.

"I just needed some answers. Who wrote the song that made my inner voice sad? What is on James Island? Blaine is not even my type; he is too perfect. Why am I so crazy about him?"

Blaine had stopped playing, and then played again. I love it. I sat next to him.

"It is beautiful, isn't it?" As he played on.

"It's just a song I found in an old book in the music library at school. It was written over hundred years for another man's passion that he had for a woman."

"Did you say a hundred years ago? When did you take piano lessons in the 1800s?"

"That's close. I need to tell you something." I looked into those beautiful pools of blue-green eyes.

"I have waited for you all of my life."

"Yeah, whatever. Does that line really work?" I rolled my eyes.

"I told you would not believe me."

"Well, not some pick up line you use on a woman to get your way."

He looked at me and I could tell he was telling the truth, but that doesn't add up.

"Ok let's say that's true. That makes you over two hundred years old. You only look as though you're in your mid-thirties"

"No, I am really two hundred and seventy-two years old."

"Ok, so let's say I believe you. Why have you been waiting for me all of your life?"

"I am what your indigenous people tell stories about. The myths and legends handed down through time. We are called immortal beings. Spirit gods of the old ways and you are one of us. The reason I say I have been waiting for you. We have soul mates. To complete us, we must find the other half. We very rarely find our soul mates in today's society because of our ancestors accepted mortals as companions out of loneliness. Deluding the blood line. I am three quarters pure blood. Your blood sings to me."

"I am an immortal?"

"You're not just an immortal; you are a purebred from an ancient bloodline."

"How do you know that?"

"We can feel the essence of the immortals."

"What do you mean to feel an immortal essence?"

"Well, our energies connect us. I know you have felt it, the feeling you know someone, the familiarity of being around certain people. Immortals have the same energies. They sense one and other. You said you have been waiting for me all your life. What does that mean?"

"Yes, well, I have waited for you all of my life. Didn't even know I could feel this way. I have been living my life, content being a player, not finding love. I never thought I would find my soul mate, so few of us do with the inbreeding with mortals. You feel it, don't you?"

"Oh, god I feel, what? Crazy for you, sexually, all the time. Oh yeah, I feel it."

I got up off the piano bench and walked into the bar. I couldn't sit there any longer with all these feelings bombarding me. I paced back-and-forth fidgeting and fighting the urge to…. how I wanted him.

"So, I'm immortal. Do I have powers?"

"Some of us have special gifts."

"Like what? I have noticed you seem to always get what you want, and women respond to you."

"Oh, yes, my gift of persuasion."

"What do you think you do well?"

"I think I can hear people's thoughts."

 "So, if you think you can hear thoughts, then you should try to focus on that and see how much more you can find out. You're a little young to control your gifts. But try it. Close your eyes, take a deep breath, blow it out. Focus..." I stopped pacing and stood still. Closed my eyes and tried to picture what he was thinking. I could feel he wanted to kiss me. Opened my eyes slowly, and he had got up and moved in front of me. His lips were just inches away. His intoxicating sent was all around me. I could feel his warm sweet breath on my mouth. I wanted to kiss him, too. He gently pressed his lips to mine. Reaching his arms around me, he pulled me snug against his hard body. With great ease, he had me wanting more. I tingled all over. I couldn't stop. I just pulled at his shirt. He pulled me closer. He reached under my butt and lifted me up. I wrapped my legs around him. I just had to have him, all of him, and it was going to happen right now... here in the club, on top of the table. He pulled back and unbuttoned my shirt. He reached behind me and unfastened my bra. The straps fell on my shoulders. Holding my arms in place. I'm not sure when he removed my shirt. He pressed his lips to my neck. Kissing his way down the top of my breast, then I felt his hot breath close to my nipple. His lips surrounded it and his teeth latched on and he began nibbling and sucking. I was about to come undone. Then he kissed his way down my belly to my core. Where he tore off my thong. His breath singed my mound. Placing one finger in my folds and circling my bud with his thumb, I released a moan. Then another finger slid into my core slowly, then another as he curled them back, hitting my G-spot repeatedly. I shattered into a million pieces. Trying to catch my breath, my heart beating out of my chest. Then in the distance I heard the phone ring, repeatedly. When I reached for it and placed it to my ear…

"Dee, are you OK?"

 It was Amanda. My head hurt. I looked around. I was in my apartment in my bed alone.

"Yeah, I think so. Why?"

"You sound terrible. Should I come over? You didn't show up at school."

"Well, no, it's Saturday!"

"Dee, it's Tuesday afternoon. You have missed two days of school."

"What? What time is it? It's really Tuesday?"

"No one has heard from you since Friday night."

There was a knock at the door.

"Just a minute" I pulled on my robe and walked over to the

door.

"Who is it?"

"Dee is Jake, let me in." I opened the door and Jake pushed in.

"Where have you been? You missed work; Mica was worried sick about you."

"Amanda, can I call you back? Jake is here."

"Yeah, sure… but call me right back."

"I don't know Jake; the last thing I remember is I was at the club…"
"He didn't need to know the rest. What if I imagined how stupid would I feel if Blaine found out?

"Dee, that was three days ago, and you really don't remember anything else?"

"Um, nope. I remember being at the club. I went to the bathroom because I was feeling sick and then the phone rang, and it was Amanda. Then you began knocking on my door."

"Did you drink anything from the bar?" Well, I stayed and had a glass of wine with Blaine, I think."

"Blaine left on Thursday night to go to Canada for a meeting. He won't be back until next week sometime."

"I just dreamt the last three days. That is not possible."

"Dee, I took him to the airport."

"No, I had a drink with him Friday night."

"No, I dropped you off at home. You had been acting weird all night and so I took you home. You said you were getting sick?"

I didn't know how to answer.

"I don't know. I must have dreamed the last three days. How is that possible?"

"I think you should be looked at by a doctor."

"No…, I'm Ok, just a little confused. What day is it and where am I supposed to be?"

"It is Tuesday afternoon, and you should be at work."

"It's the afternoon?"

"Oh well, that is'nt going to happen. Will you be short?"

"No, it will be ok, I will cover for you, and I will come by when I am done and check on you."

"Ok, I'll see you later." I let Jake out and locked the door behind him and I went to take a shower, feeling the water run across my face and down my back. *What in the hell was happening to me? I must be losing my mind. No, I know what I did last night or Friday night. I just don't know what happened in the last three days. But I'm not crazy. I think Blaine has done something to me and I'm not supposed to remember, maybe he told me too much. I'm going to find out what happened."*

Weeks had passed and everyone was overly protective of me, and Blaine was still gone on his business trip. I thought over what I thought I knew. I needed proof that Blaine and his mother had something to hide. I would start by searching the county records. Took a trip up to Mount Vernon in Skagit County. Caught an Uber to the bus station to buy a ticket to Mount Vernon. It was a couple of hour's ride. I was looking for information about James Island; it had to be the key. Wanting to look at the County records and see how far back I could find deeds and information on the island. I asked for the microfilms and any deeds around the early 1885 on James Island. Found where the Indians called the island 'A-Ka-Lat' meaning top of the rock… It was late, so I only had a couple of hours to dig through all the old films. I was just about to give up when I found a book number that was older than any of the rest of the books. It must be in the basement. The clerk had mentioned that some of the oldest books had been moved down there. I asked if she could take me down to the basement. I had a book number, and it was not up here. She grabbed her keys.

"No one has ever asked to see these old books as long as

I have worked here. What are you looking for, dear?"

"Oh, I am doing research for a final in one of my classes." Lying through my teeth and I am not very good at it, but she brought the key back with her. As we headed down the stairs to the basement, I wondered if I would find some answers. She unlocked the door and pushed the old metal door as it squealed, the smell of musty books swelled out of the basement. The room was the size of the main floor, and it went on forever. It had rows and rows of books. She said the oldest numbers were in the back on the left. I found the books on the back of the shelf. I had to dust it off as I laid it out on the table. As I opened the old book, the dust filled the air, and I sneezed. Obviously, it had not been opened in a very long time. It had some ancient plat maps and property profiles. They talked about the Rosario straits and the city of Anacortes, as I flipped through the entire old book. It was tough going because the books are almost as big as I am. The three-foot tall books were also 2 ft wide, making it difficult to maneuver them. This made the process very slow, as I could only turn one page at a time. In the middle of the last book, I found a folded old blueprint paper. On the ledger, it said house for Bluestar, dated 1861. The plate showed one hundred and thirteen acres and, as I read on, it described a piece of property just off the Rosario straits. It was the island. Then, as I unfold the blueprint, it was a house blueprint. I have had this exact house in my dreams for as long as I could remember. My dreams are not dreams; they are more like visions. As I looked back at the book, I read the house was 7500 sq ft and it had six bedrooms. I really did not think I was going to find anything before I had to head back to Seattle to work. I felt as if I had done all this before. You know one of those 'déjàvoo' moments. I took the book up to the clerk and asked her to copy a few of the pages of the book, and I stuck the blueprint in the backpack. I caught another Uber and headed back to the bus station, where I barely made the bus. I had to get to work on time so they would not worry. They all had worried enough about me, and I knew I was right. All of this happened and somehow Blaine had covered it up. However, if I was an immortal, why didn't he want me to know? I arrive back in Seattle and headed off to work.   It was Friday night. The school was out for spring break, and it would be packed at the club. Everyone was going to be working tonight. Amanda would be there Jerry and her were an item now.

I talk Mica into having some blues bands play now and then. I had heard the guy play in Austin, Texas Monte Montgomery and he was great, so she said she would try him. It just so happens. He is going to be in Seattle for two other gigs and said he was free Friday night. I opened the door, and I was the first one there, or so I thought I could hear someone in the back room I walked through turning on the lights. As I threw my backpack on the bar, I walked to the storeroom back behind the kitchen, just past the cellar door.

Chapter 4

Blaine's Story

 I have heard stories from the ancients that have passed down through the years that occasionally one of us finds an immortal soul mate, driven by pure desire and uncontrollable passion.   I have lived in this world for a very long time. Born in 1897 in Seattle, Washington, my mother Jacquelyn fell in love with a mortal Indian Chief Charles Bluestar. The other immortals found each other throughout the years and bought James Island shortly after Seattle was being built. They barged out all the material to build a home to house all the immortals, and they updated their lives and a haven for the new immortals to train as they adjust to their new life. Mom and I lived on the reservation for a time until my father was began aging. He was half Immortal, which gave him a longer life that a mortal. He was ninety-seven years old, and my mother was still looking as though she was forever twenty. She protected her secret. She should have left him many years before. But they live quietly and had few friends. If they went places, people thought mom was his daughter. She staged an accident. It left my father in a depression. The guilt was hers to bear. I lived with him, not wanting him to be a lone the rest of his mortal life. My mother had to go into hiding, so she moved to James Island where the house is large enough to hold several of us as we move in and out of the mortal lives, we touch. A beautiful place allowed us to train and read from the extensive library a place to reinvent ourselves for different lives. My father never understood the accident. Losing my mother drove him to a dark place that he never fully recovered from. She would visit me, but I could never tell my father.

As we move from place to place throughout time, we must not allow the mortal's life that we had touched to be influenced by our existence. We had to give time for them to leave this earth, always would make sure that we cleaned up all pictures and anything that might resemble a past life. Having had many years of practice and our elders have trained us well. When I reached twenty, I had discovered some strange abilities that had a strange effect on people, a persuasion of sorts not normal. I could get people to do or give me anything I wanted; no questions asked when I mentioned it to my mother. She revealed the truth that I was an immortal. She told me her story of our people and why she had to leave my dad. Dad would tell me she visited him in his dreams every night and it was

OK. She came and checked on us at night religiously. I suppose that was where the indigenous people thought the immortals were a myth being ghosts like. That they only showed themselves when they were needed. After my dad died, I went off to college, attended Stanford, Harvard, many European colleges with years of time to fill up moving around seemed the safest way. After getting many degrees, you learn a ton of information, making you better at life. I am now about 37 immortal years old: I am Two hundred and seventy-two mortal years. In all those years, I have had some relationships with mortal women and some immortal women, but I have never spent a very long time with anyone, nor have I ever fallen in love. My gifts are the ability to influence. I can make mortals do whatever I want, and immortals are a different story. I can only influence their thoughts if they accept my touch.

Until now, I held the door for the most flawless, beautiful woman. Long blond curly hair, with golden highlights, and she smelled of fresh rain and peonies. I could sense she was an immortal, and she had not yet discovered her true gifts. I could feel her strength and how powerful the energy flowed from her that was un-shielded. She was glowing like a damn beacon in the fog. As I held the door and looked into her lavender blue eyes. My heart stopped. Who was this exquisite creature? My most inner animal desires were controlling my thoughts. All I wanted to do was grab her and take her into my arms and make mad, passionate love to her. I had to look away and take a deep breath and focus. As she was walking by me, I could smell her sweet fragrance and it was driving me mad. I knew in that one moment that she had captured my heart and my life would never be the same. All I could do at this point was hurry away from the coffee shop. I waited until she had passed. Turning around, I rushed back out the door and I headed across the campus to my car. All I could think about was I had to get as far away from her as soon as possible. I got into my car and just sat there thinking about her. Remembering how her fragrance smelled when the wind blew through her hair when she passed me in the doorway. Who was she? An immortal that is so very young. Where was she from? How did she come to Seattle where I would run across her before the renegades? Did anyone else know she was here? I drove over to the club to talk to Mica and see if she could help me figure out why I was having these intense feelings about a woman that passed by me in one second of time. When I got there, Mica was busy getting the club ready for the usual dinner crowd. I walked through the door. Jerry and Jake were helping her get set up. We were a small band of immortals that looked out for one another, and they were all I had except my mother who we told everyone she was my older sister because we looked too much alike to deny another story and Jerry's girlfriend, Amanda. Jerry Malone found us when his life changed. He can feel the essence of a new mortal once they have developed some of their powers. That is how he found us with his gift. All of us come of age at different times. When the aging slows, we are frozen in time at whatever age that occurs. Jerry also can sense some future events that will happen, but the visions are not always correct; they can change based on the decisions made by who the vision is about. We all have choices to make in life, right or wrong. When we choose our own path, that can skew what he sees. He only reads immortals. He is Kind of our own fortune teller. Visions of the mortal world don't seem to happen to him. Jake Kirby showed up on Jacquelyn's door looking for answers. Jake was looking for the truth because he instinctively could do the martial arts of ancient Asian warriors and did not know how he learned the art. He thought the professor could help explain where he got these gifts when he read one of her articles on ancient Asian warriors… When Jake showed up at the University of Washington state campus he had signed up for her class and one day asked if she might help him. Immediately, my mother knew he was an immortal and yet suspected he did not know who he was. She waited until the time was right to let him in on his secret abilities and bring him to all the rest of us. He is a loner and a protector; he is skilled in combat, and he has studied the martial arts under the Dali lama. Jake was a monk where he studied many ancient marshal art forms. He meditates to remain calm and in control. Jake loves a good fight. He hides it very well. Most immortals always underestimate his strengths. With his long blonde dreadlocks and his wit, he behaves as the joker of the group, but really, you never want to make him angry. Amanda Pennington showed up for classes at the college and she can read minds. She just thought she was a fortune teller, like her mother. She worked at a traveling carnival. Yet when she notice she has stopped ageing and watched her friends and family were disappearing and she remained forever twenty seven. She, by the way of the underground, learns about her immortal abilities. She left them to seek an honest group of immortals to hang out with when she took classes with Jacquelyn. Then she read her mind and learned about us. She showed up at the club and talked to Mica. The rest is history. She is kind of young soul with a fun-loving attitude about her immortal abilities. She and Jerry have become an item. They have great fun at my expense. Mica Wentworth came to my mother many years before I was born. They are the best of friends. She is like my second mother to me. Her gift is to keep us on our toes. Mica is very strong emotionally and physically. Quick on her feet and has a temper to go with all her love for us. She has worked in the top-secret government facilities. Her military training helps. She has priority clearance, which comes in handy. Especially when changing our identity, so the mortals never catch on that we exist.

Finally, when I arrived at the club, I burst through the door. "Mica!"

"What is it, Blaine?"

"Um… I opened a door for a young immortal woman and in that moment, I knew she was the other half of my soul and her fragrance drove me insane. I just wanted her, you know."

"What? When? Where?"

"She walked through the doors at Mary's espresso. She caught me off guard. I almost lost control. I can sense she is questioning her abilities. Her essence is so very strong for someone so young. I could feel her powers. There is no mistaking she has the strongest energy I have ever come across. She is too young to understand what is happening to her. We need to protect her. I can only be around her for a while before the desire consumes me and drives me mad. Her smell is intoxicating. All my senses want her and only her. I cannot stop thinking about her. Mica, what do I do?" Blaine put his hands to his face, resting his head on the bar. Jake came out of the back room carrying a box of glasses that just arrived UPS.

"Hi Blaine, so what is going on?"

"I think I have found my soul mate."

"Who is she?"

"I don't know. Not yet."

"What do you mean you don't know?" he scoffed.

"I just ran across her at the Mary's coffee café on the

college campus. I must sound pathetic."

 "Yea, you do. I can see you have got it bad, Blaine. You need to focus. You have the strength to fight your instincts to be with her and control your emotions. Remember the focus of training we did last summer? Breathe and focus, you will be fine. Just stay away until you get it together. We will look after her for now until you get stronger." Jerry had just come into the room.

"What's wrong with the kid?" He laughed…

"Well, evidently, our Casanova has run across the ancient instinctive passion, and he is has been hit with Cupid's arrow?"

"That's ruff it aches, doesn't it? I felt that way once for a mortal, the time with her I will never forget, but she died in the early 1940s. I have never run across those feelings again. It will get easier after the first couple of times. However, for now, when you are near her, it will be tough. But you are the strongest of all of us and your mind can control all those feelings. Just practice."

 "But how can I even go near her and try to get to know her if I cannot control my urges to ravish her? How do I do that?"

"Watch her at night and be near her without her noticing. It will not be easy, but the more you are near her; you will become desensitized to the urges. But you are going to have to be very careful. Touching her will be very hard. The pure animal instinct will take over for both of you."

"Both of us."

"If you're feeling these feelings for her and she is an immortal, you can bet she just felt everything you are feeling and along with her own feelings and I'm sure she was not ready for all of that emotion to flood her system. I am thinking it caught her off guard and she is trying to dismiss it as most mortals do when they have experienced something supernatural."

"We need a plan." Mica picked up the phone.

"I'll call Amanda and have her track her down. She is the most sensitive of all of us and she will find her and not want to consume her."

"Thanks Mica." She was making fun of me, and I was not sure it was so funny, but everyone else got a kick out of my torture.

"Jerry, why didn't you see this coming?"

"You got me, kid. You know it works when it wants to."

Mica dialed Amanda's number. "Hey, we need you to track down a new immortal young woman on campus. She has long blond hair with golden highlights. She is about five foot three inches tall has the lavender blue eyes. Blaine says her essence is very strong. Well, for him anyway when you find her, call us back."

"I have already run into her this morning. I wasn't sure she blocked my attempt to read her if she didn't know her powers or who she was. Her instincts are very good."

"Well, did you ask her name?"

"Her name is Deedra Lee."

"That is a good start. I can look her name up in the tribal books and see if I can find her family. Lee's, huh? I seem to remember something about the Lees. I will check and see which tribe she comes from."

"Make sure you are in her classes. We have to protect her until she is ready to be told."

"I know. She is already in Jacquelyn's class with me and several others. Just coincidence. Or maybe fate has directed her to us."

"Perfect, we can't let renegades get to her first."

"Oh, and Blaine says she is his soul mate."

"Really, this will be interesting to watch. Think about the women he has gone through; they all think he is their lover."

"I wonder if she will be so easily convinced. I'm hoping for a really entertaining year."

"Amanda, behave yourself. You shouldn't get entertainment

from Blaine's misery."

 "I know but think about it." I could hear Amanda laughing on the other end of the phone.

"What does she find so amusing?"

"Oh…. Your Casanova days are finally over. She wonders how you will do for your desires for someone who might not be ready. For someone who might not be taken over by charisma of your gift. Then what will you do with those uncontrollable desires to have her? What if it takes years before she comes of age with her own gifts? She just thought this should be amusing, that's all."

"Well, I'm so glad all of you are so amused at my expense." They all laughed.

 "Oh, lighten up. We have your back."

A couple of weeks had gone by as I was watching her at night to keep her safe. The cat didn't like me much. He always hissed at me and growled too, giving me away. I had to be even more careful. Then I thought I would spend some time at the club-taking inventory. It was Saturday early, so no one should be there. I thought if I could forget about her for just a few minutes, it would ease the tension I was feeling. Then she came into the club. I could smell her fragrance as soon as the door opened. I stepped out of the cellar and up the stairs to the end of the bar. Standing in the dark there she was, saying hello, calling out Jake's name. I should have just left, but I couldn't. I wanted to be with her. I think I can control my behavior, so I stepped out into the light. Her eyes were full of disbelief. I said hello, talking in a low and soft, controlling voice like you would talk to a frightened child, not knowing if I could make her feel safe. She introduces herself and all I could say is, hey, I couldn't think of anything else to say.   I was trying not to freak her out. Jake walked in the door. Shoving her forward, almost knocking her down. I was never so glad to see him. I was in way over my head, and I needed the backup. Then Jerry came in the door right behind Jake. Better in numbers. She started talking about going to the island. Then I offered to be alone with her. I couldn't help myself. Jake was not much help. He offered her up as a prize possession. I got my coat from the back, and we were off, touching her hand for the first time. It was like an electric shock to my system. I was not really prepared for her to be so intoxicating; I thought I was in control of my feelings for her. I had to focus harder to keep my self-control.   I drove, trying to focus on the road. I just wanted to pull over and have my way with her. She asked many questions, and they helped keep my mind preoccupied. I could feel her trying to probe my mind. I wasn't even sure she realized she was doing it. The pain was slight, but I was sure I was making faces at her. It was obvious she was having visions and reading other thoughts. I could tell she didn't know what she was doing. It was just part of her thought process. When we reached the island, it was almost dark, and a storm was coming in. Convincing Noah into taking us for a ferry ride and then turning back just before we got there. A relief come over me. I was not ready to fill her in and I did not think she was prepared to hear it either. I could feel her trying harder to read me. She had started to figure a few things out. As I blocked her, the pain was getting excruciating. I knew I was still making a face. I could see it in her expression that she thought I was making a face at her. The ride back in the car was quiet as she just stared out the window and when I stopped in front of her apartment; I could not help myself. I wanted to see her again, stepping out onto the sidewalk with her. Placed a piece of hair behind her ear. Leaned in to kiss her, realizing she wasn't ready. Sucked in some air with a sigh and took a couple of steps back. Was afraid I didn't have that much control once I started kissing her. Wouldn't be able to stop myself. Instead, I asked when she worked next. Then told her I would see her later. Drove around the corner and waited until I saw her light go on. Then back to the club. I would just stay there in the apartment above the club where we had redone the loft many years ago for a hideaway in town. The old building had tons of room. We had bought some of the old buildings in the area in the early 1950s. The loft was hidden from everyone; it just appeared to be the storage area above the club. No one knew there was a warehouse loft… I could see Dee's apartment. The building was just across the courtyard; she was in the corner apartment. From the bedroom window,

I could watch her and make sure she was safe. We also owned the building Dee rented. Just by luck, we had an open room and Amanda directed her to it. It helped that it was so close to us for security. All I really wanted to do is let myself in and tell her the truth so I could be with her.

The next day, Jake, Jerry, Amanda, and Mica were asking questions about how our day was. "Does she know? Did we make it to the island?"

 I explained it was interesting and difficult, but I loved being with her and if she was fighting back the urge to be with me, I sensed nothing.

 Amanda smiled at me smugly,

"Maybe it is because she doesn't feel the same about you!" Jacquelyn and Mica had done some research on Deedra's tribe, and her great grandmother was an immortal one of the original immortals she live almost five hundred years ago and her powers where unremarkable like no other immortals. She was feared by the corrupt immortals and that is how they stayed inline then after she was gone the corruption took over. Her grand mother also had a soft side. She fell in love with a tribal chief that taught music and loved the simpler things in life and be grateful. His name was George Allen Lee. The powers of the current immortals in the last hundred years had diminished to only one or two abilities per immortal. This happened when ancients mated with the mundane mortals and create the highbred immortals we are today. It is interesting Deedra's parents were both mundane mortals, but her great grandmother was the original immortal with amazing gifts. She was the most powerful of all the ancients. The gene must have been waiting for her. The carvings on the door refer to Deedra's arrival. We could not translate the language on the door we have tried for many years to understand. Blaine's face was still with no emotion.

 "Deedra is the woman in the carvings on the library door at the college. So, what happens now?"

"Blaine, Deedra is 'The One.' We don't know enough to know how many gifts she has. Or if, with her young uncontrolled gifts if she even knows how to control them. We are not sure what she is capable of, and we cannot read her because that is one of her basic gifts, to block those who will try to read her. All I could think about was that she needed to know the truth. It would help her understand what was happening to her. I waited to see her that night at the club, took out the wine we had bought on our trip. I picked out the private table in the club's front and then I waited as she came to my table, where I asked her to join me later for a glass of wine. She jokes about me being her boss. She said she had better get back to work before the boss fires her and then she smiled at me. My heart just stopped at her presence, her smell intoxicating. Her smile lit up the room. The night seemed to drag on. I watched and waited for her. Finally, the night was over. I thought

I would play some music to see if she would feel more at ease around me. Her great grandfather wrote a song about her grandmother when he was courting her. I was a student of music under him. He told the story of his soul mate and the love he had for Deedra's grandmother, and so he put it to music. I never realized that Deedra would be my soul mate when he played me this song. I remember the song moved me the first time I heard it. As I played, Jerry and Amanda watched her face go white. They could see the tears streaming down her face. The music moved her far more than I had expected. They asked her if she was Ok, and she ran to the bathroom. "What happened?"

They told me about her reactions. Did she have the power to pull past the feelings of her grandfather? Deedra's grandfather wrote that song many years ago. I ran across it in some of my music I was going through last night. I thought it would make her feel safe. She came out to talk to Amanda and then she nodded, and Amanda and Jerry left. They had been hooking up for many years. I felt bad for lying to Dee, but it was necessary for now to keep her safe. Then I saw her head for the door, and I called out her name. "Dee, are you ready to have a drink with me?"

She turned and came over to sit down. She grilled me again.

And this time I could not stop myself. I wanted her to know everything, and I was having trouble controlling my passion for her. Finally, she asked if she could read people's thoughts, because she felt she was hearing bits and pieces of people's thoughts around her. I had her close her eyes. Then I got up walked over to where she was pacing. I stood still and close to her lips. I inhaled her breath. It was sweet like honey. I looked deep into her lavender blue eyes.

"See if you can read my thoughts." She closed her eyes took a deep breath. Seconds ticked by.

"You want to kiss me?" Then I pressed against her lips, and it was so powerful she pressed back and then we were ripping each other's clothes off before I knew it. I had her up on the table, taking off her clothes and her legs wrapped around me. Couldn't stop myself, her little thong I ripped off. At first just putting my fingers in her folds, stretching her so she would be comfortable when I took her and before I knew it, I was buried deep inside her all the way to the hilt. I started off slow, and then I lost it. Slamming repeatedly in and out of her, reaching down to suck on her nipple and pinching the other one as I felt her tighten around me. I tensed, then jerked, letting it flow into her. I was feeling her core milking me. The release was gratifying. I felt the room shake. It was astonishing. Somehow, I got her up to my apartment. Opened the door, lifted her up by her bum, took her into the shower. I turned on the water and held her against the shower wall. I lowered my head and kissed her, pushing my tongue into her mouth, nibbling on her lip, then kissing down her neck, down to her breast and attaching my lips to her nipple. One, then the other. Suckling and twirling my tongue. Pulling my teeth across her ever so hard nipple as she screamed out my name. Then I sat her on my shaft, pushing as far and as hard as I could get it in her. Then lifting her to the edge of my rock-hard member and dropping her down on me. Beginning to moving faster and harder. Could feel my whole body tighten, ready to explode. I couldn't hold on any longer. I liberated my erection. Rose again to fill her up. Working her core, we went on for hours. If I questioned, I was in love with her, I no longer questioned it. I had found my mate after all these years. At some point, I think she passed out from her many orgasms. As she slept in my arms, I took her back to her apartment. I needed her to forget last night. Jake could spin a pretty moral tale. Maybe with a plan we could make her forget. I called my mother to come give her a sedative to give me time to meet with the group. I went back to the club the next day and told the group I had lost control and we needed a plan to cover up how much of the truth I had told her. Deedra wasn't ready yet to know the truth. Mica, Jerry, Jake, and Amanda came up with a plan. First Mica and Amanda picked her clothes off the club floor and table. Then they went to her apartment. Put her close away and put her in leggings and t-shirt and back into bed. Jake was going to tell her she got sick, so he took her home, and whatever else she thought happened, it was all just a dream. Feeling ashamed for being so weak that we had to set up this elaborate lie. I hoped she would forgive me one day. So, with the plan in place, we lied to Deedra. I felt awful, but it was for her safety until I could decide if the news about her had been received by the cartel and if the renegades were coming for her. The cartel is a group of immortals who virtually run this country and has powerful roles all over the world. The renegades are gangsters that conduct their dirty work for the cartel, doing horrific things to mortals and gathering immortals for their army. They murder, rape, kidnapping, general destruction. Jerry pulled me out of my thoughts.

"Blaine, take off and go find out what you can from your underground sources. We will take care of everything here and make sure Dee is alright. We will get her into work telling her the story and make her feel as if she is losing her mind.

"You're sure this is how you want to play this?"

"Yes, it's the only way we can play this and keep her safe. I blew it and I told her too much information. I could feel she was overloaded and not yet ready for the truth."

"Blaine, go now. Find out if the renegades have a clue if there is a new immortal and if they have sensed her powers."

"I'll be out of here later. I want to wait until she wakes to see if we have pulled this off."

"Then I will gather some clothes and be off."

"If you need me…"

"We have got this."

"I will call soon."

"Be careful". I hugged Mica and left.

I have heard some stirring from the underground. I need to check it out. The underground was a large group of immortals that thought of themselves as gods and better than the mortals. They used their powers to take advantage and manipulate the world government, economy, stock market, drugs, pharmaceutical companies, and oil cartels. Most of the CEOs of these companies are immortal. They are corrupt & greedy, and they run most of the mortal world and not doing an excellent job of it. The world has never been this divided. I remember when the market crashed in 1929; the mood of the nation was not as bad as it is now. Then again in 2008. The corrupt immortals forced the downfall of the world economy to happen, then took advantage while the rest of the world put the economy back together. There needs to be a change in powering the immortal world. Not much hope our new president will make some changes that can make a difference. He is an immortal with mind control, like me. He can get anything he wants from anyone, mortal or immortal. Let us hope he uses his gift wisely.

I would have to be very careful about my question and

make sure no one remembers I was here. I could not risk drawing attention to myself. Deedra's life may depend on me not screwing this up. My first contact said they heard a new immortal was in town. Not much more was out on the streets yet. There was going to be a meeting of bosses I was trying to get invited to. I got hold of one of my old boss's. I convinced him to take me along with him to the meeting. They met in warehouse space in the underground of Seattle. Their meeting was about young immortals and how important it was to retrieve them with their uncommon talents to improve the renegade's forces. They talked about how they had felt a forceful presence in Seattle but had not found the source. That had to be Dee she showed like a beacon. We need to help train her... and soon. It took a couple of weeks, but I was sure they were coming for her. I called Jerry.

"I think we have only a couple of days to move Dee to the island. We need the vantage point of the island to control the renegades. It will keep them from kidnapping Dee before she is ready. They know there is a great power that has entered our world and they know they must control it. They do not know any details like her gender or age or location. I will be there tonight at the club to tell her the truth and everyone needs to be prepared."

"The truth! Are you sure... so soon after what we have done?"
"We do not have any more time... they are coming for her."

Chapter 5

The Truth

Hello anyone here?" as I walked into the club. I could hear banging going on in the cellar. I walked over to the door behind the bar and hollered down.

"Hello, is anyone down there?"

"Yeah, I'm here." I could barely hear someone talking to me from down there.

"Who's here?" I could hear a woman's voice but couldn't make it out.

"Me."

"Who is me?"

"Mica, who do you think is down here in all this mess?"

"Oh, it's Dee. What are you doing?" She stuck her head out from the cellar. Cobweb hanging in her hair, holding a box. She moved through the door and set the box on the bar. She pulled out brandy balloon with along stem glassed to be washed.

"Blaine is coming in tonight." My heart jumped into my throat, choking off anything I was about to say, and then… the anger washed over me.

"I know I have been lied to and I know what happened that night and I think everyone is in on it. I never put my clothes away. I always just throw them on the floor… They were hung up and my room was clean."

Mica kept talking. "He wanted these wine glasses out. I had to put them back because they always get broken and then when he wants to have a glass of wine in the brandy balloon because it is a full-size glass, we are always out of them. It makes him cranky."

"Blaine is coming in tonight?" She could hear in my voice as it hit a few octaves higher than normal, proving something was wrong.

"Yes, he is, is that going to be a problem?" As she set the large snifters into the dishwasher.

Exasperated, I muttered to myself.

"Problem… Why would there be a problem? He hasn't even tried to call me in a month. After all the sex, the story of being an immortal, my ancient gifts and, to top it off, how

142

he has been waiting all his life for me. What if I'm seeing the future? What if I am mad about something that hasn't even happened yet? I don't even know my mind anymore. Call the asylum. I am bat shit crazy." No warning, she just plops into my ranting mind.

"My dear Deedra, stop beating yourself up about that man. You're not seeing the future… it all happened and more. Brace yourself for the truth."

"What! Now you are giving me a heads up. Where have you been through all the lies?"

Nothing, not a sound from her.

"Dee, are you ok?"

"Humph, sure, I am just peachy."

. "What time will he be in?"

"He didn't say." Jake and Jerry came through the door.

"Big night hey Dee?"

A bewildered expression crossed my face.

"Dee, the band you have been raving about!"

"Oh, yeah, you guys are going to love him."

"What did you think I was asking about?"

"Oh… nothin." I went to the dining area in the club to set

up.

Jake followed me to the front of the club.

"Hey, I'm not letting you off that easy Dee, what is wrong?"

"Blaine is coming in tonight."

"Ok, and why is that a problem? I thought you liked him."

Jake knew I had a thing for him, but he didn't know about the other weird stuff that was happening to me, along with the dream or vision. He just knew I had lost three days.

"Are you going to be, ok?"

"Sure, why wouldn't I be?"

"No reason. If you sure you're ok."

I knew they all were trying to hide something. I just didn't know the extent of it.

The night got busy, and I forgot what time it was. Band had set up in the back by the bar and I was in the front serving food. The music started. It was good, and the crowd seemed to like it. The dinner crowd had left, and I was the only one in the front cleaning up for the next day. When I heard from behind me.

"Hey, Dee." It was Blaine, but there was an uncertainty to his voice, softer than I remember it, and not as seductive. I spun around to make sure it was him. He smiled, "I *couldn't be mad at him, dammit, why?"* I smiled back and then looked down sheepishly. I murmured "Hey."

He had two of the long stem brandy balloons in one hand and a bottle of Burning Desire in the other.

"Would you like to join me?" He walked to the small booth in the corner. I took a deep breath, sighed, and followed him over. He set the glass in front of me and filled the snifter up. He never once took his eyes off mine. I could feel him trying to read me like the part of my dream where he told me I had gifts that were young. If I have such exceptional gifts, could I focus and read his thoughts? I sat as still as a statue, trying not to show any emotion and focus on him staring into his eyes. I glimpsed a thought. Then it was as if some door had shut. His eyes narrowed. I know I was in his mind by the pained look on his face. I smiled and took a drink. *"Mmm… so smooth."*

Looking at him over the top of my glass, there was confidence in my newfound gift.

"How have you been?" he broke the silence first. It made me feel even more in control.

"I have been fine?"

"How is school?"

Thinking to myself. *"What is with the small talk?"*

"I'm glad it is spring break."

"Was he trying to make me believe the story they told me by appearing normal? To make me seem like I was insane."

I focused again on his eyes and tried to read him, then I heard. "Stop, *you are hurting me."*

His lips had not moved… I backed off my focus.

"What, did you say something?"

"You know I did, Dee stop. It hurts when you try to enter a mind that doesn't want you in their thoughts."

I was shocked he acknowledged I knew what he was referring to… I looked away to gather my thoughts and I could feel the tears running down my face. I wasn't sure I was relieved that I hadn't dreamed the week or was just upset because of the lies. Then I turned back, wiping the tears from my face. I could feel myself losing control of the anger. My voice raised a pitch higher and the volume even higher.

"You have left me here thinking I was losing my mind and everyone I care about is worrying about me. How could you do that to me? Where in the hell have you been?"

"Calm yourself, Dee, before you hurt someone with your gift. Anger is not a pleasant state of mind as a young immortal…. I will explain."

Infuriated, I yelled back.

"Like you did last time after we made love all over this club, then somehow erased it all. Made me feel I was dreaming and none of it happened. Who does that to a person they say they have been waiting for all their life… who does that, Blaine?"

"Dee, relax, it was for your own safety. Here, have some more wine. I will tell you why it all happened the way it did."

He reached across the table and took my hand. I began to unruffle and even went into that place of spinning like he was stirring my brain. I pulled my hand back. Then I glared straight into his blue green pools.

"You have to stop using your gifts on me. Maybe it does not hurt, but it is not a fair way to deal with me either."

"Dee, I don't know how to deal with you."

I looked up at him and in a whisper, with tears still running down my cheeks.

"The truth is always a good place to start."

I looked down at my glass of wine, took another sip. He poured more wine in my glass.

"It's a long story."

"Since I age one year for every thirty of all my friends and family, I have plenty of time to listen. Unless this time I don't want to wake up three days later thinking, I have lost my mind along with all of my friends."

"He smiled sheepishly and looked into my eyes. I won't be able to do that to you anymore. You are way stronger than any of us expected you would be at this age and appear to be adding to your gifts every day. You evidently embraced your gift from the beginning and that makes you likely to cause more harm in injury to all around you, not knowing the truth. Most of us take a lifetime at least fifty human years to realize everyone around us is getting older at a faster pace than we are. Then our gifts show up years later. You have even noticed that you are remaining 18 years old and never changing."

"How old are you if you do not mind me asking?"

"I am twenty-nine and turn thirty next month."

"Just a babe in immortal years."

"How old are you? You can't be that much older than me. So how old are you in mortal years?"

"I am Two hundred and seventy-two years old in mortal years. In immortal years I am thirty seven."

"Wow! That is old, I kind of remember you telling me that but must have dismissed it because you look to be in your mid-thirties…"

"Your time for explaining is up… I have questions."

"Do we stop aging at different times?"

"Yes, all of immortals age at different times. Some of us are eighteen, twenty-three, thirty-five; no one is older than fifty mortal years before the aging in immortal years begins. There are highbred immortals that age faster than immortals but live longer than most mortals."

The reason I seem to do everything better than most is because I have had plenty of years to learn how."

"Do we die?"

"Yes, when most humans die in their 80s in human years, we die in our 1200+ years. Depending on when what age we stop ageing."

"How do you blend in? You must have to move around, so no one notices you are not ageing as fast as they seem to be."

"Yes, we have homes in many places all over the world."

"The professor is an immortal?"

"Yes."

"How old is the professor?"

"She is three hundred and two years old. Is she really your sister?"

"No, she is my mother."

"Where is your dad? My father is dead. He was a one third immortal. His only gift was longevity. He died at one hundred and three. When the ancient decide to mate with the mortal world, the gifts that are passed on in the genes, shows up at random like you. You have parents are mortal, but your five times great grandparents were some of the original immortals. Grandmother had the most powerful gifts of the ancients. And your grandfather was an immortal chieftain of the Duwamish."

"I am not Cherokee, I am Duwamish?"

"Is that all you heard me tell you? You are Atlantean and Duwamish. Raise in the Cherokee beliefs. Your grandfather had one love… your grandmother. You have not even tapped into your potential. Part of the reason we did what we did to you was waiting for you to understand what you are and if you were ready to hear the truth. We had to do some research on your family."

"How did you know I was an immortal?"

"We can feel the essence. Can't you feel the energy we give off? It's like another sense we all have the ability."

 "What were you so afraid of telling me?"

"Not all immortals live within the mortal laws. There are those who abuse their gifts. They take advantage of mortals. These immortals think they are gods and have no regard for mortal or immortal life."

"How many of us exist?"

"Immortals inhabit 5% of the earth's population. We have always been here. Immortals have rules and laws. We have to go by, trying not to change the mundane mortals existence. We report to a council once a year to solve any problems we like to police ourselves. The Cartel is the guiding body of the renegade. There is a group of about thirty strong and they are headed to Seattle. They are looking to control the essence they have noticed, and that essence is you, Dee. They have heard of you through the underground Network…. Probably happened the day we almost made it to James Island. I found out in my trip to the underground that the boat captain, Noah. Is working for the Cartel, he is one of their spies."

Blaine paused.

"I think you should know. I had decided you had lied to me, and I was not sure who was in on it. I was going to prove it to myself. I was not losing my mind. I took a ride today to Mount Vernon. At the courthouse in the basement, I found a blueprint with the name Bluestar on it, and it was built in 1905. The white house in my dreams and it is on James Island. I was ready to confront you whenever you showed your face again."

"Do you know why I have been dreaming about this house all of my life?"

"I do not know. It was built after your grandfather had passed, so it's not a past vision. Maybe you can see the future like Jerry."

"I have something else to tell you."

"Okay, I'm listening."

I crossed my arms and glared deep into his blue-green eyes.

"You know when mortals say it was love at first sight"

"Yes, go on." I was releasing my aggression with him, but I did not want him to know how easy it was to manipulate me.

"You know, the animal instincts that turn on the chemistry and endorphins that come when two are in love?"

"Yea, I have heard stories, but I have never been in love."

"You have never been in love?"

"Not that I know of."

"What was he trying to say?"

"I have never felt for any woman the way I feel for you. There is something also you should know when immortals imprint it is ten times as strong as the mortal love and not very many of us ever experience it. In all my many years here on earth, you are the only one. I cannot stay away
152

from you. I have tried." My heart thawing, I trudge on with the inquisition.

"What makes you so sure I want to be with you?" He smiled smugly. "Oh, my dear Deedra, I remembering you ogling me. And you liked what you saw. Then he reached over and took my hand. I could hardly resist climbing on the table and ripping off his clothes. I pulled my hand back.

"Well, there is that! Will it always be this hard to be around you?" Blaine went on to explain,

"I really don't know. You are my first. I am told with control we can behave like everyone else."

"I am your first, so you are having uncontrollable feelings for me?"

"Oh, Dee, haven't you been listening to me? I am hopelessly in love with you. I had to take a break after being with you because I had to get back in control. Do you remember that first day when I held the door for you? I inhaled your fragrance of fresh rain and peonies, your vibrant lavender eyes, the wind in your hair. When you walked by me, it took all my self-control to make it through the door without just taking you down right there in Mary's and have my way with you in front of everyone. I have wanted no one like I did with you at that moment. I ran away and watch over you from afar."

"I smell like peony and rain? You watch me?"

"Is that what you just heard me tell you?" He shook his head and laughed.

"For months now I have watched you, from a distance, I have been keeping my eye on you."

"I knew I wasn't going mad. I felt you, but I ignored it. DC saw you, didn't he?"

"You mean your cat. Oh! Yes, you were in the shower. I could hear it running." He chuckled, lightening the mood.

I got a big smile on my face teasingly smiled.

"Why Blaine, are you a peeping tom?"

He stiffened.

"I would not do that; I was just monitoring your apartment."

"Ok, ok… I am going to need another bottle of wine. I'm overloaded."

 I just put my hands over my face. Blaine turned to Jerry, "Can you get us another bottle of cab and tell everyone to come in?" Jerry went to the cellar, grabbed a case of wine, and brought it back, along with Mica, Jake, and Amanda.

"So, everyone around me is an immortal?" How could you all deceive me like that? I thought I was just bat shit crazy!"

The tears were streaming down my face.

"Amanda, how could you?"

 "Oh, Dee, I am so very sorry, but it was for your own good. You needed a few more weeks before we told you everything. Please forgive me."

"I just heard you and you didn't move your lips."

 "Yes, it is one of your gifts. To talk to all of us in our minds, I am the only one that can continue a conversation with you. Because of my gift to read minds."

 Then Jake came over and put his arms around me. He just pulled me into a big hug.

 "Don't cry, Dee, we just wanted to keep you safe." Jerry was on the other side.

 "Hey kid, we love you, don't ya know?"

"We are so very sorry…" Mica came over and hugged me. She pulled back and looked into my eyes. Her tears were gathering, too.

 "You have the purest powers of the immortals. There are some unscrupulous immortals that want you for your gifts. To control you, so we will have to leave now and take you to the Island to protect you from the renegades.

The most debauched group of them all. Are you ready to learn about your life and what the future might hold?"

"Where's the professor?"

"Jacquelyn and Ray are getting the island ready."

"So, who is Ray?"

"He is our oldest immortal. Ray is two hundred and ninety-five years old in immortal years. That makes him forty-two years old in mortal years. Ray takes care of the island; he doesn't play well with the mundane mortals; he prefers to be alone or with immortals". Jerry poured me another glass of wine.

"Here sweetie, drink up. It could get a little rockier before it gets better."

"I cannot believe you, Amanda. I thought you were my friend."

"I am, but I also was taking care of you." She looked at Blaine.

"I was just following orders."

"Jake, I trusted you to have my back."

"Well, that shows you have an expert judge of character."

He was always making a joke that took the edge off.

"Jerry, I thought you and Amanda just met."

"I know, Dee, we are all so very sorry."

"Jerry and I have been together for years. Not like you and Blaine are, but we are very fond of one another."

"Mica… you knew the minute I walked in the door that afternoon looking for a job. Why didn't you tell me who I was?"

"We needed you to discover your own gifts or some of them. I think you have the purest of all the immortal powers. Your gifts have been handed down through the generations from the ancients."

"Ok, so what does that mean? I am some kind of super immortal?"

"We don't know yet. As you transition, your gifts will show up, usually at random."

My eyes closed. I stopped in the middle of my sentence. My amulet was getting hot around my neck. I reached up to pull it off my skin.

"They are coming."

"Who is coming?"

"I can see some men and they don't look friendly."

"Where are they?"

"Traveling in a car, they just passed the space needle headed our way" Blaine stepped back in the room.

"We had better get moving then they are closer than I had hoped." Jerry put his arm around me. "Dee, are you Ok?"

"Um… yea… a little light-headed, though. How did I do that?"

 "I'm not sure."

 Jerry spoke up, "My visions come in different images that I have to put together. Your sound like they are all together like a movie. I think you're imprinted with the powers of the original ancients to protect you if danger is near. Just a guess we will learn more about your abilities on the island in controlled situations."

Blaine stepped out from the back of the bar…

If we must fight to keep you, it needs to be on our terms, since we will be outnumbered. The renegades never travel with less than 30 men."

"Won't some of you get hurt if we fight a group of renegades?
"

"Well… we don't exactly get hurt easily. We heal at a rapid rate. Our cells regenerate our injuries. Although it can slow us down and we have to be careful not to be taken to a hospital. It would be hard to explain one minute we are in intensive care and the next we are walking out of the hospital."

 He looked at me with those sultry blue green pools, making

my toes curl, changing the subject.

"Your Monte is very good."

"I know isn't he great? I didn't know if you would like blues."

"I like all music, except maybe the 80s and 90s, not so much." I jumped back in asking more questions, as fast as I could think to ask.

"Who, told the renegades I was here? How did they know I existed? Can they feel my essence from miles away?"

"Dee, slow down. We need to go now."

"No, you need to tell me more."

"You need to tamp down that temper. I told you people get hurt if you're not careful."

He took my hand doing that thing he does to calm me.

"So, what does that have to do with you answering my questions?"

"You're hurting my head again and you may need to work on your anger issue with Jake."

"I am so very sorry. I do not want to hurt anyone. I'm just not used to all of this supernatural shit. I didn't know. I was hurting you. It was happening the whole time when we were on our car ride to the Island. That is why you made all of those faces at me, isn't it?"

"It's OK. I may have deserved some of it."

 "I really thought you just didn't like me, and I was annoying to you. Then you would ask to see me again and you did not kiss me. I thought maybe you were mental. "

I smiled and winked at him.

"Blaine mental, if you only knew the truth." Jake was laughing at us now. The music stopped in the other room. It must be 2:00 am and everyone will be leaving so we can clean up. Mica came out of the back of the bar. "Hey Blaine, we need to get moving. If they were at the space needle a half an hour ago, they are almost here."

"How is the urge to... you know, your thingy…?"

"We have it under control for now. We have to keep our distance and it seems to be easier for both of us."

 "That's good. We don't have time for the two of you to disappear to hook up." Mica was having a poke at us as well. I was so glad they could have fun at our expense… Most everyone was gone, and Jake and Jerry were gathering supplies from the cellar. They kept a stash there in case of trouble. They got everything loaded into the hummer and the rest went into Micas, Porsche Cayenne. Unbelievable. None of these immortals drove anything but the best in vehicles. I didn't even know they had released the Porches SUV. Mica informed me it was a year old and 2020 was already out. Who Knew? The boys rode together.

Mica, Amanda, and I went to my apartment to gather my things and to get DC. Jacquelyn had gathered medical supplies earlier this week. All of them had their thing to do, and I was just lost and confused. They worked like a finely tuned team, ready for whatever came their way. This time it was to protect me until I could control my gifts or figure out what they were. I grabbed some clothes, put DC in the carrier and headed to Anacortes to catch the ferry over to the island. The boys took the ferry ahead of us and we took the second one so we could have the vehicles to haul the supplies to the house. I wondered where the roads were since the island said camping only and walking no vehicles, but they must have some special state passes. It took a couple of hours to get to Anacortes, where Noah was waiting for us. I asked Mica how I could see if he was the one that told the underworld about me.

"Be very careful, not full blast."

"What in the hell is not full blast? Will I blow up his brain?"

"You must remain calm if you see anything in his mind you dislike. Do not let your emotion take control while you're in someone's thoughts or you will do them great harm."
"So, what do I do?"

"Take a deep breath, blow it out, calm your mind and focus on him, look into his eyes, and see what is there. They will come in images at first, broken pieces. But do not stay very long."

We had arrived; I was trying to look at it as a straightforward exercise. Noah was there to help us on the ferry. Looked at him and focused. I stared at him, trying to get an image, but I noticed his nose bleeding. I stopped.

"Mica, is that supposed to happen?"

 "It will hurt him if he can block your thoughts."

"What did you see? I was looking at his face and when his nose bled, I drew back."

"Well then, we do not know if we can trust him, so we don't. Search his mind on the way over if you cannot get in when we arrive; we cannot let him leave. We can't risk him telling someone that he left us on the island."

 "We will have to take him as a prisoner if you can't get in." I could not even believe it was going so fast, all this immortal shit, and now I have to take a man prisoner.

"What in the hell was happening to my seminormal life? I came here in search of the truth, but this is not what I had in mind. I thought maybe I was psychic, but no way was I thinking I was an immortal.

The ferry ride was faster than I thought and now I had to look into another person's mind. Mica came over.

 "Dee, it's time," Amanda went to get Noah.

"Hey Noah" Then I heard her voice faintly in my head.

"Now, Dee!" I looked into his blue-gray eyes. I tried not to hurt him. I saw an image of Blaine and I when we first met him a month ago on his boat. I saw how he knew I was an immortal with extraordinary gifts. His nose is bleeding again. I could hear Mica encouraging.

"Keep going. He is hiding something."

I pushed further and saw a bank deposit of $10,000. He screamed.

"Stop, you're hurting me."

He grabbed his head in agony when I stopped.

Mica shouted, "Take him and tie him up. Blaine and Jake will want to talk to him later."

Amanda got some rope from the van and tied him to the seat, then blindfolded him.

"I'm sorry Noah, but I have to know if you betrayed me, and I think you did."

He said nothing. I planted a story in the deck hands mind of Noah getting sick and he had to make the ferry runs for today. Just normal campers left on James Island. The rest of the day just kept speeding by. We arrived at the drop off point on the island. The ferry pulled up to the docks, lower the ramp to allow us off. We drove off the ferry, stopped and waited for the fairy to be out of sight before we took off up the beach. Now we were in front of the sizeable overgrown mound of blackberries and underbrush. Mica hit the button like a garage door opener in the rig, the mound moved back like a gate. Behind the mound was a road. No one would ever guess. It just looked like a mess of briers at the water's edge. Brilliant idea, tire tracks disappearing with the crashing waves, was ingenious. I would have never found it if I had walked the island as I had planned. We drove for a while up the hill until I saw the house, just like my dreams, in the middle of the beautiful grounds surrounded by evergreen trees. We pulled in around the circle driveway as Blaine was waiting on the porch. He stood and walked down the steps towards me. "How did it go?"

"Well, let's see. I have probed through a man's mind, trying not to do any damage to his cerebral cortex. I have taken a prisoner. Oh, before that I made him bleed from his nose twice, other than that I'm just peachy." Sarcastically didn't even describe my feelings.

"Oh yeah, then there's the fact I'm just a little freaked out. All I ever wanted was to discover my destiny and what life had in store for me. Not to be part of some mythical, immortal society."

I put my hands to my temples and started rubbing them lightly. Blaine reached up and touched my hands and he pulled them away from my face, then he gazed into my eyes. He leaned in and kissed me on my forehead. I put my head on his chest. I looked up, and he kissed me again. Then I heard.

"Get a room" it was Jake.

"We have work to do," as we both straightened up and gathered our self-control. We walked into the house, and it was magnificent. "Do you like it?" My smile beamed.

"Oh yes, it is so perfect, just like my dreams."

The immense staircase flowed ostentatiously down towards the entrance. Spindles twisted their way down the staircase. The windows were encircled by a clear five-quarter fir. The red oaks floor gleamed, from the light of the crystal chandelier hanging overhead. Showing the slender planks that variegated their way across the floor. Mahogany panels lined the walls with the most intricate detail.

"Make yourself at home. I think the rest are in the kitchen. I have to go help Jake deal with Noah." He leaned down and laid another smoldering kiss on my lips. I was on fire.

"I will see you later." He smiled, leaned down, kissed me again, then turned and walked outside. I knew what he meant by later. I smiled and went off to the kitchen. As I walked into the ultramodern kitchen, with my mouth open, staring at this amazing room. I heard.

"Hey Dee, welcome." The kitchen was bigger than the club

kitchen. This gourmet kitchen had beautiful maple cabinets that hung from the 10 ft ceilings with counters of white quartz with gray swirls throughout the kitchen, stainless appliances, Thermador gas eight burner drop in stovetop, with a stainless vent overhead that was big enough to suck me out with the smoke, under the stove top where warming doors, there were four ovens double stacked, two microwaves one on each side of this enormous space with a walk-in refrigerator with glass doors at the end. In the middle on the wall was a coffee station that had an espresso machine, regular coffee pot, teas in little square drawers that had labels and several types of coffee beans to grind. Amanda was sitting at the massive bar that had eight barstools, elaborately hand carved details on the seat back, arms and legs, with black leather cushioned seats.

Behind her was the great room with a fireplace. Faced with chocolate marble and a beautiful, detailed mantle. Above the fireplace was a picture of the professor and a little boy. They were dressed in early 1800s garments. I assumed the little boy was Blaine. I was staring at the painting, thinking of how old they are now, and she still looks the same. Amanda smiled, "Cute, isn't he?" She was teasing me.

" Yes, but I think he is cute now." I smiled.

"Oh brother, you have got it as bad, as he has got it for

you."

I stuck my tongue out at her and we both laughed. I joined Amanda at the bar. Jerry was pulling out meat, cheese, lettuce, tomato, mayo fixing to make up some sandwiches. I wasn't very hungry; it had been a long evening. I think it was early morning, but I could not tell it was still dark out. I was tired and ready to go to sleep.

"So… If I wanted to get cleaned up and go to sleep, where would I go? Thank you, all of you, for what you have shared with me and for protecting me. I am exhausted." Amanda stood.

"Come on Dee, I will take you upstairs to show you Blaine's room." We headed up the stairs off the kitchen. Jake barked his orders. We were not at the club anymore.

"We start early for your training. I will see you at 7am right here." Jake had an evil smile on his face. I saluted him. "Yes Sir."

I followed Amanda and headed up the stairs off the kitchen. At the top of the stairs, there were rooms on each side of the long hallway. I was in the second door, down on the right from the kitchen stairs. My stuff was already in the room with DC. He was meowing loudly to get him out of the carrier. I bent down and let him out as I picked him up and he purred.

"So, DC, what do you think?" He nuzzled me. He was glad

to be out of the crate. I sat him down so he could explore the room. I was dog-tired. "Amanda, I think I will lie down if that's alright."

"Sure, are you feeling, ok? I know it has been a lot to digest, and then we up and move you out here."

"I'm just drained. I'll see you later." Smiling, letting her know I was ok.

She turned, opened the door, pulling it closed quietly.

The fireplace was huge; from the floor to the ceiling, it was made of river rock. There was a fire going, and it was warm in the room. The ceilings were ten feet tall with crown molding that wrapped the room. I walked into the bathroom; you could tell this was Blaine's room. I could smell his spicey woodsy all man sent.

When I picked up the towel, his scent was all over it. I could not believe how gigantic the bathroom was. My complete apartment would fit inside of this room. I undressed and dropped my clothing to the tile floor with its little equiangular tiles, off whitish with light gray and light gray grout. The shower was a large walk-in with porcelain tiles, the look of distressed gray wood planks that went vertical to the ceiling. I walked into the shower as I turned on the warm water and let it run down my back. I was feeling overwhelmed by all the information I had consumed today. I had my small pity party with Blaine, but it didn't last long as I realized that all the kayos made me feel more alive than I had in many years. I had a purpose. This immortal world was amazing, and I was soon going to be a big part of it. Just maybe I wasn't crazy. The voice in my mind could be explained. I finished washing my hair with shampoo in the shower. It was Oribe. I had seen it at all high-end stores. It made my hair so soft and smelled so good; the fragrance reminded me of Calabrian bergamot, white butterfly jasmine and sandalwood. There was a blow dryer on the shelf, so I combed out my hair and used the blow dryer until my hair was dry. I pulled on some leggings and a tank top, then lay down to get some sleep. I was so tired I couldn't sleep. I heard the door open

"Dee, are you sleeping?"

It was Blaine. I wasn't sleepy anymore. My whole body was aware of his presence more than I had ever noticed before. I was vibrating; he came over to the bed and lay down beside me. I rolled over and looked into his eyes.

"Well, can I let down my guard now because I don't think I can hold back any longer?" He smiled, and then he pulled off his shirt. His body was so damn perfect, with broad shoulders, washboard abs. My eyes ran down to the slender hips and the hair that swirled down to his enormous erection pressing against his jeans. I ran my fingers down the curves of his chest. My hand glided over his muscles, and it made my heart race. Running further down his chest to his waist, I unzipped his jeans, and his unit sprang free. I encircled his member with my hand and tugged gently on it, rubbing up and down. He seemed to get harder and larger all at the same time. Blaine made a moan of satisfaction. Then I lowered my head and set my mouth on his swollen shaft. I swallowed as much as I could, then pulling back slowly and I swallowed again going down on him. I could taste the pre-come, that salty taste of a man. Blaine reached down and pulled me up.

"You're going to have to stop that, or I'll be done before we even start."

What a heady feeling to be in so much control. Wanting him like nothing else I have ever wanted in my life. I had too many clothes on. Pulling open my shirt, he pushed it down, trapping my arms. He gently pulled my breast out of my bra, displaying them. He ran his hands around my breast then reached over, twirling each nipple until they were so hard, they hurt. Then he lowered his mouth to grab hold of my nipple one at a time. He sucked, twirled his tongue, nibble with his teeth, then the other. While his finger spun and squeeze the other nipple. I came unglued and screamed his name as I broke into a million pieces with an orgasm that was among my top ten orgasms. He pulled me close and kissed my neck, moving his way down my body. His hands then removed my leggings as he finished taking off my clothes. Then he removed his jeans. Naked, we took in each other's bodies. He pulled me closer, his body pressed into mine so gently, and then his lips engulfed mine. At first soft, then more forcefully. He pushed his tongue in and out as I opened it for him. I could feel his hard chest against my extremely erect nipples; they were so sensitive to the touch of his skin. Then he rolled me on to my back kissing his way down from my lips, my neck, my chest and as he cupped my breast with his hand, he pulled my nipple into his mouth slowly sucking and rolling his tongue around it sending an electric shock wave to my core. I could feel my orgasm rising. My body tightened. I raised my hips and then it hit me. Shattered into a million stars. I screamed out his name. I could feel I was coming down from the explosion that had rocked me. My breath was slowing, and I could see again. Blaine rose over me and set his shaft at my core entrance. He slowly pushed as I eagerly wrapped my legs around him and tilted my hips up to meet him, so he was seated all the way in. Then he moved slowly and hit the spot every time I was building another orgasm that might kill me. He looked into my eyes and said "Love, are you ok?"

I moaned, "Just about to be perfect again for the fourth time." He smiled and moved faster. I was about to black out when I released, as he did. Together, we slammed into oblivion. A thin sheen of sweat was all over us and we were both breathing heavily, as if we had just sprinted home. He leans over to my side not to put his total weight on me. He pulled me into his arms. Hours had passed, and he kept holding me in his arms as the moonlight glistened through the window. I didn't know if it was the next day or if it was the same long night. All I knew was safety in his arms. I fell asleep. When I woke up, I was alone. I almost thought that maybe I was having another dream until I looked around the room and DC and I were not in the apartment anymore. We only got a couple of hours of sleep. Jake wanted to collaborate with me early this morning. Looked at the clock and it said 9:00am. I bet that is not early for Jake. I rolled out of bed and put on my leggings and t-shirt. Grabbed my tennis shoes off the floor and headed downstairs. Wasn't sure what clothing I would need for what Jake called a workout. When I hit the entrance to the kitchen, I smelled coffee. It was intoxicating. Mica was at the bar with her laptop open, doing more research.

"Doesn't anyone sleep around here?"

Chapter 6
Training Part One

"Good morning, Dee. How did you sleep?"

"Perfect, I know I am not up early enough for Jake. Is he training without me?"

"Yes, he is doing his workout said to send you down when you're ready." Mica went back to her laptop.

The bacon and coffee had a wonderful smell. I really need a ton of coffee. Last night had taken its toll on me and I was happy, sore, tired, and anxious. Coffee was what I needed. In the kitchen I found Blaine cooking as I had seen him in my dreams cooking, or was that the lie they set up? It was all running together in my mind. I need to have Jake help clear out the cobwebs. First, I was starving.

"Good morning, beautiful." I smiled up at him.

"Good morning." as I leaned up and kissed him. I snag

a piece of bacon from the plate. It was hard not to keep going. I pulled back. He smiled. As I walked to the other side of the bar, smiling in a sultry way. "You were amazing last night."

"You're not so bad yourself."

"And now your control is amazing. I have had years of practice and most of the time give in to my primitive side… but you."

"If he only knew how I wanted to climb on the kitchen bar and have my way with him. It is not as easy as it seems."

"Jake will be here in one, two, and three." Stepping out of the stairway into the kitchen.

"Hey you love birds. How are you this morning?"

"Dee, you are just glowing. Who knew Blaine had it in him?" Smiling and teasing both of us without mercy.

"Wow, that smells fantastic. When can we eat?"

"It will be done in a minute. Hey Jake… Dee knew you were coming, just like she did last night when she knew the renegades were coming towards the bar."

I blushed and tried to explain.

"It just happened so naturally, but I saw you coming up from the basement to the back stairs into the kitchen."

174

"Unheard of... that is truly remarkable in someone so young. Skills of that magnitude are gained over many years of training."

"Dee, what else can you do?" I shrugged my shoulders and smiled. "I thought that is what you are supposed to help me with. Didn't know I could do that until last night when I saw the men coming and I knew they were coming for me."

"Do your thoughts come in images?"

"You did. I saw you coming up the stairs."

"What were you doing?"

"I was kissing Blaine."

"What were you thinking about?"

"I was thinking, um…" I stopped talking, turning five shades of red. "Um, you know."

"So, it prevents you from getting caught in the act?"

"Hmm, yeah, I guess. Today anyway." I shrugged my shoulders.

"When you saw the men, when you were in the bar, you knew they were coming for you. Did you feel you were in danger at the club?"

"Yes, I felt their aggression towards me and my amulet

slightly warmed.”

“What amulet?”

“At the second gypsy camp I visited for a psychic reading. I was trying to find out who I was. She gave me a protection amulet. She told me to never take it off, for it would save my life one day. It gets hotter the more danger I am about to be in. I am really not sure how it works. I have noticed the warming or getting hot when I should be careful. It also glows soft lavender.

Jake held out his hand. “Let me see it.”

I reluctantly reached up and took it off and handed it to him.

“It’s primeval. I can feel the long forgotten magic coursing through it. It is beautiful. Then the amethyst purple grew darker. The vines swirled around the stone in his hand. He gave it back like it was on fire in his hand. I slid it back around my neck. It cooled off at once.

“Have you ever experienced anything like this before?”

“When I was little, I would dream of different things and parts of them would happen. But I saw you as if it was just part of my thought process. Kind of like when you hear someone coming into a room. You don’t stop what you are doing, you just know… I saw you coming like that; it didn’t interrupt my thoughts; it was just you up for breakfast.”

176

Mica came in with some information from the antediluvian archive. She directed her attention to me. "Dee, I have found out that the ancient gifts get stronger and stronger once the younger immortal discovered their heritage. At least it was written in a language I could read. So much of the text is in a language we have yet to translate."

"So, what kind of gifts will I have?"

"You can see the future, sort of…. anyhow, the immediate future. You seem to have figured out."

"I get small glimpses further into the future. But I have also noticed they cannot be depended on because fate determines which path you might take that will alter the future and what I see to be the truth."

"Some of the original immortals could do astonishing things like you might move inanimate objects. Your strength will increase along with speed and agility. Your senses will become more acute. You may have some kind of mind control; you could kill us with your thoughts if you choose."

"I'm not killing anyone. Stop! I don't want to hear anymore. I am beginning to feel like a mutant to all of you." Got up, went around the bar to the coffeepot, and poured another cup of coffee. Humming this time let me know she was about to intrude on my thoughts.

"Oh, Deedra you are not a mutant, but you will wheel greater gifts than any of these mere immortals have." Then

hearing nothing but the reticule of myself.

"Dee, are you with us?"

"Oh, yeah, um, sorry." I gathered my thoughts.

"This does not explain how I became this immortal with gifts beyond my years nor what I am supposed to do with them."

"Dee, we will help you embrace your gifts. Think of all the good you can do with them. Perhaps you can stop the corruption of the other immortals just with your presence."

"You're putting a lot of hope in me!"

"Should we tell her?"

"Tell me what?"

"Your arrival has been predicted in the carvings on the doors at the library for 500 years." Jacquelyn and Ray came into the kitchen.

"What are you talking about?"

"The etchings on the doors at the college library."

Jacquelyn acknowledged, "Yes, Deedra, the doors describe an immortal pure of heart and with the purest of gifts given by the original immortals. Her powers have been passed to you genetically from the first of the immortals. You're that immortal. It is your destiny."

"It is all a little too much to take in. You knew when I was trying to understand the dialect on the doors what they would tell me."

I just sat there, staring at my cup of coffee. Blaine reached across the bar, put his hand on mine.

"One step at a time, love."

This time, I loved that magical thing he did to me. It was calming. I needed to be calmed. I felt safe and it would all be okay. I smiled back at him. The room was silent and uncomfortable.

Jake busted out by saying,

"Well, the first step is to get that breakfast on the table. I'm starved, and the crowd broke into laughter."

"Yes, Dee, I am glad you are here."

I could hear her, and she didn't even move her mouth

"Can anyone else hear us? Do you hear the other voice?"

"Nope, we are the only ones who can hear each other's thoughts. What other voice?"

"Oh nothing, you should be able to communicate with anyone you want when you come into your gifts"

I was mortified she would hear my fears and my intimate thoughts about Blaine.

"It is just interesting you have total control over your thoughts. You can allow your thoughts to be heard by others, but I cannot read you. I have tried."

"Thank god!"

"So, what are you girls talking about?" I turned and looked at Jake.

"Easy… it was just your body language that gave you away."

"Oh, that Amanda is the only one who can converse with me subconsciously?"

"It appears so."

"Are you feeling any other gifts?"

"No, not really."

"Well, we will be doing some self-defense training in the gym; I'll see you there in 20"

"The gym?" I was confused where that could be. Blaine reached over, touching my hand.

"Yes, the basement is our gym, and we do a lot of training down there. I will take you there when you're ready."

"I want to see you kick Jake's ass, anyway."

"I can't kick anyone's ass!" I squeaked.

"Jake and Ray are our strongest and the most trained soldier in our unit. They also have the most training in the art of war. Ray was in the royal guard."

"Jake, it is one of his gifts. He has work with all of us on our skills to defend ourselves."

"That just ludicrous Jake outweighs me and he's taller than I am. He has the advantage. His reach is longer than mine. I am sure he will slaughter me, and I know nothing about self-defense."

The humming and then a buzzing began, and I braced for her annoying commentary. I thought she was done speaking to me more than once in a day was a record.

"Be patient. You have been given many gifts. We will most certainly kick ass today, as you say…" Then the silence I always follow when she leaves my mind. I inhaled to steady myself. Blaine took my hand.

"Are you done with breakfast? I will show you the basement." I stood; he took my hand and led me to the basement. There were stairs by the fireplace off the great room. The room was the size of the Gym down the street from the apartment. On the walls hung several ancient weapons.

"Swords, sai, escrima sticks, nunchalcus, kamas. Oh god, how did I know the name of all those weapons? My knowledge was growing as fast as my new ability, and it

was unnatural. Or was it her knowledge bleeding over in to my mind? Take deep breaths and keep it together."

Then I heard her, no warning this time, just her voice in my head.

"Don't let those boys know you're afraid. We will show them a thing or two in today's exercise."

"A thing or two? What is it you think I know?"

"Oh, silly girl, not what you know, but what I know."

"Yea, but I'm here and you're a voice in my head. I know nothing about warfare or weapons or even how to defend myself. How am I going to beat them? Uh-oh; Crap, now I'm carrying on conversations with her… nut house, here I come."

The room was full of top-of-the-line exercise equipment. The floors were hardwood like a basketball court. There was a large mat on the floor, and Jake was standing in the middle. Blaine stood on the side of the room, leaning against the wall with his hands in his faded blue jeans, looking like a model, on the front of GQ. I walked up to Jake.

Ok, now what?" He came at me. I spun around, did a cartwheel in the air before I knew it. Landed behind him, grabbing his arm, wrenching it behind him and pushing him to the floor with my knee in his back and my hand was ready to strike him. I stopped in shock. I stood up and took a couple of steps back. My face was red from embarrassment.

"Oh, my god Jake I am so sorry, are you ok? Where the hell did that come from?" By now everyone had heard Blaine laughing and when I looked up, everyone had come downstairs. They are now staring at me. Jake was rising from the floor, brushing himself off and headed at me again, this time with all his force. I could see his maneuvers this time and countered each move. Hand to hand, blow to blow once again, I flipped in the air, landing in front of Jake, catching him with a kick to the solar plexus and riding his chest to the floor. I crawled off him and backed up several steps. Apologizing as I retreated.

"I'm so sorry Jake; I can't stop myself when you attack me like that. Where is it coming from?"

The Professor stepped forward. "Deedra, like Jake, you evidently have been imprinted with antediluvian warrior skills."

"Your instincts are your greatest weapon."

Ray pointed out.

"Trust in what your body is telling you. Jake, I cannot believe you let this little girl throw you to the mat."

Muttering to myself under my breath. *"And the woman*

whose voice that is in my head and now in control of my body." I smiled sheepishly, not wanting to tell them I was just crazy.

Jake rose from the floor. His anger from what Ray said radiated off his body.

"Ray, I know your skills far surpass mine. You should give it a go. Show me how it is done."

Jake swept his left hand out to jester for Ray to take his place. Then Jake stepped over by Blaine on the wall with a smile on his face. Ray stepped up to the mat. Then, without warning, he came at me with a Martial Arts move. I moved out of his way and kicked him in the back. He spun and kicked out, just grazing my hip. If I hadn't moved, the kick would have knocked me down. Then he swung at me. I raised my arms, blocking his punch. He attacked me again. I was getting mad. He just kept coming at me. I blocked him and then cartwheeled around him and grabbed him from behind. I had him in a headlock. He broke free and then came at me again. I spun with a kick and twisting off his body in midair and sent him to the floor; I went in for my final blow. Jake grabbed me. "Dee, stop!"

He could see I was going in for the kill and forgot who I was. I looked up at him in amazement at what I was about to do.

"Oh, god I am so, so, sorry Ray. I stood and backed away.

Knowing she was in control and was about to hurt Ray terrified me.

"What in the hell do you think you're doing? This is training day, not life and death."

Ray got up, straighten his shirt and walked off. He turned back to me.

"When I first met you, I thought you looked like someone from my past. But I didn't want to believe she would be reincarnated. Now, after fighting you, I know she is. He turned and walked away. Jake came over to me with a Cheshire cat smile on his face.

"Is Ray, ok? I am so sorry. I am not sure what happened."

"He is ok, you just hurt his ego."

"I would feel so horrible if I hurt anyone in my new family. Jake, I do not think you should let me train with anyone alone. I don't know what I am capable of, and I don't want to hurt anyone."

"You need to be the trainer now. Your moves are some I have never seen before. I can't even surprise you."

"Hmm, I cheated a little; it's not your fault I read your thoughts before you moved."

"I didn't feel a thing. So, we can't tell when you have entered our minds."

"I think only Amanda can feel my presence now."

"So, there are no secrets from any of us?"

"I'm not trying to see what's on your mind. I rather not, but it appears I can, sorry."

Then what happened when you looked at Noah? He was blocking me and as I pushed through; I saw his nose bleed. I can't hurt anyone, whether they are immortal or mortal. Good or bad. I think that skill is ever evolving. Then the professor spoke in her soft voice.

"That is why you have been gifted with the ancient abilities. You're pure of heart."

 Blaine piped up.

 "Maybe you can teach me a few new moves so I can have a try at kicking the master's ass."

He was laughing with glee. Jake was watching my expressions.

 "I think Deedra needs some time to get her head around all of this." Jake could always tell when I needed a break from information overload.

"Blaine, why don't you take Dee outside for a walk? You can show her our beautiful grounds, maybe head down to the beach. We will regroup @ 1:00pm. Don't the rest of you have chores or an assignment that need completing?"

"Thanks, I am again sorry for reading your thoughts."

"Don't forget the training you just gave me."

"Awh… come on, Jake, she just handed you your ass. And you know it."

"Get some lunch and drink lots of water. We will revisit the mat."

"Never apologize for being excellent. They were supposed to be the best. Instead, they are sore losers. Hard on their egos to be beaten by a woman half your size. Ray was trained by the best. Ray is losing some of his edge."

"How do you know of Ray's training? Who are you? Is that why Ray said I was reincarnated?"

Then there was nothing but silence in my mind.

"Is everything ok? You look far away from here." He leaned in, kissed me, and took my hand. We headed up the stairs and out the front door. There were two Adirondack chairs on the porch along with a porch swing at the end facing the yard.

"Can we just sit here for a while?"

"Sure" I sat down on the porch swing. The air was cool, but the sun was out, and it felt great on my face. It did not seem so cold. "What are you thinking?"

"I'm trying not to think."

"How do you do that?"

"I'm not sure. I just emptied my thoughts and think about the sun and the smell of the ocean." I closed my eyes. I could feel Blaine's arm wrap around me. It was nice. I just focused on the sound of the ocean, and then I saw the renegades they were at the dock in Anacortes.

"They are very close, Blaine."

"Who is very close? Where are they?"

"They are at the docks in Anacortes."

"Can you hear their thoughts?

"No, they must be too far away."

"How many men did they bring?"

"I can see ten men. They are talking to the ferry captain" The others appeared upstairs on the porch with us.

"Amanda just told us." Interesting how Amanda and I are connected intuitively. So, what do we do now that they are on their way?"

"We wait." Jake pointed out.

"They are not here; they may never find us; it could be just the end of the trail for them. Let us hope they just go back to Seattle."

"Don't you think if we were to confront them, it would be better on our terms?"

"It will be on our terms when you're ready."

"Oh that…" Blaine hugged me tighter.

"Let's all go back inside." Amanda suggested.

"Dee and I will know before they even step foot on our island."

Blaine and I sat on the porch swing for a very long time. I think I took a nap in his arms. I was dreaming again of a place I have never seen. I could tell it was long ago because of the way everyone was dressed in Indian robes. They sat in a circle in some kind of room. The walls were dirt, a small fire was in the middle of the room, and a hole in the top of the room let the smoke out. The man was familiar somehow; he talked of the goodness of our people. We will help the mortals to live longer and teach some of them our ways. Then my dream was interrupted by the sound of a small boat coming to the island. I woke up and told Blaine they were coming in a small boat. We got up and went inside. On the third floor was an observation tower where we could see all sides of the island and anyone approaching. If someone saw it from the air or the land, it looked like a fire lookout. It was very rustic outside with stairs, no windows, just a lookout post. There was a door from the third-floor storage that led to the roof. Then we climbed up the outside stairs to the top of the lookout. Blaine and I headed up to the top of the tower. Jake and Amanda were already scanning the horizon for the intruders. Jake turned around and asked,

"Any sighting of them in a boat or on foot?"

"Maybe I was wrong." Then Jake spotted the boat with the binoculars

"I see only two of them. It must just be a scouting party; they won't find anything. In fact, let's try something, Deedra. When the boat is on the shore, I want you to think about them, see what they are thinking, then tell them to go. No one is here. They have searched the entire island."

"Ok, I will give it a shot." I closed my eyes and focused on the men I saw the boat land on the north shore. The two men got out of the boat, pulling the small boat up onto shore. They were talking about me. I heard my name and then touched the edge of their minds. I told them to leave and that the island was clear, no evidence of anyone living on the island, and they had searched the entire island and found nothing. I could see they were getting back into the boat and headed back to the mainland. I smiled. They are gone. Jake scanned the horizon and concluded they had left.

"You are truly astonishing." I could feel Blaine's pride.

"I wouldn't let my guard down, though. Look at what she

did to Ray." Jake elbowed him. "She may get mad at you one day and then look out." He gave a full belly laugh.

"That's not funny Jake."

I turned to Blaine, tears welling up into my eyes.

"All of this is a little uncomfortable and overwhelming." He looked deep into my eyes and reached up and with his thumb brushed away the tears from my face and hugged away all my fears.

" It will get easier, I promise." The rest of the day flew by uneventfully. Jake gave me a break. The sun was setting on the ocean. Blaine and I were in the tower watching the sunset. It was astonishing. The colors of the sunset were red, pink, and orange. Then as the sun dipped into the ocean, the green dot. I made a wish to always wake with Blaine's arms around me. Jerry was preparing dinner. The smells of roast beef wafted up from the kitchen. I looked up at Blaine. It is time for dinner. Jerry just called the others to the table. We headed down to join everyone else. There was a fire going, and the game was on the TV. Ray and Jake were watching the game. Amanda was setting the table for dinner. Mica was pouring glass full of water. Amanda asked.

"Hey Dee, how are you holding up?"

"It is getting better. It helped, with the rest of the day was quiet."

“Where's the professor?”

“She is in the library looking up all the ancient stories from the antediluvian books.”

“You don't use the internet? “

“Oh, no, the internet was developed by the immortals to watch the mortals as they move through their lives. You have heard of Big Brother. It is true it's the corrupt immortals watching everyone.”

“We only have books. They are in the ancient language, and only Ray can translate some of them. Ray has the gift to read the ancient language. Except there is a series of books no one has interpreted; they have the same language as the doors.”

“May I see them?”

“Sure, after dinner.”

I wanted to learn more and thought maybe the dream I had was in one book and I could learn more about me and my ancestors. Learn about my destiny. I had only told Amanda I could read the doors in the library. I had mentioned it to Blaine on our trip, wine tasting. Didn't think he would remember he hadn't asked me anything about it since.

Dinner was quiet as we all ate, and then the boys went back to the game while the rest of us cleaned up the kitchen. When we were done. Professor J looked at me.

"Mica tells me you would like to see the books of the ancients. If you're ready, I will take you to the library and show you the books we have."

The room was all mahogany, with shelves that ran from the floor to the ceiling. The ladder ran around a bar that ran down two sides of the room. At the end of the wall where the bar met in the corner, there was a hole in the rail, stairs leading to the second level of shelves. On the second level that another ladder hooked on a bar slide around that level. This ran around the top of the room. Where another five feet of shelves extend up to the ceiling. The room had to be 14 feet high; it was a remarkable set up. At the end of the room was this enormous fireplace. Black Lava rock covered the face of the fireplace that filled the full length of the wall. Someone had built a fire, and it made the room cozy and warm.

"Now let's see where I put that? Oh yes, here they are." She brought them over to the round table that sat at one side of the room, and she spread them out. It was the first time we had been alone in a room. I tried to gently scan her thoughts, and I got nothing. Hmm, she was blocking me, ok I will just ask.

"You don't like me much, do you?"

"Why do you say that, dear child?"

"I don't get any reading from you and all the others I can

read.”

“Well, I’m like you in that my thoughts are mine until I want you to hear me.”

“Oh! So can you read others?”

“No, that is your gift alone, I’m afraid, except what you share with Amanda.”

“So then, why do I feel so much fear and anger?”

“Well, you are also intuitive. This will be a good gift to have when we have to face those who will try to destroy you.”

“Destroy me? So, what is that all about? “

“Yes, my dear, there are those. If they cannot control your gifts, they will try to destroy you, so you cannot use your powers against them.”

“Who are they? “

“They call themselves the cartel. People with all the control over the world’s cash flow, whether it be banking, oil and natural gas, food and beverage industry, war, arms sales, stock market, insurance, pharmaceuticals, brand consumer packaging, the government, and communications.”

“Ok, ok, I get it, the world’s top 1%”

“I have no intentions of taking on any of those entities.”
194

"You may not have a choice when they find out about you. They have collected all the immortals that have extraordinary gifts. Your gifts are beyond approach. You are 'The One' They will not rest until they own you… They have immortals that are loyal to their way of thinking. If they don't know where you are, they most certainly know of your existence because of the essence you have been putting off."

"Your Essence is the strongest I have ever felt. I have noticed it is getting stronger."

"You're saying eventually I will have to face all of them?"

"We won't let that happen. We will always be by your side, but eventually they will find you, and yes, we will have to deal with them one way or the other. I'm afraid you will have to face them. That is why you are here to learn about your abilities with us, so we can help you with the unknown and to hone your skills."

"These are books with ancient stories?"

"I opened one of them just like at the courthouse. The dust swirled out into the room, and I sneezed.

"Ah-chew."

"Bless you."

"Thanks. No one has looked at these books in a while. Sorry, I should have dusted them off for you."

"No one has determined the dialect. I read from the book…

"Our people are growing old alone and as we die after many centuries of living, we will have to rely on the mortals to continue our legacy.

 "You can read the ancient dialog?" I looked up, and she had that look like I had done something astonishing.

"Ray, everyone, come Deedra can read the ancient words." Blaine came in first, "You can read from the antediluvian books?"

"Um, yeah, a little enough to tell you what it says. It is like the Cherokee language; it was a form of Kiowa-Tanoan dialect. That is what my grandfather told me. He did not speak any English and so he taught me his language. I was the only one who could communicate with him. It came easy to me when I picked it up at seven… I have a confession to make. I also caught some of what the doors mentioned, but I did not know the story was talking about me. If you don't mind, I would just like to read through these books and then we can talk about them tomorrow."

 "Oh, yes… I'm sorry, I was just so excited." Ray turned to me,

"Can you teach me the language soon?" I smiled up at him.

 "I would love to."

They all left except Blaine. He put his hand on my shoulder.
196

"Are you going to be alright?"

"Yeah, I just want to see if any of these books can help me get my head around what is happening to me. Also, I have the etchings I took from the doors at the library to see if I was reading them correctly or if there could be a different translation that Jacqueline and Ray translated."

"I'm going to go to bed. Don't spend all night here. Come up when you are done."

"Ok I won't be long, just want to read awhile." I took the books over to the couch in front of the fire. I read them all. When I woke up, it was morning. The sunlight was just making its presence known. I was still in the library on the couch. I had a stiff neck from falling asleep on the arm. The last of five books were in my lap. I got up and stretched to get the kinks out of my neck. I was staring out the window, watching the sun coming up through the fog that lay on the ocean. The sun was a spectacular sight. As I thought of the responsibilities that had been left to me, I wanted to know why me? Would I be able to make a difference with my abilities? I felt Blaine's arms around my waist. So deep in thought, I didn't hear him enter the room.

"Good morning, love. I missed you last night." I turned around and looked into his smoldering blue-green eyes.

"Why are you looking so serious, Dee?"

"I finished the books, and they told me how I had been

chosen. Or engineer from DNA of the Ancients. They hoped I could make a difference in the world. I'm not sure I am the right person for all of this responsibility."

"What did the books tell you?"

"I can only share some of it. I may not be able to give you many details. It is the future and the past. If I tell you, I will change the events that have been put into motion millennia ago."

"It will be OK. Let's get some breakfast." He took my hand and led me into the kitchen, where they all gathered around the bar. This time Mica was cooking.

"Morning Dee, did you sleep well?"

"Not really, fell asleep in the library. I have a stiff neck."

"Say no more. The couch in there has left a crick in my neck, many a night. It is impossible to get out." I laughed and nodded at her, rubbing my neck.

"Hey Jerry, what's for breakfast? Micas French toast and fresh strawberries with whipped cream. "

"Sounds delicioso."

"Coffee is over there, and I will help Mica get you a plate of French toast. "Strawberries? Whip Cream?"

"Oh yes, the works, please." I got my cup of coffee and sat

at the bar next to Blaine. Jerry set the full plate in front of me. It smelled heavily. It tasted even better. I kept eating, hoping the Professor would ask the first question. How disappointed she would be because I would not be able to tell her what was in the books. When I was done eating, I took my plate over to the sink, rinsed it off and placed it in the dishwasher. I turned to the group with no need to get their attention. They were all watching me, waiting for information. I was feeling bad about what I was about to tell them and wanting to lower my head to apologize. They were so excited to learn the ancient language. I had stalled long enough.

I heard her voice, no warning. All the buzzing and light-headedness were gone. Just her voice there in my mind…

"Hold your head high, girl. These are gifts from us and the language that was made just for you. No need to feel guilty. They will all understand… you will see… Protecting your team is your job and their job is to protect you."

Ahem, I cleared my throat to address the elephant in the room. Head held high, as my inner warrior had told me to do.

"I cannot tell you or teach any of you what is in the antediluvian text. It was created only for me to read. Revealing any of it will change what the ancients have started in motion all those millennia ago. Our team is an intricate part of the future for all immortals. I will need to keep training and discovering all my other gifts. I must work on my temper. I do not want to hurt any of you. I know when the time comes, I will be ready. Your training is important as well. Amanda, you need to have more self-defense maneuvers, so you're not left vulnerable if alone. Mica and Jacqueline that goes for the both of you, more skill is needed for this fight. I want the women in this group as tough as the men who love them. I read through the antediluvian books. Comparing the dialect to the etching from the library doors. They were written in the same language. They talk about 'The One' who will come to save the people.

Not sure, that is me! They talk about the future and the past. I cannot tell if they understood what they were doing, making a special gene made up of all five ancients, and implanting those special genes into an egg. Then putting that egg into my mother on one of her checkups at her gynecologist. My mother never knew I was implanted into her. I am not sure that I even understand what their thought process was back then. I have been engineered to be the best of all of them, with all their gifts. I think they thought the DNA would produce a boy, not me.

Here is what I do know: I have a hidden warrior in me. She speaks to me at inappropriate times and then nothing for days and talks to me when I feel threatened. She has been in my head for as long as I can remember just thinking I was a bit touched. I have no control over her, and that scares me. According to the book, they spliced her DNA

200

into my genetic makeup to protect me. Giving me all her abilities just in case, an immortal team didn't find me first. That must be the five of you who are my immortal team. I will need to control her before we leave here. I think she was the one you fought, Jake and Ray.

Ray, you made a comment about me being reincarnated. You might just be correct. Who do I remind you of? Because I have no skills like that in me or the old me didn't.

 We begin today until we have fine-tuned your defensive of this compound and all my abilities.

"Jake, even though my warrior knows many moves, I need your expertise on the mental aspect as a warrior not to react with emotion. I will need to learn how to use weapons efficiently. Professor, I think your fencing skills could come in handy. Amanda, we will need your communication and your computer skills. You are going to hack some official immortal computers to find out what they know and who is giving the last orders. Mica, you can contact some of your federal agent friend's and help Amanda." Jake's eyebrow arched above his one eye and his lips tighten.

He seemed a bit ruffled. He had always given all the orders… listening and taking orders, not so much. There she was. Just jumped into my thoughts."

 "Let see what he is made of, if he loses it, after you're done."

I smiled to myself. *"She was evil. Enjoyed poking the bear."* I kept on hearing their ideas and verbalizing them.

"I will need all of you if I am to be ready to take on anyone that comes our way. Ray will teach me the basics of explosive and tactical skills".

"No one can teach you what I already know… you have all of my gifts. The training is already in you to use. I will teach them a few things and have fun doing it. Are you ready, my dear?"

My head hurts. I didn't relax when she entered my head. I reached up to rub my temples. Blaine put his arm around me.

"You, ok? You seem tense."

I smiled sheepishly. "That's not it. She was in my head and made some sarcastic comments about what she was going to be teaching all of you. I smiled up and shrugged.

"Oh, this is going to be good." Blaine just chuckled.

"Wow, Dee, just wait a minute. When did you have time to get all of this information on all of us?"

"It just comes to me as I talk. You are all thinking of how you can contribute to the daunting task ahead and how young I am. Blaine, you need to focus on the job. I pointed my finger at him and winked. He laughed."

"I will go help Ray."

"Jake, let's get busy."

Jake and I headed downstairs to learn the art of self-control. It is tougher than I thought. We had been at it for hours and I had already left bruises on Jake. He just shrugged and said it didn't hurt or wounds heal fast enough. I felt bad.

"Jake, let's take a break before you hurt me."

 I hoped it would let him off the hook and let him keep his pride intact.

"I haven't even put a mark on you, you move too fast."

Mica came in to tell us she had just made some lunch. I had never felt how strong his passion for her was. Mica had no clue. I know she had feelings for him, but she kept them to herself.

She was busy taking care of business, just like at the club. Hmmm, I promised myself that what I hear from them I would never share with them or tell them I know. However, somehow, I wish I could help them get together. It is none of my business. I must let all things occur without my interference. The books warned me about the possibilities of changing future events. I had to be careful.

Chapter 7

Alone At last

Blaine was at the bar. I sat down beside him. I leaned over to kiss him on the cheek. Oh man, I forgot how hard it is to be so close to him and what was making it worse. I was now hearing his thoughts about what he wants to do to me. He is a bad boy, and I am a lucky girl. He put his arms around me and looked deep into my eyes. Of course, everyone started teasing us. He let go of me and turned to the group.

"If you will excuse us… Dee and I are taking our lunch upstairs." He grabbed my hand and pulled me up the stairs. We heard some boo's and hissing coming from all of them, but we really didn't care. He shut the door and undressed me as he had wrapped his lips around mine. I was pulling at his clothes and soon we were undressed, laughing, and falling on the bed. I was looking into his blue-green eyes and could see how much he loved me and that I was his life. I whispered in his ear, "I love you too." He pulled back, looking deep into my eyes. He smiled and began kissing my neck. As he kissed his way down my body, he stopped at my erect nipple, sucking and pulling with his teeth. My heart sped up, and the room spun, and his touch still sent my senses into overload. He reached into my folds. I was wet and ready for him. He slipped in his digits and pressed his thumb on my bud. His capable fingers curled to hit the G-spot, rapidly moving them in and out one more time. I broke into a million pieces, my body limp in his arms. "I will never stop loving the way you explode for me." When we were done making love as I lay beside him, I noticed some bruising on Blaine's arm. I ran my hand down to the bruise. "How did this happen? How did what happen? Oh, that's nothing." He was silent, but I read his thoughts that you did it the other day when we were making love.

" I, did this?" I sat up in the bed.

"I hate you know my every thought, even if I want to keep some things from you."

"I'm sorry… I hurt you."

"I'm ok Dee, you are very strong and getting stronger."

"Oh. Man, did I hurt you again?"

"No, I'm fine. You will get better at all of this. You need to not be afraid. Remember, we are hard to break and heal fast…" He grinned at me.

"We will all survive a little bruising until you figure out your strength." He changed the subject.

"How is the training with Jake going?"

"Oh, just peachy… he is bruising up just fine. He never complains, but I know sometimes my punches are not pulled."

I lied back down beside him.

"I like the Sai; they seem to be my inner warrior's weapon of choice."

We just laid there holding each other. "I am hearing the others' thoughts. They are placing bets on when we will appear again. I think I will give Amanda the upper hand"

"Amanda, can you hear me?"

"Yes, Dee."

"Make your bet we will not be out until tomorrow".

"Have fun." I smiled. I could hear her giggle. I snuggled up to Blaine.

"What are you smiling about?"

"I just told Amanda she would not see us until tomorrow, and she told me to have fun."

"She would." Kissing the top of my head.

"Would you like to take a shower?"

"Yes, that sounds lovely."

He got up and went to turn on the shower. I walked over and turned on the fireplace so the room would be warm when we came out. DC was sitting on the windowsill, looking outside. I think he liked it here as much as I did. I heard my name coming from the bathroom.

" Dee, are you coming?". As I walked into the shower, the water ran down both of our naked bodies as we pressed our lips into one another. The warm water felt as good as he did against my body. He washed my arms with his soapy hand. He ran his hand down across my breast and down both sides of my waist until he had reached my toes. When he was done, I turned, and he soaped up my back. He ran his hands around my butt and down the back of my legs. I turned into the water and then I soaped up his chest and ran my soapy hands down across his flat abs. I caressed every muscle as I ran my hands across his rigid shaft. I felt him moan and his shaft twitch in my hand. Then I washed all the way to his feet. My mouth passed close to his enormous member. I licked the head and pressed my lips on the tip, then slowly opened my lips to let him slide in all the way, swallowing his head down the back of my throat. He gasped and throbbed in my mouth. I pulled slowly back until I could suck hard on the head of his shaft, then I swallowed it again all the way into the back of my throat. He finally exploded. His whole body trembled as he released. Then I glided my hands down his back and slide them around his butt, then both sides of his legs all the way to his feet again. He turned into the shower and rinsed off. Then he grabbed me. He lifted me up, holding me firmly against the shower wall.

I wrapped my legs around him. He was hard again, and he pressed into me, slowly at first, then in one thrust filled me up… then once seated, he moved faster and harder and harder. Having an arduous time catching my breath, he hit the spot repeatedly until I reached rapture. My heart beating out of my chest, he held me until my breathing slowed, then he moved again, pumping one, two, three, then I was hit by another orgasm. He was so intoxicating. I never wanted it to stop. As we climaxed together, I glided down his body, holding my arms around his neck, allowing the water to rinse over us. He leaned down and kissed me again; he picked me up and turned off the shower. Then he carried me over to the bed. He began kissing me even more passionately than before. He rolled me on all fours and pushed against my core, again slipping in, and rocking harder this time as all my senses exploded in complete culmination. I have never felt so much of one man completely satisfying me. The next thing I knew, I was laying across his naked body. His velvety smooth voice pressed against my ear.

"Dee, you are the most astonishing woman I have ever

encountered."

"Really go on…" I was smiling. It was early in the morning. The day was gray and stormy. I rolled over, sat up, and got up to get in the shower. I finished my shower, grabbed a big white fluffy towel, and wrapped it around my body. Blaine was lying on the bed sheet at his waist, arms crossed above his head. Wow, he should be a model, with his dark hair messed up and those piercing blue-green eyes watching my every move. I turned back on the fire to dry my hair.

"Come back to bed." He padded the spot next to him.

"We can't, we have to get back to work."

"Are you sure?"

"Yes, they are all in the kitchen, and we wouldn't want Amanda to lose her bet. Get dressed, I will meet you downstairs."

Blaine got in the shower as I put on my clothes. He headed downstairs while I finished getting ready for the day. I dried my hair and put on workout clothes. I took the back stairs into the kitchen. I started down the stairs when I could feel something awful was about to happen. It felt like nothing I had ever experienced. It chilled me to the bone. At the bottom of the stairs, I had to grab the rail. I felt as though I was going to pass out. "DEE!!!" Blaine ran over and grabbed me before I collapsed.

"Are you all right, my love?" I reached for him for strength.

"I don't know."

"Come over here and sit down." they were all around me. I looked at Amanda and let her feel what I was feeling. She turned as white as a ghost. Jerry touched my arm. I looked up at him.

"Do you know what this is?" I shook my head.

"I think you are feeling some future event with no pictures."

"Well, that will help none of us."

"Jake, I think I need to tune up my psychic parts. I think it is on the fritz."

They all laughed. I couldn't have them worrying about me. There was a reason I saw nothing. It wasn't time yet. The books had talked about the warning before the event, so I couldn't change what was about to happen. I really didn't like this part. Not knowing what is about to happen that can cause such a chilling feeling. At least we could be on alert.

"Jerry, are you picking up any vibe of things going sideways?"

He was really my eyes to the future, but he wasn't getting anything. I think I just need some water. Maybe I am dehydrated. I have been working out hard and not eating."

"Blaine you dog."

 Jake laughed. "You need to at least feed the girl."

"Yeah… you're hilarious."

Mica pointed out; "Perhaps we should get breakfast going."

Jerry was already on it. The professor had gotten me some water.

"Here you go dear, you may just be dehydrated." Amanda just kept looking for more of what I let her feel. I shook my head at her.

"That is all I got there isn't any more."

The coffee was done. I jumped down off the stool, grabbed a cup from the cupboard. Went back to the bar with the craft. I refilled everyone else's cup. Then I took the craft back and made another pot of coffee. I turned with the cup in my hand and walked back to the bar. Blaine put his hand on mine. He always was making me feel better. I looked at him, laid my head against his chest; He reached up and ran his hand down my head and through my hair.

Chapter 8

Training Day Part two

The weeks have gone by slowly as Jake tries to train me in the art of war…. and today Jake is going to let me use a weapon. He sure is a glutton for punishment.

"Which of the weapons would you prefer to use?" I looked at him in surprise.

"I don't know."

"Sure, you do, or your inner warrior does. Just grab one and give it a try."

"Hmm, those look like you want to wheel them?" Pointing at the two Sai.

"Interesting?"

"You think she will like these basic forms of the weapon?"

Jake took them down off the wall, spinning them in his hands to explain what the weapon was. He set them on the table in front of me.

"The Sai are pointed, dagger-shaped truncheon, with two curved prongs (called yoku) projecting from the handle. The ball of the handle is called the knuckle. Contrary to popular belief, the shaft of a traditional Sai is not a blade. However, in a fight, they are very sharp. Alright, pick them up in your hands and see how they feel…. Ok, let's see you spin them."

Her voice echoes in my mind with such conceit.

"Oh, Pleeeze, just get on with it, son. I have been wheeling these for millennia. No one is better with them than I."

My inner warrior spoke up for the first time in a while, not making my head hurt, no humming or warning, just talking to Jake.

"Well, what am I expecting to do with these? Do I know how to use them? Or do you take over and I just watch?" Again, I am having a conversation with my inner warrior about a weapon I know nothing about, like she is going to teach me in mirror seconds.

"First time, you just watch me wheeled them. Muscle memory will keep, and you will be proficient as I am with the Sai."

"There she is again. I hope she is right."

"Dee, hello are you with us?"

Huh, ummm… Yea, Jake, I'm here…I am sure I will still cut myself."

"It's ok, you'll heal."

"All right, here I go." I put one in each hand and flipped them in my hands slowly at first, then faster, as though I had used them many times. I threw them at a dummy 15 ft away and nailed it. They zinged right by Jake's face and his eyes were as big as mine. I am so very sorry, Jake. I let her control them so I would not get hurt. You should have known she would show off."

"Wow, Dee, it will be alright. I know she is on our side. So, we will need to use them in combat situations. I will go suit up so you can practice on me."

"Jake I can't, I will hurt you."

"No, learn to control her or at least be one with her and not be afraid. I will be right back."

Jake came back in a full-length shirt. The shirt was made of Kevlar. It was made to protect the parts of the body that are critical from bullets, explosive fragments, and sharp knives. I hoping it was enough so I wouldn't cut him. Teasing. I walked a way looked over my shoulder. Pointing the Sai at him. I winked.

"What's wrong Jake? Don't worry, you'll heal!"

"Yeah, those Sais cut deep."

"Oh…." Jake came at me. Holding the knife moving in the same way as before. I spun out, and then the Sai hit his arm and then his back.

"Good, do it again." He came from behind. I flipped up and over his head and landed behind him, putting the Sai in his back. I could feel the power and yet knew we were training, and I was in control.

"Good, you are one with her, aren't you?"

"Yes, it appears so. I can really fight with these Sais, and it is her weapon of choice." Jake was smiling and surprised at my development for such an inexperienced immortal. "The time is at hand. We will have to fight them soon."

"How do you know that?"

"Because your training is almost complete, there isn't anything else I can teach you. The ancients have provided you with the greatest of gifts, their knowledge of combat and the sight to see your opponent's move. You are ready."

"Jake, that's not funny. I'm not ready."

"Dee, just let your inner warrior take control. If you're in a desperate situation, she will protect you. We can spare some confidence, if you like. But I am not sure it will be good for any of our confidence. Especially if you keep beating all of us. You're the best student I have ever trained for over 50 years. Let's say we are done for today.

"Well, of course she is the best.'

I smiled and shook my head.

"Is she talking to you again?"

"Yes, boasting that she is the best. Or we are the best."

Jake laughed. "She probably was. I wish she would tell you who she is."

"I wish I felt as strongly about this as you do. What if I hurt someone?"

"Dee, if you are in the position that you have to harm someone. It will be in self-defense."

"When that time comes, it will be a sad day for me. In all of my searching or who I was, I never in my wildest dream could I have imagined this truth. That I was a supernatural, immortal warrior, and I would need full combat skills to survive attacks on myself. What in the hell were the powers to be thinking? Did they think I was going to take on the Chieftains of the cartel and make them change how they behave? What exactly do I think I can do?"

"Dee, I am not sure. Maybe you will find your answers elsewhere. I don't have any answers for you."

"Why has our small band of immortals been chosen to train you and help you find answers? Too many questions and not enough answers. Let's go upstairs and join the others."

We have been on the island training for 3 weeks now and we needed to get back. If we stayed gone too long, we would draw attention to ourselves. My mother had called from Cherokee, North Carolina, and wanted to let me know a couple of young men came by and were looking for me. She told them I was at school in Washington state. Then the club called Blaine and said that a new group of men were frequently coming by the club and asking questions about Dee. We would have to deal with this eventually. Everyone had seen my inner warrior at work on Ray, and the team knew that my inner warrior would protect me if I were caught alone. So, we all agreed except for Blaine to return to Seattle tomorrow.

We still had Noah to deal with. We blind folded him and took him back to Anacortes. When we got there, I tried one gift. The book talked about mind manipulation. I should be able to make up a story of where he had been for three weeks and implant it into his mind. Therefore, I focus gently so he would not notice. I don't even know if it will work yet. The men in the boat that came to the island left after I told them they were done, and nothing was there. I worked on Noah's mind. When we left him in his boat in the Anacortes harbor. I told him he had the flu and was laid up in his boat for a couple of weeks, then caught it again, this time turned into pneumonia with the high fever. He couldn't remember anything when he awakens, he will have a headache because of the sleeping pills we slipped him. It would not matter if he suspected anything; we would be long gone back to Seattle and on our terms if he reported anything he remembers to the cartel.

Chapter 9

The Visitors

The professor had to get back to the college. She still had several classes to teach, that finished out the year. The rest of us thought I should take the rest of the year off and continue to train with Jake and work at the Club. I moved in over to the club with Blaine and the rest of the team. It was a remarkable space that was big enough for all of us. Professor only stayed during the week, spent weekends and breaks with Ray on the island. In the entryway was a black wrought iron fixture that hung from the ten-foot ceilings. Beyond that were three sky lights. They were Georgian Wire Cast Glass is a fire rated glass with an obscure pattern which contains steel mesh embedded into the glass Array of five-inch-wide warehouse oak planks made a colorful pattern across the floor. It was laid at an angle, adding tons of character to the loft. It was one great room concept. The kitchen was along the back wall. Counter space ran twenty feet down the forty-foot wall. Hickory cabinets ran up to the ceiling. Side by side refrigerator, stainless sink, and dishwasher fit into the twenty-foot counter that was black and brown swirled quartz. The reddish purple and black broken brick fireplace was to the left off center of the entry. Above it was seventy-two-inch flatscreen suspended above the knotty oak mantel. It was a large oak limb with two sides cut flat, the bark stripped. The wood underneath stained a honey color. The wall behind the mantel was painted mocha. There was a craftsman chocolate maroon leather couch with recliners on each end. There also had two craftsman recliners. Couple end tables with lamps. Small coffee table is in front of the couch.

The cooked top was on one end of the twelve by six-foot island. Ten blond oak stools set around the island. It was used as an eating area along with cooking and prep space. The Island was placed strategically off center of the back wall. Right of the entry there also was queen-size hide-a-bed against the wall in a hickory cabinet. The room was painted khaki, with five-inch white trim that framed out the doors. The door, just before the hide-a-bed, went to a wide hallway that led to the five bedrooms. Each room had a window looking either to the courtyard or the street. Blaine had a corner room, looked at my old apartment building and the courtyard. The first door to the right of our room went to stairs that accessed the rooftop, where there was a big Kahuna spa in a gazebo, a Traeger XL Wood Pellet Grill. It was bronze, it was a beauty. Jerry cooked on it, for the dinner specials for the club. And our personal food. There was a bar at the end of the hot tub. It had to be custom, stemmed glass holder overhead. With a wine cooler, small refrigerator for beer, and spirits. Chairs and recliners spread around the rooftop. Some white lights adored the gazebo for those summer evenings in Seattle. We could see the Huskie stadium. I think the guys must watch the games from up here. Jake and I trained on the rooftop. It was big and flat. That way, I broke nothing in the apartment. I was not in as much control over my inner warrior as I would like. Blaine and Jerry worked the bar and Amanda waited tables while Jake and I worked on my temper. We knew I had to be kept upstairs while there were renegades in the local area. We have been back living and working at the club for two weeks. The spring air was a pleasant change from the cold winter breezes that blew in off the Rosario straights on the island. It was the beginning of May. I was getting bored cooped up in the apartment, so I wandered down to the bar. I poured a glass of wine. Blaine was at the piano playing. No one was in the club. It was early in the day and the club opened at 4:30. The music filled the air as I walked by and set a glass of wine down for him. We still had the hardest time keeping our hands to ourselves. I caressed the back of his neck and leaned in to kiss him. The music stopped. "Don't stop playing."

"Dee, I can't play and be near you. All I want to do is…" I smiled.

 "I know. It is the same for me as well. Why deny ourselves if you are up for it?"

"You don't have to ask me twice." He picked me up. I giggled, and we disappeared up the stairs. Hours later, just before opening, we showed back up. Jake was setting up and Jerry was stocking the bar. I went to help Jake. Blaine was checking with the cook to make sure we were set up for the dinner crowd. My amulet warmed against my chest. I closed my eyes, reached out with my senses, then uttered, "Jake, two guys are going to come in the front door and two are coming in the back. They are dressed in black trench coats and have IDs from a government agency. Are caring guns, but they are tranquilizer guns. They will be here in 5 minutes." Then I opened my eyes to see Jerry coming out from behind the bar.

"I see trouble coming."

Amanda came down from upstairs.

"It's time Dee, isn't it? I can see your vision."

"So, gentlemen, how do you want to play this?"

Mica walked in from the cellar and Blaine came out of the kitchen. He looked around.

"Someone is coming, aren't they?" Blaine walked over and

wrapped his arms around me. He leaned in to kiss the top of my head.

I know no one can hurt you. You have got this."

"Blaine, you need to let her go and move away. She needs to focus."

"Dee is ready. If not, her warrior will take care of her."

"The rest of us should just observe and not bring any attention to us. They will think she is alone, and Dee remember your mental strength, no emotional response and focus on controlling your inner warrior. There could be other mundane mortals in danger, depending on how we oversee this."

It was comforting knowing that my inner warrior had my back. She was all instinct. I knew they couldn't outmaneuver me. I saw all their thoughts before they moved. Everyone took their positions. We watched as the men came in. Two sat down in the front booth. Then two more came in the back door and sat at the bar. Jerry asked, "Can I get you anything to drink?" They knew he was an immortal; one of them is a telepath.

"Is Deedra Lee working today?" I grabbed one of the big serving trays as I walked over.

"I'm Deedra, can I help you?" I was sizing them up. The blond man was over six feet tall, over two hundred and twenty pounds, and the pocked face man was larger. The big blond man flashed his badge.

"You will have to come with us, Miss." His badge was a government special affairs badge. I just shook my head.

"I don't think I will be going anywhere today." I could see the other man grab for his gun. I could smell the chemical in the tranquilizer. The pock face man was calling himself Allen. I could hear the trigger cock and then the dart swooshed as it left the gun. I leaned back and as the dart passed by my side. I grabbed it out of thin air and flipped it back at him, nailing him in the thigh. He slumped down in the seat and his head hit the bar with a clunk. I looked at the other man, smiled sweetly.

"Do you want me to go with you?"

I probed his mind, looking for who sent him. He blocked me as his nose bled. His face crinkled with pain. I heard him say, "Stop." under his breath.

"Just... Stop! You're tearing my mind apart."

"Simon, is it?" Sarcastically I asked, His face looked perplexed. I could hear him wondering how I knew his name...

"You need to go back to whoever sent you. Tell them I will come for them when I'm ready."

The two men in the front had snuck out the front door.

They came in the back. They went to grab their guns when Simon shook his head. "Unh-unh, we are done here. Just pick up Allen and take him out to the car.

Dedra, I'm sure we will see you again, sooner than later." He smiled. Jerry stepped out in front of the Bar.

"Easy, Jerry, it's over." He could hear me in his head. He stopped short of the bar. The men continued out the back door. We all took a huge breath.

"That went well, don't you think?" as I smiled and went behind the bar to stand with Jerry. Jake came out of the kitchen. Smoke coming out his ears, about to bust a vein that was bulging on his forehead. Then she plopped into my thoughts.

 "Boy, it is fun to do what he doesn't want you to do. Look at him all puffed up. Like we are intimidated by him. In what timeline did he think we would stand by and be hit with a dart?"

I tried not to laugh and encourage her as she took a jab at Jake in my thoughts. I had to cover my mouth and pretend to cough.

"That is not exactly what we talked about, Dee…"

 "I know, but my inner warrior… she still is in control of protecting me. She is very cool, don't you think? Did you see how she stepped to the side, grabbed that dart, and

224

flung it at the bigger of the two men? Down he went, kablahm." I smiled sweetly at Jake.

"Dee, you talk as if you're possessed by another person."

"If you only knew how unlike me this inner warrior is, then you would talk about her as a third person as well." Blaine, Mica, and Amanda came to the bar. Blaine came over to my side. He grabbed my hand gave it a squeeze. "You never stop amazing me."

"Ok, show over. Let's get back to work. We still have a club to run" Mica was barking orders. The night was normal after a little excitement from earlier. We all helped clean up. Mica had been making phone calls to find out what branch our four strangers came from looking through personnel pictures. Amanda has hacked into special affairs files. The men who visited were not part of any internal, special, or any other government agencies. They were using fake id. We suspected they were just renegades from the cartel. The question came up: who oversaw the Cartel these days? Rumors were they were based in Seattle underground. Mica and Amanda continued to research. I was tired and needed a shower. Jake, Jerry, and Blaine reviewed the security tape from the bar. I crawled into the shower. After my shower, I was too emotionally exhausted to stay up. I just went to bed. The next morning, I was in bed alone. I could smell the coffee brewing; I loved the smell, and I could hear voices outside my door. I got up and pulled my hair back. I opened the door and headed to the kitchen.

"Good morning, love."

"Good morning," as I leaned into kiss Blaine.

Jake was making breakfast. He was fixing his cream cheese stuffed waffles with fresh raspberry drizzled over the top.

"Where is everyone else? "

"Amanda went to school today; she had a paper due. The Professor has a class this morning and Mica is downstairs placing orders for the club. It was as if last night never happened and life was back to normal.

"Did you find out who those, gentleman were that came into the club last night? "

"No, we are still looking."

"Where is Jerry?"

"He is barbecuing a brisket on the roof for the dinner menu tonight."

"Yum, that sounds amazing." Jake asked,

"Could you tell Mica & Jerry, um, you know… with your mindie thing?"

He smiled big and showed those adorable dimples.

"Hey guys, breakfast is ready."

My ability to communicate with everyone was cool. I could talk to them in their heads, but they could not talk back to me, well telepathically, they talked plenty at me. Except Amanda, she could talk back to me mentally. I could hear everyone's thoughts, but I tried not to listen. I focused on Mica and Jerry, and then I heard the rooftop door open. Jerry was coming down from the roof and Mica headed up the stairs from the cellar. Jake made the best waffles in the world. We all sat at the Island in the loft and let him serve up his breakfast. Talk was light among us. No one talked about what happened last night. When I finished breakfast. I had to say something.

"Do you guys always have evenings like last night?"

"No, never, but we thought maybe it freaked you out and that you might not want to talk about it. You left early and went to bed and slept all night. Blaine said you had a snore that could compete with a mother bear."

"I do not snore like a mother bear; I purr like a kitten."

"What do you want to know?"

"Who in the hell were they, and when do you think they will be back?"

Jake started.

"We agree they will have to report to the cartel. Their failure will be punished and then they will examine what abilities you used and send in a different team that can capture you. They must have you now, because you did not come with them quietly. Mostly because you are a woman and you have challenged them by not responding. Their egos have been threatened. They have lost face with the chieftains of the cartel. The council also was wondering what the elders of the ancients thought of giving such gifts to a woman. Problem being, they don't know what gifts you have, and that will be to our advantage."

"I don't even know what gifts I have; they change daily."

"Dee, they want to own you and they will be back?"

"Do we have any idea when?" Just then, I heard Amanda's panicky voice in my mind.

"Dee, I'm being followed. I just headed into the cafeteria, and I need someone to get me."

Ahem, "We have a situation; someone is after Amanda. She needs us to come for her. Says she is being followed. She is in the cafeteria on campus."

Jake, Jerry, Blaine, and I headed upstairs to get geared up and then met at the hummer. Mica staffed the club. We got to the cafeteria in 10 minutes. As we pulled up, I got out of the cab. Blaine grabbed me.

"And where do you think you're going?"

"I'm getting Amanda. They only want me, and I will allow no one else to get hurt because of me…"

"No, you're staying here. Jerry and I will get Amanda. You need to get back into the hummer and wait with Jake."

"I was confused. Why so protective? I knew no one could touch me. What were they so afraid of?"

Jerry and Blaine came out of the cafeteria without Amanda. She wasn't in there.

"Are you sure?"

"Yes, I am sure she said she was hiding in the cafeteria?"

"Amanda, where are you?"

"I'm not hearing anything."

"Keep listening. We will cover the campus."

"Jake, what is happening?"

"They have figured that they can use Amanda for a trade."

"I will not let them do this; they had better not hurt her or I'll……. *"Dee, they caught me threw me in the trunk of a car."*

 "Are you Ok?"

"Yeah, for now… hurry, I'm scared."

"Jake, they have taken her. She is in a trunk of a car."

"Dee, I hear the ferry whistle!"

"Blaine, they have Amanda in a trunk somewhere down by the ferries. We will meet you at the edge of campus".

Blaine and Jerry were on the corner on the south side of campus. We picked them up and headed down to the wharf.

"This had me seeing red. How dare they take my friend?"

"You all know this is a trap, right?"

"What do you know, Dee? "

"It's going to take place in the warehouse on the wharf, and I am going in alone." Blaine looked at me. I could feel he was afraid to lose me.

"You don't understand. They will hurt Amanda and I cannot allow her to be hurt because of me. I will signal you when it is time to move in, but I am going in alone. This is what you and I have been training for. Trust in me now." Jerry was beside himself.

"You just let me know which one of them is hurting my Amanda and it will be the last thing they ever do."

"I will let all of you see everything that is happening through my thoughts. It will be OK if they don't know about my inner warrior. She won't let anything happen to me. Trust me guys, this is how this has to be. I have heard their thoughts. They only want me."

We arrived at the warehouse. I got out and Blaine grabs my arm

"You had better come back to me."

"You don't need to worry about me. Jake has trained me well. Besides, there is the little thing about knowing their thoughts." I smiled up at him. Grabbing both sides of his shirt, I pulled Blaine in for a long smoldering kiss; he still makes my toes curl. Releasing him from our kiss, I turned away from him and headed into the dark warehouse. The door was unlocked. Not even giving me a challenge. These guys are imbeciles. They are assuming I cannot take care of myself.

"Shall we show them a different point of view?" I smiled.

"You know what happens when you assume you know?"

"You get the shit kicked out of you in this case." I hated to encourage her, but she was right. "Let's kick some ass."

That even made me more infuriated that they were assuming I was a helpless female. Well, it was time they learned a lesson. The hard way.

"Amanda, I'm in the warehouse. Where are you?"

"I'm on the second floor somewhere close to the bathroom. I can smell them."

"Hang in there, I'm coming." Sliding my Sai's out of the harness on my back. One in each hand. *"Slowly now, they are just around the corner. I am here with you, but you can handle this."*

I felt one with her this time. The first of three men came at me. I released the Sai as it cart-wheeled through the air. A direct hit to the right shoulder Pinning him to the wall.

"Jerry, come get him. He is all yours. Hey grab my sai."

I used my mind to attack the other two when I turned the corner. They were rolling on the floor in pain. I didn't let them up. I had not found Amanda yet. Jake and Blaine were helping Jerry tie up the others. I went upstairs, looking through all the rooms. Finally, at the end of the hall, was a door. I knew someone had Amanda there. I kicked the door open... Simon stood there with Amanda in his arms, choking her. I lost it.... my mind took hold of him. He blocked me. Then he dropped Amanda to the floor and started towards me. *"Come on, you think you can take me?"* I could hear him. *"You little bitch."* he kept coming as he lunged at me. I flipped over his head and went to Amanda. I knelt down, took her pulse.

While I was down on one knee, I Slide a large knife I out of my boot. She lay limp but breathing on the floor.

"Jerry, get up here. Amanda needs you…" I was now out of control; I stood up with intent. I headed for this bastard. "You want me? I'll show you what a true bitch is…. with my only sai and a knife ran towards him. He stuck out his arm. Like I was going to run into it. I dropped to the floor, slid under his arm, and cut his left achilleas tendon in his left leg. Dropping him to the floor. He rose with a limp as he came at me. I headed towards him. I was swinging and stabbing until there was nothing left of him as he lay there, quivering. All I could think about was Amanda. I went over and she was still out. Jerry had made it upstairs to her.

"Jake, Blaine. We have Amanda. We are upstairs at the end of the hall."

Before my thoughts were done, they were coming in the door. Jerry was picking Amanda up. "Oh honey, wake up." She moaned and came around. "Are you Ok?"

In a scratchy whisper, "Um, aha, oh, yeah." rubbing her throat, "I will be now." She tentatively smiled.

"Thanks Dee."

I stood in horror at what I had done, letting my anger rule my every thought. Blaine came over and put his arms around me.

"Are you ok love?"

"Yes, but I kind of made a mess out of him. We won't be

able to question him." I pointed at the man quivering on the floor, shredded with cuts and stab from my sai and the knife I held in my other hand.

"Dee, how did you slay him with one sai?

I held up the knife. "I had it in my boot.

"Jake, what do we need to do now?" He walked up to me.

"Here is your other sai. You left it in bad guy number one, which you had pinned to the wall. I am not sure. Who knew you would tear that big of a guy up like that? He will heal, but it could take a couple of weeks."

"What about the rest of them? We just tied them up. Unless you want to finish them off, too."

"Oh! You're hilarious Jake. He just kept coming after me, blocking me as I tried to probe his mind. Then I heard him talking about me. Calling me a little bitch and the next thing I knew; I was showing him…. he was on the floor as you see him now. I was out of control when he dropped Amanda to the floor. I thought she was dead. Jerry looked up from Amanda.

"I think you did good, Dee; you should have finished him."

"I couldn't finish him. I regained control at some point and there he lay."

"I think we need to get him downstairs so his men can

234

take him somewhere to heal."

 "You know now they are going to send more than a four-man team next time."

 "That will be their problem. Our priority is to get Amanda home now."

"We need to go back to the Island. We are too vulnerable in town. Blaine agreed with Jake.

"We will go by and get the second crew set up at the club."

"Dee, can you let the girls know what has happened?" Sure, I focused my mind on them.

"Jacqueline, Mica… Amanda was hurt by some men trying to get to me. She is Ok but we are all headed to the Island. Jake says you need to leave the club and meet us there before they retaliate."

"Ok, we will leave within the hour. Be safe."

"Alright, we will see you guys at Anacortes." I helped Jerry get Amanda to the Hummer that we left in the warehouse lot.

Jake & Blaine took care of getting the man I shredded downstairs, untied one other man, and told them to take him back to the cartel to stop coming at us unless they want us to send them all back in body bags. Jake and Blaine took an Uber back to the club to get supplies and go south, then come back up to Anacortes in case we were followed. That would throw them off by splitting up.

Jerry and I took the hummer to Anacortes to catch the ferry. We drove through the rain for hours. Finally, Amanda came around and we could talk to her. She was healing as fast as they said she would. It was amazing to me how fast we healed. Even my bruises were almost gone. By the time we had made it to the ferry, she was talking about how they had caught her. Her voice was horse and barely there; mostly she was whispering to us. She hugged me.

"Thanks for coming to my rescue."

"I'm just glad I could hear you in my head."

"The man that had me kept asking me. Who is she? He wanted to know how many gifts you had and where you were in control of them."

"Well, he found out more than he expected. Let's say little first hand knowledge…"

"What happened? I filled her in and then Jerry made the comment "We never have to worry about Dee although we really do not want to piss her off, you should have seen the man lay on the floor shredded and quivering, it really wasn't very pretty."

"I was worried about you, Amanda; you were just lying on the floor limp. Never scare me like that again."

"I'll try not to get kidnapped". We were laughing by this point. We drove on the ferry and waited, hoping the rest of them would catch up. Professor and Mica showed up first in the Cayenne. The Professor was out with her medical bag trying to make sure Amanda was not hurt. She started taking her pulse and then listening to her heart, checked the bruises on her neck. Professor J. gave her a clean bill of health. Jerry was filling in Mica. She was staring at me. I listened in. She was proud of me, loved the way I showed those chauvinistic men from the cartel who were their superior. She was glad I saved Amanda. I backed out before she knew I was listening. Eve's dropping was becoming easy now, and no one even noticed. The professor and I had had little time to talk; she walked over to me. "Did you learn the Sai from Jake?"

 "No, not really. They are from my inner warrior; it is her choice of weapon. I have been fighting as one with her. She still terrifies me when I see what damage I did to that man, even if he deserved it!"

"The art of the Sai is very impressive, Deedra."

"Really, do you think? I'm not sure how I do it, but when I'm in battle, it just happens… I have learned to go with it. She protects me from all who would bring harm to all the ones I love. *Speaking of loves.*"

I could see the red Lexus convertible pull in line on the ferry. Blaine and Jake had arrived just in time in my car. I walked over to them and opened the door.

"Why are you in my car?"

"We figured if they were keeping track of you and we left in your car, they would follow us and not you guys."

"What took you so long?"

"We made sure we were not followed. We left going south on I-5, then came back up North on the old ninety-nine." Jake got out and went over to the ferry captain.

"Dee, don't forget the mind wipe."

I have already messed with his memory. I left a word there, so all I or any of us had to say was the trigger word. The word was "Puffins" and he forgot he dropped anyone on the Island. He only remembered campers walking onto the island with camping gear. He was a trusted immortal, but so was Noah. Who betrayed me, and I had to wipe our memories from his mind. He started his engines, and we were off. When we arrive like before, we waited until the ferry was out of sight, then we move down the beach to the large thicket that opened, then we all moved up the road. Then briers closed behind us, concealing any evidence that we had left to beach in vehicles. The drive tokes us up to the house.

The tide will wash away our tracks as if we have disappeared.

Chapter 10

Refuge

I was glad to be back at my dream house on the island. I loved it here. I was going to look in the antediluvian books again and see if it could make some sense of why I was chosen and what exactly I'm supposed to do with the cartel. If they would not stop coming at me or taking my newfound family, I was going to have to take matters into my own hands, and I wasn't sure that would help. I just knew I was tired and wanted to get some sleep and deal with my new life in the morning. Getting out of the rig, I realized how stiff my muscles were.

"Blaine, I think I'm just going to take care of DC and then take a shower. I'll see you later."

"Ok, I will check on you in a while." He leaned in and kissed me. I whispered, "Hurry, I won't last long tonight before I'm out. I am exhausted."

"I need to check in with Ray and make sure we were not followed. I won't be long." as I drug my sore body up to our room. DC was sitting in the window, looking outside. He was happy to see me wrapping himself around my legs, purring. "Did you miss me?" He meowed for some food. After feeding him, I went to the bathroom to take off my clothes, looked in the mirror still covered in blood, and this was the first time I had noticed it. I was so preoccupied with Amanda and getting all of us safely away from the downtown area. I just couldn't believe how much blood was all over me.

"What had I done to that man?"

I took off my clothes and just threw them in the trash. I climbed into the shower and wept.

"What have I got myself into? Certainly, the ancient didn't expect I could save them…. what do you want from me?" I screamed in my head. The shower was running down my face as I trembled, standing alone with my fears. So engulfed in self-pity, I didn't feel Blaine enter the room until he touched me in the shower. I flipped around, unaware of my strength, and had him pinned against the shower wall with my arm against his throat, choking him.

"Uhgg… hey easy, Dee, it's me. I like my women aggressive, but I am no sadist." He had hold of my arms, pulling away from his throat; I was horrified as I looked into his eyes.

"You can let go now. You're hurting me." He reached up and took hold of my wrists. What in the hell was I doing to the one I loved? I dropped my hands off his chest to my face and began sobbing and trembling uncontrollably. Blaine pulled my hands away from my face and put them up around his neck.

"I am so very sorry I startled you, I'm ok…"

"Don't cry, love." He pulled my face up, wiping the tears away with his thumb. I felt safe as the water ran over both of our naked bodies. The strength of his arms around me made my body feel out of harm's way. He kissed my forehead, then down my neck. He lifted my chin with one finger and pressed his lips against my mouth ever so softly in a few minutes. I had forgotten loathing and was turning my attention to the most basic of instincts: my sexual desire for him. I looked up and pressed against him. He pulled back.

"Are you sure we don't have to do this now?" I just kept pushing my body against his; he would not deny the desire. As he lifted me up. Holding me against the shower wall. I like his aggressiveness tonight. He kissed me down on my breast, pulling my hard nipple into his mouth, swirling his tongue around and then nibbling and sucking on one, then the other nipple. He sent electric shock waves through my core. I was so wet. He placed his steel hard erection against my core, then in one thrust he was seated and pumped harder and harder. I was to the edge of one more twist of my nipple and I fell off the edge, breaking into a million pieces. It was the most staggering emotion I had ever felt, so much tension leaving my body in one spontaneous moment. As I slid down his body, I wanted more. I grabbed the bar of soap and washed his body, caressing every part. I stared at his shoulder and worked my way down his chest. Then he took the soap from me and caressed every part of my body. Then he took the shampoo and washed my hair. I stepped back into the spray of water and let the water run down my naked body. His hands flowed through my hair, down over my shoulder, across my breast, then down to my hips, across to my butt and finished with my feet. The water flowed out of all five of the shower heads as we embraced again, kissing with the passion of long-lost lovers. He picked me up, carried me out, and laid me on the rug in front of the fire, he pushed into me I gasped in sheer orgasmic bliss as we undulated on the rug, he pushed deeper and harder, he was throbbing, sending me into heightened pleasure again. When we finished, I lay limp in front of the fire in Blaine's, spooning my arms around me, holding me close. He had made the day disappear. He was still inside me. I could feel him growing by the second until I was full of him, and he started moving slowly at first. Then flipped me on all fours as he thrust harder than slamming me like a jackhammer. I barely kept up. Then he hit his stride, I orgasm screaming out his name, but he didn't slow down as he hit the g-spot I was seeing stars and he pumped even harder. I must have blacked out, for when I woke up to him shuddering out his release. He was all I needed for the moment, and I was going to take in all his passion.

Exhausted, I don't know when I fell asleep or blacked out of sheer pleasure but woke up in the middle of the night in bed. I got up to get a drink of water and then went back to sleep. The next thing I knew it was morning, and I was in Blaine's arms snuggling. It felt so perfect. I didn't want to get up. Nor have the energy to deal with the day ahead and the decisions I must make. I looked up at Blaine and he was still sleeping. I watched him for a long time, thinking of the first time I saw him. How he made me feel with that one glance and he still made me feel that way. I wondered what my new day was going to bring me. How much more will I learn about my new immortality? The coffee made me feel like getting up, and I was hungry. The guys always had a big breakfast, and I hadn't eaten last night. I quietly slid out of bed not to wake Blaine. I threw on some yoga pants and a tank top, pulled my hair back into a messy bun. Then I headed down to the kitchen to get a bite to eat. Jerry was behind the counter.

"Good morning, Dee."

"Good morning Jer… how is Amanda doing this morning?"

"She is still sleeping, but I think she is good, thanks to you."

"Thanks to my inner warrior."

"Where is Blaine?"

"He is still sleeping."

Jake came in. "Hey Dee, you might have to take it easy on Blaine. You know he is two hundred plus years old and you're only twenty-nine."

I smiled and winked at Jake. "He doesn't seem to have any trouble keep up."

"Oh, Jake, you're hilarious." Blaine walked into the room. He came over, leaned in, and whispered in my ear.

"You're incredible." I looked up at him.

"Ditto."

Behind Blaine, I saw Amanda standing at the bottom of the stairs. She was still a little pale.

"Hey sweetie, are you sure you're, ok?"

" Yeah, Dee, thanks to you. I will be ok. It will take a couple of days, but the professor says I am healing well, and my esophagus has been damaged. I won't be able to talk, so can you help me out."

"Whatever you need."

"OK, tell them all good morning for me. "

"Hey guys, Amanda has to let her throat heal, so I will be talking to her for a couple of days. She says good morning, everyone. What is for breakfast? She is starving and so am I."

"Who's cooking? You are if you're up to it."

"It's my turn, isn't it? No, you go ahead Jake."

 He was behind the counter, smiling.

"I got it Dee; you sit and watch the chef at work… I'm going to make eggs Benedict. I think I will use some crab cakes I saw in the freezers if someone will get them out. What do you think?"

"We think you need to get busy."

While Jake was cooking, I was pouring coffee. Breakfast was finally done. I thought I would never get enough to eat. Jake asked if he needed to make more. I had to stop before I could not move. We retired to the living room where Blaine was sitting at the piano he played. I sat next to him on the piano bench. It was nice to hear him play the piano. The sound resonated throughout the house. Soon everyone joined us.

When he was done, I touched one key, hitting one note at a time as I played the lullaby Blaine had played that night at the club… I looked up at Blaine

"How am I doing this? He gestured me to play on.

"Go ahead." He just watched me as I played, as though I had played for years. It was mind-blowing. I kept playing and when I was done with the song, I just sat there. Tears streamed down my face. Blaine put his arm around me.

 "Dee, you must have many of the Ancients' memories and talents. They will all come together as soon as you know your purpose. We are all here to help you." I just looked up at everyone staring at me.

"Needing to be alone." I got up and went into the library. Pulled out the books in the ancient language and took out the rubbings of the doors I had done before I knew who I was. There had to be the answers I was looking for in the books and the rubbings. I stood there staring at them and nothing was coming to me. Then I felt a presence. I looked around the room and I couldn't see anyone, but I knew someone was there.

"Hello! Is anyone there?" The room was quiet. Then I saw a ghostly figure appear and then it cleared up. It was a man with a long gray braid down his back. He felt familiar.

"Do I know you?"

 "Oh… Deedra…" He laughed.

"No, but I know you. I am your great, great, great, great, great grandfather George Allen Lee."

I never dreamed that my granddaughter would be "The

One.”

“What is ‘The One’?”

“You have been given the purist of the immortal gifts because of your pure heart. You cannot be corrupted. How many of my brothers will never suspect you are ‘The One?’ It is so perfect you will have all the advantages and they will be totally blindsided.”

“What are you talking about?”

“Many years ago, when the immortals began taking advantage of their gifts as they lived with the mortals a small group of us like the band you are with now decided the day would come when one of us with the purest of gifts, a pure blood, would take charge of the cartel and stop the mayhem. “The One.” we called it. They would be from the direct bloodline of a warrior, undefeatable, with the gift of mind control, telepathy, and the ability to levitate objects. They could inflict pain with a mirror thought. We never thought “The One.” would be a little girl.”

“Now wait just a damn minute. I’m a woman, not a little girl. I may look eighteen, but I happen to be twenty-nine years old.”

“I know that. You’re a young woman and will be the best of all of them because you’re my granddaughter.”

“So, what the hell am I supposed to do against the army

of men that are coming to get me? Why do they want me? If they know I will hurt them, why won't they just leave me alone?"

"Deedra, my dear, they think "The One' is a myth, a legend of the ancient stories. Like the Indigenous people of this area, and your hometown, they're just stories not based on the truth. Yet here you are, and you really exist. When the time is right, you will go with them. When you get in front of the head of the cartel, you will need all your gifts. That their taking advantage of the immortal and mortals' lives is ending. They will have to abide by the immortal council's rule just like the rest of the immortal, who have learned to co-exist with the mortals without changing their lives."

"Wow, is that all you want me to do…. are you insane? Look at me. How am I going to intimidate any of them? I am a five foot, three-inch-tall woman and I'm sure from what I've seen, the men of the cartel think very little of women."

"You have a destiny, and you will know what to do when the time comes."

"Where will you be?"

"Remember, I am always with you and know that you are never alone."

"So, if you are with me, why don't you take care of them?"

"I can only appear to you, and we have insignificant gifts over this world."

"That is just perfect." I could feel Blaine as he opened the door, then the figure disappeared.

"Dee, who are you talking to? "

"You wouldn't believe me even if I told you."

"Try me."

"Well, um." Chewing on my lower lip.

"George, my great, great, great, great, great grandfather, the one that wrote the song George Allen Lee. You remember him, don't you?" I smiled at him.

"Oh, so that is the pure blood that runs through you. Did he help you?"

"You believe me?"

"There are stories of the chosen "The One" that he or she could talk to the dead."

"Well… they were wrong about the **he** part. As far as talking to the dead, it was one ghost. Well… or …maybe two. There was the native American princess that invited me in at Chief Lelooska lodge. She was there one minute and the next… poof, she was gone."

"In my lifetime, it has always been a story… a myth…

made up fable and handed down through generations. I never thought.

"The One" even existed until you showed up and fit the description of that legend."

"I know that is what he told me. I'm just a myth that is too my advantage."

"Too your advantage, what are you expected to do by yourself?"

"He said I had to go with them when they come this time and wait until I got in front of the head of their council."

"Do you mean the cartel?"

"I guess if that is who their council is."

Suddenly, I was blasted with all his fear and then his anger.

"They cannot be sending you to the wolves by yourself. You're not trained to take on an army. What are they thinking? You're going to waltz in, and the cartel would bow down, and that is their answer to changing everything." His ranting was sucking the oxygen out of the room, and it almost knocked me down to my knees.

"Blaine, ease up on your rage, it is just about to drop me to my knees. You have taken all the oxygen out of the room."

"Oh Dee, I'm sorry. I forgot how sensitive you are to

emotions." He took a deep breath and paused for a moment to gather his thoughts.

"There has got to be another way. We will have to talk to everyone about this first."

"Can we do that tomorrow? I don't want to deal with any more today. Can we have some fun?"

"Sure… What would you like to do?"

"Can we take a walk on the beach, with a picnic, maybe lying in the sun, fooling around?" I smiled and winked at him.

"We can do it all. Let's go have a picnic." He took my hand and led me to the kitchen. Everyone else was doing their thing. Mica was reading a book; Jerry was spending time with Amanda until she had all her strength back. Jake was meditating. Ray was taking care of the grounds; he was quite the gardener. Jacquelyn was reading and grading her finals for school. When we opened the refrigerator and pulled out cheese, apples, Blaine got a bottle of wine from the cellar, found some cold chicken, grapes, and walnuts and made some chicken salad. I put a little in a container for us and left the rest for the gang to have for lunch. I put all the goodies into a basket and went back to our room to put on my swimsuit and a pair of shorts. Blaine met me on the front porch. We let the others know where we were going out for the afternoon. There was a private bay on the backside of the Island facing only the endless ocean. The sand was warm under my feet and the light breeze made it a perfect day. We had been walking for a while when we came upon a small cabin where we set up our picnic. Blaine laid a blanket down. I sat down, leaned back as the sun shined on my face. The lapping water was calming, and I was listening to Blaine's thoughts adoring me. It was unfair of me to eavesdrop, but so comforting. I drifted off to sleep safely in a beautiful place surrounded by my love. I awoke to Amanda calling to me.

"Dee, are you there?"

"Yeah, what do you need?"

"Jake saw someone approaching in a skiff from the other side of the island and thought Blaine and you should get back to the house."

"Blaine, Amanda says someone is coming to the island and we should get back to the house."

"Dee, Jake wonders if you guys can go around the island and see if you can get close enough to get in the guest's mind and find out why he is here without him seeing you."

They want us to find out who they are, and why they have come to the island.

"Jake wants us to recon our unknown visitor." Blaine was smiling at me.

"Look at you, using tactical words like a seal team leader." he winked at me.

"All right then, let's leave our stuff here and head across the island to the other side. We can remain in the trees along the beach and will not be seen."

The skiff was on the beach by the time we got there. There wasn't any sign of anyone. I stop to focus on the thoughts, pushing my mind to listen for stranger's thoughts. I always could hear Blaine. Then I heard the thoughts of the strangers. They were a boy and an old man. They had a message for me. I contacted the boy through his mind. He would be easier to manipulate.

"Why are you here?"

"The cartel wants to meet with you on your terms."

The boy stood next to the skiff, talking to the elderly man with him.

"What is it, Dee?" Blaine placed his arms around my waist and pulled me close to his chest.

"They sent a boy and an old man. Thought I wouldn't suspect them of being part of the cartel. Figured I wouldn't harm them if I found out why they had truly come out here for. They were to tell me the cartel wanted to meet with me on my terms. How did they know where to find us? Do we have a leak? Or we are not as clever as we think we are."

"Perhaps, Dee, they have a gifted immortal that grabbed onto your beacon of power. Before you could block out the world. Could have given them coordinates of a location of energy and they were just checking the Island out for inhabitance.

"The cartel has some incredibly talented immortals. Some can find anyone, anywhere."

"I am sending them home. They found no one. You can go back and tell them I will be in touch. Leave now before I change my mind and when you land on the mainland, you will forget where the island is, who you got the message from, where you got intel, we are on James Island, just repeat the message I have told you."

Closing my eyes, took a deep breath. I am still not comfortable messing with others' memories. I reach out with my mind. Eased into the elderly gentleman, then into the boy's mind. *"You searched the Island didn't find anyone. Now get back in your boat and head back to Seattle."*

"I'm ready to head back to the house. "I need more information from George."

 "Are you talking about your grandfather?"

"Yes… this is his mess, and he needs to make me believe I know what I'm doing. He said something about the ability to levitate. Have you heard anything about the ability of an immortal to levitate?"
254

"No, but let's go back and talk to Jake. Tell him about what George has told you."

"Amanda, I sent the boy and the old man away. I will tell you about it when we get back. Have to stop and get our stuff from the beach in front of the cabin in the cove."

"Ok, see you then."

We walked in the sunlight as we went back to the others. The sun was setting, so we sat on the front porch watching for the green light and we made our wish. Then, in one moment, it was dark. We went inside where the others were waiting. Amanda spoke first. "What happened? You blocked me out."

"I did? Hmm" I just contacted the old man and boy in their minds and told to get back into the boat; they found no one on the island. Then I sent him back to Seattle. Jake, could I bother you after dinner? I need to talk to you?"

"Sure, whatever you need." Dinner was quiet and uneventful. That was a delightful change for me. Less drama was always nice. After we all cleaned up, I went for a walk with Jake.

"So, Dee, what is this all about?"

"When George came to visit me, he told me I would have all the ancient gifts and, one by one, they would manifest. He suggested I could levitate. So, what does that mean?"

"Um... Dee first, who is George?"

" Oh, that's right, you don't know about my visit from beyond. I have been visited by my great, great, great, great, great grandfather ghost in the library.

"He has informed me I was chosen, well not exactly, but put together as a science project of the original six, through DNA, choosing the purist of the ancient blood line. To produce what you call "The One" who would inherit all the gifts and he is sure the ancients would be surprised I am a woman."

 "I'm not sure. There are some stories of ancients that could move objects with their mind. Let's go to the gym where I can suit up to prevent me from getting skewered and see if you have any new gifts."

"Why Jake, you really know how to build a girl's confidence."

 "Why thank you, Dee, happy to oblige, but your track record speaks for itself."

"Ha Ha." We headed down to the gym. Blaine and the others followed to see what would happen. I went to the dressing room and got on workout clothes.

My abilities fascinated them and terrified me. My inner warrior was the most talented and the most frightening to me. Makes me feel as though I am having an out-of-body experience. She was so strong and had moves I couldn't even make up. It really isn't me at all. Fighting is appalling with every part of my being, although I have a stubborn streak and a bit of a temper. Maybe I should embrace her and not fear her. This newfound life is not a good fit for me… not in my wildest dreams did I consider I would be a supernatural being with a heritage going back millennia. From time to time, I just want to wake up from the nightmare I find myself in… except Blaine, the best part of my new family. All I can ask myself at this point is, why me? I stepped out of the dressing room on the left side of the Gym. Inside my head, I still was talking to myself.

"Earth to Dee… where are you? Are you ready to see if you can command inanimate objects?"

"Yeah, I guess. So, what do you want me to do first?"

"Just focus on the Sai's on the wall."

"What if they fly at me and stab my hand?"

"You will either catch it or you will heal when it stabs you through your hand. Come on, try it."

"What if they fly out of control and hit one of you?"

"We will move out of the way, focus." I focused on the Sai's and nothing.

"It's not working."

"Patients, picture the Sai in your hand."

"Ok." As I pictured the Sai in my hand, they wobbled on the wall, but nothing flew through the room. Then, in a split second, the Sai flew at me. I just stood there in disbelief, then my hand reached out and it landed with precision in my hand with the handle grip right where it should be for combat.

"Hmm, so can I pull the other one off the wall?" I held out my hand and with no effort, the Sai flew to my hand with the same precision as the first one, now in both hands, ready for combat. I was smiling. This was somewhat cool. Jake came over, eyes big and shaking his head.

"I have only read stories of such a warrior. I am in awe of your gifts, Dee."

"Stop Jake, your seriousness doesn't become you."

"But it's true Dee, I believe you can make a difference in the world." I dropped my hands to my side. The seriousness of Jake's words resonated through every part of me.

"My *new immortal abilities sadden me to think of the lives I may have to take to get the cartel's attention. That I am,* "The One"

I'm not just a myth. I have been sent through the generations to make the biggest change in the powers and change the greed and corruption of the immortal cartel and create an amalgamation of immortals to govern with rules to help the mortals.

"Dee, I am sorry I have upset you?"

"No, Jake, it is not you; it is the realization of the reality of what I have to do. Or more, what it will take to get all the immortals to agree?" I walked away from all of them, headed upstairs and outside to clear my head. I ran away from the house, through the dune grass, down to the beach, running along the water in the wet sand until I couldn't run any further. All the thoughts that were in my head astounded me and I fell on to the sand and lay there. Catching my breath, I rolled over and just lay there, staring at the clouds in the sky as they floated around. I knew what I had to do, and I had to do it alone. I could risk none of their lives; this was my destiny. As soon as they were all asleep, I would leave and find the underground and get inside the cartel. They would never suspect a small woman as some kind of super immortal. There are those I will have to block so they do not feel my power, but I just let my inner warrior take over and she will make the process easier if I did not fight her. I will leave in the morning and when I'm gone, I will let Amanda know they cannot follow me and to take care of DC. I will be back soon. It was perfect because I could control my thoughts and they would never figure it out. Blaine followed me out to the beach.

"Dee, are you alright?" He sat down next to me. I was staring out at the sea and plotting my next move.

"Just needed some air. Was I going to be, OK? I think I

will just sit here and watch the waves. Would you want to stay with me?" I wanted one more moment with him, the man I loved, adored, and that soothed my soul. He sat beside me on the beach. Looking deep into my eyes, he was searching to find some answer, yet he knew he couldn't hear my thoughts and yet I could hear his. He feared for me the decisions I was about to make. Yet, he did not know I was planning on leaving all of them.

After a while, we headed back to the house hand in hand, meandering. We walked to the top of the porch, and he took me in his arms as he leaned in, pressing his mouth against mine. He just took my breath away when he was so close. I opened my mouth, our tongs gliding in and out so passionately I pulled back slowly. "We should go in. The others are worried. They are wondering if you found me."

"Alright, love, we will take this up later." Then he kissed me again, making my toes curl.

"You have a date."

Jerry met us at the doorway.

"Dee, can I talk to you in private?"

"Sure, what's up Jerry, He headed to the library, waited for me to enter, and then shut the door quietly behind him.

"What are you thinking you cannot leave alone?" I spun around. "How do you know what I am planning? I just put the plan together in my head at the beach minutes ago?"

"I saw you leaving in a flash of a vision. Then saw that guy from the cartel named Simon open your door. You stepped out of you Lexus and went to a bar downtown. I have never experienced vision so vivid. You're you sneak out. I will tell Blaine and the others if you don't give up this ridiculous idea." I turned and looked up, talking to the room. Like a loon.

 "George, did you have something to do with giving Jerry a vision?"

"Dee, who is George? And who are you talking to in this room?"

 "Oh, my great, great, great, great, great grandfather who has manifested his presence to me and he says he has no powers here on earth, but I think he can do some things." Then he ghosted in. Jerry just stood there frozen. He kneeled and bowed his head. "We are honored to be in your presence."

I scoffed… whose presence? This is just my grandfather, not a king!

 "What the hell, get up Jerry?" Stepping over Jerry to get into my grandfather's face. I passionately implored him to see my point.

 "How am I to change the immortal world? When I try to

make a plan and you stop it?"

"Dee, you are not ready. It was profound the way you have accepted your responsibilities, but your temper is like your grandmother's, and it will get you killed. Jake needs to keep training you further."

"So then, you will… what… let me know when I am ready to talk to the cartel."

"You're just not very patient, just like your grandmother."

"Jerry, you will be my vessel to keep Dee in check. There will be nothing you can do without the rest of them knowing. We gave a team of immortals to help you use them."

"Oh, that's just perfect." I sat in the chair, pouting.

"I don't get it. You want me to make a change, but I cannot do that from here."

"They have tried to use all the telepathic immortals to see if they can see who you are, but they are striking out. No one can know who you are and your gifts. You instinctively block all the thoughts of the immortals that might harm you. You don't even know you are doing it. It is as natural to you as breathing. They need to be afraid before they will listen and it is not in your nature to kill, so that will not be a possibility to spread fear. Patients are the only way to win this battle. The cartel will never give until they think they have you, and your job for now is to just keep putting that off. "

"But I cannot continue to risk my friends."

"Have you ever thought that this is not your destiny alone, that this small but impressive band of immortals has been predestined to carry out the wishes of the past? Jake can teach you more of the ancient ways. I heard you once say that you noticed this team works like a well-oiled machine. Remember, you felt left out and didn't know what to do. You need to become part of that machine. You need to study the old ways and not be so, as your generation says in-your-face about the rules of your destiny. We will talk soon, and he just ghosted away.

"Dee, you are so angry and rude to your five times over great grandfather. He is legendary for all immortal kind."

"What the hell are you going on about? Legendary for what?"

"Your grandfather was the leader of the Duwamish (Lushootseed), He led The Pacific Northwest Chieftains and taught the twenty-nine federally recognized Native American tribes to live in peace. He also had many immortal gifts he never took advantage of; he lived among the Indigenous people as a mortal. Later, he taught music to immortal children. He loved one of the original six Atlanteans name Suzzallo Lee.

"Wait a minute, I am Duwamish and Atlantean?"

Dee, is that all you just heard? No, that is not all I heard you say. But has importance to who I am, and wouldn't you be traumatized, being stuck with these responsibilities, because of something in the past that the immortals couldn't get right?"

"No, I would be honored to be chosen, to lead our culture of immortals into a new future. You should listen to your grandfather. He was trying to tell you, you're not alone, we are with you, and we have your back. You're amazing, but your battle skills & strategy suck. That was where Ray and I come in."

"We need to sit with the others and let them know they have also been chosen to help in the changing of the Cartel. They need to agree to help."

"What if they feel like I do and don't want to?"

"Dee, you are still so noticeably young in your thoughts the rest of us have seen all the damage the Cartel has done and are ready to do battle, you will see. We have been together waiting to be told for what we are here to do. Now we know we have been chosen through the centuries to help you. Don't take away our destiny."

"Why don't you go get them and we can sit here in the library and tell them?" Jerry went to the rest of the group that was in the kitchen, fooling around. "Dee and I have need of all of you in the library."

"Jerry, why so serious did you see something?"

"You could say that! We will tell you in the library." They all filed into the library one at a time. Blaine came over and stood beside me as if in a show of support no matter what I was about to say. Amanda was trying to probe my mind. I smiled at her.

"In a minute, you will know with the rest."

She blushed because I knew she was trying to probe my mind, and I caught her. She went and sat on the couch in front of the fire. Jake came in and looked at me with those admiring eyes. Mica was right behind him; they sat next to each other at the table and Jacqueline and Ray sat next to them. We were all in one room, and then I looked at Jerry.

"You tell them I have no words for what we are about to invite them to do."

I took Blaine's hand and went to sit at the table as well. Jerry stood in front of the fireplace and told the story. He talked about his vision of me sneaking out alone and how George just ghosted in to talk to us, told them how George wanted me to include them and then he ghosted out, this was our entire destiny, and we were all chosen to help in my effort to fix the mess of the Elders. The room was silent; Blaine squeezed my hand and smiled at me. "I'm in; the rest had the same response. They were almost giddy with excitement, like I had never seen. Ray stood.

"I knew one day the truth would be revealed and the world would have to listen to the stories of the past. I am honored to follow you into battle. Whatever that may look like in the 21st century."

Mica came over and hugged me.

"I knew you were going to change all of our lives when I met you." The professor came over too.

"Could you please teach me the language of the ancients? That way I can continue to help you with the rubbing's translation and the books. I see you have been studying them together." Jake came over and sat next to me.

"So, tell me how your grandfather likes who you are?"

"He says I need more training. My temper will get me killed."

"A wise man indeed."

"He says I remind him of my grandmother. She was stubborn too."

"Who is your grandmother?"

"I do not know, he never said."

"Are you sure he compared you to your grandmother?"

"Yes… I'm sure that is what he said."

"The next time he ghosts in, can I meet him? He sounds like a great man."

 "Jerry kneeled at his presents."

 "Jake, you should have heard Dee. She was in his face, yelling and swearing at him. The greatest General our kind ever had, George Lee."

"In his time, you would have been thrown to the floor or, worse, beheaded for your disrespect."

 "Since he gave me his gifts, I think it would be a tossup."

Jake just shook his head. "So, tell me, what does he want me to do for you?"

 The professor stood up and came over to me.

"Wait a minute; your grandmother was married to General George Lee?"

"He just kept repeating I was just like her. Why? Do you know who my grandmother is?"

"I will have to do some research and get back to you."

Turning my attention to Jake.

 "My grandfather suggested you should work on training me for battle. I have to get my temper under control. If an opponent gets under my skin, it will be the death of me."

"We will begin out on the lawn tomorrow morning. We will start with meditation, some Sahaja yoga. This will help you contact your inner spirit. Give you self-control and perhaps make you one with your inner warrior. You might find letting go of the control will help. You need to get some rest tonight for tomorrow's training. See you in the morning." Jake left the library. I just sat there and watched him go.

"Good night, everyone. See you in the morning."

I took Blaine's hand, and we headed to our room. I just wanted to sit in front of the fire in our room and hold my cat. His purring always soothed my mind. I was petting DC and holding him like a baby. *"What was I thinking I could do without help, and what did they all think of me?"* Blaine came over and put his arm around me and we just sat there. I fell asleep, woke up in bed in Blaine's arms. As the sun came up, I knew I had to get up. Jake would be waiting for my first yoga lesson. Laid there, staring at the ceiling. I could see daylight coming in the window, slid quietly out of bed and pulled on my leggings and t-shirt. Put my hair back in a ponytail. I headed down the back stairs to the kitchen. Jerry was up with a cup of coffee and a bagel for me. He handed them to me; "Jake is waiting on the lawn for the sunrise and your yoga lesson." I took the bagel and coffee and headed out onto the front lawn. Jake had two mats set up. I finished my coffee, and we began. A couple of hours had gone by in silence and process. I felt calmer. Maybe it was working on my inner spirit. I hope so because next we are going to work out in the gym. Jake just wants to continue to push me.

Jake and I had been in training for months. He and I were left on the island and everyone else assumed their normal lives with caution, never one of them being alone. My inner warrior was really quiet lately. Professor went back to college. Mica, Amanda, and Jerry went back to work at the club. They stayed in the loft together at night.

Blaine and Ray worked on plans to protect the group both from an outside attack on the island. Back to the security system in Seattle. They had sent out Intel to track the cartel and try to guess their next move. They had picked up some noise in Victoria BC on the Island, a small band causing trouble for the locals. Blaine had been gone for two weeks. Ray and he were coming back to the island. I knew they were going to arrive hours before. The closer Blaine got, the less attention Jake got from me finally.

"I give up. I cannot compete with the hormones; Blaine obviously has taken over your brain."

"Yep, I am hopeless about anything but his thoughts. The closer he gets, the less I want to control them. I can feel all of his thoughts and we will need most of the day and tonight to get it all out of our systems so we can focus on the task at hand."

"The curse of immortal passion that Blaine and I had to

endure." I told Jake they were here and ran out to the front porch. Blaine stepped out of the rig and walked up to the top of the porch. He took me in his arms and hugged me tight. "I have missed you."

"I know" I smiled and leaned up to kiss him.

"Come with me." As he took my hand, I felt like the first time we had touched, my head spun. The electricity between us could light an entire city for months. Being apart for too long made both of us mad with desire. My desire was so intense because I allowed all his desires in my thoughts, which is like when you take more of something because taking more is much better. I had to shut him out this time. Having twice as much was more than I could manage. When we got to the stairs, Blaine picked me up into his arms and carried me to our room, pushed the door open and sat me on the bed. I reached for his shirt, grabbing both sides of his shirt buttons flying in every direction, but he took it slow, one button at a time as he removed my shirt, pushing down my arms, leaving it there, holding my arms in place. Then he stared at my lace lavender bra as my breasts were bulging against the cup holding them in. He reached behind me and released my bra, as my breast fell into his hand, then he leaned into them with a kiss so slowly and softly as though they were made of glass. He suckled, tugged, scraping his teeth across my nipple, then pulling it into his mouth and rolled it with his tongue, nibbling on one, then the other. I released a moan, almost
270

to an orgasm.

"Let go love, give me that pretty orgasm to me he whispered tugging again at my other nipple. Then I saw stars. I shivered too my toes and my breath was coming too fast. I shattered into a million pieces. As I lay limp, unable to do anything but recover my breath, he removes the rest of my clothes. He perched above me, spreading out my knees. He placed his rock-hard erection at my core, and in one swift move, was buried.

deep into me. I thrust up to get him deeper. He swayed his hips, hitting the spot until I burst into more pieces and then my pelvic muscle squeezed as he plummeted faster and faster until I felt him shutter and collapse to the side not to put his entire weight on me. We both laid there trying to catch our breaths. I rolled over and snuggled him. He reached out and pulled me close. I was so glad to have him in my arms again. I realized how much I missed him. Jake was keeping me busy with training and wiped out by the end of the day. Probably was a good thing. Blaine leaned over, kissed my forehead.

"I have never in all of my years experienced what you just did to me."

He looked so intently at me.

"I'm sorry it was too much? I mean, with our thoughts together."

"No, it was remarkably the best I have ever had, it's just I get what Jake was talking about when I first set eyes on you and was complaining about the desire to touch you, how strong it was, he pointed out to me you were having double the experience and didn't know what was happening to you. I know now I understand.

"Oh, that seems like so many years ago, and it has only been months." We laughed.

"We need to help Ray unload the rig and give Jake an update on the Intel."

"I know." We hopped into the shower one at a time; otherwise, we would be at it again. Then we got dressed and headed back downstairs, where Blaine helped Ray with the supplies and finished stocking the shelves with provisions. Blaine took a couple of cases of wine down to the cellar and Jake followed him with ammunition for the safe. Ray and I finished unloading the rig. We have our own Fort Lewis here with all the essentials in case of attack.

"How is everyone?"

"They are good. No one has been approached by the cartel."

"That is good. Has the professor deciphered the rubbing on the doors or had any luck with the dialect? After I gave her what I could remember of the alphabet."

"Yes, in fact she has some things to show you when she sees you again." Ray and I had never talked a lot until he stood up that night and gave me his honored to fight beside me. I was always afraid I upset him that day when I threw him on the mat. I was amazed at my strength. Ray is no little man, about six feet two inches tall, and I would guess he weighs in about two hundred and forty pounds, all muscle, has dark hair and dark skin with the immortal blue eyes. Dresses in his fatigues, and he always kept his navy seal workout daily. Quiet, but I could see a sensitivity that none of the rest of the group had. You could tell he was from the old world and had lived an exceptionally long time. He was the oldest of all of us. He looked about forty-five-ish and he said he didn't find out until he was twenty-seven years old, so make him five hundred forty years old, give or take a few years. His knowledge to me is valuable.

"Ray, what can you tell me about the elders in the beginning? Their beliefs would help me."

"The Ancient Elders were a respectful, fun-loving group of immortals with rules about interacting with the mortals. We had run into trouble in the past. That is why we put laws forth when interaction with the mortals is in place. Then, in every generation, comes a rebel group. However, this group took over. They started the renegades, and we could not control them. Soon the elders were voted out and the new leaders voted in, and they banished most of the Ancient Elders from the council. They are what we call the Cartel. They grew to such a size of corruption they took over. That is where you will put the cartel.

Eight in its place. Most of all of them are highbred, like most of the last five hundred years of the immortals. No one has all the abilities that you have. They will be at your mercy and then you have a talented back-up crew." He smiled, referring only to himself. I liked Ray. He was a good man to have my back.

"Thank you. I guess when George reappears to give us permission to go, we will be ready." Jake and Blaine were done, and we gathered in the library. Jake and Blaine told me about the Intel they had received from a couple of informers they have underground.

 "We would like to take a trip up to Victoria and see how well you do against a small group of renegades. The group seems to cause some trouble with the immortals up there. They are attacking the immortals in plain sight in the Pubs there, making them visible to the mortal and they have to be stopped and we need to clean up their mess. They are taking advantage of their gifts. Are you ready to give your gifts a spin?" He smiled with his dimples. How could anyone take him seriously if you didn't know him?

"I guess… when will we leave?"

"We thought we would get the float plan out tonight and head up in the morning. Ray, is that good for you?"

“Ray is going?”

“Yeah, he is our pilot. The plane is one of his pet projects. He rebuilt it. He also doesn’t let anyone fly his plane.”

“Good to know. I like my odds with the four of us.”

“I will go get the plane ready and make sure it is fully loaded and be ready in the morning.”

“So what time are we leaving?”

“6:00 am that will put us there about 8:00 am and then we can check into the Empress hotel suit that they have on hold for us. We will PUB hop and see what the renegades are up to.”

“I will see you all in the morning.” leaning into Blaine. “I’m going to go upstairs. Come up when you’re done.” I kissed him. He looked deep into my eyes. “I will see you in a while. I have to finish helping Ray and Jake with the plane.”

“Good night, guys.”

“Good night, Dee.” I headed upstairs and DC greeted me at the door he was just hanging out. I picked him up and sat in front of the fire. *“What was I supposed to do when we got in front of some renegades? Am I to kick some ass and take names later?”*

I giggled and rubbed DC until he was purring loudly and nuzzling me.

"Will I be like a comic book hero? POW! BOOM! BANG! WHA LAH… that will teach them a lesson? I laughed out loud at the how ridiculous I sounded in my head. Hm… what is it George, that you would like me to do? Then in that moment he ghosted in.

"Dee, don't be silly… there aren't any sound effects in the real life action hero." He smiled at me.

"You heard my thoughts?"

Then he laughed a big belly laugh.

"I am a ghost… I hear and see everything, even if you do not see me."

"You will become the heroes of the mortal and the immortals. Your legendary tales will be told to the younger generations. The stories will reach the cartel and then we will have their attention."

"Then… what?"

"You will be asked to come in front of the council."

"You seem so confident I will put back the rules and keep them in place. Why won't they just run me off, the way they did the ancients?"

"Because they are weakened now by their selfish inbreeding with the mortals, and you have the advantage. You're my granddaughter."

"I just waltz in and say hey bow to me. I am the great General George Lee's granddaughter. Be afraid. Are you serious?"

"When the time comes, you will see."

"I have to ask… how do we, I mean… can we die before it is our time?"

"The only way is to hurt us so bad we cannot move and cut our throats and let us bleed out. Then you must decapitate the body, remove the heart, then place heart, head and our bodies in separate tombs that are sealed for all eternity. Or we will eventually die of old age. The oldest of us was 1700 years old. I think he just closed his eyes and let the world go away."

"It sounds like you need a vampire on hand." I mumbled as he ghosted away. I was tired of the conversation anyway and I went to bed.

Chapter 11

Victoria Island

The next morning, I woke up to Blaine packing.

"Dee, it is time to get up."

Rolling over, stretching out the kinks, and crawled out of bed. Shuffled off to the shower, not awake, letting the hot water soothe me. Got dressed, then threw some close together and headed down to grab some coffee to go and a bagel. The guys were already waiting at the Hummer to drive across to the cove. The Floatplane is hidden inside a cave on the backside of the island. When we pulled up to a sheer cliff, I was puzzled by how we were going to get to the water. A small opening appeared, leading into the cave. Each of us grabbed the gear from the Hummer; we walked into the small doorway. Just a head inside the entrance were stairs going down into the ground. One hundred feet downward into the grotto, this opened up to an enormous cavern with a dock. A float plane sat in the water tied at one end of the dock and a 40-foot 1959 Chris Craft Conqueror tied up on the other end. No one would ever guess hidden in this cavern are two vintage crafts. They had brought power into the cave and had built a small storage building with a bathroom. The building had tools, workbench, and refrigerator. We loaded all the gear on the plane. Blaine and I sat in the back while Jake and Ray were in the front.

"Ray, what kind of plane is this?"

"It's a 1952 Beech D185."

"It's in amazing condition."

"Thank you. I restored it myself."

"Did you restore the Chris Craft or purchased it that way?"

"I bought it at an auction in 1962. It needed a little reconditioning to bring it up to my standards."

"They are both exceptionally done."

"That explained the workshop in the cavern." The motor revved, echoing off the rock walls. I couldn't even hear my own thoughts. This was my first floatplane experience, and I was a little nervous. The plane slowly turned and coasted on top of the water out of the cave into the wide-open water, then the acceleration as we skipped along the water it was all a little rough as my teeth chattered in my head.

Then we were up in the air. The noise was much less once we left the cave, and it was perfect in the sky. The view from up here was nothing short of extraordinary. I saw a small pod of orcas breaching. Washington State, Victoria, Vancouver, Canada, and the San Juan Islands were the most beautiful place I had ever seen. When looking back at James Island, it looked as it had many years ago. You wouldn't guess anyone lived there. The trees camouflaged the ground and the house. The only thing that was visible was the watchtower, and it looked like a rustic fire station above the tree line.

Finally, we were off; it was a sunny, beautiful morning. I had never been to Victoria. We landed a short time later and parked the plane at the Victoria Harbour Airport terminal in the Inner Harbour steps away from the downtown. The harbor also facilitated the ferries coming over from Anacortes, Port Angeles and Seattle, Washington. A man met us at the dock. He was an immortal friend of Jakes. "Bonjour Jake, it is good to see you again. What brings you to the island?"

"James, this is Blaine, Deedra, and you remember Ray, my pilot?"

"Enchante." James bowed his head in greeting us. A small wiry Frenchman, about five feet five inches tall, with brown hair. He was dressed in jeans and a t-shirt, with a levy jacket.

"Just take care of the plane."

"Ma part lors d cette visite?"

"Notre accord habituel?"

"Oui."

"I will have your gear taken to the hotel straight away."

" Merci."

"We will be staying a couple of days and I will be in touch." I could hear James's thoughts. He was not aware of me, and he didn't even have any abilities, just one of those highbred immortals who live a long life. I was curious what the arrangement between James and Jake. I eves dropped on his mind only for a moment. Jake always bought him a case of Balvenie old scotch whiskey, such a small thing to be so loyal. James was a good man.

"I just realized I had understood the conversation in French that Jake had with James."

Minutes later we were off to the hotel as we lugged some of our gear across the street. James was bringing the rest later. The hotel was an astonishing work of artistry, with all the intricate details in the finish work. It seems to be a dying art. According to the brochure I just picked up, that I read while we waited for Jake to check us in: Throughout its history, The Fairmont Empress has played host to kings, queens, movie stars and distinguished guests from around the world. In 1919, Edward, Prince of Wales, waltzed into the dawn in the Crystal Ballroom - an event considered by Victorians to be of such importance that almost 50 years later, the obituaries of elderly ladies would appear under headlines such as, "Mrs. Thornley-Hall Dies. Prince of Wales Singled Her Out."

The city was so clean and had interesting architecture. I wanted to go exploring. Do some shopping. Girl stuff seemed like a marvelous idea. It made me wish Amanda had come with us. I missed her. I listened in as Jake was greeted at the desk. "Mr. Kirby, welcome back. Are you planning a long stay with us?"

"No, only a couple of days on this trip."

"The maître d' will take your bags up to the room. We have set the penthouse suite up as per your instruction."

"Thank You." Jake tipped the attendant. After he checked in, Jake walked back to the group and gave us all room keys. We headed to the elevator while we walked through the hotel. It was very crowded with a large group of Rotarians and a soccer team.

"So, Mr. Kirby," making fun of the formality they had taken with him. "How many times have you been here?"

282

"Many times, over the last hundred years. My first visit was when they were building the hotel back in 1906. As a young immortal and looking for answers. I also needed a job. I met Francis Rattenbury. He was the designer and asked if I could have a job. He put me to work over seeing his architectural plans and then, after a while, he made me his general supervisor on the building crew. The attendant is an incredibly old friend. He was here then, also another immortal that has no abilities.

 "Yeah, I got that from him while we waited through all the informalities."

 "You could learn from the old ways, the colloquial way of show respect in the everyday language. There are too many slangs used in today's vernacular, Dee."

 "I'm sorry Jake; I didn't mean to be so flippant. You're right. I should show more respect for all of you who have been at this much longer than I have." I lowered my head in shame.

"Dee, don't be so well-mannered. It doesn't suit you." I stuck my tongue out at him. Showing how well-mannered I truly am. "Oh… your hilarious Jake." I shoved him forward. We got to the room. It was on the top floor and took a special key just to get the elevator to go there. When the elevator doors opened, we walked out into a suite that had 3 bedrooms off the great room, the view of the bay and the Olympic Mountain range that was incredible. I went into the room where a king-size bed was made up with white cotton sheets. Who knows how high the thread count was? The sheets were smartly tucked in with the five white pillows that ran across the top of the bed. The bathroom was tiled, and the countertop was black granite. Ceilings in the main room were lined with four-inch picture railing or crown molding. Finished it perfectly. Modern amenities had been tastefully added to the room for our modern convenience. The room's walls were painted a buttery color with white details on window and ceiling trim.   Furniture was classic for the time they were portraying elegant Victorian turn of the century. The guys pulled up the chairs and opened the bar and hit the remote for the TV and watched the game. "Can I go shopping? Does anyone want to come with me?" Silent came over the room. "Hey Blaine, you're going shopping with your love, aren't you?" Jake was teasing him. "Um Dee… the games on… it March madness. I have money on the game." He grunted out painfully and looked at me with a boyish expression on his face. I heard his thoughts.

"I'm sorry… can I stay with the guys? Their teasing will be relentless if you make me go with you. I promise to make it up to you tonight."

 "I got it, guys."

I can hear the loathing over the thought of going shopping with me.

"I will be ok by myself."

"Yep… have a good time. We will see you later." They had a seventy-two-inch flat screen TV that dropped from the ceiling. They were all engrossed in the game. I went over to Blaine, leaned down, and kissed him on the cheek; he never took his eyes off the TV. Just grunted… *"Be careful, love."* He is in control of the passion, and I have lost him to the game.

Then I heard.

"No one should look that good walking away in a pair of jeans."

I smiled and shook my head as I headed to the lift door. I liked the idea of going alone. Took the elevator to the lobby, then out onto the street. I walked down government street towards the bay and then up Courtney Street to some shops. It had been so long since I had some kind of normal life. I was having fun just being me, without all the immortal stuff. Just as I thought I was a human again, my immortal senses heard a small voice

"Help me, can anyone hear me?" I looked around, and I didn't see anyone in danger. I focused, reaching out with my senses.

"Help me." It was a young immortal with a weak, frightened voice. I focused and mentally responded, *"Where are you?"*

"I'm in the basement of a church."

"Which church?"

"I don't know. It was dark, and they had a hood over my head. I just heard them say…

"Leave him in the church's basement. We will come back for him later."

I walked along the street, trying to figure out where the voice was coming from. Then I saw a red brick church with white ornate trim. There was an X on the door.

"Hey, are you still there? Keep talking. What's your name?"

"My name is Demetrye."

"Hi, I'm Dee."

"Hurry, they will be coming back. Can you hear me better?"

"Yes, I think I'm outside". I grabbed hold of the door and it was locked. I walked all around the church. Down the alley, I saw another door. I turned the knob, and the door was unlocked. I opened it slowly and scanned the area for any thoughts. There didn't seem to be anyone else in the church I walked in. It was dark, kept focused so I could hear thoughts that might show up unexpectedly. I worked my way through the church until I found a door that led to the basement, opened it slowly.

"Are you there?"

"I just heard a door open."

 "Yeah, it's me." I could hear his thoughts much clearer now.

"Where are you now?" he said

"Just keep talking. I will find you." I could hear him in the hallway.

 "I'm terrified they will come back and catch both of us."

"It will be alright, I'm very close now." There was a hall and four doors. I opened one at a time and in the second, door was a young man tied up on a cot. He was blindfolded and gagged with duct tape. He couldn't have been over 19 years old. Who would do such a terrible thing to him? I untied him and pulled off the blindfold.

"This is going to hurt.

"Do I pull it off in one clean jerk, or do I let him pull it off?"

 He reached up and pulled the duct tape off that was over his mouth before I could rip it off.

 "Oh… ugh, um, thank you." He swallowed.

"Why are you down here?"

"The renegades are looking for people to join their group.

I do not qualify, so they put me in here last night after the pub closed."

"What do you mean, you don't qualify?"

"I am not immortal."

"Are you sure? I can tell you're not a mundane mortal. be patient, you will come into your gifts."

 I could sense he was an immortal, just too young to come into his gifts.

"Well, let's get you out of here and get you home Demetrye."

 We headed out of the church into the light.

"Thanks for hearing me. How did you do that?"

"Oh crap, how am I going to explain that to him without giving my secret away?"

 "I must have good hearing."

 "But I heard you too inside my head."

"You did? You must have been hallucinating."

 "How did you find me?"

"A lucky guess. You should get home. Someone must be worried."

"Yeah, thanks Dee."

"You're welcome Demetrye."

 He took off around the corner and was gone. So much for a day of normalcy. I kept shopping until it was getting late.

"Hey Dee, can you hear me" it was Blaine.

"The game is over, and we are headed out to dinner. Do you want to meet us at the Irish time Pub on the corner government and View Street?"

"Sure, I'm just around the corner. I can meet you there."

We didn't need a cell phone with me around. I could hear all of them and could talk back to them. I saw Blaine, Jake and Ray coming up the street. The men were coming out of the PUB and the men were following them. They were mad and about to attack them. Demetrye was with them.

"Jake, you're being followed."

 I could see the men that were in front of me were also going for the guys. Listening, I could also hear their thoughts.

" We have them surrounded. Get them."

I stepped off the curb…

 "Hey boys, are you going anywhere special?" The biggest one turned around and gave me a dirty look as they kept walking. They didn't think I was any threat to them. This time I sent them a mental message to them with an attitude.

"Excuse me boys, I think you're looking for me." They stopped and turned around. I had all their attention now.

"So, gentlemen, can I help you?" as I walked closer, I could see into their eyes. Jake, Blaine, and Ray were preoccupied with the men that were following them.

"I suggest you take a step back." Listening to their abhorrent thoughts,

"It's not a marvelous way to greet guest to your beautiful city." Out of know where she plopped into my thoughts. My inner warrior making commentary on the situation.

"Well, are these boys in for a surprise?"

I was hungry, and this is annoying me and didn't seem like a genuinely nice thank you for saving Demetrey. Taking a deep breath, I could feel my inner warrior and her annoyance at their thoughts of me. I thought to myself. "Don't let her take control. Someone will get hurt." I took another slower breath, trying to control my inner warrior. These men were not a threat to me, focusing just a little and probed their minds as they dropped to the ground in agony. They were just trying to stick up for Demetrye, but they were afraid I was with the renegades. I walked past them, rolling on the ground. By now, they had a severe headache. I stopped thinking of them and could see Jake, Blaine, and Ray. I walked up to join them.

There were four of us. We just stood there as one of their

men pointed a shotgun at us. Now I was truly annoyed. Is this how they wanted to thank us for helping? I since fear from them, they thought we were part of the cartel.

"Deedra, are you going to just stand there? Or are going to show them who is in charge here and now."

"I got this. I don't need your infuriating comments in my head."

I opened my hands and focused on the shotgun. Levitating it out from his hands, it flew into mine. I walked over to the wall at the edge of the bay and dropped it into the salty water.

"You boys shouldn't play with guns; someone could get hurt."

This time, my inner warrior and I agreed. Jake looked at me and shook his head.

"Dee, we have got to get. That attitude, under control." Jake retorted.

"He better not be… referring to my help…"

Why would you think he was referring to me…? You're the one with the temper." Then the silence that let me know I was alone with my thoughts.

"We had these guys right where we wanted them without your interference."

"Yeah… It looked as though you were about to get your heads blown off. I could see you had it under control…. come on, I'm starving, and these men are ruining my wonderful day." We all turned and walked towards the pub. We left the men in the street, half of them with their mouths open, the other half picking themselves off the pavement. Walking into the Irish Time Pub, the man at the door greeted us.

"Mr. Kirby, welcome back, your usual table? Oh, I see you have some guests, maybe the balcony where you can have some privacy."

"Yes please, that will work just fine."

I could hear Jake's thoughts as we climbed the stairs to the balcony, and the server led us to the back in a private room overlooking the bay. The server sat the menus down.

"I will be back to get your orders." Jake pulled out the chair at the head of the table and sat down.

"Dee, you're so casual about putting six men to their knees in a matter of seconds."

"In my defense, I had just saved their buddy and was hungry. I was having a momentous day, and they ruined it. They're lucky I didn't damage their brains."

"Thanks for the warning out there that we had a tail."

"It's ok. It was my fault. I thought I was saving a young

man tied up in the basement of the beautiful old church today. Besides…. you're my team… are you all ok?"

"Yes, Dee, they all talked at once. The gun thing you did that was hilarious and amazing."

I could hear Blaine agreeing with Ray. I never tire of hearing Blaine's thoughts. I know I shouldn't, but his thoughts were so loving and with pride behind them.

"They just ignored me as if I was just some dumb woman. We got a little annoyed at the fact they just dismissed me again… then you know what happens to my inner warrior… she takes over and makes inherent decisions naturally. I noticed they have not heard of me up here. That will make it easier to fix what is wrong. When I found Demetrye tied up in the basement of a church, I knew he was an immortal young man. He had not come into his gifts yet, or maybe he didn't have any. I felt good about helping him."

I stopped in mid-sentence. Jerry was coming up the stairs with the server.

"Hey, Jerry." I hugged him. "Is Amanda with you?"

"No, I came alone. Thought you might need backup. I saw in a vivid vision that you're going to need more help. Got on the first ferry out of Seattle."

"Really!"

Another server showed up with water on a tray.

"Can I get any of you anything to drink?" She was tall with longlegs and long blond hair. She was looking at Blaine.

"Oh… Hi long time no see… your usual?"

"Yes, the oldest scotch you have got and the wine list, please."

Ray & Jerry ordered a beer and Blaine looked over the list. He turned to the server. "Thanks. We will let you know about the wine." Blaine turned to me. My one eyebrow arched. "Who was the server, love?" he ignored the question and changed the subject.

"Do you think you want to try some of the local wine?"

"I have heard Canada hasn't perfected their wines yet. I think I would like a hard cider. Who was the server?"

He fidgeted and informed me he used to make runs with Jake. No further information came out. I was looking towards Jerry. He was in that place, where he was seeing… staring off into nothing in a trance.

"What do you see Jerry?"

"They are more of them coming. See if you can hear them?" I focused throughout my net of consciousness towards the crowd. The thoughts of everyone in the Pub were all around me. It was like a humming noise…. Bees buzzing. It made it hard to listen and center my attention until I'm outside.

"Awh…. taking in a deep breath and letting it out. I could hear them. I heard my name coming from Demetrye, the young man I un-tied early today. He is telling them I am on their side. I am a good immortal, and I should be trusted. Oh, so they are the good immortals up here could have fooled me with the welcoming party.

"Dee, what is happening?"

"They are the locals they thought we were from the cartel." Jake interrupted me.

"Well… maybe you shouldn't have been so intense and tried to listen to their thoughts first, before you put them down like a bunch of rabid dogs.

"I listened to their thoughts. Their disrespectful vocabulary was condescending to me, it exasperated me, to feel their chauvinistic attitude. It just gripes me to no end; we live in the 21st century and women can do anything that a man can do and most of the time, we do it better."

"Amen to that. That's my girl. I knew you would get there." Out of nowhere came my inner warrior, encouraging me to rage on.

"Dee, settle down. That temper of yours is going to get us killed." There goes Jake. He was gnashing his teeth about my losing control.

The twelve men walked in the pub's front door, and they

talked to the tall, picturesque, blond server. She pointed at us on the balcony. I focused on the man in front; he was the leader; he was medium height, about six feet with an athletic build, in his mid-thirties. His hair was short with salt and pepper gray going through it. I could hear him tell the others to sit at the bar. He headed up the stairs where Blaine, Ray, and Jake stood up. I sat there with Jerry, waiting for my hard cider.

"Hello, I'm Kevin O'Reilly." With his hand extended to shake Jake's hand. Jake took his hand and smiled. Kevin began with, "I would like to apologize for my men's behavior earlier. We thought you were the Cartel."

"No hard feelings. We are sorry as well." As he looked directly at me.

"Let me introduce you to my team. This is Ray, our pilot. Ray smiled." Kevin, you old dog. I thought you were in Europe?"

"I left there centuries ago and ended up owning a ship that delivers goods back and forth between Seattle and Victoria."

Ray turned to all of us.

"Kevin and I served in the Royal Guard under Suzzallo."

The guys all stiffened. *"Note to self-ask Ray about Suzzallo."*

Jake continued, "This is Jerry and Deedra. We are on a training mission. Deedra is new to our world. We heard you were having some trouble up here and thought we could help."

 "Yes, last month the Renegades came up here recruiting our younger men. We have been taking them out, locking them up and they keep sending more."

"How can we help?"

I wanted to know what "taking them out" meant…. Was he killing them?"

 I eased into his mind for some details. On how they took them out…picture of dismembering of the renegade bodies, then burned their remains. I disengaged my connection with Kevin's mind. He looked at me suddenly. Your woman is powerful. I smiled and cleared my throat.

"This woman doesn't belong to anyone, and I have a name."

 I stood up and walked toward the Kevin.

"It's Deedra Lee." Put out my hand, keeping eye contact with Kevin. Kevin smiled as he shook my hand. He looked away first.

"Forgive me, but you look familiar, and I can't place who you remind me of."

"Make them bow to you. How dare they act with such disrespect towards you? I should shame them all."

"Easy now… why are you so angry? I got this… a different century or many centuries. We don't bow here; ever… there is no royalty. I am not royalty. Who are you? "

"Well, at least they should show respect." Then nothing, just the vast silence that follows her rants. Kevin spoke to me.

"You're a telepath, aren't you? I didn't mean to insult you with my thoughts. But they are my thoughts, and it is rude to intrude in one's mind. I must admit, you are particularly good. I only felt a whisper of your mind." Then there she was again.

"Deedra, you need to practice. In the old days, no one knew I was in their mind until it was too late."

"Well, you're awful chatty suddenly. Would you like to enlighten me about what I did wrong? Or you did wrong because I thought I was reading his mind, not you."

"See, you don't even feel me, and I am in your head all the time. You need to just let it happen as a whisper, as Kevin pointed out. But not even a whisper. Total control like when I talk to you, it doesn't even cause you pain, and the buzzing has stopped… hasn't it?"

Blaine came up behind me, sliding his arms around my

waist. Just you, brief touch eased my mind. I leaned back against his firm chest. He whispered in my ear.

"Easy Dee. They mean nothing by their chauvinistic attitude. They don't know who you are, and most immortal women are not as strong in character as you are. Also, the older immortals are from a different time. You seem to be distracted, like somewhere else. Is she talking to you again?" I turned. How can you tell?"

"You look like you're listening to someone not paying attention to the surrounding crowd."

"She has a lot to say, suddenly."

I moved out of his reach so I could focus again. Turned to the table and sat down. I really needed to learn how to stop him from doing that to me. I looked up at his piercing blue eyes. He kept awfully close, with in touching distance. As Jake finished talking to Kevin. "I think we can help you. Do you have a place that is safe to make some plans?"

"Yes, we can meet you on the north shore. We have a ship in the bay. I will leave Demetrye with you since Deedra already knows him and when you're done with your dinner, he will bring you to us."

"Very well, we will see you then."

Kevin turned and went back down the stairs to his men at the bar. He pointed upstairs to all of us and Demetrye nodded his head. The rest of them followed him out the door of the pub.

"So, Dee, did you pick up any weirdness about our new friends?"

"No, they were telling the truth."

"Hi Dee," Demetrye came over and sat next to me at the table. "Gentlemen, this is Demetrye, the young man I found tied up in the church." I pointed around the table and introduced them. "This is Blaine, Jake, Jerry and Ray. This is Demetrye." They all shook hands.

"Now we are best buds. Can we please eat? You don't want to experience me on a low blood sugar." My stomach was growling, and I was getting a headache. Jake signaled to the server. She came up and finally took our orders. Then the hard cider arrived. "Demetrye, did you need something to drink?"

"I'll have a soda, thanks."

"So, do you come here often?"

"Yeah, this is a great pub; they are famous for their beer and fish and chips."

"Oh good, that is what I will order as well."

"You won't be disappointed." The food came and Demetrye was right. It was wonderful. I sat across from Jake. He had gotten quiet.

"So, Jake." I wiped my mouth with my napkin and kept chewing, swallowed a gulp of cider to wash down the steak fry I just shoved into my mouth.

"I get the impression from the server that you knew each other a long time ago."

"Thanks for asking instead of prying into my brain"

"I told you I would leave your thoughts to yourself and not try to get into your head. Unless it is a life and death situation." I laughed evilly. Jake shook his head, then went on.

"She and I had shared some quality together many years ago." That was all he will share, so I left it alone. He didn't seem to want to tell me anymore. Blaine and Jake must have had a lot of fun with other women. It was hard because I was so curious by nature not to skim his thoughts, but I told him I wouldn't. Demetrye ate with us, and he seemed genuinely nice. He had the most exquisite brown skin, and his eyes were not the immortal blue, they were a deep green, he had a bit of an accent, maybe Scottish, not sure. When it comes to guys with Scottish, Irish, Australian accents, they are hot languages, but I can't tell them apart. I guess if three men stood in front of me, one talked at a time, I could tell. His hair was a dark auburn; it was curly but just little more than wavy. When we finished Demetrye, let the door attendant know we would need the limo driver to pull around, I really could get used to all the opulent way the immortals' lived, with the suites, limos, secret homes, yachts, planes, I guess when you have lived for centuries you accumulate a ton of wealth and possessions. I was used to living frugally on the reservation with my mom and dad in North Carolina. The house wasn't any bigger than the bedroom at the house on the island. I have been in the Northwest for only six months, and I have more than anyone could ever accept to gain in a lifetime. And place with a monstrous responsibility. The Limo arrived, and we all piled in. I sat on Blaine's lap. All I wanted to do was go back to the room. I *could feel him pressing against my bum. Hear him thinking.*

"Oh God, Dee, you feel so good."

"Focus." I intruded into his thoughts, and I turned and looked into his eyes.

"I'm sorry I forget it makes it twice as hard for you. I Just need…"

"It's ok but we must stay focused on the task. I'll take care of you later, I promise." I laid a Kiss on the palm of his hand and smiled.

I was keeping my eye on Jerry's facial expressions. Making sure he wasn't picking up in added information for future events. We arrived at the bay where a small boat was waiting for us to take us to the ship where we were to meet the Victorian immortals and talk with Kevin O'Reilly, their leader. I was unsure about all of this after I had skimed his mind and saw the devastation of the renegades. What it takes to kill us, I could never do. Perhaps I will never have to. We pulled up to the big container ship in the harbor. Our boat was twenty-five feet, and it was dwarfed to the ship. It was the size of three football fields on water. A couple of men were there to help us on the ship. Blaine helped me out and then he pulled me close to his side, making sure we were touching. I was curious why so close, so I lightly skimed his thoughts. He thought if this was a trap; had to make sure I got away safely. He was so sweet he didn't realize how my gifts had grown while he was gone. I would have to protect him and make sure the whole team got out.

"We will make sure all of you get out of this if there is trouble."

There she was again, no buzzing, just her egotistical input into my thoughts.

We walked along the narrow halls to a big room inside the ship. When we got into the room where there were about twenty-nine immortals in one room, I scanned every mind quickly, looking for anything that might put the team in danger and then was watching Jerry's face to see if anything was going to happen. I felt we had it all covered. Kevin was trying to read my mind. I smiled and

said in his mind, "Unh-unh, you don't want to do that…."
He looked at me and smiled back as he understood I was
not to be challenged. Jake let Kevin tell his story about all
the renegades that had come to Victoria and the problems
they were causing with the local mortals. They had a plan
to take care of all of them and send a message to the cartel
that Victoria would not welcome them, and they need to
stay out of the country. Jake came back to us and said
they would set up a meeting with the renegades and then
they want our help to clean up. Sending that message,
they had some powerful immortals on our side. They were
going to set it up tomorrow night in town. They wanted
us to meet them down in the industrial area, down by the
docks around 7:00 pm so it would be under the cover of
darkness.

They preferred the docks, so no one would notice when all
hell broke loose. We all followed Jake back to the boat, and
we were off back to the hotel. I was tired of all the drama
and needed to go to bed. The guys stayed up to watch the
NCAA College tournament "March Madness" Washington
State Cougars, verse the Arizona wild cats were playing.
Listening to the guys talking about this would be an upset
if Arizona won. I really didn't care…just wanted to take a
shower and maybe read a little before I went to sleep, sat
next to Blaine and said goodnight. I barely got his attention
long enough for him to mutter a good night. Sometimes I
wondered if I had any effect on him anymore, whatsoever.

Then I heard his thoughts as I walked away. *"When I come to bed, I will make you scream my name."*

He looked up and winked at me. He noticed me leaving the room but didn't want the guys to give him a hard time. I smiled to myself.

"I shouldn't be listening to his thoughts. He would be very upset if he knew I did that and the fact he doesn't even know I'm in his head. My mind control exercises that Jake has had me working on have paid off. I have total control of how far I push into someone's mind before they know I'm present. I also know what it takes to cause pain and paralyze them in place. While reading Kevin's mind and seeing how they kill other immortal was gruesome and deplorable, there must be a better way than draining the blood until it is all gone and then storing the body in a tomb for all eternity. Don't we just naturally die as we age, even though it is at a slower process? I would have to ask Jake and Blaine why the draining of blood. I do remember my five times over grandfather telling me something on the same lines.

"Oh, my dear, they are correct. The only way to truly kill us is to drain the blood after beheading us, taking out the heart, then in tomb us in separate containers. We regenerate a such a fast rate that if the body parts are not separated, we will come back to life. The burning seems like a nice finish, though. But entombing the body without

Enough of those kinds of thoughts. I would not sleep. After my shower, I pulled a book out of my bag and read about the normal life of a girl in a small town. That was the way I dreamed good thoughts. Only on this night, the book didn't work. I was somewhere between dreaming and awake when as though I was standing in front of some ancient council. Yet I don't think it was me. I was someone else. They were handing down judgment on this immortal. They said her powers to read minds and to use it on the council would not be allowed and she would be sentenced to death. The room was cold and dark, and the council was dressed in ancient robes with beaded designs that must have represented their clan. I felt as though I knew the woman. It appeared to be me. Then they said her name, Suzzallo Lee, you have been sentenced to death for your betrayal of the council. It wasn't me at all, although it looked exactly like me. This must have been my great, great, great, great grandmother. She is my inner warrior. Then I awoke to the alarm clock going off. All alone, I was lying there, and it was all coming together in my mind. The knowledge flooded my mind, the pain she inflicted without a thought. The death in her wake as she reined her people with horror. I saw them take me or her to a man they called Rajani. He used my grandfather to capture her, and she allowed them to kill her to stop them from killing him. They let him live because they knew he would just go away in grief. Knowing the love of his life was gone. She has been guiding me all this time to avenge her death and to bring the immortals to justice for what they did to her. She also had a warning not to be trapped by my love for Blaine and the others. Not to trust like she did and be deceived by people she thought were her friends.

What was I supposed to do with Jerry watching the future and knowing when I was to make any wrong decision with the help of my great grandfather George? Confused, I got up to tell the team about my vision of the past and have them help me with the translation of information. We still had to deal with these other immortals tonight, so I waited to tell them when we get back to the island where I'm hoping the professor can help me with some facts that she might have discovered. For now, I would just focus on the up-and-coming battle and try to keep everyone safe. I could smell the coffee and got dressed and headed out the door. "Good morning sleepy head," the guys teased me.

"Good morning, gentlemen. So, why didn't you wake me?"

"You needed to finish something in your dreams." Jerry explained.

"Do you want to tell us what the two of you know that the rest of us don't?"

Jake teased.

"Maybe Blaine and Amanda should be worried?"

"Oh, your hilarious Jake…. I will tell you when we get back. For now, I just want to focus on the task at hand. I think I should go alone."

"Alone! are you crazy?" Jake ranted…. Ray laughed.

"So, our little princess thinks she is ready to take on the renegades on your own? Jake, we asked you to train her, not make a monster out of her."

"Seriously, I don't want any of you to get hurt."

"Dee…." Blaine walked over and put his arms around me. My mind turned to mush. I pushed him away.

"I love you, but today you must keep your distance. I cannot focus when you touch me like that." He looked at me like I just kicked him.

"I am sorry, but I can't."

All I wanted to say was.

"We have been at this much longer than you and we are still here. What makes you think we will get hurt? Did you see something in the dream you want to tell us about?"

"No, it's just I couldn't live with myself if any of you were hurt. "Jerry, is she telling us the truth."

"Jerry not a word!" no one noticed as I gave him the look that he better not give away my secret. "Um nope, she just

cares about us. She worries about one of us getting hurt because of her."

"Thank you. I don't think they're ready to find out my inner warrior is Suzzallo."

We headed down to the docks, where we joined up with the others and waited for the renegades. The first one that showed up was the guys that I had already met at the club back in Seattle. The big one that took Amanda came in behind them. Then a few others there were twelve all together. Was already in warrior mode the minute I saw my old friend Simon. I moved out in front of the others. I felt a hand on my shoulder. It was Jake.

"And just where in the hell do you think you're going?"

"Jake, it's the same group that hurt Amanda."

"I can see that… you didn't stop them the first time. What is it you think you can do this time?"

"I will aim for the jugular," I stopped. That wasn't me talking, it was her. I looked at all their faces and I could see they couldn't believe that came out of my mouth and neither could I… Jerry step forward.

"That wasn't Dee that is her warrior being verbal." Blaine came over and touched me, soothing me, keeping me grounded.

Kevin turned around, looking at Jake.

"What is wrong with her?"

"Just a minor complication." I pushed Blaine away again.

"I have her under control now."

"Are you sure?"

"Yes, I'm sure. It won't happen again tonight." Jake and Kevin met with the others to let them know they had only one choice to leave or go home in body bags. I could feel my warrior or grandmother. Seething about how she would just as soon kill them all. Her comment landing in my mind. *"Send them home in body bags."*

She was in my head. *"Dee don't hold back. No one can beat you."*

"I think you need to be quiet. Sit tight and we will talk later."

"Awh, man, now not only do I hear the surrounding thoughts, I have to listen to Suzzallo Lee, the most ruthless of all the ancients, and she is my great, great, great grandmother.

Jake and Kevin came back; they have gone back to talk to the others about the choice.

"Dee, can you hear their minds? What are they saying?" I pushed out my energy to listen to all their thoughts. "Most of them want to fight, and Simon has a grudge against me."

"Who?"

"Simon, you remember the one who took Amanda. I shredded him. He is telling them if I'm with you then they don't have a chance."

"Let me go talk to him. Jake, just let me step out into the open. I will keep in control. Maybe it will prevent a fight and they will just leave."

"Ok, but slowly, we don't want them to use you as leverage against us."

"That will not happen." There she was again.

I stepped out slowly with my hands out in front of me, a friendly gesture. The streetlight shone on me in the open. I could hear them perfectly.

"Simon, nice to see you again. What brings you to Canada?"

One of Simon's cronies spouted off.

"Look at her; you're afraid of a woman." Some laughter went through the crowd that Simon had with him.

"Leave it alone. Let's go, it's not worth it. I'm not sure why she let me live the first time I tangled with her. The second in command shouted out she doesn't look so tough, and he stepped out into the light.

"It's your funeral Johnny." He was medium built. Six foot

180 lbs. of lean young immortal. He stepped forward. I smiled.

"Really?" I step into my fight stance. Holding my arm out, curled fingers back towards my hand, signaling a challenge.

"You, want me… come and get me."

"You have this wimp… if he gets the upper hand …I will take over… but Deedra, you have got this."

He came at me with a knife. I stepped to the side and swung my heel and caught him in the middle of the back, sending him flying into some crates on the dock. He got up and came at me again. His face was red and the veins in his neck bulged. I just stood there again and with his momentum, I swung my arm up and caught him in the throat. He ended up flat on his back. I put my boot on his chest as he gasped for air. "Are we done because if this is your best? I am bored." I turned my back on him and started towards Simon. Johnny got up and came at me again. I turned slowly around just before he grabbed me. I raised one hand up, twisted my fingers to a fist and then turned my wrist and thought, broken legs, then I heard the bone snap, crunch, pop. It was a horrible sound, and then the screaming from him was worse. I just shook my head, standing in front of Simon. Then out of no-where was another voice with an accent I couldn't place.

"You tell Rajani I am coming for him." Two of the other men came out and picked Johnny up and dragged him back to the shadows. I turned and said to the group,

"This is over now, and they are leaving to go back to the Cartel. Don't forget my message, Simon."

Kevin and Ray both looked at me. Simon and his men were departing the south end of the pier. Jake, Jerry, Ray and Kevin walked over to me. Jake taking hold of my arm, shaking me.

"Deedra are you there?"

"Um, I am now. Wow, that was weird. She had never completely taken over like that. Did I have an accent? And my voice was lower?"

"What did you or she say to Simon that turned him so white?"

"How I or she was coming after someone named Rajani?"

Ray and Kevin both took a step back, turning white. Ray stuttered, "Are you sure she said Rajani?"

"Yes, but I can ask her if you like… she might answer me. She has been a little chatty lately."

They both just stood there, looking at me.

"Dee, we will pick this up back home in a safer environment."

I shrugged my shoulder.

"Okay." I walked back to Blaine; he enfolded me in to his powerful arms.

Kevin murmured… "Blaine is braver than I am. If she holds the ancient spirit, the only female was Suzzallo; I wouldn't be cuddling up to her." He laughed as he walked off with his men. He turned.

"Thank you for the help. He bowed his head and then they disappeared into the shadows, too. We headed back to the hotel to gather our gear and we would be leaving at first light. Ray and James got the plane ready for our departure in the morning. I was wiped out. Too many of my gifts were used and she, taking me over, was draining. I was thinking of what my parents had said to me. Maybe I was possessed. They were partially right. When I got back to my room, I yelled, "George, why haven't we had this conversation about my inner warrior?" There was nothing. He didn't ghost in or anything. Maybe he is stuck in the library on the Island. I wonder if he is attached to the ancients' books. I heard a knock at the door… "Yeah, come in."

"It's just me Dee. Are you OK?" It was Jerry.

"Why do you ask?"

"Well, I sense from this evening you now know who your inner warrior is, and she is in contact with you on some level. Do you need any help?"

"I am not sure I really understand who she is, but I will understand it when I get hold of George. What I need is to be back at the island to see if the Professor can help me. I must find more answers to what happened back when they ran off the ancients. Why could they not keep control over the renegades and the cartel when they had more gifts among them? We don't want to make the same mistakes. I will talk to everyone else back on the island."

"Alright, as you wish. I will wish you a good night, Dee"

"Good night, Jerry. I hugged him, and he went back out with Jake and Blaine. I tuned out their conversation because it was about me and I didn't want to listen to their fears that I was losing control of who I was. After a while, Blaine came in and sat next to me on the bed. "Are you going to be alright Dee?" as I looked into his eyes, I knew it was only him and I in the room. I could only hear his thought of touching me and what he was going to do next as he leaned in to kiss me and wrapped his arms around my waist. I just melted back into the bed, allowing him to take control. He was kissing me with all the passion, as though it was our first kiss. It was always a first kiss for us. I pushed back with the same eagerness as I pulled his shirt off. He was out of his pants and my clothes were already on the floor. Our naked bodies were entwined. With his enormous hard cock pressed against my core, he pushed harder until he filled me up and was deep within me. My muscles tightened, milking him in the anticipation of the heightened pleasure he was about to bring me and the deeper he pushed, repeatedly slamming harder each time, the throbbing need sent me over the edge. This went on for hours as we did our first night. Lying beside him trying to catch my breath. He was still inside me, growing harder and larger by the minute. Swinging his hips back and forth as he spooned me. I couldn't think of anything but him. Then, hitting the g-spot continually, I exploded into the stratosphere and then I blacked out. When I awoke

Blaine laid there still in the night. He was breathing slowly, knowing he was asleep. I rolled over to watch him. I was so caught up in all that was going on I forgot how beautiful he was to stare at, how his face was so perfect, and the muscles that ran down his body. How very flawless they are. I moved in closer to cuddle with him. He wrapped his arms around me, and we drifted off to sleep.

The morning came way too early. Blaine got up first. He was in the shower, and I got up and joined him. As I stepped into the shower, Blaine bent down, water spraying me in the face, then his head blocked the spray. He kissed me slow and meaningfully. He reached down, picking me up, holding me against the shower wall and set me on his rock hard shaft, swinging his hips up, hitting the g-spot again within all my swollen tissue. I had an orgasm before I could moan. My heart sped up. I took a deep breath and his

316

body trembled and his muscles tighten then he jerked and released. Then, as my breathing slowed, I heard Jerry.

"We will never get out of here if we are waiting on the lovebirds. Did you hear the banging going on in their room last night? She needs to take it easy on the old guy."

I giggled as Blaine release my body and let it slide down his.

"What is so funny?"

"The guys are talking about you getting old again."

"Ah! Not that again with the old guy shit. Can't they come up with something else?"

"They made some comments. They thought we were a little noisy." We hurried not to keep them waiting on us. We walked down to the bay where the plane was ready and waiting. Ray was already on board and when we boarded, the jokes began. We were trapped at their mercy with their teasing for the entire ride home. Blaine looked around the plane.

"It appears to me that you are jealous. Looks like I am the only one among us getting any?"

I shook my head and elbowed him. *"That will not stop the abuse."* I was sure Blaine, and I would choose better roommate's next time. We arrived and Mica, Amanda and Jacquelyn met us in the cave. "Looks like the girls missed

317

us." Jerry pointed out. We pulled in and unloaded the plane, taking all the gear up to the vehicles at the top of the stairs. It was good to be back on the island and to have women around me again, and especially Amanda, where I could just think to her, and she answered in our thoughts without interruption we had a lot to get caught up on, then I had to repeat it to the others, anyway. Once we got back to the house.   I was excited to love on that damn cat. He was happier to see me. He kept meowing and rubbing on me in circles as he followed me throughout the house as to tell me of his days without me.

It was lunchtime, and Mica had prepared a feast for us in the enormous kitchen. We all sat around the bar and let her, and the others serve it up. She had made her famous chicken soup with homemade noodles, and fresh homemade cinnamon rolls. The house smelled amazing. Jacqueline seemed very excited, more so than I have ever seen her. In conversation, she had mentioned she had something to show me after we cleaned up lunch.

"Is everyone done? I have something to share with all of you in the library. We all filed into the library where on the wall hanging above the fireplace was a large oil painting of a woman all dress in red leather armor. As I stared in disbelief, it was me. Well, not me. It was my grandmother, I assumed. But it could have been me. Jacquelyn interjected into my thoughts.

"Dee, do you know who this is?"

"It's… my grandmother." I said with uncertainty.

"It looks so much like me."

"We were renovating the library at the college, and we found a secret room in the attic. The contractor was fixing the ceiling and when he broke through; he could see it was on the upper floor. The electrician was above him and had just broken into the wall where he found the room. Then they looked for the hidden door in the back of a storage closet. They called me right away. I came over to the project, in this 10 x10 room where a trunk of journals and six oil paintings. Four men and one woman were all dressed in armor wielding shields with their coat of arms. And one portrait of all the original six Atlanteans. I couldn't believe how much it looked like Deedra. Lucky for us, the contractor is immortal, and the journals need to be in the right hands. It tells the story in your grandmother's words of the days that lead up to her death. Deedra, you will want to read through them. They will help you with your own destiny. The other paintings are just as grand as those of the ancients that used to reside on the cartel council. The paintings are thirty-six by sixty-two, framed in 24 carat gold filigree.

My eyes rolled to the back of my head and as I stood there, the voice that came out was not mine. The professor step up and addressed Suzzallo is it you?

"Yes, I was the only woman with the gifts of the ancient. I had fallen in love with George, one of the greatest immortal chieftains of the indigenous tribes. Though my gifts were greater than all of theirs put together. George and I... were betrayed by one of our servants. The rules said we could not have sexual relationships with the leaders of the tribes. We had to show our strengths, but you grandfather and I couldn't stay apart. We tried for many years, but the ancient passion boiled inside of us. We finally gave in to it. Rajani was furious. How dare I soil my genetic purity by sleeping with a tribal immortal? They were going to kill George if I didn't give up my quest to destroy all of them, so I allowed them to murder me in exchange for his life. I could not let them destroy the man I loved. Then George Ghosted in. Suzzallo, I was destroyed without you. I lived a very long and lonely life. She drifted out of my body and walked over to him. They both ghosted away. I could feel my knees give way and I hit the floor. Blaine was there holding me in his arms. "Dee, are you alright?"

"Um, ya, I think so that was. Eerie, are they gone?"

"Yes, it seems so."

"How do you feel?"

"Good, alone with my own thoughts."

"Is she gone now?"

"I'm not sure."

Jacqueline spoke up and turned to me.

"I read part of the first journal that was written to you by your grandmother, who must have been able to see the future… That is why you have been brought here to take her place."

"Oh Great! I'm supposed to be what… the queen of the immortal world. They need to give up now. Turn themselves over to the cartel and just give up. There is no way I can do the things my grandmother did. I did not sign up for any ruling of the kingdoms…. or of the immortal world. How about we vote in a new group of leaders and behave like we are living in the 21st century?"

I stepped out of the library and out onto the porch. I sat on the porch swing and as I was watching the sunset. I thought to myself.   *"What if she took all of her powers with her and I am not strong enough to do anything?* About then I heard her say,

"Thank you Deedra. I am with the man I love, and you have all my gifts. I just borrowed them to protect you until you were ready. You are and will always be the best of all the ancients. Your gifts have been selected carefully and left for you to live your life as you see fit. Remember, we will be watching. Avenge my death. I love you…. "

Then silence…. I just sat there wondering what I was going to tell everyone else. Finally, I concluded. Nothing, for now. I just wanted to watch the sunset holding DC in my lap, swinging back and forth. Blaine came out, slowed the swing and sat next to me and put his loving arms around me. My heart skipped a beat. I leaned in the warmth of his arms and just sat with him as we watched the sunset together.

"Dee, so what are you thinking? "I should read the journals and find out about my family and how this might help us end this reign of terrible men. I am afraid of failing and one of us getting hurt."

"The temper thing was it her, or is that really you?"

"A little of both of us, I am afraid."

Chapter 12

The Journals

Knowing that my grandmother's journals were in the library, I was hoping to get some perspective on what my destiny truly was. After dinner, which was silent. I went into the library. Fire was blazing; the room was warm. The old trunk they found sat next to the shelf on the left. Opening it up, I could smell leather with a hint of fir. I picked up one journal. Flipped open to first entry.

June 1, 1909,

The sun was warm on my face as the trees and the flowers were coming out to welcome in the summer months. I'm in Seattle with the leaders of the immortals dealing with some problems that had arisen with a band of young immortals with some unusual new talents. The World's Fair is here and made a brilliant cover because of the thousands of people visiting from all over the world. Seattle's Underground city that happened in 1889 after the fire destroyed twenty-five city blocks approximately 120 acres. The immortals had taken it over during the pneumonic plague in 1907. Seattle's politicians condemned the underground city and sent all its deplorable citizens there. It filled up with the ill and abandoned humans. Soon the immortals saw profit in the humans and were less fortunate and started moving in and used the area for speakeasies, gambling, opium dens, and alcohol production. During prohibition, they set up a transportation network up from Portland to Seattle. The homeless that were left from the plague worked for the renegades in distribution of goods and services of the immortals above Seattle's underground. It was the beginning of the Renegades.

There was also a group of gifted immortals had come to this area many years ago and they became some of the Native Indians gods. We were here to check on the immortal's population and deal with the renegades.

June 2, 1909, I went out riding in the woods and came across a meadow. There was a man walking in the woods, just the other side of the meadow along the tree line. Tall and dark, with the most magnificent features. I could tell he was an immortal by the energy he was emitting. My horse slowed as we approached. I could see in his eyes that he was drawn to me. I gently skimed his thoughts. It amazed me at the passion of his heart and how he had been living with the mortals as a spiritual guide. His name was George. He was of Duwamish-Muckleshoot descent, some of the most powerful of our kind. He was dressed in the soft leather and the aroma of his skin was calling to me. Forbidden to contact the immortals of this region, but I could not stop the passion I was feeling. I have heard the ancient stories of finding one true love for all eternity, but I never thought after all these years I would ever be exposed to such a gift of passion. I was so surprised at how out of control my feelings were.

I turned my horse around, left as fast as the horse could carry me back to town, where I was late in meeting the others to pronounce judgment on the immortal we disciplined. We voted three to two to put the accused to death for breaking the rules. I never voted to kill anyone. In my mind, I was still in the meadow. I wasn't even present... The others made plans to take the train back to Chicago, and I wanted to stay for a while longer. The fair was a great excuse.

June 7th, 1905

I stayed behind and was looking at all the furs that had been brought in on the shops. Was having a seal fur coat made from handpicked furs. I was waiting to be sized by the store tailor. Then I heard the doorbell ring when I looked up. There he was again, in the same trading post.

He was trading beaver pelts he had trapped, there were so beautiful. I had to have another coat made of the beaver pelts he brought in. He introduced himself to me as George Lee. He took my hand and laid a kiss up on it. We stepped to the back of the tailor shop so not to be noticed.

He stepped forward, wrapped his arm around my waist, and pulled me close. It was very improper, but I was lost in the passion. Laying my hand on his firm chest through his leathers, He lifted my chin up and leaned into kiss me. Soft sensual kiss with his tongue pushing into my mouth. It made me breathless. We pulled back, both of us shocked at how far we had let our passion go in public. I stepped away. "Ahem, my name is Suzzallow. I saw you in the meadow. Sorry, I left without talking to you. I was late for a meeting."

"Could you feel the pull of the passion?"

"Yes, it was so strong it scared me. I am part of the original immortals. We are not a loud to associate with the mundane. It is a death sentence. I am the only woman in our group. They watch me." He told me more about himself. We talked for an hour before the tailor interrupted to get my measurements.

I asked why he lived so simply. He shrugged... "I needed little more than a roof over my head and food to fill his stomach. I enjoyed helping my mortal friends."

"The mortal tribes are outlandish. We can never mix our immortal blood. You understand? That is a death sentence." He just smiled at me. "Can I meet with you again?"

"I am not sure. I am being watched. Rajani doesn't trust that I have moral judgment. He thinks he is saving me for him one day."

"Is he?"

"Oh, heavens no, I would never consider him to be my mate. I don't care how pure his blood line is. He is a jackass. Sorry for the un-lady like words, but that best describes him."

I must have sounded uppity to him with the mixing of our blood lines comment. Feeling strangely bewildered after seeing him again. Heading for the door, I turned.

"If I can get away without being followed..., how will I contact you?"

"I am here every Thursday with my furs."

I left and went back to the hotel. I couldn't stop thinking about this simpleton. How it infuriated me to think a simple immortal intrigued me. I must put him out of my head. and Yet I couldn't. He had great powers of persuasion and he was mentally the strongest man I had ever known. Could inflict such great pain, and yet he never used his gifts for his own profit. He lived a mortal life, and he worked alongside the common people. What purpose could this serve? Without knowing what was driving such an immortal man to the basics of society when he could have had a rich life with the wealth of Seattle at his feet. I had to leave Seattle and go back home.

July 20, 1905, I am back in Chicago. I have brought my extra fur coats back with me. I had to wait until winter, but when I pulled them out to wear, I would be the envy of all my friends.

July 26, 1905, Council met. All had attended with Adrasteia, Damayanti, Deimos, Govia and Rajani. He was the head of the council. He made most of the decision. They left me around, the only woman, because they need my special gifts, to read the future and to see into the minds of all they found to be an enemy.

July 28, 1905, I saw last night they were at the end of their time they were dying. I saw the renegades sent the youngest and strongest to destroy them. The end of our reign is coming.

Then I flipped through to

September 2, 1915, I am in Seattle again. The city is now a growing metropolis. I wonder if the meadow is still there. I took a horse ride, trying to remember the location of the meadow. Reaching an opening in the trees, I heard a man's voice. I scanned the woods. I saw the sunlight shine on the edge of the tree line. There he stood, frozen in time, still as mystifying as he was 10 years ago. I stopped when I got to the meadow. He walked over to me. The closer he got, the harder it was to focus on his thoughts and when he reached me. He put out his hands and offered to help me down off the horse. The rush of desire I had for a perfect stranger fascinated me. I allowed him to place his hands around my waist and set me down in front of him. I was so close to his chest the hardness of my nipples skimed his rock-hard abs. All my senses where electrified. He was taking over my mind and body. As I was about to be killed in the future, I knew my future was bad. I had already sensed it. I want to taste life and live in this world before I die, for I had truly wasted my time here on earth. His strength was amazing. We walked for a time into the woods. I started the questions. Curious, why is life so simple? He responded with kindest, soft, joyful voice I have ever heard. I wanted to live the life of the mundane mortal because I learned long ago, they live life to the fullest. Their life span is so short for them. They take in the world and all its beauty. I had found myself early on not appreciating the simple things in life and not being grateful for all that I had because there are so many less fortunate. The mortals have a faith that I found to be intriguing. We immortals live too long. We gave up our souls. He stopped with a look in my direction. I could read his thoughts. He wondered if I thought he might have gone mad. …

I reached up and touched his face. He leaned in close, his breath touching my skin. I closed my eyes. His lips touched mine. Gentle, at first, then with a hunger. He took my hand and led me to a teepee in the woods. A fire burned in the middle. Pelts cover the ground. We continued to kiss. He pulled off his leathers. First his top. I stood there, admiring his body. With his broad shoulders, narrow waist, hair on his chest made an arrow to the significant bulge in his pants. I ran my hands down his chest. I rubbed on the outside of the leathers. Running my hand over his bulge, un-tying his leather pants, letting his unit spring free. He was well endowed; I placed my hand around his shaft. Soft skin met my hand with a hard core. He was warm in my hand. His shaft grew harder and larger. He spun me around and untied my dress, then corset dropping them to the pelts. I stepped out of the hoops and pressed my body tightly to his and kissed him. He pulled up from the kiss. At arm's length, he finished undressing me. Standing naked in front of him, his eyes wondered the full length of my body landing on my full breast. Pulling me back into his arms, whispering into my ear…

"I have to be inside you." He picked me up and laid me on the fur bedding. Placing his arms on each side of my head, holding his body over me. Lowered his head, pulled one nipple, then the other, into his mouth. Sucking and twirling his tongue. I moaned his name. I felt him spread my legs wide open. Then his member was at my core. Pressing so gently at first. Nudging an inch at a time, then a little more. Allowing me to adjust to his size. Slow yet meticulously inch at a time until he filled me. Then pulling out, leaving the tip of his shaft just inside me, then pushing in again until I was full. Repeating this… harder and harder until I shattered in to a million pieces, seeing stars. I laid there in his arms. We made love all afternoon. Naked, we walk to the falls to wash off.

April 17, 1913, my love for George is out of control. I have bought a home here where I frequently visit in Seattle. I informed the other ancients I will stay for 6 months this time. I love the spring and summers out here and I'm 3 months pregnant. No one could find out I was with George's baby. The council of ancients will put us to Death. Rajani will not allow me to be tainted by another. The next 6 months passed too quickly. I delivered Anthony to this world, and I knew as soon as he was here, I would have to leave him with the love of my life and move them to a safe place that no one could ever find them. My future was already insurmountable, but I couldn't let that spill over on the two loves of my entire existence. It horrified me I would never see my son reach adulthood and never know the man I left behind in the mountains of North Carolina to disappear from this earth to protect our love that we created in our son. They suspect the many trips it has taken me to Seattle over the last ten years.

Flipping further in the journal.

September 30, 1925, my servant betrayed me. My anger got the best of me. She is dead. They couldn't do anything to stop me.

October 25, 1925, Rajani has captured George. He tried to come see me and I cannot help him, or they will kill him for sure. I will surrender to Rajani to prevent George from being killed. He must live to take care of our son and let them do as they wish with me. I give up…

It was the last entry in the journal. But then I began flipping back.

February 2, 1913, I found out I was with child. I will have to stay here and have the child. I will go to hiding. No one must know.

May 25, 1913, George, and I have disappeared into the Olympic Forest to wait until I have his child and he will have to raise him here in the West.

I was skipping forward.

September 13, 1914, our son Anthony is delivered to us. I have to leave tomorrow. I have been gone too long and I can see my days are numbered.

June 2, 1913, I saw my death at the hand of Rajani. He was so angry to have found out that I would love such a mundane immortal and not him. He always fancies himself as my mate. I never fancied him at all. To die at his hand is a small price to pay to save my family and the love of my life. I can only thank George for helping me learn how to be alive.

June 6, 1913, I have seen my future and the future of my granddaughter that will follow in my footsteps. I know I do not have the strength to fight this uncontrollable passion that has ignited my soul. Before they suspect my body is changing, I have to return to him. I am not even showing, but I know I will soon.

I shut the journals. I could only guess the rest of the story was all about the power of the one Rajani and his jealousy for my grandfather. He was angry at not having my grandmother's love and affection. Who was the woman that betrayed her? When did the renegades take their place at the top? It appeared back in 1920 during prohibition. That was their primary income for bootlegging and running speakeasies in the underground city of Seattle.

I would have to dig further tomorrow to find out who it was. This wasn't helping me out because I was tired. I knew more about my grandparents' love. I understood the passion they had for one another because I have found that passion in Blaine. But I found nothing that might help me change the Cartel of today. Standing alone in the library staring at the picture of my grams

"What do you want me to do?"

I turned and walked out into the kitchen and Jerry was there cleaning up the dinner dishes and Amanda was watching him; they were in a moment. I skimed through their thoughts on my way by. Jerry was in denial and Amanda was in love. Ray was with Jacquelyn in front of the fire in the great room, and Jake was flirting with Mica. I wanted so badly to skim their thoughts and see if she felt anything for him. Oh, what the hell. On my way upstairs, I tried to peek into her mind. Hearing nothing… her wall around her mind was solid. Oh… well… Her feelings are her business, not mine. I just want Jake to be happy. But I promised I would not intrude on his thoughts.

I opened the door to the bedroom, and Blaine was reading in front of the fire. I went and sat with him. He stopped and looked up and asked,

"Having any luck going through the journals?"

"Mostly… she describes some history of Seattle, its underground population. My grandmother's passion for my grandfather is eating her up. They had a son that she left with George to raise alone in my hometown. That makes Anthony their son, my grandfathers, great grandfather. The beginning of the Cartel and the raising of the renegades. They have been in charge for 100 years. But nothing that would help me put a stop to them today. I think I will look further in the morning. Would you like to help? If all of us take a journal, maybe we will find the weakness of them."

"Why don't you put that book away and come to bed." Blaine lay down the book and followed me to bed. He held me all night even though his thoughts drove me crazy. I finally blocked them out and fell asleep.

I was dreaming now. It was safe and warm in this dream. The woods of my mother's home are in North Carolina. I was walking hand in hand with George, but he was younger. He was very handsome. I could see a little boy running in front of us. It's not me… I gasped… I'm my grandmother. I could feel all her love for them and the enormous sadness that she was feeling was so heartbreaking I had to wake up abruptly. I couldn't take the strength of her despair that she was feeling. How was the vision of the despair of my grandmother going to help me? What was I supposed to do? I looked over at the clock. It was 2:00 am, and I got up and went to the library. The truth had to be here somewhere in these journals. A letter fell to the floor after I grabbed one for the bottom of the pile. I went and sat on the couch in front of the slow embers of the fire. I put a couple more logs on the embers and the fire roared back to life. The fire was warm in the library's darkness. The moon was hidden behind the clouds, making the room very dark except for the firelight.

I opened the envelope, took out what looked to be a letter, and read it out loud.

My darling granduaghter, I hav waited solong for you to find out the truth of my existence. To learn why you inherit so many of the gifts of the ancients. I have seen the destruction of the ancients by the renegades after my death, the problem being there is one of us left, and Rajani is still alive in the depths of the Seattle underground. He rules from there and makes all the decisions as he has done for hundreds of years. Dethroning him is the only way to make sure the Renegades don't repeat history. Now.... Your council is very respectful of the ancient laws. They do not take advantage of their gifts for selfish pleasure. Rajani is very dangerous. Do not mistake his gifts but you are now his equal as I was.... His only weakness is he must touch you to read your thoughts. You must find him and destroy him, not in vengeance that I feel as I am alive within you, but to save you and all the immortals that are left. Your numbers are decreasing because of the inbreeding with the mortals, but you are the only one of pure blood line that will have the strength to defeat our enemies. It is your legacy and all your friend's future. Choose wisely, my granddaughter, for your life will influence many who are alive today and reshape their life for the future. I am so sorry I left all of this on your shoulders, but remember I am with you until then very end..."

All my love, your grandmother, Suzzallo

Well, that's just perfect as tears slide down my face.

"Do you think you can give me a guide on how I'm supposed to do this?" I yelled into the library.

At that moment, the book on the couch next to me fell on the floor, face up. There was a page with drawings on it. I picked up the book, and it appeared to be drawings of

the underground city, a perfect map with each block that went on for many pages with minor notes of hidden alleys and slip through hidden doors for shortcuts. As I studied the book, the sun was coming up, and I was not sure how much of this I should share. Although I knew if I didn't and I was wrong about sharing the information with the group, my Grandfather George would alert Jerry with some kind of vision. I took the book and the letter to the kitchen. It was about 4:30 am. Started the coffee, and I treated everyone with my quiche. I don't think they even knew I could cook. I got the ingredients out of the refrigerator and used the leftover vegetables. We had goose eggs from the Saturday market, and they always made the quiche rise taller and goose eggs were rich in flavor, making the quiche more delicious. I found four fresh cheeses. I shredded the cheese and mixed it all together, whipped the eggs and cream with salt and pepper, then blended the eggs and cheese mixture poured it over the veggies and mushrooms in a large cake size glass dish. Setting the oven to 350 degrees and the timer for 45 minutes, I shoved dish into the oven to bake. I place bacon on a rack inside of a cookie sheet and placed it next to the quiche in the oven. I was working on sour dough biscuits, got them all cut out on a pan; Letting them rest; Decided in a hollandaise sauce that would complement the eggs. The pantry had a powder mix on the shelf. Melting the butter in the microwave. Jake came to the kitchen.

"What smells sooooo good…?" His dimples were showing in a big grin of mockery, about my ability to prepare a meal.

"I didn't know you knew what a kitchen was. You do cook?"

I flung him a dirty look, hitting him with the dish towel off the counter. He raised his hand palms out in a defensive stance, and he backed up slowly and sat at the bar, watching me.

"Awh, yes, I cook." I smiled.

The rest of my new family appeared from the other parts of the house.

"Good morning, Wow, you cook!" Thoughts from Amanda made me smile. Then the arms that wrapped around me had me melting, toes curling, almost forgot I was cooking.

"Can I help you with anything, my love?"

Then he leaned over and kissed my neck. I turned to him, stepped away and pointed my finger to behind the bar with Jake. He gave me his pouty face.

"You, Mr. Insatiable, can help by sitting on the other side of the bar so I can focus and finish breakfast, and not you."

The others laughed and teased him.

"Maybe you're losing your touch, old man." Jake boosted, as he loved to tease Blaine because of his extreme gift to persuade. Not very many could resist him. But with a few tricks, I had learned to resist. I was very proud of that.

 "So, Dee…. What is with all the cooking?" I smiled, adding the biscuits to the oven for the last 15 minutes so all the food would be done at the same time. The hollandaise sauce was hot. I left on the burner to keep warm.

"I wanted to give back to all of you because you're my new family. Even though you did it in a mendacious manner, I wanted to say thank you for saving me. You took you sweet time, before you told the truth about my immortality. Amanda already knew I was going to show them my newest find in the journal. Everyone ate and seemed so happy I hated to dampen the mood with the letter and the journals of the underground. I cleared my throat to speak and then I could see I had all of their attention.

"I have found this in the journals. Ray, Jake, and the other will want to look at this journal. It seems to be maps of the underground."

 Ray grabbed it out of my hand and laid it on the counter.

 "Let me see. I have never seen these areas in any of my surveillance films. Nor Have I seen any of these doors while I was undercover down there. I work years mapping the blocks of burnt areas of the cities underground. Are you sure that is what this is?"

"No." Shaking my head and laughing, "I'm not sure of

anything. All I know is when asked out loud in the library last night how this helps me? The book slides off on the floor."

"So, you're telling us you think this journal is a sign?"

"Ok, yes, I think it is a sign from my grams."

There is also a letter. After they all read the letter. Then they all started staring at me. Ray was the first to bow his head, then Jake and even Blaine.

"What! No! Stop with the bowing." I hissed… No bowing, which is not why I gave you the letter."

Jacquelyn spoke first, her soft voice and unthreatening as she approached me and put her arm around me to make me feel less weird about the staring the bowing of heads.

"When our ancestors shared with us stories of 'The One,' we didn't understand what that meant. Not really. Your royalty, my dear, that's all… we are wondering how you feel about that. You must forgive some of our ways of respect" I could feel the anger brewing under my skin. I didn't like being labeled. I didn't want the responsibility that royalty had tied to it.

"I feel nothing about being of royal descent, because it is an archaic title."

I continued to hiss at the idea. I turned away from all of them. Blaine came over and put his arms around my
340

waist. I could feel the anger leaving me and I regained my composure.

Deedra, in his soft comforting voice. "What we are trying to convey to you is now you will be the head of the immortal council with no argument of the others to your blood line and this letter is all the proof we will need. They cannot deny you your seat at the council. Where you can help to form our laws and uphold our values.

"What about Rajani?" I scowled.

"How would your grandmother from the past know he is still alive today?" Ray argued.

"Because she is an aberrational ghost that can travel and spy on the living. I know you might find this hard to believe, however I think she or I wrote this today. I am trying to explain the past couple of hours. Grams is my inner warrior and a ghost."

"What does that mean?"

"When I was dreaming it was about her, I was her and then I woke up and went to the library. I notice laps in time after I got to the library or when I remember getting there. I looked at the clock as I left the bedroom. It was 2:00 am and when I got to the library, it was 3:00 am. I picked up that journal and an hour had passed. What happened to that hour?"

"You need to know she is inside of me, anyway. Her spirit is there, and she can take me over easily. When I would talk of the inner warrior, and I now know it is Suzzallo..." I paused and looked to see all their faces.

"We, I mean, grams and I or me, if you prefer have been having many conversations with George. You know the ghost of my many times great grandfather and Suzzallo were lovers. I don't think George knows she is here within me. She can block all others' thoughts but mine. No one can know she is here. My life may depend on it."

Jake was the first to lighten the mood.

"Well, that explains a ton. The way you move, the knowledge of Sai and sometimes the aggressive attitude, I'm glad to know you're not as gifted as I thought that you're getting help. I never suspected the warrior Suzzallo, though you can read of her in many of the ancient books. No more reading. We need to put together a plan of attack. Please, I must destroy Rajani before we will be free of the corruption from the cartel. The room went silent again. Blaine moved in and calmed me with his touch. Ray and Mica were now studying the book. I can pull up the city sewer blueprints, and we can try to overlay this old mapped to what we know exists today and see if we can find this cavern where Rajani lives. Amanda was already fast at work on the computer. She was pulling everything about the underground for the database and imprinting the old drawings over them. Sure enough, there are many secret passages and the entrance to the middle of the city

"Look here. One of them seems to be in the club behind the cellar wall. The rack is a doorway. Did any of you know that?"

Everyone looked back and forth at one another, and they all were shaking their heads no.

"Now what?"

I asked with impatience, but that wasn't really me. The impatient personality was all Suzzallo. I could feel her slide forward in my mind,

"Easy grams, my mind, remember you have to let me make these decisions."

She retreated to the back of my head. It was so weird I wasn't afraid of her, but her dominance was strong, and I knew it was intertwined with mine. How much power I really had without her was not so easy to figure out. Very little, I would guess. It was ok for now because I would need all of her strength and anger to defeat Rajani, warlord of the ancients.

"I have one question. I know you have told me before in gruesome detail how we are killed, But Rajani is an ancient. How exactly, do you really kill an ancient immortal? I thought we regenerated faster than any immortal and recovered. They all turned and looked at me, again making me very uncomfortable. Jacquelyn began the story as if she was giving a great lecture in the hall at the college. Once an immortal is down or injured, like shot, stabbed, blown up, on fire, etcetera…. You only have about thirty minutes before full regeneration takes place. We can heal most any injuries quickly making a full recovery, but if while we are weakened and down you can drain the blood out, chop off our head and cut out the heart, place them in separate containers like a tomb and they are lost forever. Then mummification can take place."

"Do you mean the mummies of the Egyptians are immortals that have died?"

"Yes, that was our way of making sure the mortals didn't know of our existence. Many of the stories that have been told over the thousands of years are to cover up our existence to preserve the Laws of the ancestors, not to interfere with the mortals' lives. To live among them in harmony was the law. Then came the Reign of your Rajani and the six of them, including your grandmother. They believed they were the privileged one and the superior to both immortal and mundane mortal, and they thought of themselves as gods among the rest of the world. They reigned over the land until late into the 1920s, yet you are telling me Rajani still lives. How is that possible? "

"I don't know. I'm just the messenger. Remember, I am

a small-town girl just looking to explain the unexplainable things that were happening to me and now I am in this supernatural realm and haven't got a clue."

"That's not what I meant. Could you allow Suzzallo to come forward so I could ask her some questions?"

Hmm, I thought for a moment and then I could feel her burst through the very front of my thoughts. It was my voice, but she was talking through me. It was strange to hear my voice, but they were not my words. She gave me her heavy Greek accent.

"Yes, my child, what do you wish to inquire about?"

"Suzzallo?"

"Yes, who else do you think you're talking to?"

In a superior tone that rattles the bookcase.

"Um... where is Deedra?"

"Oh, she is here. Do you wish to talk to her?"

"Um... No, that is ok. I was just startled... You took over so fast. Your legend is very well known among us who study about the ancients."

Suzzallo hung her head. "Yes, I suppose it is, but the last part of my life changed me. I mean, my love for George did. He valued the law to live in harmony and cherish the simple things in life. I am sure they didn't cover the change in me in the stories they shared. I Know I was a horrifying, shallow person to believe I was better than the rest of the world and somehow entitled to have more than anyone deserved. But George and his love for me transformed me to know that the greatest gift you can give is to give of yourself. I apologize for all the pain I have caused. I am hoping to set my wrong right with the help of all of you and my lovely granddaughter who reminds me so much of her grandfather. They all stood there with their mouths open as she and I looked around the room.

"Hey grams, your presence alone scares all of them to death. The fact I look like you makes it seem more real to them. Your essence alone has sent all their instincts into defense mode. It is an overload to them. Come back and let me talk now. You can tell me what you want them to know, and I will deliver your message. Your presence is too much."

I cleared my throat as I could feel her retreat to my subconscious. "It's all right. I'm back. She won't do that again. You all tensed up like you were ready to be slaughtered."

Blaine touched my arm again

"Dee, is it really you?"

"Yes, it is really me" I scanned the room in their thoughts

where images of the bloodbath my grandmother used to inflict before she would leave a room when she was questioned about anything. I shook my head.

"Oh…my…. God…" I whispered softly under my breath….

"I did not know she kept that part out of my head. She has a lot to make up for. No wonder her spirit has not rested in five-hundred years. By helping us rid the world of Rajani is how she plans to reach for her misgivings and her uncaring, unscrupulous behavior over the centuries. She was looking for forgiveness for her soul. Do any of you have questions for her? I will remain and just answer as she tells me. Jacquelyn stood and faced me.

"Not at this time Dee, we are all a little in shock and apologize for disturbing her."

Waving my hand at her.

"Oh, pish-posh… She owes all of you. Now I know what she has done over the ages. It helps explain a ton."

Chapter 13

The Underground

Hours later, Ray was still all in a huff over the new maps that I have found in the journals. He has Amanda and Mica working overtime trying to overlay the two maps he had of the underground city, covering twenty-five entire blocks and the hundred and twenty acres of burnt-out city. The computer program that Mica had was not working as well as they wanted it to, so Amanda tap into one of the older satellite and pulled up a map of the city and laid it over the newly drawn map from the pages of the journal. No one ever spoke of the underground city, and I was curious as to why? I asked.

"Ray, why has no one told me about the underground city before today?"

Ray paused and cleared his throat and looked at Blaine. The gaze was permission to speak in so many exchanged looks. Blaine gave a nod, and he spoke.

"The underground city is not a place for a lady. It is a place of evil and mayhem, thieves and thugs, gangs and drugs. Not a safe place for any law-abiding mortal or immortal these days. Mostly immortals and what were left of the renegades that were out of control roam it dark and dank streets."

"The underground is a need-to-know existence, and you didn't need to know."

Jake stepped up to join in the conversation.

"We decided it wasn't best for you to know about the stronghold of the cartel and the renegades until you were trained."

"You decided I wasn't privy to that information because I would go with none of you and check it out. I might give the cartel and the renegades exactly what they wanted… me."

"And I needed to be sure that you were ready to handle it without losing control."

 "You wanted to make sure I was in control of Suzzallo." Blaine jumped in. "We didn't even know that you were possessed by someone until just a few days ago, remember you called it your 'inner warrior'. Now she has a name and the rest of us have seen her as well."

"She won't be a problem anymore. I have made her sit in my subconscious, kind of a timeout."

"Until the next time she gets a bee in her bonnet and terrifies someone. Ask Ray, he lived through Suzzallo temper tantrums. Go ahead have him in enlighten you to your grandmother's mood swings."

"Jake, shame on you…."

I felt a little like they were ganging up on me. Amanda picked up on it right away and she growled at all of them.

"You need to leave Dee alone. She is doing the best she can with the destiny of life has given her. You are treating her like she is Suzzallo, and that's not fair. She is still our Deedra, remember?"

I was embarrassed that she felt the need to defend me, and I just got up and left the room.

"Oh, my dear Deedra, he is right about me. I used to leave many rooms bloody. I never really controlled my temper, I just let it happen and with my gifts, many suffered under my reign."

Ray looked at everyone. "This is getting us nowhere. Let's leave the past in the past. I suggest we decide on getting back to the city and see if these maps are correct. If they are, we have our own entrance into their world behind the wine rack on the east wall."

"Ok, you heard him. Let's move. We leave at first light."

Everyone packed. I was still sulking on the front porch. Blaine stepped on to the porch. "There you are." he came and sat next to me on the swing. "It was a little rough there. I'm sorry we just…" I place my hand in his.

"I know…. Suzzallo, she must have been really a horrifying person.

And with me looking just like her, it seems more real to all of you. I get it… Nonetheless, not my fault that a few ancient, genetically made me in her image. She even made that comment to me while Jake was going off. She told me she was atrocious."

"Well, let's say she wasn't the most patient of people. Not sure even narcissists really give her justice. She decided punishment based on whatever mood she was in."

"I saw the awfulness in all of your eyes as I let her move forward and take over my body. The images that you transmitted to me unknowingly were repulsive. That… will never happen again. I don't want any of you to be afraid of me." Tears filled my eyes. Then they ran down my cheeks. He reached up placing his hands on each side of my face and with his thumbs, wiped away my tears.

"I believe you, my love." when he touched me, that released

all the tension of the day.

"Everyone else is really sorry too Dee… they all feel just dreadful for being so prejudice over someone who has been dead over 100 years. It will take a little getting used to." I turned and smiled. They lived it, I only saw their memories, and I couldn't hold it against them. I stood up, looking into Blaine's eyes, holding out my hand. "We should go pack."

Back in our room, I went over to get the bags out of the closet. These days I left DC on the island. He loved it here, and I knew he would be safe. I could return as soon as all of this was done. I love it here and I thought it would be better than living above the bar and everyone else agreed. We just packed as though we were staying overnight in town. Blaine and Mica had hired some new people to manage the club in our absence. It helped keep the club open. The next morning at sunrise, we all gathered at the dock in the underground cavern, loaded up in the boat to head back to the city. Rays Chris-Craft was superlative. The ride across the sound was quiet. The seagulls and the puffins flew by, a couple of dolphins jumped in the water. A pod of killer whales breached. It almost made the appending terror go away and seemed more like a normal site seeing day. The rigs were waiting in the lot as we docked in Anacortes. They moored the boat there as needed. Jake had two new hires drive our rigs over last night. He told them to put dinner on his tab at the restaurant. It had taken a couple of hours to cross over from the island to Anacortes. Blaine and I took the Lexus. Jake, Ray, Amanda, and Mica took the Hummer back to the club. Jerry and Jaqueline had headed back earlier, the professor had a class to teach. They picked up the jeep at the dock. We arrived staying together for safety. It was warm out away from the ocean and the wind blew lightly across my face. I grabbed my bag and started in the front door of the club. As I approached the door, I stopped, knowing the renegades had been back looking for me. My sense of smell was very acute, and I was totally aware of the intensity of my other sense as well. Each of us had an odor.

The immortals had a sweeter fragrance than the mundane mortals. I had first noticed it with Blaine when I first met him. I had paid little attention until now. What is it? Blaine asked. "

 "We have had visitors recently." I saw they were here when I touched the door. Amanda ran past me into the club. I ran in after them in case there was trouble.

 Nothing and no one was in the club. I heard some noise up the stairs. "Jerry?" Amanda called out. "Yeah, I'm up here."

 "Oh, thank god." I let out a sigh. I wasn't ready for more drama today.

 "Hey Jerry, was anything off when you arrived?"

 "Not that I noticed." He was already coming back down to

the club.

"I feel the renegades have been here recently. I felt it when I touched the front door and then I smelled the scent of them when we came in the door. Jake and Jerry stood there and stared at me.

"Dee, are your senses increasing? It seems strange you know odors of the others and the touch of a door thing? Is that a new sense?"

I paused for a moment, which seemed a long time as my mind separated the question and looked back through my memory of doing any of the same things.

"I think you must be right. I didn't even think about it. It just came to me when I touched my hand to the door. I just knew the renegades had been here."

I sat down for a minute thinking about how advanced my abilities had come and now were taking on their own life inside of me. I didn't want anyone to be afraid of me.

"Just some more superhero stuff. No need to worry. It will come in handy sometime soon." They laughed. I hoped they would just ignore it. I went upstairs and unloaded my bag. The smell of them was everywhere. They were looking for something. I went down to get Ray. We need to look for the door in our cellar now. He understood, and we went to the basement cellar. It smelled like wine and there was a sweet smell of whiskey or rum. I walked along in

354

the dark. I could see perfectly. Ray was fumbling around, trying to find the light. I got to the back wall where I saw a loose brick. I reached up and pulled out an old brick in the wall. Inside of the brick was a button I pushed on it. The wall with the wine rack on it went the full length of the wall. It wiggled and rattled. The bottles were making the sound of music as they clinked together. Then the shelf split. It moved out about three feet, then they slid sideways. A cloud of dust rolled into the air, and cobwebs hung in the opening off the shelves. Ray got the lights on and came towards me with his mouth open.

"Awh ah Dee, umm…, how did you know about that? He pointed towards the opening in the wall.

"I didn't know. I saw a loose brick. Maybe she is guiding me."

"Oh! You mean Suzzallo."

"Um hmm" biting my lower lip. I looked down; afraid I was scaring him again. He picked up on my shame. Put his finger under my chin raised it up until we were eye level.

"Dee, it's Ok, it just takes a little getting used to. There is no shame on your part. You have done nothing to earn that shame. "He put his arm around me to comfort me. Jake and the rest came downstairs when they heard the racket, to see what caused the rumbling in the floor upstairs.

"Wow, you got the doorway or wall in the cellar to the

underground opened just as the journals had said." Jake walked over, pushed the cobwebs out of the way, and started down the steps in a very narrow hall. The musty smell of the sewer and smoke wafted up from below. They went about 20 ft and stopped at another door. Jake put his shoulder into the door the corner appeared stuck. He pushed harder and the door open slowly. It opened into a bigger room. Jake called out, "Hey can you bring a flashlight down please? Mica handed the flashlight to me, and I went down the stairs. I didn't need the light. I saw fine without it. When I got to Jake, I looked around the room before he turned to make a sweep with the light. I had already made sure no one was waiting for us in the dark. I hesitated to let him know I could see without the flashlight, my gifts were changing and getting stronger. I didn't want them to know anything anymore. I could still picture the horror I saw in their eyes when Suzzallo talked to them as she talked through me. I know they just aren't sure they can trust me. It makes me very sad and puts me into a difficult situation. Jake found the light switch on the wall at the bottom of the stairs and turned on the light. The room was lined with racks of bottles of whiskey and rum. They were covered in a thick film of dust and cobwebs. They had been there many years. Jake was excited because he found an old bottle of Scotch and he had been looking for it for centuries. The shelves were stuffed with wooden crates with labels on them such as Jim Beam, Jack Daniels sour mash whiskey, Old Forester, Old crow.

Bottles in tubes read, Whipple Creek Corn whiskey, Mac Calhan, DEW Irish Whiskey, the one Jake is holding, said Little Taylor Company, Portland, Oregon.

"What is this place, Jake?"

 "Well, it appears to be a holding room to disperse whiskey, rum and scotch during prohibition and someone forgot this room after the fires."

   "Lucky for us, Ray spouted." I had never seen him so happy. Blaine came in and smiled in awe, like a kid in a candy store.

"Who knew when we bought this place all those years ago, not only one of the finest wine cellars in Seattle, but all this to boot?" Blaine was as excited as the rest of the boys. I cleared my throat

 "Ok, back to earth. Where is the door out of here into the underground city?"

They looked at me as though I had just ruined their party. Jake looked puzzled as he turned and looked at each wall carefully. It appeared there was no way out. Dee, do your abilities allow you to find the opening?"

"Not sure what abilities you think I'm getting. But no, I don't see a door. But I might sense people on the other side of the wall. This time, I had to focus on my hearing. I listened with impressive control. I could hear movement outside the left wall. As I moved around the room, I touched the walls. Nothing, then a soft faint noise of men talking. I stopped. I was about 20 feet in on the furthest wall from the stairs. Brushing the wall with my hand. When the dust settled, you could see where the opening was bricked up. Jake asked if I could see on the other side of the wall. I hesitated to answer. I took in a deep breath and blew it out with a heavy sigh. Laughing at him under my breath.

"I can't see through the wall like superman if that is what you're asking. But I hear them passing by. I think it is an alleyway. I can hear people passing by no one seem to stop."

Jake said with enthusiasm.

"Great, let us know when it is quiet."

"Blaine, do we have a sledgehammer around here?"

"Ray, we are going to need a metal door to put in after we make the opening. Maybe the old salvage yard. Make sure it is solid so we can secure our position. They left looking for the tools and the door we needed to make this work. Hours passed. I wasn't sure what time it was, but it had got quiet in the alleyway. Ray swung the fifteen-pound sledgehammer with little effort and broke the fragile bricks into a pile with one blow of the hammer. Jake and Blaine got the door in place and with little or no time they had the opening secure. The doorway to our side had a heavy iron shaft as wide as the door that swung into place so no one could enter. We opened the door and looked down the alley both ways. The alley was narrow and had twelve-foot brick walls with no doors except the one we just made. The alley went for two-hundred feet both ways and seemed to open into streets on both sides. You could see bodies in the dark walking back and forth on both sides of the alley. The scent of the renegades, their sweaty, musky, unpleasant smell of unlikable immortals. I cringed at their odor. It was so strong. Jake looked at me

"Are you Ok, what is it?"

"Can't you smell them? Their odor is so awful."

"Awful how? With the strangest look on his face, as though he knew I was evolving. I looked down again. Shaking my head, I have to remember they can't know how much more I have changed. I cleared my throat to speak, and it was dry and scratchy.

"It's nothing." Jake turned and put his hands on my shoulders. "You have to be honest with me. I will not judge you. Have all six of your senses increased?"

"Yes, please don't tell Blaine and the others you have noticed my mutation. You were all so afraid of me it breaks my heart."

"It's just between you and me, but you must tell me everything that is happening to you now."

"Well… when we got back to the club, remember I told you they had been in the club?"

"Yes."

"I smelled them. They smell different from us. We have hints of vanilla and almonds and are sweet to the senses, all different but sweet. And the Renegades have the smell of sweat and musky stench, like going into a men's locker room only ten times as potent. It is very distasteful to me and hard to be around. It truly gives me a headache, as if I am allergic to their scent."

"What else?" He looked into my eyes to make sure I would tell him everything.

"It seems all of my senses are very acute now: hearing, sight, smell, taste and touch. The way I move, I feel more like a cat, graceful and aware of my surroundings more than a human. It is the only way I can describe it."

"Are you leaving anything out?" He used his authorities' voice. It made me feel like a little girl that had just done something wrong and now I had to confess.

"Jake, I am changing as we speak with new abilities, evolving into a warrior, I think. It just keeps coming. I don't even know what is happening until I am using one of these new senses. I don't need the flashlight anymore. Can see perfectly in the dark as if I were seeing for the first time. The figures in the alley, I can flawlessly see every line on their face, the smell of the close they have on, if they are innocents or if they are part of the cartel. It is like a computer in my head, narrowing in on them and passing judgment. My mind seems to work at a faster pace. My thoughts and my reactions to anything are much faster than it has ever been. No second-guessing any of my decisions on how to continue. I just know. All of it is very natural. I think that's it for now."

 Jake just stood there. I could tell he was trying to control his emotion, yet I could see his mind and he was amazed and afraid.

"Jake, you're afraid of me."

"Dam it… Dee, stay out of my head."

"I don't control that anymore, either. It is another feature that just comes to me."

 Jake looked profoundly serious.

"All I can say is I'm glad you're on our side."

 In my sarcastic humor, I muttered.

"Great, that makes me feel better."

Then intensely I looked at Jake,

"No one can know. If you're afraid of me, they won't be able to deal with their feelings about my newest abilities.

Do you understand me? I will leave."

"No… No… Dee, you cannot possibly think we would let you go alone into the city or anywhere alone. We are your team."

You couldn't stop me if that is what I decide to do. You know that now, don't you?"

 "I guess I do, but I beg of you to let us work together. It will destroy Blaine if anything happens to you."

"I know that. It is why I haven't left. I could never do that to him and the others. I don't want the others to think I have let Suzzallo take over and be frightened of me."

Jake looked me in the eye and smiled, placed his hand on my shoulder.

"It will remain our secret for now."

"You promise."

"Yes, Deedra I will keep it just between you and me."

I sighed with a heavy heart that I had to keep this from Blaine, but I knew it was for the best.

"Thanks." We both turned and went back upstairs to the club. Jake had grabbed the bottle of Scotch when we hit the bar. He opened it and poured himself a glass. He swirled the gold liquid in the bottom of a barrel glass, raised to his lips and sipped and then sat the glass down while he savored the taste.

"Oh…uhm…awh… he sighed. That is excellent."

Standing in the silence alone, I could read his thoughts about how worried he was for all of us, and then Mica came into the room. Jake's thought scrambled. I watched as she walked behind the bar. She leaned in close to Jake's ear and whispered. "Do you have a glass of that for me?" Then she reached out and picked up his glass, pressed the glass against her lips. She sipped, taking a small taste, and then she made the same delicious noises Jake had made.

 "Umm. oh, this is marvelous and so smooth. "It was such an intimate act. I just stood perfectly still, and she hadn't noticed me in the shadows. I stepped into the light, and she jumped.

"Dee, where in the hell did you come from?" I could see I startled her.

"I have just been standing here awhile." I was now silent in my movement, just like a cat. Jake turned to Mica.

 "Dee and I have been in the sub-cellar where I brought out this fine bottle of aged whisky, talking about our next move, haven't we, Dee?" I nodded

 "She was probably deep in thought. That is why she seemed so quiet and why you hadn't noticed her. I looked at him and smiled. I knew he was protecting my secret the best way he could, and he also acknowledged that this was another change. Who would've thought I could be so quiet? My grandfather used to comment on how I walked so heavily. It seemed like a lifetime ago when I left North Carolina in search of the truth. I just wanted to be in love and happy in Blain's arms on the Island in the beautiful white house of my dreams. I wondered if that was ever going to be possible now.

Chapter 14

The Old World of the underground

I wondered the next morning what the underground city looked like. What kind of goods did the marketplace have? Was it a town just like the upper part of the City of Seattle, or was it like going back in time, or a much different place than the world above? I would soon find out we were going to make a trip in to see if the journal maps matched up. We needed to make sure when we made our moved, we would have all our escape routes down. Also, know all the shortcuts back to the club. Jake wasn't taking any chances, and neither was Ray. The rest of us relied on them to make the military planning and to keep us all safe. We are scheduled to go at the same time as it was last night after midnight when the alley wasn't so busy. I needed some fresh air, so I headed up to the rooftop and sat down on the patio furniture that was there. The sun was out today. It was late Indian summer, about 80 degrees, with the sun high in the sky and the smell of the salty air was refreshing. Mica and Amanda had planted some Jasmine on the wall that surrounded the rooftop when the wind blew through it. The sweet smell swirled and circled my senses. I closed my eyes and dreamed of another time when I first met all of them. Blaine with his intensity and the passion we have for one and other, that is where I wanted to be today. Leaving all the others to make the plans for whatever danger we were about to be in soon. Blaine, I thought to myself and as if I had called him to the roof; I felt his hands on my face. I opened my eyes to his beautiful face and his crystal blue eyes gazing so loving into mine. How could someone so wonderful be so in love with me? How could I do this without protecting him from me? I was so afraid that I was going to hurt him. The pain I felt when my grandmother left my grandfather, I couldn't make the same mistake. I could not allow the cartel, the renegades, and Rajani to win.

I knew only one thing: Blaine's touch was amazing, and I let him take me to a place of sheer enjoyment. As soon as his full lips touched mine, I reached out, pulling him closer. His fragrance is as sweet as the jasmine that in gulf both of us. He unbuttoned my shirt and then my jeans he left in my lace bra and purple matching panties.

"Oh, I love these on you, you're so gorgeous and your breasts are so beautiful in how they fill the lace. He ran his finger around the edge of my bra, then to the back, where he unhooked it and let my breast fall and the bra came off my shoulders. Kneeled and pulled my nipple into his mouth and rolled it around with his tongue, then nibbled with his teeth. He was twirling the other nipple between his two fingers. I release a moan and press myself up against his bulge. I reached to release him from his jeans and when they were off, he was completely naked and ready. He was so magnificent with his broad shoulders, narrow hips, and a small patch of hair that arrowed down his flat abs to his shaft. Oh, my, how large he was. I thought of only him and then he picked me up as our lips continued to move even more passionately as he lay me down on the chase lounge. We were in the most passionate embraces of our life. He reached to my core, sliding a finger in,

"Awh! You're so wet."

He positioned his body over mine and pushed my legs apart to touch my core. He eased in until I was so full of him the pressure was all I could manage and then lifted my legs up over my head, holding my ankles to go deeper and then he began a rhythm that hit the G-spot. At this pace, I wouldn't last very long. I was ready to let go. I was going crazy, grabbing and scratching his back and thrusting my hips with his. He whispered in my ear, let it go, my love, just let it go. I have got you. He kept the rhythm while I came apart until I couldn't scream anymore; I was gasping for air. He picked up his rhythm and slammed into me until I let go of another orgasm. Then he released a growl, his whole-body racked, he stiffened as he throbbed inside of me. Releasing with a grunt. Then falling softly beside me, rolling on his back, pulling me on top of him while he was still inside of me. He pulled back to look into my eyes and with a smile I could fill him growing inside me again. I reached out with my mind and the door on the roof shut and locked. The rest of the world would have to wait. I was going to make this last late into the night. My thoughts I gave completely to Blaine, making the experience for both of us something beyond the real world; it was truly supernatural. Our bodies moved like a sonata with the orchestra working towards the Crescendo. The way we fit together and in the same rhythm as in the score of passionate music. The composition rose in harmonious arrangement as it filled our souls. It came with no effort and the score rose to the passion of my heart.

I lay in Blaine's arms, and I could feel the warm breeze flipping off the rooftop. The sun was in the western sky, getting ready to set into the ocean for another day. I didn't want any of this to stop. I could hear the others now. They were ready.

"Blaine, it's time we have to help the others."

He looked for a long time into my eyes before he let me

know.

"I love you, never forget that, and without you, my life is not worth living. Please keep my heart safe."

"I love you too, with all my heart and soul. You take care of my heart as well."

All I could do was smile and press my lips to his in assurance no one loved him more than I did, and his and the others' safety was all that mattered to me. I could feel the tears welling up in my eyes and my stomach turning in knots, as I knew the next couple of days were going to be full of uncertainties for all of us. Whatever lay ahead of us, I knew in this moment that our love would hold the test of time no matter what happened.

I could feel my grams agreed with me as her love for my grandfather was still in her soul. We headed downstairs when Blaine got the door; he pulled on it and it was still locked. He looked at me with one eyebrow raised. I shrugged my shoulders, and the door opened. "Your abilities have improved and come in handy now."

"Yes, they are, and aren't you a lucky man?" I winked at him.

"Hm." he smiled and headed downstairs. As we entered the primary area in the loft. Jake chuckled.

"Ok, let's get this show on the road. The love birds have

surfaced."

He passed out copies of the maps to all of us and we each had two doors to confirm that really existed and that they led us back to the alley by the club. I would know if anyone was in trouble. But Jake told everyone we would be back at the club at 3:00pm to cover my abilities, so we all synchronize our watches. We took off in pairs through our door to the alley of the underground passageway.

We were paired off, Blaine and I, Jake and Mica, Jacquelyn and Ray, Amanda, and Jerry.

Amanda's mind was loud with emotion. *"Be safe, Dee, come back in one piece. We all are depending on your abilities, and we all love you."*

I nodded and smiled.

"That is the only way I plan on coming back. I love you too."

Down in the underground's stench, we descended to a level where we split up and went in different directions. Blaine and I headed to a lower level; I was feeling grams wanting to take over. I pushed her back just far enough she was now just giving me direction. The streets had vendors on both sides displaying the wares. Museum grade artwork lined the streets. Bootleg music in shops, knock offs or where the real designers' goods. Drugs of any persuasion stacked on walls with labels like a pharmacy. The label told you how much an ounce and price per ounce are on each shelf. Further down the street, I could see there were food venders with fruits and vegetables, the fresh catch of the day. The world down here was much like the city above grade. They were musicians playing a familiar blues song in what appeared to be a small club. Blaine and I stopped in the doorway to take it in for a minute. They were good. The first doorway we found we had to break it open. It had not been used in many years; it was a tunnel back the way we had come. I led the way into the dark of the tunnel. I found a switch on the wall a couple of feet in. The light glow was weak but ran the full length of the tunnel. The lights in the tunnel lined up down the middle. Then, around a corner at the end was another door opened, and the entrance was bricked up like the one to the club. Blaine gave it a light kick and down the old bricks crumbled. It was in the alley by the club. One down, we head back into the tunnel where we started and came out on the street and moved about five more blocks. We evidently had entered what I assumed was the red-light district where the women were really looking at Blaine. I couldn't blame them; he was so stupefying to look at. I just smiled and sent a small warning in their mind. They all had a distinct fear in their eyes as I walked by, and I was enjoying it this time. Blaine turned and looked at me

"Dee stopped doing that because we don't want to draw any attention."

"Yeah, I know it was just a baby bump of fear."

"Save it for when we really need it."

My man was all business now. It was endearing how he wanted to protect me if he only knew what my abilities had turned into. I wondered if he would still be so sweet. The street narrowed like the alley but darker. It was sloping downward. How deep did this go before we would be under the sound? Blaine looked concerned. "I don't think we are ready to go down this alley. Does the map go this way?" He took it out of his pocket and this alley wasn't on the map. Blaine pulled a pin from his pocket and drew in the alley on the map that we saw the guard come out of. We would need the exact place to show the others.

I asked *"Grams, does this look familiar?"* She pushed forward in my thoughts.

"I'm not sure. What are you feeling?" I pushed out my senses. My amulet got hot on my chest, sending out a lavender glow.

"Danger, urgency, anger, fear. I want to turn around and leave."

"Then you need to leave here now."

"Blaine, we have to leave now. I am getting a bad feeling."

He didn't argue as we began walking out. A group of men were coming out behind us, and we stopped in a
372

small alcove that held both of us and observed them. They seemed to organize, like soldiers. It was a guard to something, or someone at the end of the alley. Blaine put his arms around me to hold me back, calming the thoughts that were swirling in my head. I was trembling with her anger.

"Rajani is the only one who needed a guard down here." Grams was now screaming at me in the back of my mind. I had to focus to keep her from coming any closer to the front of my mind and taking over my body. Blaine's arms kept me calm and focus, as they always do. The guards had moved by us.

"Dee, are you in control? He waited for my answer before he was going to let up on his hold on me.

 "I'm ok but thanks. We have two more doors to find. We can deal with this later, after we regroup with the others. He isn't going anywhere." Blaine released me and I turned to hug him and whispered in his ear.

 "Without you, she might have been able to take me over. She is determined to get her revenge on Rajani"

"Dee, I'm sure you are stronger than you give yourself credit for. But I'm always here for you…"

"Ok, let's look at this map. Which way now?"

 Blaine pointed the opposite direction where we had been.

"Let's head back to the first door we have in the market on the south side of the map. Then backtrack to the next doorway."

It had been a couple of hours; we had found the other doors all bricked up and easily opened just like the other doorways, then headed back to the club. We met the others at the wall in the alley. Everyone went through and locked it behind us. Metal bars swung shut on the door. The stench of the underground was all over us; the smell of sweat, cigars, damp sewage, and a musty skunk was truly unbearable to me. I hated the stench and was obsessive about taking a shower. I cleared my throat.

"Can all of you shower and wash your clothes? The smell of the renegades and the underground stench is on all of you and your scents are much more pleasant to be around."

They all looked at me as though I had lost my mind.

"Kind of weird huh…..." I explained…

"My sense of smell has gotten very acute, and it makes it easier to let you know when the renegades show up in a crowd if you don't smell like them."

I heard all of their thoughts." They all seemed to get it… I saw them nod their heads and their thoughts were all in agreement. I was getting stronger in my abilities. I just felt like the Freak, trying to explain my odd ability without causing them fear. I could hear their thoughts without

374

reaching out to their minds. I had to close myself off to each of their energies, not hear them. Just allow the humming sound, but not let their thoughts threw.

I showered first in the club; we only had two bathrooms. I was done out in the kitchen, drying my hair off with a towel. Amanda and Mica approached me.

"Did you find anything about Rajani while you were down there?"

I nodded…

"Blaine and I ran across a tunnel or alleyway that led down, not sure how far. When we headed back out, we think we saw the royal guard coming up a narrow tunnel at the end of the city. We hid in an alcove and watched them pass. There must have been 30 of them. My grams went crazy in my mind, but I held her thanks to Blaine."

"I wasn't ready for that suicide mission yet without a plan and some backup."

"Yeah, that is good to hear."

Amanda smiled and thought, *"That is smart of you."* Everyone joined us at the bar.

Jake started with the details of his official ability as our strategic planner.

"We found all the doors and short cuts through the alleys

down there. Ray has updated the maps and Amanda is applying it to the new GPSs. We will be caring about the latest technology we good get from a source of Rays tied to the military. When we are down in the underground city from this day forward, we will all have GPS trackers with us. Did anything else happen we should know about? Blaine told them about the guard in the narrow tunnel.

"It looks like only One-way in one-way out."

"We knew getting to an ancient that had lived this long would not be easy. We need to get into that chamber to see what we are up against. If we can see into the chamber, we will make a better plan of attack. Do you mind asking Suzzallo if there is another way in the chamber?

I could feel her move forward in my mind. "Easy grams…" she stopped and talked to me.

The royals always have an exit strategy. They give one guard the privileged information of a royal. They would go nowhere alone. Probe the guards and you will find your answer."

Jake touched my arm.

I shook my head to clear it so I could talk to Jake.

"Suzzallo says there is always an exit route. She said I should probe the guard's minds". Ray came into the room.

"What are you two talking about?"
376

"Well, Dee was just telling me that Suzzallo said the ancients are never left alone."

"That would be correct when I was in royal guard. I was always assigned to the ancient that would leave and need protection."

Ray, you know my grandmother Suzzallo?"

Ray was a man of few words; he would only state the facts.

Ray paused and looked at me. "Yes, I knew her."

Jake looked at me.

"Have you ever probed from a distance?"

"No, they have always been close, or at least within sight."

"Let us get some rest and we will try it in the morning."

I was glad to wait to probe at a distance because controlling grams is exhausting, and I was not up to exert my mind over a long distance. Jake and Mica opened the 80-year-old scotch and poured several glasses full, passing them around to all of us. Jake raised his glass.

"To our success at finding and defeating Rajani and safe return for all of us."

"Here... Here..." clinking our glasses together.

We all toasted in agreement we need all the help we could

get. Amanda and Jerry had disappeared upstairs. Blaine sat at the piano and played some old blues songs; I got a bottle of Malbec from behind the bar and poured a glass and ask Blaine if I could get him a glass too.

"I would love one."

"I was really glad you were holding me today. I wasn't sure I was strong enough to hold her back when she was so close to having what she wanted. I think I'm going to head upstairs and get some sleep. I am wiped out."

I leaned in, kissed him on the cheek, and said goodnight. Then, as I passed Jake and Mica, they said.

"Sleep tight Dee."

I nodded, and I went up the stairs to our bedroom. It got quiet. I must have been tired.

The next morning came, and I was just not ready to get up yet. I was alone and didn't even know what time it was. It looks to be another beautiful day in September.

Chapter 15

Without Warning

I could smell the coffee that was my body was my alarm clock, making me want to drag my butt out of bed. I stretch and then stood up; Feeling wobbly, strange, took a step, and had to steady myself on the wall. Looking and examined every inch of my body, and everything still looked normal. Just wondering what had changed in the night. I put on my leggings and a tank top. I noticed my amulet was glowing purple. "This is not a good sign."

I headed out to the great room. No one was around. The coffee must have been set on automatic to brew this morning. I grabbed some coffee and headed downstairs to the club. Still no one. Hmm… I went back up to the loft, looking for a note or something. Finally, I thought of Amanda.

"Hey where is everyone?"

I listen… nothing…no humming…no buzzing, just silence.

I could only hear grams.

"Careful… not like them to leave without letting you know where they are going. Your amulet is trying to tell you something."

The amulet glowed purple, hot against my skin. It sure was trying to warn me I was in trouble, panicked; I couldn't hear any of them. All I could hear was my rapid heart beating. I was awake now, and I opened the door to Jerry and Amanda's room. A potent smell hit my senses. I recognized it. Katamine… the horse tranquilizers Simon and his thugs tried to use on me months ago. Then an unfamiliar odor must be the new assailants. Not the renegades, not sewer from the underground. An ambient smell like heather floated in the air. Who or what came for us? Grams pulled forward in my mind.

"Red heather was believed to be bad luck. The ancient believed it grew out of the blood of their enemies. Death would surely follow."

"Thanks grams, that wasn't helpful."

"Sorry, Deedra, I just was trying to remember the old stories. Why would an enemy carry the scent of heather with them? Trying to figure out who came in the night that I did not see."

"Witchcraft could be involved. They still have druids in this

time, don't they?"

"I know the Professor knows a witch. She put a ward around the island to gives us some warning when someone is coming near the house and to deter the campers from continuing up too far on to the island.

"Magic has been eliminated by science for most people. The Wiccan religion is still around. But not sure spell casting is."

I went to Jake's room found the same scent and smell; every room I opened had the same distinct odors, and no one left an image of what happened. Until I got to Ray's room. When I touched the door handle, then the doorjamb, I saw how he didn't go down on the first dose from the tranquilizer gun. I could see how he fought the three men off. They were all dressed in black; they wore hoods, so I couldn't see their faces, but the smell was not like ours, that mossy woody scent of pine, the smell of heather permeated the loft, along with the katamine odor. Their minds were silent. They just kept hitting him with the tranquilizers until I watched him drop to the ground, but he uttered one word before the drug took over…. "Guard."

What was he trying to tell me? Was this part of Rajani's royal guard? Why leave me? I was the one they were truly after. How did they get Blaine out of our bed without me knowing? What time was it? I looked at the clock and it was 3:00pm late in the afternoon. My arm was stiff. I looked at the holes where they must have dosed me with the tranquilizer gun. I was starting to really come around all my senses in play now they had drugged me as well. But why didn't I know in advance? How could they do all of this without some kind of warning? Why couldn't I have stopped this…? What is happening? I heightened my senses, passing quick back and forth. The phone rang down in the club. I raced down the stairs and picked up the phone. Picking up the phone breathlessly, I answered.

"Hello BJ's, can I help you?" There was a silence on the other end. I couldn't hear a mind, and no one spoke.

"Who is this?" The voice rose out of the darkness, slow and deliberate.

"Deedra…. I have waited too long to talk with you."

Said, an old, awfully familiar voice. Maybe not to me, but grams raised her head and sneered. *"Rajani."*

"Deedra, do not let him know I am here. Shut down your mind… NOW!"

  I took a deep breath and blew it out. Cleared my mind and locked it down.

"Who is this?" uncertain what to do next.

"Awe, yes, we have not been formally introduced; I had wished to do this in person. I am Rajani, the leader of this world, and I understand you have been causing some problems for my men."

"What do you want, and where is my team?"

"Patients, my dear, I have your friends in a safe place for now… kind of my insurance policy, so you will do what I want."

"So, what is it, that you want, Rajani?"

"I want you to join my family."

I hissed, shaking my head.

"What does that mean?"

"Oh, my dear, you know what I mean. Join me and I will think about letting your friends go."

"I really hated the way he is addressing me with "My dear… I'll show him my dear…"

He was still talking.

"I understand you are quite gifted from the reports I have received."

"Where are my friends, and how do they fit into this deal?"

"I have them safely put away, and I will release them when you come to me."

"Where and when?"

"Tonight, at the pioneer square, I will have my men meet you. You already know Simon. He will be there to bring you to me.

Don't be late, my dear, and come alone. If I see anyone, I will kill your team one by one just for fun. I will send you the video. Starting with your little boyfriend. What's his name? Blaine."

The phone went dead.

"Grams, how is he doing this? I thought you and the ancients covered all the bases to make me invincible"?

"It appears he has sensed you after you were in the underground, and he blocked all of our senses before he had everyone tranquilized. However, I should have seen them coming."

"Yes, you should have."

"I'm not sure, unless he has gained someone with the gift to block for moments in time, rendering all of our senses long enough to assault your team. I had heard of ancients that could block all their prey just before they attacked".

"Grams, that would have been helpful when you and your cronies were engineering my DNA. Did you miss something?"

"No, this has never been DNA or a gift, just a training of one's mind. Only no one could accomplish this level of control it in my time."

"Well, someone has done it now… Grams, I'm calling in backup.

I got on the phone and called Kevin.

"Hello."

"Kevin, this is Deedra. Remember me? We met in Victoria?"

"Awe Yes, Deedra. What can I do for you?"

"I overheard you greeting to Ray."

"Oh yes, how is Raymond?"

"Well, that is what this call is about. They took Ray and the others, but on his way down, he said one word: Guard… I assumed he was talking about you. I need your help."

My voice was shaky, and I was about to cry. I was scared and all alone. I cleared my throat.

"Someone came in the night and has taken everyone. They want to trade me for the rest of my team. They will never give up any of them. I need all the people you can find." I was rambling on and on.

"I will have all of my teams to you within the hour. Deedra, no need to fret."

"Thank you; please bring them to the club here in Seattle."

"Deedra, who has taken all of your team?"

"Rajani… I will need your people to get all of them out, and I will be the distraction. Can I count on you… now you know who has them?"

"Rajani, how does... how is he still live?" confusion rang in Kevin's words.

"I will tell the entire story when you get here. Hurry, please."

"Yes, Deedra, we are on our way as I speak to you."

"The address here is 2258 NE 65th for the club. I will see you soon. Just use the alley door and let yourself in."

I hung up the phone, and I went into Jake's room and dug out all the gear, weapons, the GPS, and maps of the underground. My Sais were in their leather back halters. I grabbed the protective clothing Jake had warned when we were sparring on the island in the gym. I pulled on the long sleeve shirt, reached deep into the back of the closet. There was a trunk with strange ancient writing on it. It looks like the scrolling on the amulet around my neck. I would have to ask Jake about it later. Pulled the trunk out. I thought it might have some more gear in it. The trunk was vibrating... a humming sound like my amulet was doing. In touched the latch. The humming stopped. My scrolling on my forearms glowed and swirled around. Opening the lid inside was the set of blood red leather armor. It was my grandmothers. I had seen her wear it in the painting. I dug it out and set it on the bed. It was a bustier with stays that made it stiff. It laced up the front to make it tight after pulling it on over my head, put on her red leather armor over the top of the Kevlar protection gear. I pulled on the black leather pants. I could feel grams moving forward to help me place the armor in the right place on my
386

body to protect me. There were leather wrist bands that held small throwing knifes. I picked up the knife from a case. The handle was weighted for an accurate throw. I bet they were enchanted and never missed their target. There also was a half jacket, like a welding jacket, that was fitted. I grabbed the backpack and loaded it up with explosives and ammo. I strapped a Glock 17 to my leg. almost heard Amanda; she must come out of the drug. It was all foggy and then nothing.

"They are keeping them drugged so they cannot communicate with me. Grams, any ideas?"

"Try to focus on the guards. One of them will know how to get in undetected. You might even see where they are in a guard's mind."

I finished dressing, sat down, and closed my eyes and focused. It took a couple of minutes, but I could see the underground market. I was walking down the alley where Blaine and I had seen the guard. I could smell their stench. As each guard passed, I skimed their thoughts. Nothing, nothing, one by one and still nothing, then the last one out of the door. He was Rajani's private, most trusted guard. His name was Daniel; he was so incredibly young and enormous. Blond, long hair and muscle protruding, think Viking of long a go, everywhere he walked without fear. He knew of me, and he was ready to take me on if ordered to do so.

"No one will take me on without losing their life or limb or both, if they cross my path this evening; I thought to myself, or grams did not sure whose mind was on destroying."

 I could see that from Pioneer Square, there was an entrance to the underground through Doc Maynard's Bar, I was in the back of the bar through a door down some stairs, that opened to the city below, then trailed north there was a door with two guards at it; he pause nodded his head then he entered. Then it all went dark. They blocked my mind sweep once in that room. So much for seeing where they have my team, other than we know they are in the underground. The back door was open when I heard it. I stood up, went down, and stood on the stairs; Kevin entering the back door. I stepped down and stood behind the bar.

 "Hey Kevin, I am so glad you came!" Demetrye was standing behind him. I smiled and nodded my head.

"Deedra, we owe you. What can we do?" as they all piled into the club. There were about fifty men and women.

"Wow!!! You brought more people; we are going to need them all."

 I turned to the crowd.
"Thank you for coming. Please make yourselves at home. The bar is open."

"Kevin, can you follow me upstairs?"

We went to Jake's room and showed him the maps of the underground and the GPSs. They need to break into teams.

I explained how we found the door to the city in the cellar and where it opened into a room, and then the back door opened into the alleyway of the underground. The secret short cuts back to the club were on the maps I showed him. Also showed him the alleyway to the chamber of Rajani. In addition, where I was headed, and I could contact them through Demetrye's mind, as his mind was already familiar. He could let you know what is happening. We must get to the others. They have been heavily drugged with ketamine, and they are keeping them that way, so I cannot find them. I heard Amanda faintly. Then they must have given her more. I will keep trying to listen to them. Ray said guard before he dropped, I didn't recognize the attackers, and they didn't seem familiar, and their minds were silent."

Kevin looked at me, perplexed.

"I recognize that armor. Just realize how much you look like, Suzzallo? I was one of her many guards.

"Yes… I will end this; I guess it's time you know what is going on. I am the granddaughter of Suzzallo and George Lee."

 He gasped and took a step back and looked down, showing respect from long ago.

 "No, Kevin, it is not like that. Please don't behave that way. I am of the royal blood, but do not want you to treat me any different from the first time we met."

"But I was so rude talking down to you."

"Stop, Please Stop…"

"Whatever you need, we are here at your command."

"Stop it…" I hissed.

"Deedra, allow the man to show respect. It is the way all of them should behave in your presence."

He sighed.

"I am from the old school like Raymond. We served together in the royal guard. We knew your grandmother and Rajani. They had no mercy for disrespect. It is a little hard to forget."

 "I understand, but I need you to be my equal and fight beside me. Ray needs us both if they are going to return alive. Do not worry about me; I have taken on all of both my grandparent's abilities and some of my own."

 I smiled then, looking at him. I saw the fear in his eyes that I had seen in the others, and I reached out to put my hands on his shoulders.

"I am on your side; remember that as long as you don't cross me, your life is good!"

He lightened up and his body language became more relaxed, but his mind was still in awe of my presence.

"Oh yeah, good thing. I will get my people ready and pass out the maps and GPS. We will wait for your orders downstairs.

Bowing his head as he backed away. Then he looked up and smiled and winked.

"Old habits are hard to break." We laughed.

I took a deep breath.

"Please don't tell your people who I am. I would like to do that myself."

He headed downstairs to the bar, only to have an hour left, and I would be leading a battle. I wasn't sure I could win, but I would not allow Rajani to win this time either. I would not die, and I wasn't ready to lose my new family or the man I loved unconditionally. The tears were streaming down my face, my hands were shaking, my stomach was in knots. I loaded the Sais in the back strap of the armor. Looked in the mirror and saw a different woman. I had become a warrior.

"Oh grams."

I could feel her as she moved forward in my mind, even with my own thoughts.

"Deedra, here is where I will remain until you are safe. Remember, we are now one, and you are the best shot all of them have, even the fifty men and women downstairs. Let's keep it together and, Deedra, remember how proud of you I am, and I love you."

"Love you too, grams."

I wiped the tears from my face and walked downstairs to the bar. As I cleared my throat, you could see I had been crying. I could hear the thoughts of all that gathered here, and they wanted to know why they had been summoned.

"I would like to thank you all for coming on such short notice. The Renegades have taken my family, my team, and most of all; they have taken my soul mate. They only want me. I must tell you why, so if when you hear my story, you may choose to leave or to stay and fight with me for all of our freedom."

I heard some grumbling from the crowd. I stepped up, stood tall, and stated my case.

"I am the granddaughter of Suzzallo and George Lee. The crowd was silent. They lowered their heads, bowing in respect.

"Please don't lower your heads to me. I have not earned your respect. I am one of you. I want to stop the renegades from ruling. I want our council to work, and I want all of us to live in peace and harmony with the mortals we walk among. Rajani's reign must end before he destroys all that the ancient's work so hard to put in place for us to live by. We must uphold the rules and laws of the immortals to live in this world with the mortals. We must put the council back in charge and abide by the ancient rules. Getting exposed to the mortals is not
392

a good idea. We have always protected our existence by our amazing stories like the city of Atlantis, the mummies of great pyramids, gods of the old world, Zeus, Pluto, Cerberus, Uranus and Gaia."

They all looked up as I scanned their faces in disbelief and suspicion. I went on.

"This is not about me, but you. You all know Ray, Jake, Blaine, Jerry, Amanda, Mica, and let's not forget the professor she has guided some of you through your beginning in the immortal world. They are the best of the immortals, and you all know them. Please help me save them and free all of us from the rule of Rajani."

Kevin steps forward just as Ray had done months ago. I couldn't believe how moved I was by his support. I got choked up, and the tears streamed down my face and my hands shook. Thinking back about our first meeting, I remember him thinking of me as an insignificant woman that didn't know her place. Kevin stood beside me, putting his hand on my forearm. He was speaking from his heart, with the conviction of a leader that he was.

"It would be an honor to fight next to someone so great, Deedra, granddaughter of George Lee and Suzzallo. You are 'The One', are you not? His eyes smiled as he announced to all of them.

"Deedra is 'The One' in the stories that we have been told for many centuries. She is 'The One' that will be sent to save us all. Who will stand with us to fight for our freedom?"

The crowd was silent again. The looks got even more intense. Their minds were loud. I had to tune them out. I spoke out.

"Yes, Kevin, I am in all the ancient books and the legends that you and your generations have told. 'The One' is coming with the gifts from the Gods. So first off, my gifts have let my friends be taken so don't believe everything your legends have told, and secondly I just want to be one of you and I need your help as an immortal trying to make this world better for all of us."

I heard one after the other. "I'm in." and a few murmured

"I'm out of here, not my fight."

A few left. We still had thirty-five men and women to help me save my family.

As they filed out of the club, I replaced all their memories of a band they came to Seattle to listen to in BJ's.

"Before I turn you over to Kevin, I just want to thank you for staying and fighting with me. Kevin, ther're all yours. Hand out our new equipment and tell them our plan. Oh, one more thing, Kevin, the room you go through in the sub-basement is Jake's rum and whiskey collection. He knows every bottle. Let your people know they are not to touch or take. He has cameras in the room to watch his alcohol. He says it to make sure no one breaks through the door from the underground. I smiled and laughed.

 I turned to Demetrye.

"I will be in contact with you in your mind. You will hear and see all that I am doing. You must keep Kevin updated. Kevin will know what to do with this knowledge. You will also be able to let me know when you have found the others. Good luck."

I turned and headed out the door. I climbed into the Lexus and headed downtown. I could smell Blaine in the car, and I was having a hard time keeping it together.

"Deedra sweetie, focus all those feelings on our task at hand."

"I know, grams, I'm trying but, are you sure I can do this?"

"We shall see you are stronger than you know. You haven't even tapped into all you were gifted."

"Know this, if Rajani sees your affections for Blaine, he will kill him before you have time to save him. You must not lose your focus."

 "I won't grams, I'm ready."

The traffic was relentless as always and the closer I got to Pioneer Square.

Doc Maynard's Bar was just around the corner. I could hear

Simon. Then when I turned the corner to park, I could see him. He was pacing back and forth. Then I heard his thoughts. Ugh!

"Where is she? It's my head this time. If the bitch tries to pull something, she had better show up."

Pulled in and parked at the curb across the street, got out of the car. There were about fifteen of Simon's men around the square. I could smell them and read each of their thoughts. I walked up to Simon

"Good evening, Miss Deedra, nice outfit. What war are you going to defend in that getup?"

Simon smiles as he lowered his head.

"All I wanted to do was wipe that smug look off his face. I should have killed him the first time I had him."

"Good evening, Simon. Where to now?"

"Let us step into Doc's for a drink… shall we?"

He put his hand on the back of my arm; I pulled it away and glared at him.

"Do not touch me." I sneered.

I walked in front of him, and his men followed. The man in front of me led us to the back corner to a table

"Sit here."

396

He pointed to the seat in the corner. We all sat down. Something to drink

 "No thank you. Let's get on with it."

We will wait and go in with the tour. It is less conspicuous," Simon mumbled.

Kevin and the rest had found the cellar door and were headed into the Underground through the alley doorway. They split up into teams, looking for the others in the twenty-five blocks of the city below, hoping to find them before I could make my move. Demetrye was letting me know they were in, and they were looking for them. They questioned some immortals below. Not all of them were renegades, some of them just didn't know any other way of life. Their families have been living underground for centuries. They had passed on the business such as they were; from generation to generation, they still made their living off what they knew. Finally, Kevin asked a shopkeeper if they had seen some unusual activity. An older man with gray hair looked to be in his sixties, but as an immortal he had to have been six hundred plus years. He was up late unloading his latest score.

"Yeah, I saw some guys were dragging seven body bags into the church about ten blocks north. Demetrye was thinking as fast as he could, trying to keep me posted.

 "Dee, did you hear? We are headed to the old church."

There was a woman with him, she said

"They moved them this morning to the cellar on the far side of the city into the forbidden blocks. No one goes there… ever."

She gave a looked of fear for those blocks. Kevin took half the group to cover the church, and the rest headed to the cellar beyond the city blocks. I was feeling better because they had some idea where to find the others. I was still waiting with Simon for the tour that was about to begin. A man stood on the bar, and he told the story of the Fire in Seattle.

"The great Seattle fire was June 6, 1889, after the twenty-five blocks burnt town was rebuilt of stone and the underground city was formed. If you will all stand, I will lead you down the back stairs to see the past as it is today."

They all stood up, and we filed down the stairs single file, going into the lower city. When we got to the first alley, we headed away from the tour. There seemed to be a fake underground city set that was mostly rubble and one city block with a jail cell and a hat shop. This was the mortal tour of Seattle's underground city. We were headed into the immortal's real underground as we headed down the narrow alley where Blaine and I had stopped and watched the royal guard. I knew exactly where they were taking me. We finally got to the door. It opened from the inside and Simon, and I were the only ones allowed in. The room looked like a modern-day penthouse condo in Alki point. Seventy-two -inch flat screen tv, ultramodern stainless kitchen, bar, several rooms off the main room. Old paintings on the wall had to be an original Monet. There was vintage furniture that was in excellent shape. Over the fireplace was the painting of the six ancients with my Grams in the middle and seeing my image in the old painting was a little eerie. Out of the corner of my eye, I saw a man enter from another room. The chills ran through my body clean through to my bones. I felt the pain my grandmother endured under his knife as he cut her throat when he murdered her. The memories are still fresh in her mind and now in mine. I was horrified, angry and thought of even standing in the presence of such monsters made me ill. This monster had my new family and the man I loved.

"Deedra, how you resemble your grandmother, yet I see your grandfather's eyes. How exquisite you have become." He said in a heavy accent.

He smiled with evil intent.

"I thought no one could be more beautiful than Suzzallo."

His words pierced my heart. I looked at him in distaste. Then grams spoke.

"Rajani, I have waited too many years for this."

His eyes got big, and his face turned white.

"Suzzallo?"

"Yes, it is I, Rajani. I have come to settle our score."

He stopped in his place.

"Suzzallo, it has been many years, and I was a young, foolish man. I was out of control. I have never forgiven myself for what I did to you."

"It's too late. You need to be stopped."

He laughed. His eyes were not pools of blue water like the rest of the immortals; they were dark pools of evil. There was no life in his eyes, just darkness.

"And you sent this little girl to take vengeance on me and save the weak, immortal world?" He boastfully laughed.

Then I could not take it anymore. I spoke up with an attitude.

"Oh, boy, do you have so much to learn about this little girl?" As I took a defensive stance. I pushed grams back into my mind.

"Where are my friends?"

"Who am I talking to now?"

"You are talking to Deedra, and I want some answers. I want my friends set free. You have what you wanted…. I am here." I could hear Demetrye

"Dee, we have found the others but—"

He paused. "Um, Blaine is not with the others." I talked to Demetrye fast, not to let Rajani know what I was up to.

"When Amanda comes around, ask her if she knows what happened to Blaine."

Rajani was watching me awfully close. Now my stance was ready to take him out and he could, since I had a lot of anger brewing up. Not sure whose emotions were coming through mine or Grams.

"Is there something wrong, my dear? I see you are wearing your grandmother's old armor."

I looked at him like I would kill him if he called me my dear one more time.

"Yes, I thought it would be appropriate when I kill you and get her revenge on how you took her life. Enough about me. Where is Blaine?"

"He is with the others, my dear."

 "No, he is not. I will only ask you one more time, where is Blaine?"

"You need to calm down. I am sure he must be around here somewhere."

I saw the door open, behind Rajani and a young woman came in. I could read her mind. She was Rajani's daughter, Priscilla, and she had Blaine. She was extraordinarily beautiful; tall and thin with long blonde hair and blue eyes. She walked in and stood beside her father.

Rajani asked her,

"Priscilla, where is Blaine?"

"Oh father, he is so exquisite I want to keep him, please."

I could feel my blood boiling, wanted to maim her... focused on her. I wanted to make her understand I was going to take her head off if she didn't return him.

"Deedra, easy…. you do not want to show our hand just yet. Stop what you're doing."

I drew back. Grams was right. I did not want to make her same fatal mistakes. I took a deep breath and look fiercely at her.

"Oh! Daddy, is this the woman that is causing all the trouble?"

"Yes, Priscilla, this is Deedra."

"She looks very familiar."

Then she looked up at the painting above their fireplace. The painting was of the original six immortals from hundreds of years ago. Suzzallo was the only woman in the middle of all the men who reigned in that time.

"Oh, so is she one of the pure bloods? I thought you and I were the only ones left. She looks just like the painting. The resemblance is uncanny."

"I know Priscilla. She resembles her grandmother, but we

have yet to determine if she is pure blood.”

My thoughts were only of Blaine and not all of her royal gibberish.

“I want to know where Blaine is, and I will not ask you again?”

I said calmly, trying not to show my hand and make the mistake my grandmother made giving up any weakness they could play on. I could not make a move until he was safe.

“Father, who does this woman think she is talking to?”

“Priscilla, you need to be incredibly careful. We are not sure what abilities our new guest has. I have heard some of them are exceedingly special. So, honey, where is the man she is referring to? Where is this, Blaine?”

Priscilla looked at me and I had no more patience with her. I focused on her mind, and her nose bled. She wiped it and said.

“Is that all you got” That was it. I hit her mind hard, with my opinion of what I thought of her.

“If you don’t want to be a fucking vegetable, the rest of your life you will walk out that door and when you come back, you will bring me Blaine un- harmed do I make myself clear?”

I smiled. Before Rajani could react to me, Priscilla turned and walked out the door.

"Ladies, now let's behave, Priscilla. Where are you going?"

She ignored him and kept walking.

 "What did you do to her?" he was showing the fear I had done damage to her mind.

Grams moved forward and whisper to me.

"That is his weakness, his daughter, and we will use it to control him as he did me with your grandfather and my son."

"Why do you think I did anything to her?" I was feeling rather self-righteous.

 I could see I had evoked some fear for his daughter. A couple of minutes later, two guards and Priscilla returned with Blaine. Dragging him in and dropping him at my feet.

"Freeze, Deedra, don't show any emotion on your face. Don't let them see any weakness. Deedra, take a deep slow breath. I know he is ok. Listen to his heartbeat."

Grams was yelling at me not to move. I could hear Blaine breathing, but he was still out.

 "What have you done to him?" I demanded in a royal voice that was much like my grandmother's, and yet it was my voice.

 "He will be out for a couple of hours. I had to give him more sedative. He woke up and fought with my guards."

Priscilla smiled. I stepped forward over Blaine's body and my heart raced as the rage built. The feelings were not just mine; they were a mix of grams now. It was also my own, and I felt as though I was ready to explode, knowing I would hurt everyone in the room, including Blaine.

"Deedra stop, I am sorry I will try not to let my emotions join with yours, breathe, easy now you don't want to hurt them you will have to live with the shame of their deaths just as I have for too many years…. take a deep breath and calm yourself."

"I am not sure there would be any shame in taking out such evil."

Grams had taken control of my mind and she was holding me back.

I stopped in front of Blain's lifeless body but never took my eyes off the two guards standing with Priscilla and Rajani.

"It appears we are in a predicament. What do you want to do?"

"Well, Rajani, I think you should just let Blaine and I walk out that door if you don't want this to end badly."

Then I spun in front of Blaine and pushed into their minds. Everyone dropped in pain to the floor except Rajani. As I walked by the others, I pulled the Sais from their leather carrier on my back and approached him. I read his thoughts; I hit him and knocked him to the ground, then from the back room came more guards. They were firing rounds from colt M4s. I was focusing without thought; the bullets stopped in midair and dropped to the ground. Then I pushed into all of their minds. They dropped, grabbing their heads, and screaming in excruciating agony like the other guards did. That were rolling on the ground. Then I turned Rajani now up on his feet again and he was trying to get into my head. I shook my head and his nose bled. I stepped forward in order to protect Blaine, who was still lying unconscious on the ground. My Sais were still drawn in my hands, and I was prepared for anything they could throw my way. Grams yelled, *"Locked all the doors into the subterranean room! NOW!"*

 I hear the locks clicking shut. The hammering on the doors started.

"Rajani, you will never beat me. I have all the gifts of the ancients, and I can inflict pain on anyone who enters this room. Are you ready to die?"

He looked up at me with superciliousness.

"You are very good, but you forget one thing: I have never lost a battle to any immortal, and you will not be any threat to me, either."

"Really, as old as you, I am sure I won't have any trouble taking you down."

Grams stepped to the front of my mind and took over. She still was much stronger than I was mentally, and she pushed me to the back of my mind to watch her wrath.

"Rajani, you may think my granddaughter is an easy mark, but you forget I can beat you and I am about to do it again without mercy."

"Suzzallo, you are still here with your granddaughter?

"So, what will it be, Rajani, your death for the safety of your daughter? The choice you gave me."

I could hear Demetrye and the others fighting with the guards and were almost to the chamber now.

Grams stop; we will not lower ourselves to be at his level. Not today will harm his family because that will make us no better than him. We will leave this judgment to the council. You stopped me in my rage. Now let me stop you.

Grams paused and in her Royal judgmental tone, as though she was declaring her rule

"Disband your guard and leave the underground. You must take the punishment of the council delegates and you must live within all the immortals' laws.

If you cannot do this, then you leave us no choice but to destroy you and all who follow you. So, what will it be, Rajani?"

I was not horrified any longer as she was behaving as though my thoughts were her thoughts. Rajani moved closer, and I stood my ground. He was now in our face.

"So, you think you are going to stop me from walking out that door? You and what army you are all by yourself?"

"Well…." Just then I unlocked the back door and in came Kevin and Ray and most of the others.

"Not by myself."

Rajani looked surprised to see Kevin and Ray.

"Gentlemen, just like old times."

He smiled with egotism. Ray moved in beside me and bent down to check on Blaine and make sure he was ok. Kevin stepped on the other side like two giant gods ready to destroy anyone who dare look sideways at me. Then Ray stood back up. I could feel Ray's relief that Blaine was ok.

"Not like old times, Rajani. We are here with Deedra, and we do her bidding now."

"So Rajani, what is your decision?"

"You have to release my Daughter Priscilla." I didn't really want to let her go; she needed to understand who she was dealing with.

"Dee let her go; she will remember you for a very long time". I drew back from her mind and then Priscilla stood up, pulled on her clothes, straightening them, and standing next to her father.

"Take them and all who follow them to the docks. Hold them until we can get them to council for judgment."

Kevin and his men obeyed and took the others with them back to his ship in the harbor. He assured me that his cells in the ship would hold them. Ray cleared his throat and added,

"You should sedate them when you get to the docks to keep them in control until council has begun. I looked at the two of them.

"You will not try to escape. That will be a break in our understanding, and I will be forced to destroy you both. Do I make myself clear?"

Rajani and Priscilla both nodded. They went with the others willingly.

"Deedra, he cannot be trusted. They went too easy." Ray reminded me.

"Kevin, will you make sure your best men are guarding them?"

"Yes, Deedra, I will see to it myself."

Kevin's men led them out of the room through an underground cellar and up through Doc Maynard's Bar. There was a black suburban waiting to take them to a warehouse on the docks. When they got to the docks, a doctor was waiting to sedate all of them so they would not cause any more trouble until they could take them in front of the council. I leaned down and I could hear Blaine coming around.

"Hey there, baby, wake up."

"Dee, where are we?"

Ray and Kevin laughed.

"Hey big guy, you missed all the fun laying on the floor at Dee's feet." Ray and Kevin reached down, picked Blaine up. It took both of them to hold him up. He kept going in and out of consciousness. He was swaying back and forth; Ray and Kevin had to help him walk out to the Hummer, where Jerry was waiting with Amanda, Mica, and Jacqueline. She had her medical bag and her stethoscope in hand. As soon as Blaine was loaded in the rig, she was checking him over. Ray got in the back with Kevin.

"See you all at the club. I shut the door."

I walked down and got in the Lexus that was parked around the corner where I had left it. As we entered the front of the club, I could hear the others again. It was good to have them all back, humming in my head. I loved hearing all of their thoughts in my mind. Amanda was the first to hug me and then the rest piled into the bar. Jake was the first to speak.

"What in the hell happened? I remember having a drink going upstairs to bed and then nothing until the Canadians freed us and were helping us wake up giving us coffee at Doc Maynard's?"

Chapter 16

Escape Plan

Well, you better get out some of the famous scotch you came upon in the hidden room before the underground. It's a long story."

"How do you know about the scotch in our hidden cellar?"

I had to pass through it with my team to save your ass. Let me tell you, I had to threaten them with their lives not to commandeer your stash

Ray and Kevin brought the others up to speed. I was holding on to Blaine as he started to really come around. I leaned up to kiss him and hug him and didn't want to let go.

"Blaine, how are you feeling?"

He still seemed a little groggy and his speech was a little slurred from the drugs

"I am feeling more and more like me. Could I get some coffee?"

Mica was behind the bar and poured him a cup. He listened as the others told the story of the events that had taken place and how Blaine almost became Priscilla's pet.

 Jake complained,

 "Why is it always Blaine that the girls want as a pet? What about me?" Blaine was coming back to his normal sense of humor.

"They are not sure what is growing under all of that hair."

They all laughed.

Then Grams started talking.

"Deedra, we should check on Rajani and make sure Priscilla and her father have been taken care of before we get too far in this celebration."

I leaned into Kevin,

"Where did you take Rajani and his daughter?"

"They were placed in the brig on the ship in the harbor. After the doctor drugged them for safekeeping. Why do you ask?"

I focused on the guards who were with Rajani & Priscilla. The guards were out lying on the ground at the docks they had been murdered. I could see Priscilla with Rajani. They were leaving the harbor with Kevin's ship. I focused on Priscilla. I saw the ship. It was not in the harbor anymore; it was in the sound and was moving it through the passageway out to the open sea.

"Kevin, did you know your ship was moving through the sound?"

"What are you talking about?"

"I can see it through Priscilla's eyes; she is the least unsuspecting for me to probe. Grams alerted me."

"Kevin, are you sure they were your men?"

"Yes!"

Kevin's cell phone was ringing.

"Hello, the man on the other end was letting Kevin know he had been overtaken and the ship was gone.

"I see, thank you."

Then he put the phone in his pocket and turned to me.

"They were waiting at the dock. They took out most of my men and took the captain under their control and they took my ship."

"What the hell!!!!! The incompetence of today's help..." Grams shouted. She was in control now...

"I should have killed him when we had the chance. I knew he couldn't be trusted."

"Take it easy, grams."

Everyone was silent and just staring at me. They heard Grams ranting through me.

"Grams, stop what you are doing. Can't you see the fear you are still inflicting on these people that have helped us this far, and you're scaring my friends?"

She moved to let me take control again. I smiled and cleared my throat.

I put my hand out in the jester of friendship.

"Hey, I'm back, it's me. She has gone to the back of my mind again. I'm sorry, but she is right. We had them. We gave them a chance to take judgment from our council. They have to be destroyed." Blaine reached over and put his arm around me. This time we take them down as a team."

Jake commanded the room.

"Kevin, does the ship have a GPS or maritime tracker?

"Yes… I installed the best ASI 6800 tracking in real time. Comes with an app on my phone."

"Great, then you get with Amanda. Give her the passwords,

see if we can find your ship."

Amanda and Kevin were on it; they were upstairs seeing if we could track the ship. Sure enough, the GPS's signature was located by satellite. They could see the ship as it headed up the inside passage to Alaska. Grams moved forward in my mind.

"Dee, see if you can see the captain's mind focus. Ok, then what? Let me use your mind. I can make him do whatever I want and so can you."
I focused and saw through Captain Scott's eyes saw. Daniel was on the bridge with him.

"Captain Scott, don't be alarmed. It is Deedra Lee. Can you get control of the cabin?"

"Have you seen the guard that is here?"

"Yes, I will distract him, but you have to knock him out and tie him up. Can you do that?"

"Yes, I think I can."

"Good, wait till you see his nose bleed, then hit him with everything you have got. You will only get one chance."

Grams and I focused on Daniel. I see the pain we were causing him, but he fought us.

"Get out of my head."

He screamed as he put both of his hands to his head, holding his ears, then the thud and he was out.

"Good job, Captain Scott. Now lock the doors and turn the ship slowly around so no one knows you have changed direction and get back here to Seattle."

I heard Amanda telling Kevin the ship seems to have turned around. It is heading back to Seattle. Someone must be on our side and taking the ship back. Jake looked up and knew I had something to do with it. He walked over and leaned in close so no one could hear.

"Dee, did you have anything to do with this? I smiled and nodded.

"I'll explain later. I have to focus now."

I was trying to make sure the captain Scott didn't have any visitors. Grams suggests we put the crew into a sleep state. Working off her knowledge and together, I hoped to keep all of them in a dream state until we took the ship back over in a couple of hours in the harbor. Jake, Blaine, Ray, and Kevin were getting ready to leave for the docks.

"Grams, can you hold the focus for a minute?"

"Yes, but not long without you."

"I'll be right back."

I stepped into the room.

"You're not leaving without me, but once in the rig, please do not talk to me."

Jake took me out and set me in the Hummer.

"Suzzallo and I are keeping the ship in a dream state. Everyone except Captain Scott he has taken back the bridge."

I looked up

"We have to hurry. I don't know how much longer we can keep the ship in a dream state."

I got into the hummer in the back seat and then back to grams to help her with keeping everyone in the dream world and a sleep as the ship moved closer to the docks. I didn't know how long we had been at the docks when from inside the ship I could see we were pulling in the slip in the Seattle harbor.

"Grams, I have to go with the others. Have you got it alone? Yes sweetie, hurry and get Rajani."

"I will."

"Are we ready to board?" I could see relief on Blaine's face.

"Dee, you're back. You had me worried for a minute. You're so pale. Are you sure you're strong enough to take on Rajani?"

"Come on, we have to hurry and get to Rajani while Grams is

holding the crew asleep. She can't hold them much longer by herself."

We boarded the ship. I could see Rajani was waking up. He was in the captain's stateroom. Had taken it over. He will never change, and I will have to kill him, so no one will ever have to endure his cruelty as my grams did.

Kevin led the way down to his room.

"I pushed Kevin out of the way. He is all mine. I saw Rajani turn and go down the hallway. The lights flickered and then went out. I followed him down into the bottom of the ship and it kept getting darker, and I could not see him, but I could feel him. The smell of oil and gas was so strong, but somewhere in all the smells of the machine room, I could smell the stench of Rajani. His evil darkness was all around me, as he was all around me. I called to him

"What is the great and powerful Rajani afraid of running from little old me?"

"You have mistaken me for someone else, and I am leading you to your death."

"It's my death. Why don't you come forth, you coward? Are you going to kill me like you killed all the elders, so you were the only ancient left?"

418

I stepped around a large tank. Still, I could not pin him down.

"Oh, my dear, you are not an ancient. You're a new immortal with some incredibly special gifts, but you're no pure blood."

"So, what are you afraid of, if I am no match for you?"

"You will be killed too easily."

"So, why don't you come out and fight if I'm so easy? You're not afraid of this little girl. Are you? Or is it Suzzallo you're truly afraid of?"

He stepped out and lunged at me. He caught my arm as he passed, and I hit his back with the butt of the Sai. Again, he came at me. This time, he hit my legs as I swung at him, and I cut his arm. He never flinched. But my pain was excruciating. I turned, and there he was in front of me as I spun too close to his blade. He tore another slice at my middle. Cutting right through the armor and Kevlar I had on. I hit the floor like a ton of bricks. Was this it? I evidently was not up to overpowering him; he moved like a ghost. I didn't have the gifts to defeat him. I turned my head to watch as he struck his final blow. My forearm burned. The tattoo swirled to life. My amulet glowed a deep purple light. My forearms glowed, swirling to life.

The enchanted swirled markings they were on fire. Then, from within me, I felt Grams step out of me. I saw Grams standing in front of me solid, not a ghost. She dressed in the red leather bustier with black leather pant. Suzzallo summoned the Sai's. They flew into her hands, and she blocked the blow that would have ended my life.

"I am sorry, my dear granddaughter, but I cannot allow you to finish this. He is mine. It is my revenge to take and his death to add to the other souls I have taken."

I lay there almost comatose. I could feel the blood run down my arm and leg. It pooled at my stomach where my skin lay open. I watched as the Suzzallo moved repeatedly with the gracefulness of a ballet dancer. Rajani just stood there in shock at that moment as she had already slit his throat, hitting his jugular with the accuracy of a skilled surgeon. Rajani dropped to the floor. His head was askew. She had almost sliced it completely off. Lying on the floor bleeding, unable to move. Only feeling my wounds and not sure if I was conscious or unconscious watching the floor fill up with blood. I hoped it was pouring from Rajani's still quivering body and not mine. I could hear the last few flutters of his heartbeat then it stopped. Blaine was looking for me, and I could hear him calling. I wasn't sure I had any strength to summon him and let him know where I was. The next thing I remember, Ray was carrying me up out of the ship. I don't even know if I was hallucinating about Grams killing Rajani. How could a ghost kill a living immortal? Did I finish him while she moved forward in my mind, or did I watch her finish him?

420

"Ray, you must put me down." I muttered to him.

 "But Dee, you're bleeding. Your insides are close to falling out. I need to get you to the professor."

"Ray, stop, Is Rajani dead?

"Yes, you have completed your destiny." At the top of the stairs, I heard Blaine call my name. He ran up to Ray, his face was white.

"Oh god, Dee the blood, we have to get her to my mother."

"I have tried she insists I put her down. She keeps mumbling about Rajani."

"Blaine I will be ok, but we have some unfinished business to take care of if Ray will put me down."

 "I could hear Priscilla coming down the hallway screaming and crying No… No… Not my father, as she pushed her way past us to her father. Get her out of here. We have to remove his body at once before his cells regenerate and produce more blood. We only have minutes."

I shouted at them all. Blaine came to me and just put his arms around me to help hold me up while Ray and some men wrapped Rajani's body up for transport.

 "The rest of them can manage this; let me take you back to the club."

"No!"

 I pulled away

"This is my destiny and my responsibility, and I will stay here until this is done and Rajani can no longer hurt anyone."

Softly Blaine whispered.

"Suzzallo, is that you? Where is Dee?"

"We are here together, and we will finish what we have been sent here to do. We are the only ones that know what we have to do to secure Rajani's body. Hurry, we have little time left."

"Take Priscilla and the others and lock them in a well-guarded and fortified holding cell. Make sure you tranquilized heavily so she cannot use her gifts. I will deal with her later."

 In her Royal voice commanding, she was in control of me.

"Ray, Kevin, Jake and Blaine, we have to take Rajani to the underground and place him in the vault. Ray looked up at us.

"What vault?"

 "I will show you the way." Blaine still had his arm around me. Holding me up with his hand, holding a towel on my stomach.

422

"I'm coming. You can barely walk."

"Fine, have it your way."

"Grams, be nicer. He is the man I love."

I talked to Blaine in his mind.

"Blaine, thank you. I will need you to carry me when she lets me go from her control."

I looked at him so he could see it was me, not grams.

He looked worried.

"It's Ok don't worry. She is only doing what she thinks is best for all of us."

They loaded Rajani up and I could still hear Priscilla yelling at the guard that was taking her away. She was threatening all of them. I could hear her thoughts

"I will get you, Deedra. I will have my father's revenge. One day, when you least expect it, I will make sure I avenge my father's death. Do you hear me, Deedra? You better keep looking over your shoulder because one day you will get what is coming to you for destroying my father. This isn't over yet. You will see I will get my day."

Then they must have drugged her to shut her up. I couldn't hear anymore.

"Do whatever work to get her locked down before I have to kill her, too?"

We arrived back at Pioneer Square. I got out with Blaine's arms around me to hold me up, and we headed slowly into Maynard's bar. It was closed for the evening, so we picked the lock and moved quietly through to the back staircase. Walked into the back down the stairs. We could go back to the club, but Doc Maynard Public House was closer to the church. Then headed to the church at the end of the 25 blocks deep into the city. The further we walked, the stronger I became. I was healing at a faster rate than any immortals with such fatal wounds. This is what Grams was talking about with Rajani; he will begin soon to regenerate his tissue. We entered the church. Kevin, Jake, Ray and Jerry were carrying Rajani into the church. I strolled down the aisle to the enormous altars at the head of the room. I kneeled down and turned the rosette on the side of the carve altar. The enormous slab of marble slowly slid open and below were some stairs. I walked down the stairs as the others followed. I grabbed the torch off the wall and Blaine lit it. We were beneath the church floors in a subterranean chamber at least another twenty feet below the underground city. I walked along the forty-foot chamber and lit more of the torches that lined the chamber's walls. Walking along the south wall you could see in the chamber were six sarcophaguses in them where the remains of all the ancients. Chiseled on the tops of them were the names of all the ancients that were encased here.

Damayanti had the power to subdue his prey just before he killed them, showing no mercy.

Govua could conjure the wind, water and fire at will, causing a great storm with tornados to confuse his enemies.

Kreios was always the lord and head of his kingdoms.

Deimos wrecked terror everywhere he ruled.

Then there was Suzzallo. She was the only woman, and she had most of the gifts. She was selfish and had no conscience.

 Let's not forget Rajani. He was always the Dark One. He prayed on the mortal or immortal. Not caring only wanted to rule the world.

The sarcophagus on the end had the lid off, it was for Rajani. Ray, Kevin, Jake, Jerry, and Blaine stood with their mouths open in awe of the liturgical room with all the ancient treasures, ornate vases in gold, marking the time of the ancients and the end of their rule. Paintings on the wall told of the rituals of a time that had passed, but how vivid a reminder to Ray and Kevin, who remember that time oh too well. The room was filled with ancient artifacts of the time when the world was a different place.   The room with all of its treasures was worth millions of dollars on the black market. I turned around and looked into their faces.

"Before you place him, remove his heart and take off his head." Ray pulled out a very sharp sword, not sure where he was keeping it hidden. With one swing, Rajani's head was removed. Kevin took it by the hair and placed it in the box, then secured the lid. The square boxes against the other wall were for their heads and on the adjacent wall were smaller square boxes, all made of stone for their hearts. Ray pulled a large knife out of his boot. He drove it into Rajani's chest and cut out his heart. Ray lifted it up and carried it to the little boxes on the other wall. Opening the lid marked Rajani; he placed the heart in the box and secured the lid. Then they all lifted the headless, heartless body and placed the final ancient sarcophagus and pulled the lid shut. They didn't have to drain the blood. He lost most of it where Grams had laid open his jugular.

Without his heart, head, no sun or air, he cannot regenerate."

"Grams, is that really you in that sarcophagus with your name on it?"

"Yes, sweetie, I am afraid so. I wish it weren't. I always wanted to be with your grandfather."

She was done and moved out of the front of my mind and moved to the back. I could hardly sense her now, letting me back to regaining control of my body and mind.

"Oh, ouch, I hurt all over."

"Dee, are you back? Here, let me help you."

Blaine had his arm around me, helping me stand and looked at him smile. "It only hurts a little, like I have been hit by a truck."

"We should go now before we are discovered. I'm sure the underworld has heard of what we have done and someone else is looking forward to trying their hand at ruling the underground. I will have to make some kind of warning to all of them in the marketplace. Before we get to the club, I have a few items to finish.

"Wait a minute; we need to secure this place." Ray pointed out.

I smiled at them.

They were all looking at me now. Jake confirmed.

"Your going to make us forget?" with an unsure look on his face.

His mind loudly expressed his unhappiness of me messing around in his mind.

"It will be painless, and I will replace the memory with another one." Ray and Kevin laughed out loud.

"It's ok; we probably have had it done to us when we were

guards. Someone had to bring all the ancients to this place."

"Yes, you both have had your memories altered. You have both been in this chamber before when you place my grandmother, and you also helped in placing the others here many years ago. See, it works, you are not damaged, and yet you have no memory of this place."

"We need to get back before someone discovers us down here."

I could feel Grams' power was weaker, and she was fading further away into the back of my mind.

"Yes sweetie, my work is done."

"Don't leave me just yet. Can't you stay just a little longer? I still have to face the council! I'll try, but you have nothing to fear. You are the most powerful immortal alive today, and no one will challenge you, not after today."

"Please… stay."

"Ok, but I have to move on soon."

"Dee, Hello Dee … I could feel hands on my arms. It was Blaine. He was shaking me.

"Dee, are you there?"

I looked up, and Blaine was shaking me.

"Yes, where else would I be?" Jake abruptly pointed out.

"Well, we can never tell if it is you or Suzzallo."

I turned and looked at the others.

"I suppose in some ways this has been harder for you than me. We need to get out of here and back to the Island. We have to prepare for the hearing in front of the council, and I will need to know what to say."

As we all headed out of the bowels of the underground, we passed the market place. A crowd had gathered there. The stench of sweat and dirt filled my lungs until I could not breathe.

"Wait, I must address this crowd."

Jake snapped off, "You or your grandmother?"

I gave him a malicious look.

"Enough Jake, I am the only one here, Grams is very weak, and I am sure she would respond to your accusation if she were so inclined, but you're going to have to just deal with me from here on out.

"Sorry, Dee, I will work on being more respectful of you."

Kevin, Ray, Blaine, Jerry, and Jake spread out on both sides of me like a royal guard. It was hard to get used to, but I was glad to have the backup. The illusion of strength getting no more immortals hurt was my goal.

I tried to clear my throat, but the thick air and the musty smell made my voice crack. I tried to speak with some kind of authority.

"I am Deedra Lee, granddaughter to Suzzallo and George Lee."

The marketplace got silent, and they all bowed their heads. I could feel the fear of just uttering the word Suzzallo, brought images of her bloody reign to their minds. "I am here to let you know Rajani's reign has ended. Please rise, I am an immortal, just like any of you. There is a council in place for the judgment of our behavior, and we must live in harmony once again, unseen by the mortals of this world. The ancients have provided me with some gifts that I will not take advantage of. However, do not mistake my behavior as meek. I will do what is needed to keep this world from the corruption of the past. Rajani is gone and his followers must disband or face the consequences. We will be watching the underground and communicating with the council. If there is any trouble, you will see me again with my team."

The crowd talked among themselves. I could hear most of them were glad, yet a few were going to challenge me, but not today. The crowd was dispersing.

"Well, that went well, don't you think?"

Jake laughed. "Not bad for your first command, but it will only be good for now until the next time someone challenges you, then what?"

Ray turned to all of us.

"We live our destiny as we help Deedra manage the immortal world. We are now the team to keep peace.

Jake smiled, dimples showing. "It will make life a little more exciting than the last hundred years or so."

The guys laughed and were horsing around as we walked back towards the alley that led to the secret door below the club. Someone would have to take Kevin back to his van in Pioneer Square later. I needed to take a long shower alone to gather my thoughts.

I could hear the grams softly whisper.

"It's time to make them forget. Remember, just a whisper will do"

When they stepped into the cellar out of the alley, I stopped them with my thoughts.

As everyone passed me in the doorway, Grams guided me in replacing their memories; of what we had done with Rajani's body. As I was the last one in, I slid the steel lock in place and climbed the stairs back into the wine cellar; we shut the shelves of wine for good, hoping to never have to open that door to the world of the underground for a long time.

Chapter 17

In Loving Arms

When I hit the top of the stairs, I collapsed. Blaine and Jake grabbed me just before I hit the floor. My clothes were a shredded. I was a bloody mess. Blaine carried me upstairs, he laid me on the bed and the professor came over and inspected my wounds. Only most of them were healed and just the small remnants of scars remained that were disappearing in front of her eyes.

 "Oh my!" In a shrill, shocking tone in her voice.

"What is it? I will not make it, will I? He just kept coming at me and when he hit me, the pain was like nothing I had ever felt. He cut through the layers of Armor and Kevlar. His sword must have been enchanted steel. It burned as if his blade was made of fire."

The Professor laughed.

"Oh, Deedra, you are going to be fine. You can regenerate at an extremely fast rate. I have read about the ancient's ability to rejuvenate but never thought I would witness it firsthand. It is miraculous."

"So… I'm…. Ok."

"Deedra, you will be fine. Just sleep. It will help you finish healing."

She kissed me on the forehead and left the room.

When I woke, I could see it was dark out and the full moonlight made the room look like we were in the city with a streetlight on, trying to wake up, stiff and sore but able to get out of bed. I couldn't believe they let me lay there in the bloody clothes and the stench of the underground all over me. Pulling the sheets off the bed to wash. I took a quick shower and then threw on some clothes and headed out to where everyone was; they were still celebrating our conquest. I just watched, no one noticed me, the happiness on all of their faces. Knowing we had all made a difference in so many lives. In the mortal and immortal world, it was a great day to celebrate and remember how bad it could have turned out. Ray and Jacquelyn were having a private moment, and I was trying to tune them out.

Mica and Jake seem to flirt a little, but still holding back. Amanda and Jerry were in the middle of a conversation when Amanda was the first to since my presence in the room.

 "Dee, you're up. How are you feeling?"

I smiled at all of them. "I am a little stiff but good and I could eat a horse."

Blaine came over and put his arms around me.

"Oh Ouch… easy, I'm not sure there isn't one place on my body that isn't sore."

"I'm sorry. I will be gentle. What can I get for you?"

Jake rubbed me softly.

"Is eating a horse one of your new abilities?"

"Oh, you're so hilarious, No… I am starving. What time is it?"

"Dee, it appears you have been asleep for 24 hours. That must be the tradeoff for healing so fast you have no wounds, no scars it as if your stomach weren't even touched."

"Um, yeah, I don't have any wounds." I ran my hand across my stomach where Rajani had laid my stomach wide open with his blade. Not even a scar.

"I have been sleeping for a whole day. That explains the headache and why I am so starving. I feel like I tied one on last night and had a superlative time."

Jerry was in the kitchen and yelled,

"I heard you're hungry. Give me a minute. I will have some eggs up ready for you to eat."

 Jake asked, would you like "a cup of coffee?"

        "Um, that sounds good."

"You just sit at the bar, and I will get you some."

"Where are Kevin and his men?"

"They have gone back to the docks, boarded their ship where the celebration had gone on all night. That crew knows how to celebrate in the grand fashion with a case of whiskey, scotch, and I am sure they have found a couple of women. They were going to leave after the council meeting.

They thought you might need backup."

"I wanted to thank Kevin for coming and helping us."

"We have already done that. Jake gave them a case of the old scotch we found in the cellar."

Jerry came out of the kitchen and the eggs smelled wonderful.

"Thanks Jerry." he smiled and went back over to Amanda. They left for the evening. I smiled, knowing what they were going to be doing.

"What are you smiling about, Dee?"

"Oh nothing, it is just I never thought my life would be exactly like this."

Blaine sat next to me at the bar.

"Would you like to hear some music while you eat?"

"That would be very nice."

Blaine sat at the piano and played while I finished my eggs. It was so nice to feel normal and loved again. I almost forgot about the underground, and what I had done over the last week. I walked over from the bar and sat next to Blaine at the piano.

"Shall we call it a night? I'm exhausted."

"Dee, are you OK? should I get the professor? You just slept for 24 hours and now you want to go back to bed?"

I looked at him and smiled as I let some of my thoughts enter his mind.

Blaine didn't have to be asked twice. He stood up and grabbed me in his arms. Then carefully lifting me up and carrying me to our room above the club. He sat me on the bed and went to turn the shower on. I could hear the water running and wondered in the bathroom to find Blaine already in the shower waiting for me. I took off my clothes, stepped into the shower. The water was running

436

all over our bodies as I pressed against him. He turned and soaped my tired body with his hands, running them down my breast making my nipples erect and sensitive to his touch. The soapy water rinsed away in the shower spray. He lowered his head and pulled my hard nipple into his mouth, sucking and rolling his tongue around my erect knob. He then dragged his teeth, adding pressure until there was a gentle pain. I rose to a climax, then, grabbing my bottom, he lifted me up and sliding into my core with one smooth motion. He began drifting in and out, hit the G-spot. Pressed me gently against the shower wall. As he pushed in until he was seated, then rocking his hips with the movement of a piston harder and harder. I just hung on for the ride, then a small current of electrical waves of energy wracked my body until we climaxed together. Trying to catch my breath, He let my body slide down as he continued to kiss my mouth, never letting me go, and the water still spraying both of our naked bodies. He reached down and picked me up again, this time with more force as he penetrated me and pushed harder, causing a wetness and tingling that I could feel all over my body just as it had been the first time; we made love, that uncontrollable feeling while doing it repeatedly. Climaxing together, repeatedly, never missing a beat. The water got cold, and I focused with my thoughts turning off the water. Then Blaine carried me to the bedroom, never leaving my lips and laid me down on the bed, flipped me over and pushed into me, causing the most intense sensation between my legs as a rush of moisture ran down from my core. I had never felt this kind of intensity. He reached around me and rolled my nipples between his fingers and then moved one down to rub my button until I was climbing off the edge. I was beyond an orgasmic experience into an unexplained realm of sexual satisfaction of the superhuman levels. This was the ultimate place of enjoyment. Trying to catch our breath, he kept up the rhythm. He was pushing in and out harder and harder until he tensed, then him jerk and unload all he had to give me. Next thing I knew, it was morning just like any other morning except I felt road hard and put away wet. What a lovely feeling. The coffee smell wafted in our room, off the loft area, and I felt as though I was awake from a dream for one minute in time. I was just a woman in love with a man and the rest of the world, and my responsibility was something in my nightmares. Then I sensed I was not alone any longer. I could hear the humming of everyone's thoughts, wondering if we were ever going to come out of the bedroom. It was 3:00PM in the afternoon. Blaine and I had slept all day, not that we didn't deserve it, but I was hungry, and the coffee smelled so good. I rolled over and nudged Blaine with a kiss, and he mumbled something I couldn't understand. He was still totally out of it.

"Blaine, we need to get up. The rest of the gang is waiting for us. Remember, I still have to go in front of the council."

I sat up and stretched and put on a pair of shorts and

t-shirt and pulled my hair back and stumbled out to the kitchen, where they all sat around the bar like it should be.

"Good morning sleepy head or afternoon." Jake likes to point out the obvious.

Jerry was cooking, and it appeared to be bacon and eggs. I grab a cup of coffee and sat down. They started in on the old jokes about the young super immortal should take it easy on the old guy as Blaine came out of the bedroom.

"Enough with the old guy already. I was the one who was drugged repeatedly."

 "Yeah, to be Priscilla's pet." Ray laughed.

The room was alive with chatter and laughter, and it was great to have it this way again, the way it had always been. Jacquelyn stepped into the room.

"I have an announcement. Attention everyone, the council will preside next Monday at 11:00 am at the wharf in the Seattle harbor. They will use Kevin's ship for the proceedings. Deedra, you have been summoned to appear in front of the council for your part in killing a fellow immortal."

The room got too quiet, and they all looked at me.

"What?" Jake spoke up.

"It's just the council is not a place you want to go, unless you have committed a crime, and they are passing judgment."

 Grams... was at the front of my thoughts and in control and was extremely angry. My body paced back and forth.

"How dare they summon me? I will show them who oversee their small, insufficient council. How soon you all forget who I am... summing me to the council. I am the only one that is qualified to be on that dam board."

"Good morning, grams. You still know how to scare a room full of people."

"Sorry Deedra, I forget I'm using your body from time to time".

Her anger was hard to suppress, but she was growing weaker because it was easy to push her back into the silence in my mind, so she could not take me over any further.

 "Ah... Um, sorry guys... grams forgets she is only borrowing this body from time to time." The look on their faces of fear when she speaks, and the head bowing was so unnerving.

"Please stop with the head bowing- I'm not my grandmother, and I will never take advantage of the gifts that I have."

 Ray came over and put his arm around me.

"We will work on not remembering the atrocity that your

grandmother inflicted on us so many years ago, deal." I smiled at him as the room lightened up.

"Deal." We shook hands.

 With the relief that I was not my grandmother, nor did I ever want to leave a legacy so violent and so fearful.

Monday was going to come too soon. I wasn't sure what to expect from the council, and what I was supposed to say to them. Grams just wanted to tell them where to go but, I would like to be a little more diplomatic and see what they have to say about what has transpired in the last couple of months and if I have done enough to make a difference. I wonder how long it will take for the news to travel and be heard throughout the cartel.

How long will we all have before other immortal challenges me?

"Dee, are you ok? You seem so deep in thought."

"I was just thinking about going in front of the council. I think I would like to go back to the island to spend the weekend before I come back to face the council if that's ok with everyone."

"I would like that too." Blaine hugged me and looked at the others. Dee and I are going back to the island until Monday."

Jake came over. "I think we all should go with the two of

you just for your protection.

Everyone agreed from this day forward we would all be together.

"We leave this afternoon as soon as we are all ready. I will let the staff know there additional hours. Will that work for you?"

"Great, I will go pack. Perhaps Ray and Mica should look at the supplies; we might need to take some with us to restock. "

"You do not need to worry about any of that Mica, Jerry and Amanda are already prepared to return to the island.

 Jake said, "All you need to worry about is resting and packing all of your clothes."

I just wanted to sleep for weeks, take a long bath, and hold my cat on the porch swing and be with Blaine. I also needed to get back to the library to help my grams find George. Maybe I could summon him, and so they could somehow be together forever. Anyhow, that was my goal of having my grandmother and grandfather together for all eternity. Focusing, keep it away from her. I know she aches for him. I can feel all of her feelings, and I can separate them from mine now. She is lonely and oh so sad to be without him. When we get back to the island, I'm going to the library right away and I hope he will show himself. There was knocking at the door. Jake came into our room.

"Dee, it's time we are all loaded up and Blaine is waiting for you in the Lexus."

"Really, we are taking the convertible, yes!!" I clapped.

I loved going for a ride with Blaine in the Lexus. It brought back the memories of our first date. I listened to Blaine's thoughts. We were taking the long way to Anacortes and would catch the ferry over to the island. And everyone else was taking the boat back to the island, and we were going to meet the others there. They were going to leave the Hummer for us at the dock to get it on the ferry and take both rigs back to the island.

I grabbed my bag and smiling from ear to ear; I headed downstairs to the club front door where Blaine was waiting in the car. The roof was down, and I threw my bag in the back. Blaine was giving me that look like I had been in his head.

"Ok, confessing… I just skimed your thoughts. I just wanted to know what to wear."

 I winked at him, as if I ever cared about dressing for the occasion. We both broke out in laughter. He knew I was lying and so did I.

It was a beautiful September day. The air was cooled yet the sun was still warm on your face, leaves had changed, and it was magnificent, the colors of red, orange, and yellow against the blue sky. The East coast has nothing on the Northwest. I sat back and watched the scenery go by. It was so relaxing. Grams was silent. I know I have to hurry to get her with George, but I was so enjoying my afternoon. Soon we arrived at the dock in Anacortes. The ferry was waiting to take us across to the island.

"Blaine, I think I would like to get some more of the Malbac from the restaurant." The hummer was where Ray had left it for us.

"While you're doing that, I will get the rigs on the ferry."

He pulled the Hummer on first. Then pulled the Lexus on behind. Then he went to talk to the captain. I walked into the tasting room at the back of the restaurant and the wine steward remembered me.

"Hello Ms. Lee. How are you today? Can I get you anything?"

"Yes, I would like a case mix of Malbec and Rock Island Red. We picked up the last time we were here."

I could hear her thoughts, and she wanted to know where Blaine was here, and if we were still together.

"Blaine is at the dock waiting for me, and yes we are still together, but thanks for asking."

Her eyes got enormous, her face turned white, and she was now staring at me.

"I'm sorry. I didn't mean to answer your thoughts."

 She just kept staring at me.

I whispered. *"Forget I said anything."*

 She brightened up and put back on her smile.

I cleared my throat…. "The wine please!"

"Oh yes, right away, will a case be enough?"

"Yes, 6 bottles of each. That will be fine."

I paid for the wine and added fifty dollars for being naughty with my gift. Then her boss came in. He was an immortal and told her who I was, and then I had to tune her out too much of OMG and some nonsense about being with royalty.

Blaine was standing on the ferry. Leaning on the skipper's cabin looking like a model off of a page in GQ magazine.

"What took you so long?

"Oh, I was having some fun with the wine steward."

"Dee…. he said with a warning tone. She has been working there for a long time."

"I know. I tipped her well. She also has had a crush on you for an exceedingly long time."

I smiled at him as he took the case out of my arms and

carried it on and set it down on the ferry deck.

The ride to the island went fast. The weather was perfect, and the water was calm.

I said Puffin our trigger word for the captains to forget they deliver vehicles to the Island, just as I drove the Lexus off the ferry, while Blaine followed in the Hummer. The ferry left us. We still waited for it to go out of sight. Then we drove up the beach to the briers that slid sideways, and we headed up the driveway through the camouflage gate and up the hill toward the house.

"Grams, are you there?"

It was silent.

"Grams, where are you?" I was panicking…. We arrived at the house. Blaine stepped out of the Hummer. He came over to me.

"What's wrong, Dee?"

 "It's Grams; I can't feel her anymore. She can't have left me, not yet. I have one more thing to show her."

I opened the door, jumped out, and I ran in the house and up the front stairs to the porch and then down the hallway to the library. Whipped opened the doors and stepped into the room.

"George… George… George as I spun around scanning

the room with all of my senses looking for him to be ghosted in, then he appeared as I had hoped.

"What is all the hoopla about, my dear granddaughter?"

As I stood there, the thoughts filled my head.

"Grams, are you there?"

"Dee, who are you talking to?"

"George, I need to bring you up to speed Suzzallo has been with me, and she helped me get through the last couple of months, and I wanted to bring her back to be with you, but she was frail, and I can't find her inside my head anymore."

Then I could feel her, but this time I looked, and she was standing next to me, all Ghostly like George. I watched as he held out his hand; they touched and gazed into each other's eyes the way Blaine and I do from time to time. The tears of pure joy welled up in my eyes as I not only could feel all of Grams' feeling but watched the love that had been lost all those years ago together at last. All the sadness I have been feeling for months was gone and with their spirits together, I felt they were complete. I couldn't stop staring at the glow that was all around them now. They turned towards me for one last time. They were young and stunning, both of them. George had white leathers on, and she wore an incandescent white sheer gown. I could hear Grams in my head.

"Thanks to you, Deedra, I am with the man I love, and you have all of my gifts and a few more of your own. I just borrowed them to protect you until you were ready. You are ready and will always be the best of all the ancients. Your gifts have been selected carefully and left for you to live your life as you see fit. Remember, we will always be with you in your heart. You are the best of both your parents and your grandfather and I. Stand tall and do not let the council intimidate you, I love you…. Oh, the swirled workings on both your forearms they carry some powerful magic. I'm not sure how or when you will use it in the future, but it added to my gifts to allow me to become solid and finish Rajani. "She walked over to me. My amulet glowed a deep purple, and the tattoos swirled around my arms. She leaned forward and placed a kiss on my for head. "You will be just extraordinary." She murmured. I could feel her lips touch my forehead. It was magic.

Grams turned, took George's hand, laid her lips to the back of his hand, and they walked off into oblivion. There was complete silence in my head, alone with my thoughts going to take some getting used to. I always have had a sounding board to make my decisions, now they are all my own.

Blaine came barging through the doors, followed by the others.

"Dee, what in the hell is going on?"

448

"Oh, I'm sorry; I had to hurry so I could give Grams a chance to be with George. I thought she was gone when she wasn't answering my questions. She showed up outside my body. She was magnificently dressed in a white gown that sort of flowed around her, and George and her were young again. When he took her hand and hugged her, they glowed. It was the most amazing thing I have ever witnessed. Then they disappeared into the light. It was the most loving thing I could have done for her."

"Suzzallo is gone and her powers?" Jake asked.

"Gone with her. It's just me, Dee. You know some mind control a few tricks, but just me."

"Couldn't let them know I was the most powerful of all the immortals alive today. I just wanted to be Dee to them and nothing Royal. Thinking it would be better that way, and if I need some extra abilities, I could use them with none of their knowledge. I cannot fool Jake for long; he would insist on training none stop. I will let him figure it out. Until then I am just Dee, friend, lover, and I was going to need help with the council when I got in front of them, and I will tell them I am not all-powerful and that I am just an immortal like them, nothing special. Maybe they will not be too hard on me.

They all just stood there looking at me."

"What is wrong?"

"Nothing" Jake emphasized.

"Then why are all of you looking at me like you are not sure if I'm Dee or Suzzallo?" Well, something is different about you the way you stand, and you look more like a goddess."

"What are you talking about?"

Jacquelyn brought in a mirror, and as I gazed into the mirror, I didn't recognize the stunning woman that stood there with the confidence of a queen. And I reached out to touch the mirror, and it was me all right, but I was different, not a college student from North Carolina, but a woman with responsibilities.

I just stood there. Blaine came over beside me. Together, we looked like George and Grams did when they left. Blaine leaned in and whispered.

"Astonishingly the most beautiful woman in the world and you are all mine, my queen. I think you're even more irresistible now than the first time I saw you at the college." Putting his arm around me, pulling me closer to kiss me, and my toes curled.

"Thanks Grams. You had to leave me with the aura of a pure blood descendent, didn't you?"

Of cores there was no answer, just the silence of my own thoughts.

"Well, this look is going to be harder than I had planned. I

thought I could come off like simple little ole me, Deedra Lee, and nothing special. But no grams had to leave me with all of this." As I gazed into the mirror, I saw an immortal woman with the aura of a beautiful, powerful leader. Even I had to admit I had grown up and changed.

Jake laughed to let me know he knew I was Deedra with all the gifts of the ancients, and I would not be dismissed easily by the council, either.

"Ok, so I now have this look about me. So, what am I supposed to do with it?"

"Nothing, my queen, absolutely nothing. Just be yourself."

As Blaine lowered his head, rolled his arm out and bowed, teasing me… I didn't find it very amusing as the others did but went along with it because that is what the old Dee would have done.

"I really did not find it amusing. It infuriated me, but that is how grams would have reacted and I was always a good sport. How did I get so serious? Still, no one is answering me. Just silence. It was going to take some getting used to."

Chapter 18

The Council

It was early Monday morning; I could hear the ocean. I wasn't afraid to admit to myself. I was a little apprehensive about today's meeting with the council. Ray was going to fly me in, so I didn't have to leave last night with everyone else. Blaine and Ray stayed behind to come in with me just in case something went wrong. They were going to want to protect me, and I was going to have to get used to it. Couldn't let them know I was powerful like the ancients of the past. I couldn't live with myself knowing they would fear me as they did Suzzallo. Needing coffee before I got ready to go to Seattle, went down to the kitchen, and I was alone. I could smell the aroma of the coffee. I reached for a cup out of the cupboard and there was a sticky note on the pot.

"Dee, I made you some coffee.

Your meeting with the council will be OK.

You can always scare the hell out of them

with all the abilities the ancients left you...

I will see you there.   Love Jake."

Grabbed a cup of coffee, pulled the sticky note off, crumpled it up and tossed it in the garbage can. Then I went back upstairs to take a shower.

Jake was letting me know he knew I was as gifted as any of ancient was and that he would keep my secret. I knew Jake would not fall for the small white lie I had told the others, that I had lost all the ancient powers. He was the only one that knew how much I had changed. I suppose I will let him keep my secret. I could always erase his memory as we did before. However, it was good that someone knew who I was and not totally afraid of me, maybe because he knew Suzzallo. I am also the only one that can beat him in a fight. Hmm... I smiled smugly to myself. Blaine came into the room.

"Dee, it's time to go soon. I will be downstairs when you're ready."

Blaine and Ray must have been at the cave making sure the plane was ready to go. I went into the bathroom and turned on the shower, letting the water heat. When I stepped into the shower, I was all alone with my thoughts. The immortal world was going to have to make a few adjustments. Now that my team and I had been chosen. Would there be more immortals to challenge me? Would the council decide on how to take care of any problems with my team? Jacquelyn could let them know how we were proceeding. Would they let go of the power to rule in the old way?

I got out of the shower, while I was drying my hair, I pondered the most important thing that I was worried about, what do you wear to a council meeting and how formal were they.

How old were some of the council members? How many of them were there? Was it like going to court or something more ancient? Who would I ask?

I thought for a moment and then wondered if Amanda could hear me in Seattle.

I focused on her mind…. "Amanda!"

Then I heard.

"Wow…. Dee, I can hear you as if you were standing next to me." "What can I do for you?"

"So…. what do I wear?"

"Jacquelyn hung a dress in the closet of your room. She hopes you like it. See you soon."

I was afraid of what it might look like. I was a jeans and t-shirt kind of girl. The professor was wearing a formal suit.

I walked over to the closet, hanging in a garment bag. It was a royal purple dress, short just above the knee, fitted with sheer sleeves that buttoned at the cuff. The V-neckline was simple, yet elegant. My amulet looked good. Patent black leather heels, Kari 90 Jimmy Choo's were on the chair with a note.

"See you there... Love J"

"Amanda, tell Jacquelyn I didn't miss the Royal Purple color of the dress and the Jimmy Choo's cost more than a month's rent at my old apartment. Thank you." I sighed.

I left my hair down, twirled it around to the side in a curly side ponytail. I heard the door open downstairs. It was Blaine.

"Dee, are you ready?" as he walked through the door into our room, he stopped and just stared, looking me up and down. Then he smiled.

"What, I look ridiculous?"

"Um, no, you're so beautiful. I had to just stop and take it all in."

"Oh, is that right?" I blushed.

"Yeah." He pulled me close and kissed me

"Your mom left the dress and shoes for me."

"It is perfect. I have something for you."

He handed me a box. I open it to find a beautiful amethyst dangle tear dropped shaped earrings that matched my necklace.

"Oh my, they are beautiful. Are these enchanted also?"

"I don't know. I found them at a flea market in the underground. "

I took them out of the box with no tingling or humming of my amulet. I put them on. They finished my outfit perfectly.

"Well, you look rather yummy in that Sotheby's suit." Blaine was dressed in a black suit, a white shirt with a black tie. James Bond has got nothing on Blaine.

As I ran my hands down the front of the dress, it was silk and made me feel pretty. Given my dress, one more look in the mirror.

 "You're sure I'm not overdressed?"

I was feeling uncomfortable. He was staring at me as if I

was something yummy to eat. I could hear his thoughts and all he wanted was me out of the dress.

"Oh, know you're going to blow them away."

"I'm not sure I want the council blown away?" He smiled and put his arms around me and kissed me softly.

"Come on, Dee, we need to get going. Ray has the plane running and waiting for us. You do not want to be late."

I walked down to the Hummer. Blaine was already ahead of me, holding the door. He took my hand and helped me into the Rig. He bowed his head and looked up, winked, and smiled. I gave him a dirty look; he knows I do not want to be treated as a royal.

 "But you will always be my queen." He reached over and kissed the top of my hand.

His words were velvety smooth. He could soothe me even with all of my abilities and melt my heart and make everything seem normal when it never will be again. I was hoping he would always soften my heart and keep me calm with his touch. Just like Grams and George.

We arrived at the cavern, and the motor was running when I got on the plane. I could hear Ray's thoughts.

"Well... miss Lee, you look incredible. They will never suspect you an ancient in that dress..."

I just looked at him and smiled. "Ray, you don't look so bad yourself."

Jacquelyn must have dressed him or told no fatigues. The flight was brief and all I could think of was, what is in store for me and the others?

The plane had begun its descent to the Seattle harbor; we were landing already as Ray pulled up next to Kevin's ship. Ray cut the engines, and it was silent. All I could hear was the water lapping against the planes float. Ray was securing the plane with the help of one man from the ship. Blaine helped me to the edge of the float. Just then, one of Kevin's men put his hand out to help me step off the float on to the small deck at water level. I was blocking all thoughts now with no effort. The silence was weird but pleasant at the same time. The men on the ship were behaving as though the president just set foot on their ship not a salute, but all the head bowing as I passed all of them. Blaine had gotten out behind me and then Ray followed. Kevin's man led us down to the meeting room where the council waited. There were two men guarding the door. When they saw me approach, they opened the doors. Blaine touched the backside of my arm.

"You'll be, just fine."

"Aren't you coming?"

"No, we have to wait here. You'll be all right."

458

I walked into the room. There was a table with six men and one woman. Just like the ancient council, my Grams was on. *"Mistake number one, repeating the past. Only one woman at the head table."*

That was going to have to change, for pity's sake. It is the twenty-first century. As the ancients looked, they seemed to all look the same. They all had the aquamarine eyes, but they were of all different nationalities, they were not the ancients that left Atlantis. They had that look of pure blood. Yet they all had the attitude of the ancients, like my Grams and Rajani. Let's hope they have a different way of dealing with people other than intimidation. That would not work on me. I had to be cool, though I didn't want them to be afraid of me. I walked about 20 feet. I took a deep breath. The twenty steps seemed to take forever and all of it was in slow motion. I stopped short of the panel behind a chair that sat in front of all of them. I could hear some of their thoughts. They almost gasped as I entered the room. I could hear them saying she looks like Suzzallo. Jacquelyn stood up to introduce me.

"Council Members, this is Deedra Lee, the great, great, great, great, great granddaughter of Suzzallo and George Lee."

The council stood, and all bowed their heads. Then they all sat down. The man in the middle pointed towards the chair.

"Please sit here." He gestured with his hand.

It was mind-blowing at how stunningly handsome all the men were. They could have been models. There is something about an immortal man. They never get that mortal pot belly. The first man spoke directly to me.

"Hello Deedra, welcome to the council. I understand you have had a spirit guide along your journey to us."

"Yes." I smiled, thinking how nice it would be to have her here for this.

"Is she present with you today?"

"Unfortunately, no." I could feel the tension in the room lighten. The room warmed up. They also were a little afraid of me, I will think of it as respect.

"My name is Michael; I'm the eldest in this council. Have lived 450 mortal years. Was here when your grandmother was murdered. I was also new to all the ancients. and was here when they were all

de-throne by the cartel."

"On my left is Mathew." He bowed his head.

"Next to Mathew is Vincent," *again the head bowing.*

"On my right, you know Jacquelyn. Next to her are Wesley and finally Urey. He also remembers the atrocities of the time."

"We have brought you here to hear your story and your thoughts."

I cleared my throat, looked down, and then I heard my grams.

"Hold your head up high. You are royalty, whether or not you like it. Stand and tell them how you intend to lead them into a new reign of equals. Let them know what your part in all of this council will be. Make me proud." then nothing totally alone in my head. But I felt her presence not far away.

With a tear in the corner of my eye missing her desperately, I smiled and raised my head high. As I spoke, their eyes got big and wide, and I knew I was using my gram's authoritative royal voice, but it was in me and now part of who I was, so I let my voice be heard.

"I am only here to uphold the immortals' rules. I do not wish to be part of this council. Your board is and will always be a source of expert knowledge. I will remain on the island with my team and work at our club when needed. Jacquelyn and I will work on the ancients' books, journals and other written words. I'm hoping to help her, and Ray interpret the dialog.

Jacqueline will be in contact with you. She will keep my seat at your council. You will contact me only through her.

You will add more women until the council is fifty-fifty. We must learn from our past. You only have one woman on the council now, just as the original six did. Don't you think with a more diverse opinion our judgment of our people could be better justified? Maybe the original six would not have been destroyed with an equitable knowledge base to pull from.   I know keeping reign on the immortals has been a challenge. Upholding of the rules you have set forth for centuries will not be easy. With Rajani gone, we have only just begun. There will always be someone who will challenge me. I will continue to hone my abilities with my trainer Jake and my team, and we will continue to be the council's enforcers."

Urey interrupted me.

"So, your abilities are not like your grandmothers?" I held up my hand. I looked directly at him.

"When I am done talking, you may ask your questions. Interrupting me shows no respect. Respect will be vital as we move forward to bringing this council into the 21st century. "

"Hmm, wonder how that sits in these dinosaurs' craw? They are fishing to see how many abilities I have. I am leaving them guessing."

"My abilities are always changing."

"Where is Rajani?"

Urey spoke up again with attitude. My grams would have slapped him down for addressing her in such a manner. Good thing she was gone. But in today's society, mansplaining was not accepted by me either.

"You do not need to worry about him; he is with the other ancients in a safe place."

"So, you don't plan on giving us any more information than that?" Wesley snapped.

"It is a need to know, and none of you need to know."

"You are very sure of yourself, young lady," said Matthew.

"I am the only one who knows, and that is my cross to bear. No one can know their location. If they were to be awakened, they would destroy the world."

They all just sat there, staring at me. I probed their thoughts and saw what they were really thinking of me. It was a need to know on my behalf. The kind of immortal I would be dealing with. I was so good at it now that they wouldn't even know I was in their minds, not even Jacquelyn. Slowly, I listened.

Matthew was horrified. I reminded him too much of Suzzallo and he didn't trust me not to strike out in violence.

Vincent was impressed by someone so young in the immortal world and so sure of myself; he admired my strength and remembered the stories of 'The One' that would come.

Michael was not impressed and wondered if I had any of my grandmother's abilities at all, especially now that she was not present. Jacquelyn had told them the story of George and her ghosting away in the library.

Wesley was one of the youngest of the council; he wasn't sure someone so small and with the resemblance of the great Suzzallo should be allowed to command anyone on the council.

Urey was not impressed at all and wanted to ask more questions. He was not satisfied with any of my answers. He was about to speak.

I held up my hand, and I interrupted him, so he understood they couldn't keep anything away from me.

"Urey, you are concerned that I am not what you have heard and wish to ask me more questions?"

"He smiled, bowed his head and said,

"You have just given me enough proof, my lady."

Jacquelyn just smiled, as proud as if I were her own daughter. All I got from her mind were loving thoughts. Oh my! And thoughts of her lovely grandchildren. Hmm, I wonder what is up with all that. I disconnected. I wanted no more thoughts of grandchildren.

I looked at the council. Again, I addressed them with my royal voice.

"If there is nothing else, I would like to address some of your concerns about my abilities. It is true, Suzzallo spirit is gone, but she left me with her abilities and a few new ones of my own. I do not want this information to leave this council. I do not want to be treated any different from a regular immortal following the rules. You must keep my secret, so I may use it to protect the honor of the immortal population to live in harmony with the mortals we walk among. Do I have your word? I need you to swear in front of god and these witnesses that you will keep my secret."

Jacquelyn spoke first.

"May I address the council?"

They all nodded.

"Thank you. I believe we should promise Deedra that her secret is safe with all of us. It would not be wise of us to cross her. Remember, just by looking at her, she is the perfect descendent of Suzzallo. Even her mannerisms and her style are all classic Suzzallo."

The council all looked at each other, and as they nodded in agreement. I could feel their terror, and I knew they would never betray me. The council is some of the oldest immortals alive today, and they remember the reign of Suzzallo."

"We agree." They all said in unison.

Before I addressed them. I whispered; *"Forget you know of my gifts and abilities. I am just a young normal immortal. You are giving me all your respect and trust."* I pushed that out into all of their minds. If grams taught me right, they would never know I had been there.

"Well, now that we have that unpleasantness out of the way, I would like to leave and start living my new life as normal as possible. Do I have your permission to leave?" As I nodded my head showing great respect to all of them.

Jacquelyn stood. "Does the council have any further questions of Deedra?"

The room was silent. I can speak for all of us.

"We are glad you're here and on our side."

She came over, hugged me, and whispered.

"You were perfect, as I knew you would be even without your gram's help. See you at home."

As I left the room, the others were not as happy as she was, but they were too afraid to challenge what they did not know or understand about me. I don't know if that is a good thing or a bad thing. But respect was offered. That's what mattered. The doors in front of me opened and Ray, Jake, Jerry, Blaine, and Kevin were standing there like guards they had not moved, and they escorted me to the plane. Kevin took my hand.

"Deedra it, has been my honor to fight at your side, call on me anytime you have my number, he bowed his head, winked at me and laid a kiss on the back of my hand."

"Thank you, Kevin, I couldn't have done any of this without your help and the help of your men and women who are loyal to you."

"And now they are loyal to you, Dee."

 "Raymond, I have a good feeling the next century will be interesting. See you soon, my friend." Kevin and Ray shook hands, then pulled each other into a man hug.

Blaine laughed as he took my hand as I got on the plane. Jacqueline, Mica and Amanda were on the plane waiting for the rest of us. Ray got in last, secured the door, sat in the pilot seat, put the plane in motion and we flew off.

I sat there staring out the window and thought about how it went with the council. Wondered how long it would take the stories to reach the population of immortals and someone to want proof I was as gifted as the stories told. I was sure it would always be like this. I was the only pure blood descended from the immortal ancient world. Our new world was just beginning. So was my life with Blaine and the others.

Only the future was not so easy to see now. Jerry and

I would have to be ever ready when the peacefulness of today would change. I was sure it would transform knowing the supernatural world we live in, but for now, I was going to enjoy the tranquility that had been given to me. Watching the ocean below me and seeing the island in the distance, my life was now and forever changed by the ancient blood that ran through me. What challenges awaited all of us? But at this moment, I was going to enjoy the unobtrusiveness of the rest of my day. When we landed outside the cavern that held the plane, I was looking forward to a nap on the porch swing. We unloaded, and I headed up to the hummer at the top of the landing. Waiting for everyone to pile in so we could drive up to the house. Finally, home, I got out and went to sit on the porch swing. I leaned back against the pillow. The sun in my face and just sat there. Blaine came over and sat with me. He lifted me into his lap, holding me close I fell asleep. As I drifted off, listening to the ocean, the salty air soothed my soul. I wasn't sure how long I had slept. I heard off in the distance.

"If you can hear me, Deedra, I will avenge my father's death. I am coming for you."

Amanda burst onto the porch. "What the hell Dee, who is that calling to you?"

Characteristics of an Immortal:

*T*hey all have these aquamarine eyes, physically perfect, they stop aging; they are different nationalities, extreme intelligence, talented in everything they do. Own fortune five hundred companies. The House and Senate have members. They sit on the Supreme court. They are ten percent of the richest population in the world. They are people of mystery and don't like to be noticed; it allows them to live among the mortals' lives and not get involved in changing their lives. They have a council of elders that governs them to keep the rules. Breaking the rules is punished by death.

The original Six Ancients:

Rajani: The Dark One. He prayed on all. The mundane mortal and immortal; Rule and influenced the mortal world.

Damayanti: The king of men with the power to subdue his prey just. Before he killed them, he showed no mercy.

Govua: He could control the elements. He could conjure the wind at will, causing a great dust storm to confuse his enemies. Or a fire tornado, waterspouts in the desert. He could suck oxygen out of the air.

Kreios: He could wheel lighting and electricity in the new age.

Deimos: He could physically change his appearance. Able to slip in behind enemy lines and destroy from within. Had mind control. He was always the lord and expert in his kingdoms.

Suzzallo: She was the most powerful immortal alive. She could read your mind, inflict pain, break bones, and drive you mad with one thought. Skilled in combat. Her choice of weapon was the Sai's. No one challenged her. She could telepathically control objects to move at will. The originals had only one woman. She was selfish and had no conscience. She would leave a room in a bloodbath for any emotional reason. No one questioned her. And no one knew truly how many gifts she possessed because she kept them to herself. She is Deedra Lees' inner warrior and grandmother.

George Lee: His immortal abilities were equal to Suzzallo, but his kindness and a gentle spirit were his true gifts. Being an immortal that loved the indigenous mundane mortal race so much, he lived among them as they lived. Never used his immortal gifts; he had many but remained spiritually pure. He loved Suzzallo, even though her royal blood line would not allow her to be with him. Their passion for one another could not be denied. They fell in love and there were great consequences. He was also Deedra's great, great, great, great, great grandfather.

Deedra Lee: Was twenty-nine, looked all of eighteen. New to the immortal world but distend to lead and fight for the freedom of her kind. 'The One', keeping the corrupted immortals in check. But there were still those who would take advantage of their abilities for their own gain.

Blaine Bluestar: thirty-seven years old, Part owner of the club BJ's, a Casanova, has the power of persuasion, lived a very different life until he saw Deedra one day on campus. Has mastered the piano, has a master's degree in international economics. Loves the arts and the finer things in life. He is two hundred and twenty-seven years in immortal years.

Jacquelyn Bluestar: forty three-year, the mother of Blaine but looks like his sister; she is two hundred and nine five immortal years old.

Professor at the University of Washington. She teaches Indian legend of Washington State, physician, archeologists, and. Blocks immortal thoughts.

Jake Kirby: thirty-nine years old, a server in the Club, a martial art expert, strong, military strategist, fast, combat ready. He is two hundred and seventy-three immortal years old. He trains Deedra for battle. Jake is her confidant.

Jerry Malone: thirty-two years old bartender at the club, sees the future, helps keep Deedra safe from herself. He is two hundred and one immortal years old.

Amanda Pennington: thirty years old. Is a student at U

of W, keep an eye on Deedra until she is ready to know the truth. She reads minds, speaks to Deedra through her thoughts. Was the Youngest immortal at one hundred and ten immortal years until Deedra shows up.

Raymond Anthony: Ray is forty-two years old Caretaker of the home on James Island. He served with the royal guard when Suzzallo was in rein. Navy Seal for decades, extremely strong, expert in his craft to defend. Abilities are limited to his strength and honor. He is in his immortal years two hundred and ninety-five immortal years old.

Mica Wentworth: Thirty-eight years old. She keeps the group on task to behave like mortals. She runs the club. Strong, trained by the CIA, has security clearance. She has the mind of a genius. She is in her Immortal, two hundred and seventy-nine immortal years old.

Kevin O' Reilly: forty-seven years old, Owner of container vessel, Is a Canadian immortal from Victoria. He served with Ray in the Royal guard and saw all the hateful, selfish atrocities that the ancient brought down on immortal and mortals alike for their own greed. He is three hundred years old.

Charles: The Owner of the PUB, in Victoria

Noah: Ferry captain Betrayed Deedra and Blaine.

Captain Scott: He commands Kevin's ship.

Demetrye Spalicek: The young Canadian man the Deedra saves in the church and communicates with in saving the group from Rajani wrath.

Simon Casteil: Did the syndicate bidding and grew to hate Deedra

Allen Freeport: Worked for Simon

James: He was a very old French mundane immortal. He took care of Jake when he visited Victoria.

Priscilla Meier: She is twenty-five in mundane mortal years and one hundred and seventeen immortal years. She can control minds to do her bidding. The Daughter of the Dark one, Rajani. Granddaughter to the Meier and Frank fortune in Portland, Oregon.

Council Members:

Michael 450-years-old

Mathew 402-years-old

Wesley 375-years-old

Vincent 370-years-old

Urey 320-years-old

Jacquelyn 272-years-old

www.ingramcontent.com/pod-product-compliance
Lightning Source LLC
Chambersburg PA
CBHW030657190726
48286CB00001B/61